THE KOALA OF DEATH

THE KOALA OF DEATH

BETTY WEBB

WORLDWIDE.

TORONTO • NEW YORK • LONDON
AMSTERDAM • PARIS • SYDNEY • HAMBURG
STOCKHOLM • ATHENS • TOKYO • MILAN
MADRID • WARSAW • BUDAPEST • AUCKLAND

For Wanchu and her sisters.
And especially to Notch and Half-Ear—long may they and
their endangered cousins contribute to the beauty of this Earth.

Recycling programs
for this product may
not exist in your area.

The Koala of Death

A Worldwide Mystery/July 2015

First published by Poisoned Pen Press

ISBN-13: 978-0-373-26950-1

Acknowledgments

Writing may be a solitary process but whipping all those words into shape is not. For the improvements they suggested, my thanks go out to the glorious Barbara Peters at Poisoned Pen Press who wanted "more koala," the Sheridan Street Irregulars, Marge Purcell, Debra McCarthy, and Robert C. Kezer. Louise Signorelli provided much-needed technical advice. Bravo to you all!

On the zoo front, more thanks are due the Phoenix Zoo and John Sills, the zoo's Collection Manager, Birds, who patiently explained the intricacies of the Great Flamingo Round-Up (and had me laughing as he did so); and to Paige McNickle, the zoo's Senior Keeper, Hoofstock Trail, who took me behind the scenes and introduced me to Notch and Half-Ear, the white rhinos who appear in this book.

My continued admiration (and envy) goes out to the happy liveaboarders at Moss Landing, California—mosslandingchamber.com—and to Yohn and Melanie Gideon, of the marvelous Captain's Inn—captainsinn.com—who showed my husband and me such warm hospitality.

Special thanks go to Eileen Brady, my bowling partner at the Bowling for Rhinos fundraiser. (Yes, folks, that event is real). We may not have won that bronzed rhino dung trophy, but we sure had fun, didn't we?

As for the rest—any errors that appear in this book are my fault alone, not those of the helpful folks listed above.

ONE

I AWOKE DURING a pearly dawn to hear something bump against the *Merilee*'s hull. A brief glance at my bunkside clock gave the time as 5:24. Before I could pull the covers back over my head, DJ Bonz, my three-legged dog, slapped a wet tongue across my face, while at the foot of the bunk, Miss Priss mewed, *Feed me, feed me, feed me.*

"I can't have just six more minutes?"

No, you can't, they thought at me.

Miss Priss, a mostly Persian who had weighed a whisker-thin three pounds when I rescued her from the same shelter I'd rescued Bonz, marched up my leg, across my stomach, and onto my chest. Now a whopping ten pounds, she shoved the small terrier mix out of the way so she could glare down at me through her one remaining eye. *Feed me, feed me, feed me.*

"I can take a hint." With a groan, I threw off the eiderdown comforter—even in June, Gunn Landing Harbor mornings can be chilly—and rolled out of the bunk. "Now you guys just settle down for a minute while I…"

Bump, ba-ba-bump.

There it was again, the sound that had wakened me. Portside. Surely not Maureen. The sea otter never showed until 5:45 a.m., so punctual I could set a clock by her. Maybe, like me, she'd had a rough night. Ignoring my pets' ever-louder demands, I slipped on some sweats before removing a herring from the galley's small refrigerator. Thus steeled against the chill, I stepped out on deck and drew a deep breath of Pacific Ocean air. Sounding only yards away, gulls shrieked, but I couldn't see them.

Grayness swirled around me in a fog so thick that only the outline of the boat next to mine was visible. A blue and white CrisCraft twice the size of my *Merilee*, the *Gutterball* bobbed gently in the harbor's calm water. The night before, its owners, Doris and Sam Grimaldi, had thrown a noisy party that lasted far too late. I'd stayed until ten, then came back home to the *Merilee* to get some sleep, but found myself still awake at one, listening to a boat full of drunks guffaw at jokes so ancient they should have died with the dinosaurs.

Casting a dirty look at the now quiet *Gutterball*, I leaned over the *Merilee*'s rail, herring in hand. For a moment, the fog parted just enough that I could see, in the oily water below, a patch of sable brown fur heading for the boat again. Then the fog closed in.

"Early today, aren't you, Maureen?" I held the herring out, waiting for her to break surface. Even if she couldn't see the fish, she would smell it.

Feeding resident wildlife was just one of the joys of harbor living. My quarters on the *Merilee*, a 1979 thirty-four-foot CHB trawler—or "powerboat," to landlubbers—might be cramped, but the view was terrific. Once the mist cleared, anyway.

Despite my waving the herring around, Maureen didn't respond. The otter just thunked into the *Merilee*'s hull, eighteen inches below the final "E." That was odd, too. She usually surfaced under the "M."

"Maureen?"

By rights, she should have already stuck her head out of the water, chattered at me, then executed a flirtatious belly roll to earn her breakfast. Not today, which gave me some concern. In the past few years, the Central California coast had seen a rise in sea otter deaths due to *Sarcocystis neurona*, a protozoan found in innkeeper worms and clams, which were among the otters' favorite meals. Could Maureen…?

Truly alarmed now, I leaned farther forward, intending to grab Maureen by the scruff of the neck and haul her aboard, to be followed by a quick trip—if it wasn't too late—to the vet. But as the fog parted again, I saw something that a clear day would have revealed earlier: otters don't wear pink dresses or tie their long hair back with festive silver ribbons.

"Help!" I yelled. "Anyone! Woman overboard!"

Without waiting for an answer, I plunged into the dirty harbor water and hooked my arm around the woman's neck, tipping her blue-tinged face out of the water. Although my soaked sweats weighed me down, I was able to maneuver her over to the *Merilee*'s ladder. I tried not to fasten on the phrase "dead weight," but as she dangled limp and cold in my arms, I suspected that the rescue had already been too late. Yet I couldn't let her go.

"Help!" I yelled again. "Someone get a rope or boat hook! She's too heavy for me to lift! Call 9-1-1!"

The *Gutterball* remained silent, but from the boat slip on the other side of the dock, a woman called out, "On my way with a rope!" It was Linda Cushing, the owner of the *Tea 4 Two*. Then I heard hurried footfalls. Seconds later, the *Merilee* rolled to starboard as Linda stepped on deck. "Damned fog, can't see a thing. Where are you, Teddy?"

"In the water near the stern. Hurry! Just in case." Just in case, what? Just in case the dead could rise again?

A splash next to me as Linda threw down one end of the rope. "Slip it under her arms, tie it tight, and help me ease her up," she ordered.

With much grunting and gasping, we two women pulled

and pushed our helpless third up the chrome-slick ladder and onto the *Merilee*'s deck, where she flopped across the teak as if boneless. Linda cocked a critical eye. "If you're thinking about giving her CPR, forget it. That's about as dead as I've ever seen." Although dismayed by Linda's seeming heartlessness, I had to agree. The woman was indeed dead, her body slightly swollen from an hours-long immersion in the water. And now that tendrils of dark brown hair no longer covered her face, I recognized her, too.

Kate Nido, also known as Koala Kate. The new koala keeper at the Gunn Zoo.

TWO

"ARE YOU TELLING me you didn't hear Ms. Nido go into the water?" Sheriff Joe Rejas asked, his blue eyes searching mine.

I hated it when my boyfriend became official with me, but in this case it was understandable, so I repeated myself for the third or maybe fourth time. "As I've been saying, Joe, the noise from the party kept me up past one, but after that, I fell dead…" I swallowed. "…fell asleep. I didn't wake up until she bumped against the *Merilee*."

An injury to Kate's head must have accounted for the thin red smear across my soaked sweatshirt, which for some reason, Joe demanded I turn over to him along with my sweatpants. His request left me standing on the deck wrapped only in a terry cloth robe that had seen better days. I tried not to watch as two hefty EMTs casually zipped Kate into a body bag, then just as casually carted her off toward a waiting ambulance. This just-another-day-at-the-office attitude seemed all wrong. Now that the fog was beginning to dissipate, I saw that the tourists gathered at the rail overlooking the harbor didn't seem particularly disturbed, either. When had the world become so indifferent?

Remaining in sheriff mode, Joe asked, "Ms. Nido's the one they call 'Koala Kate,' isn't she? Has that TV segment on *Good Morning, San Sebastian*? Called '*Koala Kate's Kuddly Kritters*' ?"

"The zoo hired her two months ago, just before the new

koala exhibit opened up," I explained. "That TV show was only part of her duties."

Who would call the station to tell them Kate wouldn't appear tomorrow or ever again? Zorah Vega, the zoo director? A former zookeeper herself, Zorah was great with animals, but social niceties seemed beyond her. She'd delegate the job, perhaps even to me, since the owner of the TV station was an acquaintance of my mother's. Oh, God. That meant… "Who was there?" For some reason, Joe had taken out a note pad and was writing in it.

I pulled myself together. "Who was where?"

"At the Grimaldis' party, Teddy."

"Liveaboarders from the harbor. And zookeepers."

He looked up from his note pad. "Why would zookeepers—besides yourself, of course, since you live here—attend a harbor beer bash?"

I swallowed again. The fact that I'd just pulled a co-worker out of the water was beginning to hit home. Kate had felt so cold. So…so *dead.*

"Teddy? Answer me."

"They…uh, Sam and Doris Grimaldi are hosting this years' Bowling for Rhinos fundraiser at their bowling alley, and they wanted…they wanted to treat the committee volunteers. They don't live at the harbor, so they probably left for their house in S-S-San Sebastian once the p-party was…was…"

"Sit down." Joe eased me onto a deck chair and hovered. "Take deep breaths."

I followed his advice, and as soon as my head cleared, stood back up. "I'm fine, don't fuss. This thing, it's just a shock, that's all. Nobody expects to…" *Get a grip, Teddy.* I forced my voice to sound steadier than I felt. "The party. You want to know who was there. Besides the BFR committee, there was Linda Cushing, whom you just met. Linda's lived at the harbor for ages and can tell you anything you need to know about anyone. Besides Linda, there was Walt MacAdams, Larry DuFries, myself, and a couple of other liveaboarders from around here."

"I need the zookeepers' names, too, Teddy."

One by one I counted them off on shaking fingers. "Buster Daltry. Since he's the rhino keeper, he's also Chairman of Bowling for Rhinos. And there was Robin Chase, big cats; Jack Spence, bears; Myra Sebrowski, great apes. Oh, and Lex Yarnell, the park ranger. He's on the committee, too. And Zorah, of course."

Joe stopped writing. "Zorah Vega, the zoo director?"

"I'm afraid so." Not that long ago, Joe had arrested Zorah for suspicion of murder. Someone else had been proven guilty of the crime, but I knew she still carried a grudge against him for the time she'd spent in jail.

"Anyone else at the party besides the neighbors and the zoo folks?"

I searched my mind, but it refused to cooperate. "If I think of anyone else, I'll let you know. But what difference does it make? It was an accident, wasn't it? Kate probably had too much to drink, then slipped and fell into the harbor. I guess she hit her head and that's why she didn't call for help, even though you'd think…"

"How much did you have to drink last night, Ms. Bentley?" He'd become official again, and I hated it.

"One-and-a-half beers."

"You didn't hear anything unusual?"

"No."

"Cries of distress? Anything that sounded like a struggle?"

"Hey, what's all this…?"

"Thank you, Ms. Bentley. That'll be all." He stepped

onto the dock and walked toward his deputies, leaving me standing on the *Merilee*'s deck with my mouth open.

MY NAME IS Theodora Esmeralda Iona Bentley, but most people call me Teddy. I've been a zookeeper at the Gunn Zoo for around a year, mostly working with the giant ant-eater and various small primates, sometimes helping out with the Mexican gray wolves and the marsupials in Down Under, the zoo's Australian section.

As work places go, the Gunn Zoo is ideal. Located four miles inland from Gunn Landing Harbor, it escapes most of the coastal fog, so my workdays tend to be sunny and bright. But every now and then, Aster Edwina Gunn, administrator of the Gunn Family Trust, which founded the privately-owned zoo decades earlier, limos over to spread fear and gloom among employees and animals alike. Given what had happened to Kate, today would be one of those days.

Despite the sad business of the morning, I arrived at work well before seven and was zipping along one of the wider zoo paths in my zebra-striped cart toward Down Under. When I had phoned the zoo director to tell her about Kate's death, she'd told me to start my day with the marsupials before taking care of my own charges.

"I'll call Bill, but you know how he is," she'd said. "He was probably tending bar at the Amiable Avocado last night and has his phone turned off. In the meantime, the less the marsupials' routines are disturbed, the better off they'll be, so get down there first thing." Known to zoo visitors as "Outback Bill" because of his heavy Aussie accent, Bill was a part-time keeper who at one time had dated Kate. Recently their relationship had ended, and Bill had been seen around the local bars with a series of other women. Given their estrangement, I doubted Bill would grieve too hard over her death, especially since it meant that Zorah might now hire him full-time. Originally a keeper at the Sydney Zoo, Bill could tell the difference between a nail-tail wallaby and a rock wallaby. Even better, the koalas liked him almost as much as they'd liked Kate. When my cart screeched to a halt outside the service entrance to the koala enclosure, I at first didn't see them. Normally, Wanchu, the female, would be sleeping in a tree, with her mate, Nyee, snoring nearby. But when I climbed out of the cart, I saw Wanchu waddling across the enclosure toward me.

"Morning, cutie!" I called. "Ready for some fresh eucalyptus browse?"

She looked up with those big brown koala eyes. *Yes*, she thought at me. *Hurry up so I can get back to sleep.*

Koalas look adorable with their Teddy-bear builds and googoo eyes. The Aboriginal people of Australia believe koalas are the reincarnation of lost children, a belief that— given the animals' sweet dispositions—makes sense. Even wild koalas allow strangers to pick them up. Part of their docility stems from not only their temperament, but from the fact that koalas are almost always drowsy. If they're not already asleep, they're thinking about sleeping, because their diet of eucalyptus leaves is so poor in protein that they have to eat a pound of leaves per day merely to stay alive. All that chewing exhausts them so much that they wind up sleeping 75 percent of the time.

Wanchu was one of the only Gunn Zoo animals we keepers were encouraged to touch. Zoo-born and orphaned only days after she'd left her mother's pouch, she had been hand-raised by an overly doting zookeeper. Now full-grown, she still loved to cuddled.

"Come to Mama, sweetness," I cooed, grasping her by her forearms.

Wanchu pulled herself up and curled around my torso

much as she would have around a tree trunk. Because of her heavy eucalyptus intake, she smelled like cough drops. After nestling against me for a few minutes while I sang a few bars of "Waltzing Matilda," she lifted her head, gazed soulfully into my eyes, and chirped, "Eeep, eeep, eeep!"

"Yes, and I'm glad to see you, too, Wanchu. You're my favoritest female koala." I didn't want to make Nyee jealous.

"Eeep?"

"You're hungry? Well, your wish is my command. A large serving of eucalyptus browse coming right up."

She snuggled again. "Eeep?"

"Yes, I'll give Nyee some, too."

"Eeep."

Putting a koala down can be difficult, not only because you don't want to, but because koalas cling. Wanchu finally allowed me to place her in the crook of her tree so I could return to my cart for a large bundle of wrapped eucalyptus leaves. I was tying them to her tree when I heard another cart screech to a halt on the other side of the fence.

Seconds later, Bill, all six feet four, two-hundred-and-twenty pounds of him, charged through the gate. "Rack off on your own bizzo, Teddy, and leave the walla to me."

Fortunately, due to once having an Australian stepfather, I could translate: *Go mind your own business, Teddy, and leave the koala to me.*

"Hi, Bill. Zorah told you about Kate?"

"That she carked it? Yeh." Translation: *That she died. Yeah.* He flapped his hand in a go-away gesture and started toward the koalas, but not before I saw a haunted look in his eyes. Did he still care for Kate?

Before I could ask, another cart pulled up. When the brakes didn't squeal, I guessed it was Zorah, glorying in her recent promotion to zoo director by requisitioning the zoo's newest cart.

My guess proved right. A big woman, both in height and breadth, Zorah's arms were covered with tattoos of the animals she'd cared for prior to her promotion: a Bengal tiger, a black-maned lion, a jaguar, and various and sundry great apes. Zorah was nothing if not colorful.

"Teddy, I need to talk to Bill. Privately."

To offer him a full-time job, I hoped. God knows the man needed the work. Besides his three-nights-a-week stint as bartender at the Amiable Avocado, he was also bagging groceries at a Monterey supermarket. Strange, considering he'd resigned from a full-time job as marsupial keeper at the San Diego Zoo to move up here. Not to follow Kate, I hoped, because if that had been his motive he'd shown more heart than brains, since their relationship hadn't survived the move.

"Okay, I'm gone," I said to Zorah. "If either of you need anything, call me on the radio."

She didn't answer, just started talking to Bill in a low voice. I steered my cart out of the Down Under enclosure and headed toward Tropics Trail.

The three-hundred-acre Gunn Zoo is always beautiful, but in the early mornings it is pure magic. Surrounded by twenty-five hundred acres of blue gum eucalyptus forests and vineyards, the zoo is further buffered from the outside world by a ring of hills high enough to hold back most of the coast's fog. No sound of civilization's hubbub intrudes. Instead, we fortunate zookeepers are treated to the serenade of waking animals: the lilting music of larks and jays in the aviaries, the eerie calls of New Guinea singing dogs, and from the large animal sanctuary that encircles the entire zoo, elephants trumpeting their joy at just being alive.

How anyone could work in an office was beyond me.

By now visitors were trickling in, so I drove with care in order to keep from mowing them down. Most were headed

toward the giant anteater enclosure. Thanks to recent publicity, much of it generated by Kate, who had also taken care
of the zoo's PR, Lucy and her baby had become celebrities.

A few tendrils of morning fog had unexpectedly made
their way over the surrounding hills, and wisps of it clung
to the tall eucalyptus trees that ringed the grounds. I loved
these rare mornings, when fog hushed the visitors' chatter,
thus encouraging the animals to venture away from their
resting spots and get closer to the fence. As I passed through
Tropics Trail, I noticed Willy, one of the Andean bears,
waving a furry paw at an admiring crowd as he sat on his
rump at the edge of his moat. He was looking one teenager
in the eye, a most un-animal thing to do. "Look, he's saying hello!" said one woman to another, as she nibbled on a
bag labeled Poppy's Kettle Korn. "Isn't that sweet?" Willy
was merely begging. Since visitors didn't always obey the
signs telling them not to feed the animals, the bear had developed a taste for popcorn.

More begging was going on in the iguana exhibit. Lilliana, the female, flicked her tongue at the crowd in the
hopes that they would toss her a big fat bug. From time to
time she'd attempt a wave but an iguana isn't as agile as a
bear, so the effort failed. Her elderly mate, Reynaldo, ignored Lilliana's act and continued his snooze-fest by a rock.

I felt privileged to work here, surrounded by friends both
human and animal, spending my time outdoors under the
California sky instead of some stuffy office. As I drove
along, the scents of animals, popcorn, and salt air blended
together in a pleasant potpourri and helped ease the sting
of the morning's tragedy.

Monkey Mania was a quarter-acre open-air enclosure
where twenty squirrel monkeys named after various movie
stars mingled freely with zoo visitors. Such an arrangement
could never have worked if it weren't for the many volun-

teers who kept human hands away from monkey tails, and in turn, monkey teeth from nipping at human hands. Bernice Unser, one of those volunteers, met me at the exhibit's entrance gate, her face creased in concern.

"Why's the zoo so weird this morning?" she asked. "I can't get anyone to talk to me or even look me in the eye. On my way through the parking lot, I saw Aster Edwina's limo pulling up, too. What's going on?" The other volunteers crowded around her, eager to hear my answer.

I had three choices: tell the truth, play dumb, or plead the Fifth. I chose the latter. "There'll be an announcement later, but for the time being, sorry, I can't say anything."

"Did somebody escape?" another volunteer asked, one of the high school seniors enrolled in our ZooTeen program. From his avid expression, he hoped somebody had. Somebody big, like a lion or a rhino. Oh, the thrills.

"Nothing like that. You're all perfectly safe. Now, if you'll excuse me, I need to release the monkeys."

As the boy's face fell in disappointment, I slipped past him and took the service road path down to the monkeys' night house. Marlon, the troop's alpha male, stood shrieking inside, with the females and adolescents providing an atonal chorus. Lana, a new mother whose baby clung to her back in a milk-induced stupor, plucked at the leg of my cargo pants as if to say, "Hurry up!" while I unlocked the door. As soon as it swung open, they scampered toward the red feeding buckets that swung from the enclosure's trees. All except for Marlon, who stayed near the door until I fetched a bag of Purina monkey chow from my cart.

"Is this what you're waiting for, handsome?"

He flashed his teeth, a gesture which people not familiar with primates often mistake for a smile. Experience had taught me better. "Bite me, Marlon, and I'll visit

First Aid before I feed you guys, which'll take, oh, maybe a half hour."

While he didn't understand the words, he did understand my warning tone, so he spun around and chased after his troop, complaining all the way.

It doesn't take long to feed squirrel monkeys. After I'd piled monkey chow pellets into the red buckets and topped off each with portions of fresh fruit, I waded through the monkey swarm and returned to their night house.

A zookeeper's job consists largely of sweeping up poop, poop, and more poop, but I didn't mind. Especially not today, because concentrating on mundane tasks was preferable to remembering what had happened to Kate. She had barely reached her thirties, but now her family would be making her funeral arrangements. Come to think of it, where did her people live? In the few conversations we had shared, she'd never mentioned parents or siblings.

As soon as I finished cleaning the night house, I set off toward Down Under again. When I arrived, I saw Wanchu perched in the crook of Bill's arm, her forearms wrapped around his massive bicep.

"Ooo's my good sheila?" he cooed.

Wanchu appeared more interested in searching for fleas in her coarse coat than conversing with Bill, but he didn't seem to care, not even if a stray flea hopped over from Wanchu to visit. In that, he was much like Kate. A bit stand-offish with humans, she'd been a bleeding heart with her koalas.

When I alit from the cart and started down to the enclosure fence, Bill looked my way. His eyes, usually a clear blue, now looked wary. "You, again."

Who had he been expecting, Godzilla? "How are things going?"

"Bonzer." *Great.*

"How much did Zorah tell you?"

He focused on Wanchu, who had doubled around on herself and was licking her behind. "Just that Kate drowned in Gunn Harbor and you fished her out. Yabber like that."

"Nothing else?"

"Yeh. She asked if I wanted to accept a full-time position."

"And?"

"Told her yeh on the animals, no on the telly thing. Not that she asked about that."

No, Bill wouldn't have been asked. For various reasons, he was unsuited to the task. Kate had been a natural, which was why she'd been hired in the first place. On TV, her eyes sparkled and the words flowed. Her Tuesday *Koala Kate's Kuddly Kritters* segment was one of the most watched portions on *Good Morning, San Sebastian*. So far, she had showcased no amphibians, no invertebrates, just the most cuddly and photogenic of mammals. The standard people-pleasers. "Too bad about the TV show," I said. "It brought the zoo a lot of business."

"Not my prob. Ready for more tucker, sook?" *Ready for more food?* This last comment was addressed to Wanchu, not me.

I kept waiting for Bill to ask me more about Kate: was I certain she'd been dead when I pulled her from the water: did I perform CPR; did I think she'd suffered; had the fish nibbled on her? But, no. Still cooing sweet nothings to the koala, he drifted away from the fence toward Wanchu's favorite tree, where he'd replenished the eucalyptus browse I'd left earlier. He set her down on a limb and watched as she began busily stripping the leaves.

Bill dealt with grief amazingly well, I thought.

LATER THAT MORNING Zorah put out a radio call for all keepers to assemble in the auditorium at noon, so at the appointed time I and around forty others sat hunched over our sandwiches, trying to gossip and eat at the same time as we waited for Zorah to show. "Kate got drunk and drowned, there's nothing else to know," sniped Myra Sebrowski, the darkly beautiful great apes keeper. She had never liked Kate, and the antipathy had appeared mutual.

"She didn't look drunk to me," said Buster Daltry, a rhino and elephant keeper almost as bulky as his charges. He had been an early arrival at the Grimaldis' party, and even before I'd left, he'd put away numerous beers. Today his eyes were bleary and his hands trembled, but I imagined he could still whip Hulk Hogan in a body-slam contest.

"Oh, come on. Kate was lit." This, from Robin Chase, the big cat keeper.

Myra's physical opposite, Robin was an unattractive, big-boned woman who abstained from anything she considered unhealthy, which included non-vegan foodstuffs. I'd often wondered how she could bear throwing raw beef-steaks to her beloved big cats. "I watched her chug at least three beers," Robin continued. "And I'm sure she had more. That's probably why she fell overboard."

"Three beers isn't that much," Buster said.

"Not for you, maybe, but for someone Kate's size, it was a lot. Like I said, there's a good chance she had even more."

The conversation was interrupted when Zorah entered the room with Aster Edwina right behind her. The elderly president of the Gunn Trust looked sad, but she leaned calmly enough on her cane as Zorah walked up to the podium. The only other emotion she showed was the thin smile of recognition she threw in my direction. At least I think it was a smile. With Aster Edwina, it was hard to tell.

In contrast to her boss, Zorah's round face was red, and a tic marred the standard placidity of her brown eyes. The tiger tattoo on her muscular forearm twitched, too. After fussing with the podium mike for a moment, she bluntly announced, "Kate Nido died last night."

By now, most people had heard of Kate's death through the zoo grapevine, so there were few utterances of actual shock, merely a few murmurs of regret. After all, Kate was a new employee and hadn't yet made many friends. As Zorah led us in a moment of silence out of respect for her memory, I spotted Bill leaning against the back wall, his arms crossed over his chest. His face was so devoid of emotion that he could have been attending a used-car auction, not that he had the money to buy a car. His only form of transportation was the fourth-hand bicycle he pedaled to work from the nearby town of Castroville.

When the moment of silence ended, Zorah began to describe the temporary staffing changes necessitated by Kate's death. Aster Edwina had given her permission to offer Bill a full-time job as Head Marsupial Keeper. "This means there's now an opening for a part-time keeper," Zorah said. "Does anyone know someone who might be interested?"

While people shouted out names, I cast my mind back to last night's party and its deadly aftermath.

Why hadn't I heard Kate go into the water?

She must have hit her head pretty hard, either against a mooring or the edge of the Grimaldis' boat, but the second she started her fall, she should have had time to cry out even if she'd been under the influence. Come to think about it, I'd never heard of Kate getting drunk. If anything, she'd been more like Robin, so tightly-wrapped she never seemed to have any fun. No, that wasn't quite accurate. Kate had enjoyed her TV appearances, and she'd certainly enjoyed writing ZooNews, the zoo's newsletter.

My musings were interrupted when Zorah said, "To close this sad meeting with one happy announcement, I'm pleased to inform you that Aster Edwina has chosen Teddy Bentley as the new presenter of *Koala Kate's Kuddly Kritters*, the weekly Gunn Zoo segment on *Good Morning, San Sebastian...*"

"What!?" Only my experience in working with easily startled animals kept me from shrieking the word. Zorah hadn't said anything about the TV show to me, and I certainly hadn't volunteered. "...as well as all of Kate's PR work, so let's give our Teddy a great big hand!"

The ensuing applause sounded genuine, although Myra Sebrowski's hands remained in her lap. The look she shot me wasn't congratulatory, either.

Zorah wasn't finished. "Teddy, stop by my office so we can go over Kate's notes for tomorrow's program."

Before I could argue, she put down the mike and exited the auditorium four paces behind Aster Edwina.

"How long have you been angling for this?" Myra said, stopping me at the door just as I was about to dash after Zorah.

"C'mon, Myra. It's as big a surprise to me as anyone else. You think I enjoy the prospect of making a fool of myself on live TV?"

"I'm sure you'll pull it off with your usual aristocratic aplomb." With that parting shot, she stalked up the hill toward her apes, her back stiff with anger.

Great. Now I had an enemy. Not only that, but an enemy who could handle a full-grown mountain gorilla easier than I could handle Miss Priss. But how to handle Aster Edwina's command? Besides taking care of the koalas, Kate's duties had included updating the zoo's web site, posting to the zoo's blog, writing the bimonthly newsletter, and appearing on the weekly television segment. A full workload. My own duties were already just as heavy. As a full-time zookeeper for several animals and a frequent fill-in for sick or vacationing keepers, there was no way I could handle extra work.

I caught up with Zorah at the top of the hill leading to the administration building. Aster Edwina was no longer with her. The old woman had limoed back home to plot more mischief.

Butting up against the real wall of the administration building was the large enclosure where we kept the squirrel monkeys considered too old or "nippy" to be turned loose in Monkey Mania. They kept up a raucous chorus as I pled my case. When I began listing the impossibility of longer work hours, Zorah nodded sympathetically.

"A keeper's life is a hard one, isn't it, Teddy? Oh, how well I remember. Not that those days were all bad. Truth to tell, I miss them. But you're not here to listen to my problems, are you? Let's go inside and talk."

Confident that I'd stated my case successfully, I followed the zoo director to her paper-strewn office, where photographs of her former charges lined the wall. Zorah had once been the zoo's head keeper, with a special love for great apes, so I briefly admired the pictures she'd taken of hairy heads and huge hands. Cuddliness arrived via close-ups of various monkey, orangutan, and gorilla babies clinging to their mothers' backs. From the room's large, safety glass-plated window, I could see some of the photographs' subjects staring in. They looked like they wanted to come in and play.

"I'm jealous of Myra," Zorah said, pushing aside a stack of papers. "After my run-in with the snippy great apes keeper, Zorah's comment startled me. "Why?"

"Because she spends most of her time with her apes, not behind a desk. For that matter, I'm jealous of you, too."

"Then you understand why I can't do the TV program.

Speaking of Myra, she seems interested in the job. And she's certainly more photogenic than I am."

"Wrong temperament."

Well, there was that. On Myra's best days, she wasn't exactly sunny, so perhaps Zorah was right. "Outback Bill, then. Given his long experience with animals, especially marsupials, he's Kate's obvious replacement."

"Mr. Sewer Mouth? Just the thought of that man discussing animals' mating rituals on live TV gives me the shudders. Even if he could be trained to withhold the F-bomb, that thick Aussie accent of his would be indecipherable to most viewers. So, no, Teddy. Neither Myra nor Bill is the right person to take over for Kate. You are."

I shook my head. "Frankly, Zorah, the idea of going on camera makes me feel ill. I'll blank out and look stupid."

"Don't give me that," she chuckled. "I've seen you handle the school tours, and there's not a question you can't answer. Stop arguing about it, because Aster Edwina's mind is made up, and you know how she is. Anyway, for tomorrow, here's the plan. The station wants to do an animal-related tribute to Koala Kate, so here are the animals…"

Maybe I hadn't made my point clearly enough. "Call Aster Edwina and tell her I don't have any television experience, that I'll screw everything up and make the zoo look bad."

A sly look crossed Zora's face. "Sorry, but I'm with Aster Edwina on this. What about last year, when that KTSS-TV reporter got the jump on you outside the giant anteater enclosure? You did a great job on something that could have turned into a disaster for the zoo. Before that, how about the time you and that bay mare of yours won the open jumping competition in Texas and you wound up on the national news? Who interviewed you then? Was it Katie Couric?"

"Diane Sawyer," I muttered, worried about the direction the conversation had taken.

"Then there was that debutante ball over in Monterey—bet you never guessed I watch that kind of coverage, did you? You were the only girl in the Simper Brigade who didn't sound like a jackass."

"Okay, so I've been on TV before. But what I said earlier holds. With my work load…"

She ignored my protests. "Save your breath, Teddy. Aster Edwina asked for you personally. And the TV station owner seconded it."

I groaned. Ford Bronson was a new neighbor of my mother's, whom I frequently saw jogging around Gunn Landing Harbor where he kept his yacht. A dot-com billionaire turned media mogul, Bronson was used to getting his way. But not with me. "You'll have to tell both Bronson and Aster Edwina both no, Zorah. My work load…"

"Not a problem. On your way down to the station every Tuesday, you'll clock in here. If you need to add several extra hours to take care of your keeper duties, you'll get paid time-and-a-half. You always did say you'd work here seven days a week if we'd let you. Now's your chance to make good on that." I started to say something about federal and state employment regulations, then remembered the condition of the *Merilee*'s engine. Long past overhaul territory, it needed to be replaced, and a new engine would cost thousands of dollars that I didn't have. "Pay me double-time."

"Done." Her answer came so swiftly that I realized I'd been had. Sighing, I said, "How long will I need to continue this?"

"At least until you've bought a new engine for the *Merilee*." Zoos are just like small towns; everybody knows everybody's business.

Conceding defeat by a superior adversary, I moved on. "You said the station wants this week's program to be a tribute to Kate. I guess that means you want me to take a koala over there."

Zorah stretched out her muscular arms in a gesture that seemed to take in the entire zoo. "I envision a fuller program, with a koala, a wombat, a wallaby, and a numbat— just to add one nonmarsupial to the mix. No frilled lizard; too excitable. Same for the Tasmanian devil we have on loan from San Diego. He's liable to chew off the anchorwoman's head. Just give viewers some pertinent facts about each animal as you hold it, and talk about their disappearing habitats. Oh, and before the segment ends, be sure and get in a plug for our Name-the-Baby-Anteater contest. Thanks to all the publicity we've received, Mama Lucy's a big star."

"Zorah, four animals are too much to handle. And a wombat? They weigh around forty pounds!"

She waved away my concern. "We'll give you an adolescent, one who weighs less than twenty. Besides, you'll have two assistants with you. And every animal you're taking is very well behaved. Wanchu, the female koala, is placid-to-comatose, and she'll have eaten before you pick her up, so she might even sleep through the entire program. She's sure to fart a lot, though, so make sure you turn her bottom away from AnnaLee what's-her-name, the anchorwoman. Just lift Wanchu out of her cage, cuddle her for a minute—while hyping our Down Under exhibit and sounding terribly, terribly sorry about Koala Kate, of course— then put her away. The wombat might sleep through the segment, too, since they all have the energy of Rip Van Winkle. Malka-Malka, the striped numbat I saw you talking to the other day. He's a different story. Very active, but he's no bigger than a squirrel. He's such a doll that the audience will fall in love with him. If he starts acting up, just give him a handful of termites, tell him he's beautiful, and put him away. That's it! I expect you here tomorrow at…"

"Aren't you forgetting someone?"

A bland smile. "Noooo, I think I covered everyone."

"The wallaby, Zorah."

She smiled. "No problem there, I know you like the wallabies. I've even heard you singing to them! Nice soprano, by the way. Tell you what, I'll give you Abim. He's the smallest of the mob, less than two feet high. Looks just like a joey, a baby kangaroo. Big, big eyes and the sweetest expression you ever saw. He'll be on a stretchable leash. Don't worry, he's been trained to it, and as long as you don't drop the leash, you'll do fine. Hey, if you can handle a thousand-pound horse, you can handle a wee wallaby, right?"

I frowned, remembering that the translations from Aborigine to English on the Down Under signage informed zoo visitors that Abim meant *devil*.

Maybe I was just being paranoid.

THREE

Tuesday morning began well, which just goes to show.

Down at the harbor, the morning fog wasn't as heavy as usual, and by the time I'd fed DJ Bonz and Miss Priss and gone topside to toss the otter her morning herring, it was already clear enough to walk my dog through Gunn Park without once bumping into a trash can.

Gunn Landing, population 592, had been settled in the nineteenth century by Edwin Gunn, the wealthy railroad baron who later founded the zoo. Located on a tiny strip of land forty miles north of Monterey, the village was little more than a harbor. Its only actual houses were in Old Town, situated on a high bluff on the other side of Highway One. Because of their expense—upwards of seven million dollars each—we peons hunkered down on our much cheaper boats. But we had big yards: the Pacific Ocean to the west and Gunn Park to the east.

On my way past the restrooms and showers provided for the liveaboarders' use, my cell phone rang. With Bonz panting happily at my feet, I settled myself on a picnic bench and spent the next five minutes listening to Joe's sexy voice, not his official one. He'd fantasized about me as he took his morning shower, he purred, and could hardly wait until our dinner date that night and the follow-up next Monday, the only full day off we shared. "Me, too," I purred back. "I'll chill some Reisling. But it would be nice if we could see each other more than twice a week, especially now that you don't have any more big cases." Joe himself had recently suggested an increase in face time, although the prospect had its difficulties. As sheriff of San Sebastian County, he was always on call, and as a widower with two young children, he spent most of his free hours entertaining them, not his girlfriend.

The purring ceased. "Big cases?"

"Like those murders a few months ago."

"Hmm."

"Just highway accidents, which are sad enough."

"Hmm."

I would have been more alert to his change in tone if it hadn't been for Bonz's loud bark. Coming through the fading mist toward us was Hans, Linda Cushing's aging German shepherd. He had slipped his leash again. Infuriated at this intrusion onto what Bonz saw as his own turf, my dog lunged toward Hans as best as he could, given that he only had three legs. Ordinarily, the terrier-sized Bonz is timid, but he knew from previous encounters that Hans, despite his imposing bulk, was an even bigger chicken. As Bonz snarled on, the shepherd shrank back against a rusty Volkswagen parked near the harbor gate, and vented a pathetic howl.

"What's going on?" Joe yelled through the phone. "Need me to send over a squad car?"

Through the din, I yelled back, "Just Bonz threatening Hans again. Talk to you later." I rang off, then leaned down and closed my hand gently around Bonz's muzzle. "No, dog. Hans is a friend. *Friend.*"

Bonz gave me a defiant look, but before he could bark again, I heard Linda's voice. "Hans! Shut that racket up!"

"We're over here by the gate. Bonz has him cornered."

"Can't keep a leash on the damned dog these days," she muttered, coming toward us, leash and collar dangling in her hands.

"Either he needs a smaller collar or you need to fatten him up."

She humphed. "Vet's got him on a diet."

Remembering her financial problems—these days nearly everyone in the harbor is broke—I said, "I've got a spare that'll fit him. Want it?"

"If you don't need it."

Sensing rescue at hand, Hans stopped his howling and waved his tail. She bent down and kissed him on the nose. Bonz growled.

"You shut up too, Bonz," Linda said, but with a dog-loving smile, "or your mama will chop you up for otter food."

My aborted conversation with Joe forgotten, I opened the harbor gate with my key card and we walked our dogs along the dock. When we stopped in front of the *Merilee*, she recounted what little information she'd been able to give Joe about the Grimaldis' party. "Kate seemed sober enough to me, but maybe she started knocking them back after I left."

"What time did you leave?" I asked.

"Around midnight."

"Kate was still there?"

She nodded. "Yeah, but trust me, that girl was sober."

"Did you tell Joe?"

"Of course. I also gave him that full guest list I promised. Maybe the Grimaldis know how much she drank after I left. After all, they were the ones supplying the beer. There was one bottle of Cutty Sark on hand, but it disappeared early," she cackled. "I helped with that, although to be honest, Doris was the one who was really knocking it back."

"That's odd. I've never seen her drink much, either." Doris Grimaldi, along with her husband Sam, owned Lucky Lanes, where the zoo was holding its Bowling for Rhinos fundraiser. Sam, the younger and better-looking of the two, provided Lucky Lanes' bonhomie, leaving Doris to handle the business side of things. Like many successful people, she was more bookkeeper than partier.

Linda snorted. "If you'd stayed longer, you'd have seen what I mean. By the time I left, she was looking pretty happy."

"Doris always looks happy."

"That's what you think."

Before I could ask what she meant, she said, "That dog collar you promised?"

"Coming right up." I hurried below deck and snatched the collar out of a galley drawer.

Linda received it gratefully, and fastened it around her dog's neck. "Well, kid, I gotta take Hans back to the *Tea 4 Two*. Have a nice day at the zoo, and don't let the bears eat you."

ZORAH HAD INFORMED me that she'd split my morning duties between two other keepers, so an hour later, when I clocked in, I looked camera-ready in my freshly ironed uniform. The koala, wombat, wallaby, and numbat were dozing peacefully on top of burlap sacks in their respective carriers inside the Animal Care Center, but I saw no sign of the two assistants I'd been promised. "I can't handle all these animals by myself," I complained to Dr. Francks, our new vet. A rather snappish man with a wild beard and hair that made him resemble Rasputin, he'd emerged from retirement when one of our other vets decamped with her family to the San Diego Zoo.

He looked up from the anesthetized Bengal tiger whose fangs he was cleaning. "Zorah called a couple of minutes ago, said someone's on the way."

"Some *one*?"

He gestured toward the small cages by the door. "I don't

think you're in any danger from those guys. Are you afraid
the koala will fall asleep on your face and smother you? Or
that the wombat will scratch your eyes out? If you're all
that nervous, maybe you should transfer to the children's
zoo where you could work with the sheep." At that, the vet
techs helping him giggled until he silenced them with a
growl worthy of the Bengal.

Thus squelched, I held my silence while my mind rehearsed the logistics of lugging around four different cages,
and the prospect of keeping all the animals calm during the
show. Having only one assistant would be stretching it, but
an experienced animal keeper should be able to handle the
job. Maybe Zorah was lending me Bill. His mouth might
not be ready for prime time, but it didn't bother the Down
Under animals.

My hopes were dashed when five minutes later, Bernice
Unser, the Monkey Mania volunteer, walked through the
door. She must have seen the disappointment on my face
because she said, "Sorry, but there was some kind of sched-
uling snafu this morning and Zorah asked me to help out."

It could have been worse. Although no actual animal
keeper, most of whom had master's degrees in the biologi-
cal sciences, Bernice had completed several of the zoo's
Small Animal Care classes and knew which end was the
biting end. She was also strong, which would help with
the lugging.

"Any experience in Down Under?" I asked her.

"Six months, before I transferred to Monkey Mania.
That's when I learned that most marsupials sleep all day.
Since I can only volunteer in the mornings, I wanted to
spend that time with animals who are actually awake."

She smiled. I smiled back. The situation wasn't perfect,
but it would have to do.

THIRTY MINUTES LATER, while Bernice and I waited with the drowsy marsupials in the Green Room at KTSS-TV, Suzi Lovejoy, the assistant producer of *Good Morning, San Sebastian*, a harassed-looking young woman who seemed little more than a teenager, peered into the cages.

"Are they dead?"

"Just sleeping," I explained.

Frowning, Suzi explained the segment's logistics. Gesturing toward Bernice with an ink-stained finger, she said, "Bess here will…"

"My name is *Bernice*."

"Yeah. Bess will stay out of camera range and keep the animals in their cages until the zookeeper…"

"Call me Teddy."

"Right. Until you say you're ready for another one. Then Bess will take out the animal and pass it to you. I don't want Bess to say anything 'cause you, whatsyournameagain, should do most of the talking at least when…"

"Teddy."

"Uh huh. Anyway, Letty, AnnaLee Harris will be your interviewer, and she'll start off the segment with a brief Koala Kate eulogy, then she'll introduce you. Make sure to say you're heartbroken about Kate and how wonderful she was to work with and what a tragedy blah-blah-blah, then tell Bess to pass you that bear thingy. Once she does, give the viewers some basic information about him."

"My helper's name is *Bernice*, Suzi. And the koala's a female named Wanchu. She's not a bear, she's a marsupial."

"Whatever. Then we'll break for commercial, which will be two-and-a-half minutes. When we come back, AnnaLee will ask you some follow-up of questions about the bear."

This time I let the mistakes slide. With Bernice paying close attention, Suzi prattled on, listing the order in which she wanted the animals introduced. After the "bear thingy," she wanted the "striped thingy"—I took that to mean the numbat; and then the "disgusting fat thingy"—probably the poor wombat. Last up would be the "baby kangaroo." Sighing, I said, "He's an adult wallaby, Suzi. His species tops out at two feet high."

"Uh huh. So let the baby kangaroo hop around some, 'cause our viewers like to see animals in action, not just laying there like they're dead or something."

I assured her I'd let the wallaby give a few hops, if he was awake. He'd been snoring when we lugged him in from the van. "Then give him a good kick to wake him up, just don't let the viewer see it. They tend to overreact to that sort of thing." Bernice frowned. She didn't like the idea of a kicked wallaby any more than I did.

I gave Suzi my best glare but she was so busy looking at her watch that she didn't notice. Bernice and I started to settle back down on the brown vinyl couch but were interrupted in midsquat when Suzi said, "Commercial. Let's get those fur balls out there. Stay at my side until I tell you to move."

She opened the Green Room door and ushered us into the studio.

The studio was so dark I could see little in its cavernous space, only the set itself where AnnaLee Harris, wearing enough makeup to sink the *Titanic* all over again, sat under glaring lights on a small sofa. She was holding a book up to the camera. Across from her sat a bewildered-looking elderly man, whom I took to be the author.

"As Mr. Greenwald here has so movingly pointed out," AnnaLee was saying, an unsettling smile on her face. "*Growing Up on an Arkansas Chicken Farm,* which he will be signing today at noon at the Book Beast in San

Sebastian, makes delightful reading for those who wish to return to those less-pressured days of yesteryear…"

"Oh, I wouldn't say less pressured…" the author began, then a voice in the darkness interrupted him. "And we're out for commercial!"

The smile left AnnaLee's face as she turned away from the author like he no longer existed. "Next!" she snapped to Suzi.

Suzi rushed forward, hauled the author off the sofa and pushed him toward the Green Room. Once he'd disappeared, muttering to himself, she said to Bernice, "Give whatshername the bear now."

"Teddy. Koala." Bernice opened Wanchu's cage.

As Bernice picked her up, Wanchu gave a grunt and opened her eyes. *Where in the world am I?* she appeared to be thinking. When Bernice handed her to me, she snuggled against my neck and fell back asleep.

"Get over there," Suzi said, shoving me toward the sofa. "You're on in thirty seconds."

For a moment, I panicked. "What'll I say?"

"Follow AnnaLee's lead. And for God's sake, do what you're told. If you don't, she'll take it out on me."

Another shove, and suddenly there I was, sitting on the sofa with twenty pounds of dozing koala wrapped around my neck, staring at a red light on a camera that seemed to be looking up my nose.

"Five, four, three, two…" Suzi counted.

"Welcome back to *Good Morning, San Sebastian!*" crowed AnnaLee, smiling again. Then, as if someone had flipped on the Sadness Switch, her face assumed a tragic expression. "As KTSS-TV reported yesterday, the accidental drowning of my dear, dear friend Koala Kate, everyone's favorite zookeeper, has profoundly affected us all. I first met Kate when…" AnnaLee continued to describe Kate in such glowing terms that I suspected she'd not known her outside the studio.

When she turned to me, her mad smile was back. "But now the baton has passed to my new friend…" She checked her notes, "…zookeeper Theodora Esmeralda Iona Bentley, but who prefers to be known as plain old 'Teddy.' Tell me, Teddy, are you one of the famous Gunn Landing Bentleys?"

Oh, dear. Surely she wouldn't ask about my father. "Uh, yes, I am."

"Well, I'm certain that you had no knowledge of your father's criminal activities, but tell me…"

Oh, crap. "No knowledge whatsoever, AnnaLee, and look whom I've brought you today. Wanchu, one of the Gunn Zoo's most popular koalas! Now let me tell you about this adorable Australian marsupial. As I'm certain you know, a koala's diet consists purely of eucalyptus leaves, which makes them difficult to care for in most zoos, but our zoo is fortunate in that the Gunn estate has a large blue gum eucalyptus forest situated right next door." Before she could start up on my father again, I jiggled Wanchu awake. As she gazed sleepily around, I continued jabbering about koalas and their rapidly diminishing natural habitat.

Just as I finished describing a koala's backwards-facing pouch, Wanchu roused herself, loosened her sphincter, and deposited a load on my lap. It didn't faze me. "One of the great things about taking care of koalas like Wanchu is that they're so easy to clean up after. See how tidy their fecal pellets are? Why, you just brush them away like cookie crumbs!"

Smiling madly away, AnnaLee turned to the camera. "And now a word from our sponsor, Harmon's Boat Works at Gunn Landing Harbor. You sink 'em, Harmon resurrects 'em."

Bernice sprang forward, and with a paper towel, cleaned

the koala pellets off my lap. Wanchu, deciding that she'd done enough work for one day, started snoring again.

"Do koalas always sleep this much?" AnnaLee said, when we went back on the air.

"From nineteen to twenty hours a day. If you want to see an active koala, visit the Gunn Zoo in late afternoon. That's when they wake up and bounce around. We have two koalas, by the way, Wanchu here, and her mate, Nyee. We're very hopeful that one day we'll have a baby koala— known as a pup, by the way—to increase the Gunn Zoo's koala population to three."

"Fascinating."

I jiggled Wanchu. "Wake up, pretty girl, and tell the viewers hello."

As if on cue, Wanchu opened her eyes, stared at the glowing red light, and said, "Eeep!"

"Awwwww!" the studio technicians chorused. Gratified, Wanchu went back to sleep.

Recognizing that Wanchu's act was over, AnnaLee asked, "What else have you brought for us, Teddy?"

Bernice rushed forward, snatched Wanchu away, then returned with Malka-Malka, the numbat. Unlike Wanchu, the non-marsupial numbat was wide awake and wriggling his snout in curiosity.

More *awwwww*'s from the dark shapes in the studio. "My, he's a lively one!" AnnaLee said. "What's his story?" While the squirrel-sized Malka-Malka struggled in my lap—I suspected he wanted to play with AnnaLee's flappy artificial eyelashes—I gave the viewers a condensed version of numbat lore, ending with a segue I thought quite clever. "Because of a numbat's diet, which consists almost entirely of termites, you could call them Australia's version of a giant anteater. And as I'm sure you know, KTSS viewers, the Gunn Zoo is holding a naming contest for the giant anteater's baby. Whoever wins gets a free one-year pass to the zoo, so mail in those entries today!"

Another mad smile from AnnaLee. "And now a word from our sponsor, The Foot Fetish, more than two hundred sexy styles, located in beautiful downtown San Sebastian."

As soon as the red light blinked off, AnnaLee leaned forward and scratched Malka-Malka on the head. He thanked her by embracing her wrist with his long, sticky tongue, then struggled toward her eyelashes. Before he could reach them, Bernice sprang forward again, wiped numbat spittle off AnnaLee's hand, and with a lightning-quick movement, snatched him up. A few seconds later she staggered onto the set lugging Tuang. The wombat looked barely conscious. By now my earlier anxiety had vanished, and although Tuang was obviously no adolescent—he had to weigh at least forty pounds—I settled him as comfortably as possible in my lap.

"Back again, this time with something called a wombat!" AnnaLee couldn't have sounded more excited if she'd just won the Powerball. "Tell us about that big boy, Teddy! He looks like a giant gopher!"

As Tuang dozed peacefully, I ruffled his thick fur and delivered a basic run-down on Southern hairy-nosed wombat habits and habitat. They were grass-grazing, burrowing marsupials, and like koalas, seldom drank water because they received most of their moisture needs from plant life. Wombats were like koalas in another way, too, in that they were rapidly losing so much of their native habitat that their species had become highly endangered. Once during my spiel, Tuang roused himself enough to crap on my lap, but I didn't mind because it gave me another talking point. "See Tuang's fecal matter, AnnaLee? Unlike the koala's, it's cube-shaped and is about the size of gambling dice. Cool, huh? Scientists believe this unusual shape keeps the fecal matter from rolling away on a slope, thus aiding wild wombats to successfully mark their territory. But kids, don't try making fecal cubes at home!"

"Uh, and now a word from our sponsors, Cappuccino & Chowder."

I was feeling good. Confident. Knowledgeable. A credit to Gunn Zoo. A keeper able to work on live TV, regardless of whatever organic matter an animal deposited on me. But I'd forgotten an important life lesson. During my teen years at Miss Pridewell's Academy for Young Ladies, I'd been taught that the Greeks called this kind of confidence *hubris*, known to us contemporary folk as the pride which goeth before a fall. Alas, I'd been so thrilled with my interview skills that I neglected to remain cautious, because away went the placid Tuang and here came Abim the wallaby. Looking alert, he hopped slowly ahead of Bernice, with a blue rhinestone-studded leash attached to his matching collar. Goody, he wouldn't defecate on my lap; he'd go on the floor.

Bernice handed me the leash. "Better be carefu…"

"We're back!" AnnaLee trilled, flapping those immense eyelashes as the red light blinked on and Bernice faded tactfully into the shadows. "Oh, look what we have here! A baby kangaroo! You folks sitting at your breakfast tables or sipping your full-bodied coffee drink at the nearest Cappuccino & Chowder location, isn't he simply the most adorable thing? And look at his pretty collar and leash! Why, they're just as sparkly as he is! Teddy, I'm going to walk him…"

Before I could explain that Abim was a full-grown wallaby and not a baby kangaroo, and say that no, of course I wouldn't let a stranger walk him, AnnaLee snatched the leash from my hand and stood up. She made it two steps from the sofa before all hell broke loose.

After one tentative hop, Abim looked behind him only

to see that neither Bernice nor I held the other end of his leash. Instead, his handler was a vividly dressed, garish-cheeked creature with flapping eyelashes the size of an Australian bird-eating spider. With a coughing sound—the wallaby version of "Holy shit!"—Abim gathered himself and gave a great, arcing leap, ripping the leash from An-naLee's hand. Once loose, he bounded off the well-lit set and into the darkness beyond, fear-coughing as he went.

I flashed a quick smile at the red light, and with an Aussie accent, yipped, "Crikey, mates! Wallaby on the loose!" Leaving AnnaLee looking at her empty hand as if she hadn't yet figured out what had just happened, I hurried after him, Bernice following close behind.

Once out of the spotlight's glare, it took a moment for my eyes to grow accustomed to the relative darkness. I was kept apprised of Abim's general whereabouts by the series of shrieks and curses spreading throughout the studio. Keeping silent myself, since my voice would simply add more noise to the chaos, I quick-stepped toward the loudest screams. Considering that the wallaby was so small, it was surprising to see two grown men cowering in the corner. What did they think Abim was going to do? Nibble their pinkies with his tiny teeth? Hoping to quell their whimpering because it would further frighten the wallaby, I put my finger to my lips. At that, the duo fell silent. One even made an excuse for his wussiness, saying, "Oh, we were just getting out of his way." Only one cameraman remained at his post, pivoting his camera to follow the wallaby's hopping progress through the studio. Oops; make that camera *woman*. Taking my cue from the direction in which her camera was pointing, I spotted Abim hopping toward a glowing red Exit sign. Fortunately, a line of desks barred his way.

No problem for the wallaby. Abim did what wallabies are

famous for. He gave his greatest leap yet and bounded onto the center desk, sending papers and coffee mugs flying.

"Huh-huh! Huh-huh!" he coughed, his distress growing.

His feet started a tap-dance, another sign of wallaby terror. After splashing coffee all over the room, he leapt down to the ground and continued bounding his way toward the Exit sign as if he was trying to get back to the zoo.

But before Abim could reach the door, he caught his leash between two of the many cables that snaked across the floor. His head disappeared briefly from sight. Then I heard another cough, followed by a straining grunt, then a crash. Freed, Abim appeared again, hopping on until he managed to trap himself in the corner by the Exit door. His chest heaved in and out, and his forepaws trembled. I knew that if I approached him, it would frighten him even further, and I didn't want the poor thing to have a heart attack, which had been known to happen with terrified animals.

Then I remembered something. Abim was an adult wallaby, but during times of fear even the adults often regress and seek security in anything that resembled a pouch. Keeping my voice low, I said to Bernice, "Bring me that burlap sack from his carrier."

"Gotcha," she whispered back, then tiptoed away.

Mere seconds later Bernice was back, sack in hand. Humming the tune to "Waltzing Matilda"—marsupials particularly liked my rendition—I unfolded it slowly, facing the dark opening toward Abim.

"Hey, baby," I murmured. "Come to Mama's big, soft pouch." The wallaby blinked at the sack a couple of times, then looked around nervously. Except for the camerawoman still filming, the now-silent station crew remained frozen in place.

Abim cocked his head and gave a tentative hop forward. Encouraged, I began to sing.

"Waltzing Abim-boy, waltzing Abim-boy You'll come a-waltzing Abim-boy, with me.

And he sang as he shoved that jumbuck in his tucker bag, You'll come a-waltzing Abim-boy, with me."

Another hop and he was in.

As the camera crew erupted into applause, I closed the sack, handed Abim off to Bernice, then walked back to AnnaLee with the camerawoman swiveling to follow me.

"And that's how you catch a runaway wallaby, mates," I said, smiling at the red light.

FOUR

AFTER RETURNING TO the zoo, Bernice and I left the animals in the Animal Care Center for Dr. Francks to check out, then she made her way back to Monkey Mania. I headed up to the administration building, where I found the zoo director eating her way through a cheese-and-anchovy pizza while the squirrel monkeys watched from the other side of the window.

"Want some pizza, Teddy?" Zorah asked, as I plopped myself in the visitor's chair.

I shook my head. "There's tomato sauce on your chin."

She swiped at the spot with a paper napkin, only further smearing the red stuff. I might be wrong, but I'd swear I saw one of the monkeys waggle his tongue toward it. Maybe he wanted a taste.

"Saw you on *Good Morning, San Sebastian*," Zorah said, ignoring him. Pizza wasn't good for monkeys.

"Then you know my TV career is over." *And wasn't I relieved.*

"You're kidding, right? I just got a call from the program manager and he told me that the station's phones have been ringing off the hook. People are asking when that cute redheaded zookeeper will be back and what animals will she bring next time because they want to set their TiVo's to record. We took a couple dozen calls here, too. The president of the Monterey Bay Beneficent Women's Society called and asked if you'd personally conduct the group on a guided tour of the Down Under exhibit.

"She hinted at a donation in return, which could be size-able, seeing as how all those broads, ah, *ladies,* have serious money." She looked at her watch. "She's due here any minute to discuss a luncheon on zoo grounds, too. I told her you'd be more than willing to give a talk."

None of this made any sense. My talk show debut had been a disaster. "Zorah, I wound up with shit all over my lap."

"As if that ever bothered you. You're failing to see the bright side, girlfriend. Yes, we lost Kate, and yes, it's tragic, but weirdly enough, you've turned out to be a bigger hit than she was. A lot funnier, one of our callers said." Her smile disappeared. "Speaking of, your sheriff boyfriend's in Down Under, talking to Bill. Tell me the truth. When you hauled Kate out of the water, did anything seem funny to you?"

"Funny? As in ha-ha?"

"Bad choice of words, but you know what I mean. Did her death truly look like an accident? Or could she have been, well, killed?" She took another bite of pizza, leaving a string of cheese hanging from her bottom lip. The monkey outside the window cocked his head, studying it.

"Kate *was* killed, Zorah. She fell off the *Gutterball,* cracked her head on something, and drowned."

"I must be having trouble making myself understood. What I'm asking is, could she have been murdered?"

The question, delivered so baldly, shocked me. "Of course not!"

"Then why'd Sheriff Rejas look so grim when he came in here?"

My heart gave a leap that had nothing to do with love. "Was Joe accompanied by a deputy?"

"Not that I could see."

Having a sheriff for a boyfriend had taught me a few things about criminal investigation. When an arrest was imminent, the arrester never showed up alone, especially when the arrestee was a man as big as Bill. "Then he just wants to talk to him. But isn't all this worry a bit premature? Kate's death was accidental. I'm certain of it."

"Hmm."

"Tell you what. Before I start on my rounds, I'll drop by Down Under and see what's happening."

"Pump the sheriff for more information, okay?"

I stood up. "I can try. Oh, Zorah? You'd better take a look in the mirror before you see president of the Monterey Bay Beneficent Women's Society. You've got more pizza on you than in you."

When I left, she was hurrying toward the ladies' room.

JOE, LOOKING HANDSOME as ever in his sheriff's khakis, was walking away from Bill when I braked my zebra-striped zoo cart in front of Down Under. He looked thoughtful; Bill looked smug.

Catching sight of me, Joe smiled. "Fancy meeting you here."

"Shouldn't come as a surprise since I'm here six days a week. How're things going?" In anticipation of the probing questions I was about to ask, I kept my voice casual.

Joe's face closed in. "Mom's fine, and so are the kids."

"I meant about poor Kate."

His eyebrows lifted slightly. "What about her?"

"Autopsy done yet?"

"This morning, as a matter of fact."

"And?"

"Did I ever tell you that I love it when you're interested in my job?"

Hints weren't working, so I came right out with it. "The medical examiner didn't find anything suspicious about Kate's death, did he?"

"That information will be released to the media tomorrow. By the way, are we on for tonight?"

"Tonight?"

"It's Tuesday, Teddy. Dinner date."

"Oh. That."

The smile returned. "Yes, that."

"How about instead of going out, I just fry up some fresh fish at the *Merilee*, and we eat on deck? And sip wine. And, well, maybe have some dessert."

A broader smile. "See you at seven. I'll bring the wine." When he hurried away without another word, I realized I'd been punked. Joe had had no intention of sharing any details about Kate's death. Oh, well. Two can play that manipulation game. He might have won this round but I'd turn the tables tonight.

Not so optimistic about my chances with Bill, I nonetheless stepped into the koala enclosure. He was busy cuddling Wanchu, but to my surprise he was willing to talk, just not about Kate.

"You think you're taking one of me babies onto fookin' telly again, you got another think coming, you silly sheila. Letting that drongo grab Abim's leash like that, what're you playin' at? Me and me mates was watching telly over in the employees' lounge, and it near sent me into a Technicolor yawn." Translation: *Silly Teddy can't take another Down Under animal back to the F-bombing television studio; anchorwoman AnnaLee Harris is a fool; watching the runaway wallaby fiasco made me want to vomit.*

"Bill, I'm truly sorry about what happened, and I promise to be better prepared for anchor interference next time. But not to worry. The Aussie animals have had their fifteen minutes of fame, and we'll be moving on to another continent." And to something more manageable. Like a grizzly.

Somewhat mollified, Bill gave Wanchu a final pat and

lifted the koala into the crook of her favorite tree. "Just dropped by to say yer sorry, then?"

"Yes, but I couldn't help noticing that Sheriff Rejas was talking to you. What'd he want?"

"Not having kangaroos loose in me top paddock, I won't be tellin' the sheriff's sheila anything." Translation: *I'm not crazy enough to give any information to the sheriff's girlfriend.*

"I was just…"

"Yeh, yeh, you wasn't really snoopin' around. Now rack off and let me get back to work, which is something you should be doing yerself, rather than wasting yer time yabbering."

I racked off.

Watching Zorah gobble down that pizza had reminded me it was lunchtime, so I wandered over to the Congo Café and purchased a foot-long smothered in chili, onions, and mustard. For dessert, I chose a strawberry smoothie topped with a tablespoon of wheat germ; we keepers have to watch our health. I was about to sit down at one of the umbrella tables when I was hailed by rhino keeper Buster Daltry, who was carrying a cardboard lunch tray heaped with burgers and fries. Trailing him were Robin Chase, big cats; Jack Spence, bears; Myra Sebrowski, great apes; Manny Salinas, birds; and Lex Yarnell, a spectacularly hunky park ranger most of the female zookeepers had shown interest in at one time or another.

"Look, it's the big TV star!" Lex quipped. "Descend from your throne, oh magnificent one, and join your loyal subjects in the employees' lounge."

Happy not to be eating alone, I grabbed my things and followed the group along the Africa Trail. Although Tuesday wasn't the zoo's busiest day, children from several Monterey day camps were crowding around the mountain gorilla's habitat, while a group of teens whose tee-shirts identified them as summer-schoolers from San Jose pretended to be bored. Balozi, the male silverback, who normally kept to the rear of the exhibit, had approached the Plexiglas barrier. He was aping them.

Hoping that Balozi would mind his manners—you can never tell what an ape will do when faced with tattooed and nose-ringed teens—we continued on.

The employees' lounge was located at the northeast corner of the zoo, but despite its lofty title, the building was little more than a shack. Outside, its plain lines were softened by a flowering castor bean bush and several banana trees, while inside, the decor was what you might call Zoo Modern: comfortable but mismatched furniture, walls brightened by posters of endangered animals. Scattered along the tables were years-old issues of *National Geographic, Cat Fancy, Audubon, Wildlife Conservation*, and *The South African Journal of Wildlife Research*. In the corner stood a battered old television set which, on occasion, actually worked.

Nothing being hungrier than a hungry zookeeper, we settled at the scuffed dining table and started shoving food into our mouths. For a while, all you could hear was the sound of munching, but as soon as Robin finished her soy burger, she voiced her disapproval of the way I had handled the runaway wallaby situation.

"That leash was awful, Teddy. You're lucky he didn't break his neck."

"The leash wasn't my idea, Robin. Besides, it was stretchable." Beautiful Myra joined in. Since men were present, and she liked men, she was careful not to sound waspish.

"Couldn't you have done something about that rhinestone collar? The poor little thing."

"Same answer."

Seeing the men nodding in agreement, she heightened her criticism. "Well, you need to know that when Zorah told me she was picking you to replace Kate, I voiced my concerns about your ability."

"Myra, for God's sa…" Buster began, but she cut him off.

"I warned Zorah about Kate, too, but she paid no attention." At this, Lex spoke up, his bright blue eyes flashing. "What Kate did in her own time is none of your business, Myra." Shocked—there had been rumors that Myra had a crush him—she fell silent.

But her comment made me curious. What did she "warn" Zorah about? Besides being a good zookeeper, Kate had always performed well on her *Good Morning, San Sebastian* segments. And from all accounts, she had done well at her other PR duties, too.

Did Myra know something I didn't?

Chancing the danger of irritating her further, I said, "Kate carried a fairly heavy workload. Did you think she was letting some of her tasks slide?"

Myra, having learned her lesson, remained silent, but Robin said, "Kate had plenty of time left over to cause trouble with that damned blog of hers."

The comment puzzled me. Besides writing *ZooNews*, the zoo's newsletter, Kate had also written *Koala Kate's Outback Telegraph*, the zoo's online blog, or "diary," where her descriptions of a zookeeper's typical day ranged from the hilarious to the downright terrifying. When I'd checked her site's stat counter once, I wasn't surprised to see that the blog's regular readers numbered in the tens of thousands nationwide. Apparently most people, especially wildlife-starved urban types, enjoyed reading about animals.

"Oh, c'mon, Robin," I said. *"The Outback Telegraph* is fun. How could it possibly cause trouble for anyone?"

Everyone stared at me in amazement. "What's wrong?" I asked.

"That's not the blog Robin was talking about, Teddy," Buster said gently. "She meant the other one."

"There was another blog?"

Under his voice, Lex mumbled something about what people didn't know couldn't hurt them, then changed the subject. "So, you zookeeper people, what new animals are coming in?"

"We're getting a new female Hamadryas," Myra offered. For Lex, she explained, "That's a baboon. From North Africa."

"And a breeding pair of golden eagles," said Manny Salinas, who up until now had sat quietly. "Those'll be fun. They're going into the area where the Watusi cattle used to be before we built their larger enclosure."

"Don't forget the new snow leopard," Robin said, happy to turn the attention to her beloved big cats. "I've seen pictures, and he's a beauty."

I wanted to ask again about that other blog Kate reputedly wrote, but by then, the others had resumed their chatter, so I filed the question away for later.

The rest of the day proved uneventful. Lucy and Baby Boy Anteater were dozing when I dropped by to replenish their termite supply, and the squirrel monkeys were calmer than usual. Between tasks, I thought about Kate. Dying alone at night, in a place where she hadn't had time enough to make true friends. That was the problem with a mobile society. When you disappeared, hardly anyone noticed. I would have spent more time getting to know Kate, but we had worked competing schedules.

Still, I wondered who her people were and sympathized for the pain they must have felt when receiving the news about her death.

I decided to ask Zorah about Kate's family when clocking out for the day. Although we'd been only nodding acquaintances, I wanted to send them a condolence card and flowers. White roses, for a woman who had died too young. But at six o'clock, when I returned to the Administration Building to clock out, Zorah was holed up in a meeting with the Monterey Bay Women's Beneficent Society. I left for home, intending to speak to her the next day.

As HARBORS GO, Gunn Landing's is considered small, but it's actually the largest commercial fishing harbor in the Monterey Bay area. A natural three-quarter moon shape, the harbor is sheltered at the flat end by a mile-long sandbar where seabirds flourish and harbor seals doze. Liveaboarders like myself make up about one-fifth of the harbor population. Most of us live here not only because we love seaside living, but also because even if we wanted to live inland, we couldn't afford the rent. Other than the refurbished garbage scows and sailboats that made up the liveaboard fleet, most of the other boats were commercial trawlers and pleasure craft, the sole exception being the large research vessel that belonged to the Gunn Landing Marine Institute.

I love the social mix that harbor life offers. Marine biologists, fishermen, whale watch skippers, Sunday sailors, bikers-turned-seadogs, scrimping liveaboarders, and a few folks like me—refugees from well meaning but manipulative mothers. Notwithstanding our varied population, life at the harbor tends to be peaceful. However, we aren't without the standard problems that plague the rest of the human race.

Once at the *Merilee*, I fed Bonz and Miss Priss and refreshed the kitty litter. When Bonz finished eating, I grabbed his leash.

"Ready for walkies?"

Yes, yes! he yipped.

As we strolled down the dock toward Gunn Park, I heard Linda Cushing, owner of the *Tea 4 Two*, arguing with Hector "Heck" Liddell, owner of the ill-named *My Fancy*, the rusty trawler he'd turned into an ill-kept houseboat. Curses flew fast and furious, most of them coming from Linda. In only three years at the harbor, Heck had managed to rile just about everyone, but the animosity between the two was particularly intense. This time, Heck claimed that Linda's dog, Hans, had peed against *My Fancy*'s stern. Linda counter-claimed that the other night, Heck himself had done the same thing to *Tea 4 Two*. "That garbage scow of yours ain't worth pissin' on!" Heck snapped.

"Don't insult my boat, you old fart, or I'll…"

I closed my ears to the rest and concentrated on getting Bonz to the park before he added more urine to the argument. Fortunately, we made it. As Bonz happily relieved himself against a trash can, I saw the über-rich Ford Bronson taking his regular evening jog along the harbor's southern promenade. I waved, he waved. But he kept on moving, probably in a hurry to finish his run and get back to making billions.

By the time Bonz and I returned to the *Merilee*, Linda and Heck had retired to their respective boats, and peace reigned once again. Having already showered at the zoo—I'd long ago transformed the *Merilee*'s tiny shower into a closet—I dressed in my latest wardrobe addition from Sissie's Second-Hand Stash, an ankle-length cheongsam. Although the dress's bright crimson clashed badly with my orange-red hair, I knew Joe would appreciate the slit up the side. All gussied up, I went on deck and relaxed with a glass of Riesling and awaited his arrival.

Unfortunately, Mother arrived first. I knew why she was here. Yesterday morning, before I'd left for the zoo,

I'd called and told her what happened, stressing that Kate's drowning was an accident. After recovering from her shock at a death taking place so close to the *Merilee*, she asked if I'd hurt myself dragging the body out of the dirty harbor water. I assured her I was fine, but given our past history, I knew that wouldn't be the end of it.

As always, Mother looked beautiful and was dressed far, far better than I. Rocking a beige Proenza Schouler crêpe de Chine pants suit accessorized by a gold and ivory Galliano necklace and a green-striped Balenciaga tote with matching espadrilles, she was the very picture of Central Coast chic. The only thing strange thing about her ensemble was Mr. Trifle, her new Chihuahua, who was poking his trembling head out of the Balenciaga. His beige jacket and beret perfectly matched her own.

"Hi, Mother. Want some Riesling?"

"Theodora, how many times do I have to tell you to call me Caro? 'Mother' is so aging. And no, I don't want any Riesling, since you never serve anything other than the cheap stuff." Sermon delivered, she perched her size two butt on a deck chair, but only after dusting it off with a monogrammed hanky.

"That so-called 'cheap stuff' is all I can afford."

"It doesn't have to be that way. I keep a marvelous cellar." Here we go again. Since I'd taken up residence on the *Merilee* last year, Caro had started nagging me to move back into the family home in the Old Town section of Gunn Landing. She not only considered my job beneath the dignity of a Bentley, but feared that the work was too dangerous for her precious only child. Every time an animal so much as sneezed on me, she renewed her pleas.

"I don't need a marvelous cellar, Caro."

"Yes, you do."

"No, I don't. This Riesling is delicious." I found it

peculiar that she had nothing to say about my appearance on *Good Morning, San Sebastian*, because she never missed the program. Maybe she thought that a Bentley getting pooped on in full view of several hundred thousand viewers was beneath mention.

"Your taste buds have atrophied, Theodora."

"No, they're… Say, Joe's on his way over," I said, to break up the monotony.

"That awful sheriff of yours? I don't want to talk about him. I'm just here to remind you that you promised to attend my soirée Friday night. Considering the state of your wardrobe…"

She flicked a disapproving eye at my crimson cheongsam, "… I bought you something nice to wear. When I was in Monterey yesterday, I saw this adorable Basso & Brooke that had *you* written all over it, so I snapped it up. Multiprint gauze over black silk, with a sweetheart neckline. Devastating. You must come up to the house and see it." She glanced around my boat and sniffed. "Since you don't have room for it here."

For some time Caro had been attempting to marry me off to someone she believed was more suitable for a Bentley; thus the endless soirées where she introduced me to a string of eligible bachelors. While I enjoyed our visits, I liked "that awful sheriff" just fine, thank you very much.

"The dress sounds lovely, Caro, but you didn't have to… Hey, how long has Mr. Trifle been doing that?"

The Chihuahua had stopped trembling and was lifting his upper lip in a silent snarl. If he'd been ten times bigger, he might have scared me.

She glanced down. "Oh, that. It started last week. I've got an appointment next Monday afternoon with that new dog psychic in San Sebastian, and I'm sure she'll sort him out in no time. But Mr. Trifle won't bite Miss Theodora, will he?" Cooing, she leaned over the Balenciaga tote, almost touching his nose with her own.

The expression on the Chihuahua's face made me suspect that Mr. Trifle wanted to chew off Miss Nose. "Pull your face away, Caro. Dog bites can turn serious."

Still cooing, she chucked the poor creature under his chin. "Mr. Veterinarian gave Mr. Trifle all his shots."

"Shots won't protect you from bacteria. Ever hear of necrotizing fasciitis, the flesh-eating disease? First the derma goes, then the subcutaneous tissue starts…"

She jerked her head away. "I saw some Fendi strap pumps, so I picked up those, too. And of course I'll loan you my diamonds. We need to make an impression, don't we?"

No, we don't. I was going to point that fact out to her, but then I spied a San Sebastian County sheriff's cruiser pull into the parking lot. "Oh, how nice! Joe will be so glad to see you."

My mother and Joe had, as the saying goes, *issues*. She had broken up our teenage romance by sending me away to a boarding school in Virginia. Years later, Joe married Sonia, and I married Michael. One divorce and one murder later, we were back together. Not that Caro accepted the situation.

She gave a quick look at her watch and stood up. "My, my. How time flies. I must be going."

Keeping a wary eye on Mr. Trifle's tiny fangs, I gave her a peck on each cheek. "Love you, Mother."

"Caro," she corrected, as she strutted away.

Seconds later, Joe stepped on deck. He had changed into civvies, but I could see the outline of his handgun under his blue windbreaker. As always, it made him look even sexier. After a deep kiss that took my breath away, he said, "I ran into your mother in the parking lot and she actually said hello. Quite an improvement for her, wouldn't you say?"

"Don't kid yourself. Caro can't bear the idea of her

daughter dating the grandson of a migrant worker; she's just getting more subtle. She's holding another Let's-Find-Teddy-A-Suitable-Husband party Friday night. Want to be my date?"

He sat down on the same deck chair Caro had vacated. "As much fun as that would be, I have to work."

I scooted my chair closer to his and was rewarded with another breath-stealing kiss. Once I'd recovered, I said, "That's right. Friday's a big night for law enforcement. All those drunken brawls and domestic spats, so predictable. It's too bad you don't have any good cases to challenge that fine mind of yours, isn't it?" When he didn't answer, I shot him a look. I knew him well enough to know something was up, and it made me uneasy. "What?" His face assumed an expression of feigned innocence. "You didn't answer my question."

"Wasn't it purely rhetorical? Hey, what's for dinner? I'm starved."

I didn't want to say it, but I had to. "There's a problem with Kate's death, isn't there?"

"If you don't want to cook, let's walk over to Fred's Fish Market. I'll treat you to the works. Chowder, lobster…"

"That makes two questions you didn't answer."

"What questions?"

I swallowed. "Stop dancing around, Joe. Kate didn't drown, did she?"

His innocent expression slid away, revealing a blankness I found unsettling. "You know I can't discuss an ongoing case with you, Teddy. Now let's go get something to eat."

There. He'd said it. *Case.*

What I'd begun to suspect was true. Kate had been murdered.

FIVE

ALTHOUGH OUTBACK BILL was now the interim head keeper of Down Under and my services there were no longer required, I made a beeline for Wallaby Walkabout as soon as I arrived at the zoo the next morning.

Entering Down Under was like taking a microtrip to Australia. Taking up approximately five acres, the area was surrounded by tall eucalyptus trees, and every time visitors opened the Aboriginal art-decorated gate the music of a didgeridoo wafted from speakers hidden among their branches. The Aussie animals lived in large, separate enclosures that mimicked their individual native habitats. Besides the stars of yesterday's television program, the zoo boasted four dingoes; several tiger cats; a mating pair of Tasmanian devils, both thankfully untouched by the horrific cancer that was decimating their Australian relatives; and various rodents. Wallaby Walkabout was set up much the same as Monkey Mania, with the animals roaming free and sometimes even hopping across the visitors' path.

I wandered through Down Under until I arrived at Wallaby Walkabout, where I found Abim hopping in tight circles around Bill's feet. The nervy look in Abim's eyes showed that he hadn't yet recovered from yesterday's experience.

Poor Abim wasn't doing much roaming today. Instead, he clung to Bill's shadow. Wherever Bill went, so did he.

"Don't come bargin' round here trying to get on my good side," Bill groused, as he tossed chopped fruit on top of a tub of compressed nutrient pellets. "Like I said yesterday, yer not takin' any more of me animals back down to the telly station. You came a gutser once and yer not doin' it again." *Came a gutser*, meaning that I'd screwed up.

"And a bright good morning to you, too. Have most of them settled down yet?" Not bothering to go around to the service entrance, I stepped through the visitors' gate.

"All 'cept for Abim, as any drongo can plainly see. I've told Zorah that I don't want 'em out on display for 'nother week."

I raised my eyebrows. "She agreed to that?"

The string of curses that issued from his mouth hinted that she didn't.

"I understand you're upset, Bill, but Zorah knows that after yesterday people will be flocking down here to see them. Especially Abim."

The wallaby now stood frozen in the shadow of Bill's left leg. Good thing the dingoes were two exhibits over. In their homeland, wallabies were a favorite food source.

"That's another thing carks me off, Teddy, a bunch of strange galah's always gawking around."

"Well, it *is* a zoo. Say, are you going to be speaking to Sheriff Rejas again?"

"Why would I do that? He might look a sex god to you daft sheilas, but to me he's just a big pain in the arse."

Sheilas? As in plural? A stab of jealousy crept up my spine before I realized that Bill intended his words to discomfit me. A bit of a sex god himself, albeit less sleek than either Joe or Lex, he had seemed disappointed when I hadn't swooned over him, as did every other single woman at the zoo.

Forcing down my annoyance at the Aussie's outsized ego, I said, "The thing is, I have a feeling Joe thinks there's something suspicious about Kate's death."

"No problem o' mine." He sounded unconcerned, but his eyes suddenly looked like Abim's.

Trying to talk to him further was unsuccessful, so I gave up. As I climbed back into my cart, I asked myself what I really knew about Bill. Only that, as his nickname implied, he'd been born and raised in the Australian outback, and had been an animal keeper at the Sydney Zoo, where he had met Kate, who'd been part of the San Diego Zoo's exchange program. When she returned to San Diego, Bill had been right behind her, somehow managing to snag a job as assistant marsupial keeper. From what else I'd heard on the ever-alert zoo grapevine, their relationship continued for a while, but then Kate abruptly left the San Diego Zoo for the much less lucrative Gunn. When Bill followed her this time, he discovered that the Gunn had no more openings. Thus began his financial problems.

Had the employment inequity caused their breakup? Bill's pride, always outsized, must have suffered a blow to find that his girlfriend could find work when he couldn't. But with Kate's death, his luck had changed, hadn't it? He no longer had to work three jobs to stay afloat.

Growing increasingly uncomfortable about Bill's turn of luck, I steered my cart up the hill toward Monkey Mania, only to have two slowly traveling San Sebastian Sheriff's squad cars pass me, headed in the opposite direction. In the lead car sat Joe and a deputy, both looking grim; two more deputies followed in the other. This was no casual visit.

Even though I knew Joe would be furious, I turned my cart around.

Battery-operated zoo carts don't move very fast, so by the time I arrived back at Wallaby Walkabout, Joe, flanked by his deputies, had already exited the squad car. When I saw Joe's hand resting on his holster, I knew the worst was about to happen.

As soon as Bill spotted the law officers headed his way, his shoulders tensed and he wheeled around toward the service trail. He stopped dead when Abim hopped up beside him. After muttering something I couldn't hear to the wallaby, Bill darted a look to the left, where a large mob of wallabies lay basking in the sun, then to the right, where a smaller group was doing the same. Bill leaned forward and shifted his weight to the balls of his feet. But when Abim hopped closer and sniffed at his ankle, the Aussie's shoulders slumped. Not willing to risk his animals' safety, he raised his hands in the classic "I surrender" position.

I watched helplessly as Joe recited the Miranda while one of his deputies cuffed Bill. As they hustled him to the squad car, he yelled, "Teddy! Take care of me mates! Them wallabies need fresh water, and I didn't get to the other animals yet."

"Got it covered," I yelled back.

As the squad car rolled slowly past me, Joe's face, so warm and loving the night before, appeared set in stone.

TWO HOURS LATER, I had finished feeding and watering all the Down Under animals, and was on my way to the anteater enclosure. It had been a frustrating time, because every few minutes my radio would squawk out questions from keepers who wanted to know what was going on. The most upsetting of these calls had been the closed-channel call from Zorah. She admitted that she'd known Bill's arrest was imminent, but had been ordered to keep quiet.

"The sheriff phoned me at home this morning and said to have the back entrance gate open for him and his deputies, so what was I supposed to do? Tip Bill off so he could leg it back to Australia? He'd never have made it to the airport, anyway, might even have been shot first. At least he's safe. As jails go, San Sebastian's isn't too bad,

I guess, but now we're short one keeper again. God, how I hate this job! Anyway, I already sent Myra to Monkey Mania to cover for you there, but until I can find someone to replace Bill, you're on permanent Down Under duty. Zoo One, signing off."

"Don't sign off yet! Did Joe say why he thinks Kate was murdered?"

"Of course he didn't tell me. But on *Good Morning, San Sebastian* a few minutes ago, the newscaster announced that a source over at the medical examiner's office said it couldn't have been an accident because Kate was dead before she went into the water. They can tell that?"

"Sure, if there was no water in the lungs." You learn details like that when you date a cop.

"Ugh. Zoo One, signing off."

As I entered Tropics Trail where Lucy and Baby Boy Anteater lived, I shoved the morning's events out of my mind. Since I'd arrived late, Lucy was napping in her great Dane-sized night house. When my cart rounded the corner she ambled out and flicked her long blue tongue through the holding pen's chain-link fence.

"Is my sweet girl hungry?"

"Mmm-mmm-mmm." Anteaters aren't great conversationalists. "And how about my even sweeter Baby Boy?" This, directed to the tot riding on Lucy's back.

Baby Boy didn't say a word, just stared at me through beady eyes. Like Bill—*no, Teddy, don't think about Bill*—Baby Boy was the strong, silent type.

After throwing the little anteater a kiss, I grabbed a container of termites off the cart, along with my safety board—thanks to their four-inch-long talons, anteaters are more dangerous than they appear—and entered the large enclosure. With Lucy and Baby Boy safely in their holding pen, it didn't take me long to stuff the termites into several fake logs and sweep up piles of anteater poop. These chores accomplished, I picked up my safety board and opened the lock to the holding pen. With a squeak, Lucy rushed out, headed to the closest log, and settled in for some serious termite lapping. Once out of her sight, I zipped into the pen, re-locked the gate, and swept up more poop. Then I refreshed the straw in her bedding, and let myself out of the rear exit.

It was lunch time already, but not feeling up to the inquisition I was certain to receive in the employees' lounge, I purchased a couple of tacos from the Amazon Appetito concession and retreated to the deep brush behind the jaguar enclosure. While eating, I pondered the complexities of Bill's situation.

With no relatives in the States and a boatload of legal woes in the offing, the Aussie needed all the friends he could get. Ordinarily, a zoo is one big family, but the combination of his gruff manner and his only part-time schedule at the zoo had kept most of the male zookeepers from inviting him out for a beer. Myself, I liked the man—his take-no-prisoners demeanor reminded me of Cisco, our feisty Mexican gray wolf—but even I had to admit that Bill could be his own worst enemy. How would his confrontational temperament come across in the San Sebastian Country Jail, where his every move and every word would be recorded on video camera?

As I was trying to decide whether a jail visit from me would help or hurt him, an agitated roar from Lucero, our highly territorial male jaguar, signaled that I was no longer alone. Within seconds, Robin Chase poked her head through the brush.

"What are you doing here?" the big cat keeper demanded.

"Eating lunch."

"Well, go away. That dead animal you're eating is bothering Lucero."

I looked down at my taco. "Why? He's not a vegan."

"Are you mocking me?"

Wanting to smack myself for forgetting that Robin *was* a vegan, I made the rest of the taco disappear into my mouth. "All finished. But you're worrying unnecessarily. In the five years Lucero's been here he's smelled everything from barbecued pork to banana daiquiris."

"I don't want you eating anywhere near the big cat exhibits. Ever."

Robin had always been testy, but lately she'd become even more irritable. What was wrong with her? Money woes? Perhaps, but these days, almost everyone had them. Love woes? Again, join the club, but even I had to admit that the big-boned Robin, with her blotchy complexion and mousy hair, would have trouble attracting most men. Once Bill, in a particularly cruel comment, had said that she reminded him of old photographs he'd seen of genetically challenged Russian peasants.

Feeling more pity than anger, I stood up. "Message received, Robin."

She wasn't through. Her face, which had already turned red with fury when she found me gobbling a taco, grew even blotchier. "Guess you think you're pretty smart, Teddy."

"Excuse me?"

"With Kate dead, you inherited the TV show and now Down Under. Things are going just the way you planned, aren't they? That bitch Myra was right. You've only been here a year, and already you've got everyone wrapped around your finger. Are you aiming for Zorah's job next, planning to use it as a steppingstone for the directorship of an even bigger zoo? The San Diego, maybe? The National?

Your rampant ambition knows no bounds! Drowning Kate and railroading poor Bill just so you could get what you want! I used to think you were just another ditzy Central Coast dilettante, but I've changed my mind. You're slick, Teddy. Machiavelli himself had nothing on you."

Stung, I replied, "Zorah made both those decisions. As for killing Kate…"

"You pretend to be one of us by living on some old boat down at the harbor, but I've seen that poor-little-rich-girl act before and I'm not buying it. I'm warning you. Don't mess with me and my big cats or you'll find yourself in the kind of trouble that neither your rich stupid mother, your crooked-ass father, or your cop boyfriend can get you out of."

Threat delivered, she gave my sleeve a yank that almost toppled me, and then disappeared into the brush, leaving me with my mouth hanging open.

Shaken from the confrontation, I returned to my rounds. The animals had a calming effect and by quitting time, my mood had turned to curious. While standing in line to clock out, I tried to understand Robin's sudden dislike of me. Had I inadvertently said something or done something to incur her animosity? No matter how I searched my memory, nothing popped up.

I put Robin aside and wondered what motive Bill might have for killing Kate. An acrimonious breakup? No one at the zoo knew for certain what had gone on during the final weeks of their relationship, but it was pretty much agreed that he had been the one to dump Kate. It was usually the dumpee who killed, not the dumper—wasn't it? Even more puzzling was why Bill would peddle his bicycle twelve miles from Castroville, where he lived in one of those rent-by-the-week motels, all the way down to the harbor, and then lurk in the shadows until she left the party. Why not just kill her in her own nearby Castroville apartment?

I was mulling over the logistics when I arrived home at Gunn Landing Harbor. After sliding my card key into the electronic gate that led down to the docks, I realized that gaining access to the *Gutterball* would have been a problem for Bill, too. Only boat owners were issued card keys. When they wanted to invite non-harbor residents to parties, they sometimes stationed a friend at the gate to allow other revelers in. A few rebels simply propped the gate open with a rock, but woe betide them if the harbormaster found out. Which had the Grimaldis done?

I had my chance to find out when I saw Doris and Sam Grimaldi sipping their evening daiquiris on the *Gutterball*'s deck. They didn't look happy.

"Permission to come aboard, Grimaldis?" I called.

Doris's usual smile was nowhere in evidence as waved me aboard. "Oh, Teddy, I can't begin to tell you how sorry we both are for what you had to go through the other morning. Finding Kate like that. I wish we'd been here to help, but as soon as the last person left the party, we went back home."

Even in the evening's dimming light, I could see that her eyes were swollen and stress lines marred her face. Somewhere in her fifties, she was around fifteen years older than her husband. Despite her salon-tinted hair and expert makeup, she actually looked twenty more. Sam was no beauty himself, but he made up for his no-more-than-average appearance by a warm voice and engaging manner. With those qualities and the help of his workhorse wife, he'd turned Lucky Lanes from a failed bowling alley into one of San Sebastian County's most popular gathering spots.

"You've got nothing to apologize for, Doris," I told her.

"That's what I've been trying to convince her of, Teddy," Sam seconded. "But she blames herself for inviting Kate to the party in the first place. She couldn't have known that the woman would get drunk and drown."

On my way home from the zoo I'd heard the basics of Bill's arrest on KRSS-AM. No doubt the television stations were also featuring it. "You haven't been listening to the news?"

Sam shook his head. "Too depressing, what with the economy, the terrorists, the…"

I raised my hand to stop him. "KRSS is reporting that Kate was murdered, and the authorities already have a suspect in custody." For now, I wanted to leave Bill's name out of it.

After a moment of shocked silence, Sam said, "Murdered? I don't believe it! Who would hurt such a sweet girl? Every time I…"

"Sam. Don't." Doris gave her husband a warning frown. To me she said, "Thanks for telling us, Teddy, but we have to get over to Lucky Lanes now, don't we, Sam?"

"We do?" Sam's face was a study in confusion.

"Don't you remember? Super Strikes, that league from Castroville? They changed their regular night to Wednesdays and that's going to be too much for Evelyn and Carlos to handle by themselves. Let's get going." Doris all but hauled her husband out of his chair.

Having worn out my welcome, I excused myself and headed over to the *Merilee* and the more soothing company of DJ Bonz and Miss Priss.

Later, as I took Bonz for his evening constitutional through Gunn Park, I reflected on my conversation with the Grimaldis. Bear keeper Jack Spence was a member of Super Strikes. During our afternoon break, he'd bragged about picking up a seven-ten split the night before, thus winning the evening's eighty-two dollar jackpot, so Doris had been lying.

As the evening fog drifted toward the harbor, I realized that I'd not asked the Grimaldis the question I'd originally meant to ask.

Had one of them opened the electronic harbor gate for Bill? If not, who had?

SIX

FRIDAY EVENING, after taking care of my own animals, I drove up to Old Town to get ready for Mother's Let's-Find-Teddy-a-Suitable-Husband soirée. While I disliked these parties, my attendance at them kept most of her manipulations down to a dull roar.

The problem was this.

I had been born into money. The Pipers, my mother's family, were one of the area's founding families, and for around a hundred years, had accumulated piles of the green stuff via their ranching and shipping concerns. But like so many families, they'd lost it all during the Depression. Fortunately, the Piper women tended to be beautiful and were able to snag rich husbands. Mother met my very wealthy father when he was a judge in the Miss San Sebastian Beauty Pageant—she won, of course—and married him soon afterward.

Unfortunately, several years later my father, who was as dishonest as he was rich, embezzled millions from the family brokerage firm of Bentley, Bentley, Haight and Busby, then decamped to Costa Rica with the loot. When the Feds were through with Caro, she had lost her house, the cars, the diamonds, the furs, and for all intents and purposes, was penniless. Well, there *was* that sub rosa offshore account Dad set up for us. Unfortunately, it would raise the curiosity of the Feds if it were accessed too frequently, so being a Piper and still beautiful, Caro married rich again. And again. And again. Each succeeding husband had more money than the previous one, and in no time, Caro had re-couped the family finances, even buying back the family home the Feds had snatched out from under us. Now she was able to live high on the hog without making too many suspicious withdrawals.

I took a different path. Once I finished college, I mar-ried a young and very *un*rich attorney and moved to San Francisco with him, but was eventually deserted for an-other woman. Since I had not inherited the Piper family beauty, I knuckled down to support myself by teaching. After finding that San Francisco held too many bad mem-ories, I moved back to Caro's house in the Old Town sec-tion of Gunn Landing, and shortly thereafter found myself working at the zoo. To my surprise, I adored it.

Caro didn't. Every day while I got ready for work, she would nag at me about my chosen profession until I hur-ried out of the house only half-dressed in my zoo khakis. To get away from the constant nagging, I'd moved onto the *Merilee,* where I fell in love with harbor life.

But the devil demanded her due. To make Caro leave me alone, I'd agreed to show up at her Let's-Find-Teddy-a-Suitable-Husband parties as long as said parties didn't happen more than twice a year.

With fingers tightened around the steering wheel of my old Nissan pickup, I wound my way up the hill to Old Town, where the family home sat at the end of a eucalyp-tus-lined lane. A cupola-sprouting Greek revival built in an era when full-time household help was cheap, it consisted of eighteen rooms, only six of which Caro actually used. The other rooms served as storage areas for the furniture that had been accumulated down through the centuries by various Bentleys and Pipers: a Queen Anne armoire here, a Romanov settee there. The living room was three times as long as the entirety of the *Merilee* but considerably stuffier, cluttered as it was with Victorian sofas and arm-chairs. At least it offered plenty of seating for my mother's well-heeled guests.

After greeting me warmly, Caro had the valet hide my truck in the back, then led me upstairs to my old room, where she, her hairdresser, and her cosmetician proceeded to turn me into a different person. My frizzy red hair disappeared underneath smooth waves, and my rabbity eyelashes were darkened with mascara. The freckles Joe so loved were paved over by Mme. Cherie's *Masque de Bisque*. I resembled a gargoyle trying to look like Barbie.

Once encased in the revealing gauze-over-silk Basso & Brooke dress Caro had bought me, I steeled myself and walked downstairs to find guests already milling about and a string quartet from San Sebastian Community College playing bastardized Vivaldi. Judging from the leers proffered by my wanna-be-date, the dress was a success.

"That's so hot," Jason Jackman McIlhenny Forbes IV slurred, as he downed another martini he didn't need. His bleary eyes didn't once leave my chest, and it was all I could do not to toss my glass of Gunn Vineyard's prize-winning '03 Merlot in his face.

"How nice that you like my dress," I muttered between clenched teeth. Boy, Caro sure could pick 'em.

"I wasn't talking about your dress, sweet stuff, just what's peeking out from under there. Say, why don't we sneak out of this snooze fest and take a drive along the coast in my new Alpha Romeo? Not only will I show you what it can do, but I'll show you what *I* can do, too. You'll like it. All the girls do."

"Oh, look! There's Aster Edwina Gunn! I must talk to her!" Leaving the inebriated dolt behind, I jostled my way through the crowd.

At the far end the room, Aster Edwina held court on a

red velvet chair designed to look like a lesser royal's throne. The eighty-something head of the powerful Gunn family was deep in discussion with my mother and Ford Bronson, the billionaire who owned KTSS-TV, as well as other media outlets across the country. Before I could veer off in another direction, Aster Edwina waved me over. "Ah, the girl of the hour."

"Hello, Aster Edwina," I said. Then, at Caro's prompting, I added, "Thank you for that promotion at the zoo, not that I wanted it."

If Aster Edwina's smile had been any thinner, it would have cut off her tongue. "The television program will be good for you, dear, definitely more in keeping with your talents."

Caro nudged me. "See, Teddy? She only wants the best for you." Like the lion knows what's best for the gazelle. "Well, it's been nice chatting with you, but I was just passing by on my way to the food table."

That thin smile again. "The food table is in the opposite direction, Theodora, right behind that awful Forbes boy your mother hopes will be your next husband."

She made it sound like I'd been married as many times as Caro, but I always tried to be polite to Aster Edwina, because as the power behind the mighty Gunn Trust she was, in effect, my boss. "Okay, you caught me in a fib. Now if you'll just excuse…"

"I was telling dear Ford here that you acquitted yourself quite well on *Good Morning, San Sebastian* the other day, and that he should not only keep you on, but give you your own show. A half hour, at least."

"We'll appoint her Chief Wallaby Wrangler," he quipped, winking at me.

Despite myself, I winked back.

Only a few months ago Ford Bronson, the founder of SoftSol, a computer software company, had made national news while testifying before Congress about pirated software and intellectual property theft. He was best known for his many philanthropic efforts, which had brought him to the attention of *Central Coast Style*, where he'd been the subject of a six-page full-color spread. The first photo showed him playing golf with the President of the United States. In the second, he was standing among his collection of Cubists, which included a Braque and a Picasso. Another photo showed him in his Old Town library holding a first edition of Oscar Wilde's *The Picture of Dorian Gray*, in which Wilde had drawn a very naughty cartoon. Another showed him at the finish line of the Boston Marathon, completing the grueling twenty-six-point-two miles in an admirable three hours and twenty-seven minutes. Several other photographs revealed the sumptuousness of *Lady B Good*, his yacht moored in Gunn Landing Harbor; it was the size of a small country. But even more impressive was the photo of him piloting his company jet, an elegant Gulfstream G550.

As if all that wealth and talent wasn't enough, the forty-ish Bronson was also devastatingly handsome, with male model features, gently graying black hair, and eyes so blue they almost looked fake. At his birth, the angels must have burst forth in a chorus of hosannas.

I swallowed my own hosannas when he followed up his Wallaby Wrangler quip by saying, "A full half-hour for Teddy, eh? To tell you the truth, after watching the tape of her with those animals, I started kicking around that very same idea. She has a lot of personality and animal shows are getting strong Nielsens this season."

"There's no way I can handle anything like that," I protested. "My dance card at the zoo is full."

All traces of warmth left Aster Edwina's gray eyes. "You'll do whatever's good for the zoo, Theodora. As you know, I've ordered Zorah to have you take over all of Kate's other PR work, too. You can use a computer, can't you?"

Whoever had said you can't go home again didn't know what he was talking about. You can go home, you just may not like it once you get there. History has a tendency to repeat itself; only the players change. Desperate to escape my interfering mother, I'd married Michael and moved away. Now I was back, only to find myself under Aster Edwina's thumb.

Preferring a change of subject, however grim, I said, "Of course I can use a computer. I was a teacher, remember? By the way, isn't it horrible what happened to Kate Nido?"

Aster Edwina narrowed her eyes but said nothing.

Bronson shook his head sadly. "Horrible is the word, all right. So young. So full of promise."

"Did you know her well?"

"Not really. I don't get down to the station all that often these days, and when I do, it's for some dull executive meeting, not to hobnob with the talent. But Kate and I did chat briefly, once, when we met in the hallway. I found her to be a genial person."

I nodded. "Me, too. That's why it's strange that such a genial person would get herself murdered."

"I hope you're not getting any ideas, Theodora," Aster Edwina said, her voice stern.

Startled, I asked, "What do you mean?"

"Sticking your nose into other people's business. There's been an arrest in the case, and sadly, it was one of Gunn Zoo's own. However unfortunate that may be, that's the end of it. Your mother doesn't need any more scares." Her eyes rested on Caro, who was trying to wrest a martini from Jason Jackman McIlhenny Forbes IV's sweaty paw.

Considering what had happened in another Gunn Landing murder case, Aster Edwina's apprehension on behalf of my mother was understandable. The last time I'd stuck my nose into other people's business, I'd wound up in the hospital. Caro hadn't taken it well.

"As you say, Aster Edwina, there's already been an arrest. Sheriff Rejas doesn't need my help."

"He didn't need it last time, either!" she snapped. "Furthermore…"

Discomfited, Bronson interjected, "Does anyone know what's happening with the funeral arrangements? I, and others from the station, plan to attend."

There was a brief silence, and then Aster Edwina said, "Zorah Vega, our zoo director, has been trying to reach Kate's next of kin, but so far she's been unsuccessful. Seems the phone number Kate gave for her parents in Sausalito is out of service, and the address is that of a construction company."

Bronson raised his eyebrows. "How odd."

I wasn't so sure. "We live in a mobile society. Not everyone stays in the same town where they were brought up."

Aster Edwina sniffed. "They would if they knew what was good for them."

"Some people want to better themselves." I flicked a quick look at Caro. "And some feel the need to get away from dysfunctional families."

Caro's eyes shot daggers. I just smiled.

Aster Edwina *humphed*. "The *Koala Kate's Kuddly Kritters* segment. There's another thing I'd like to discuss with you, Ford. Whatever it turns out to be, it's going to require a new title. I suggest *The Gunn Zoo's Animal Kingdom* to highlight the Gunn Trust's involvement, of which the family is very proud."

Bronson looked amused at Aster Edwina's intrusion into his own territory, but was too polite to rebuke her. Instead, he put forth an idea of his own, *Tiger Teddy's Amazing*

Animals. Using the old lady's subsequent argument as cover, I headed for the hors d'oeuvre table. Caro sidled up to me as I popped a jumbo shrimp into my mouth. Even at the age of fifty-five, she looked stunning in her aqua, six-inches-above-the-knee Pilotto dress and white diamond choker. Former beauty queens age more gently than the rest of us, especially when cosmetic surgery is involved. "All right, Theodora, I'm prepared to admit that Jason Jackman McIlhenny Forbes IV might have been a mistake," she said, forestalling any criticism. "But he has an older brother, Howard Jackman McIlhenny Forbes, and the timing couldn't be better. You can catch Howard between divorces."

I swallowed the shrimp. "He sounds like quite the catch. What's this sauce, by the way? It's delicious."

"Ask the caterers."

"Where's Mr. Trifle?"

"Upstairs, having a Time Out."

"What's the poor dog being punished for? Trembling too much?"

"For piddling in my Balenciaga tote."

"Dogs piddle, Caro. That's why they shouldn't be carried around in handbags."

"Tote. Not to change the subject, dear, but I saw you talking to Aster Edwina just now."

"I was surprised to see her here. Did you two sign a peace treaty or something?" Caro and Aster Edwina had both fallen in love with the same man—my father—and the ensuing range war had continued down through the decades, even though the man in question had long since fled with the Feds hot on his larcenous heels. To smuggle him out of the country, the two had made up briefly, but as soon as he was safe in Costa Rica, their old animosity returned.

"Aster Edwina is my dearest, dearest friend, Theodora."

"Then I'm happy for you both."

"You know, I was just thinking."

"Really?" With Caro, "thinking" is always a bad sign.

"Ford Bronson is single."

"Forget it."

"I don't know anything about his people, but Aster Edwina could help me there. She has more contacts than I do."

To Mother, marriage isn't as much about money as it is about animal husbandry. Bloodlines counted.

"Caro, Ford Bronson has expressed absolutely no interest in me. Besides, *Central Coast Style* wrote that he's been seeing Izzy Van Stoeller since he and Uma Thurman broke up."

"Oh. Well. It's hopeless then."

Isabel "Izzy" Marian Jacqueline Van Stoeller, of the Montecito Van Stoellers, was almost as pretty as Bronson. She was a tall, slim, natural blonde with a flawless complexion that could wear any color, something the fashion photographers had long since noticed. You couldn't open up a copy of *Central Coast Style* without finding at least one photo of her wearing something ridiculously expensive. Whatever Bronson's bloodlines turned out to be—Nobel Prize-winners, New Jersey telemarketers, New Guinea headhunters—in my mind the two were a perfect match.

Grateful for my frizzy red hair and freckles, I grinned. "Hopeless is right. Here, have a shrimp."

AFTER SO MANY forced smiles at Caro's party the muscles around my mouth had begun to hurt, so it was a relief to relax on the *Merilee*'s deck two hours later. It being almost midnight on a Friday, the harbor was lively. From the music and laughter floating my way, the *Tipsy Teepee, Cruisin 4 A Bruisin*, the *Mickey* and *Tumbling Dice* all hosted parties. At the north end of the harbor, Delta Force, the local blues band, rocked out at Fred's Fish Market.

As difficult as liveaboard life could be—cold, damp mornings and ever-present mildew were just some of the drawbacks—the rewards were considerable. These included being part of a community of like-minded people, a constant supply of fresh sea air, and the gentle rocking of the tide lulling you to sleep at night.

And then there was the sky, the ever-changing sky.

I sipped my chamomile tea and gazed up at the stars. Due to a freshening wind, the night was clear and the new moon glowed like a silver cat's whisker. Constellations blazed. Ursa Minor spangled the sky. Eons of light years closer to Earth, a satellite tracked its way across the dark.

Paradise, anyone?

My mood lifted further when my cell phone chimed out the chorus of "Born Free." When I flipped it open, caller ID flashed Joe's home number. He'd made it home before three, a rarity on a weekend.

"The natives weren't restless tonight?" I asked.

"Nope. Except for a couple of DUIs we pulled in, everyone was remarkably well-behaved. How was your mother's party?"

I answered the question he'd actually wanted to ask. "Have no fear; Jason Jackman McIlhenny Forbes IV turned out to be a drunken oaf."

"She fixed you up with *him*? Unbelievable. Mr. Four happens to be one of the DUIs we arrested tonight. In fact, the little creep has paid so many DUI fines in this county that he's almost bought us a new jail wing. Doesn't your mother read the 'Mean Streets' crime column in the *San Sebastian Gazette*? He's been mentioned at least five times, and that's just this year."

I had to laugh. "Caro only reads the Society page."

"Wait a minute. Do I hear music?"

"Friday is party night down here, as you well know. At

one time or another, you've arrested half the folks in the harbor."

"Don't exaggerate. I just tell them to turn the music down and remind them there's a five-hundred-dollar fine for skinny-dipping."

The mention of skinny-dipping turned the conversation to more personal topics for the next few minutes, so it wasn't until we were about to hang up that I remembered to ask Joe some questions of my own.

"Joe, how did Kate die?"

"Teddy…"

"You might as well tell me because it must have been on the news. I just haven't had a chance to catch it."

A sigh. "Her body was somewhat bloated by the time you fished her out, so you couldn't see the red mark around her neck, but she'd been strangled. The medical examiner found flecks of metal in the wound, so the thinking is that the killer used a wire garrote. The advantage of that kind of weapon is its silence. The victims' airways are immediately compressed. They can't cry out for help."

I digested that grim piece of information for a moment, then asked, "You're certain there was no chance of an accident, like, once she fell into the harbor she got tangled up in some kind of wire?"

"Of course not. And there are other reasons I arrested your buddy."

I started to protest that Bill wasn't my buddy, that I'd only known him for a couple of months, but stopped before the disloyal statement left my mouth. Instead, I asked, "What other reasons?"

"I'm not going to tell you, Teddy."

"Did he confess?"

"Nope. He didn't have to. Believe me, we've got plenty of evidence."

"Does he have an attorney?"

"The county will appoint him one."

I asked the question I'd meant to ask the Grimaldis. "How did he get through the electronic harbor gate? He doesn't have a key card."

"Teddy, you know those key cards go missing all the time. Now let's change the subject. Did your mother buy you a new dress?"

"Of course she did. She always dresses her little piggy up for market."

"Wear it Monday, okay? I'm taking you to brunch at Jacqueline's."

Jacqueline's Bistro was the San Sebastian eatery Joe likes to dine at on special occasions. After tonight's party, I wasn't up to more formality, so I suggested a late breakfast at Fred's Fish Market instead.

With a laugh, Joe agreed, adding, "You are such a barbarian."

"More than you realize. Caro once hired a genealogist who managed to trace the family bloodline all the way back to the Visigoths."

"Now *that* I can believe."

More laughter. Then we billed and cooed until we finally hung up, after which I went below deck and joined Bonz and Miss Priss on sea-scented sheets.

Just before I fell asleep, a discomfiting thought popped into my mind. If Bill had ridden his bike twelve miles from Castroville to Gunn Landing Harbor, surely someone must have seen him peddling along Highway One. A farm supplies salesman, coming back from his rounds. A waitress, having finished her shift. Or even a harbor dweller, heading home to his boat after a late night at work.

Did Joe have a witness?

SEVEN

SATURDAY WAS THE designated day for the zoo's Great Flamingo Round-Up, and I had promised Manny Salinas, the head bird keeper, that I would help. Our forty Chilean flamingos were due for their West Nile virus vaccinations, and getting them treated entailed two hours of personnel-intensive labor. Because having the public there might complicate the process, Manny wanted the work completed before the zoo opened.

I arrived promptly at six and went straight to Flamingo Lagoon, the wedge-shaped enclosure situated across the visitors' walkway from Gunn Zoo Lake. A four-foot wire fence is all that separated the birds from the public, but since our flamingos' wings have been pinioned so that they can't fly, this fencing is more than adequate. At the northern end of the enclosure stood an eight-foot-high masonry wall that kept the birds from pecking at their neighbors, the alpacas. Other than that one high wall, Flamingo Lagoon offered the birds all the comforts of home: an acre to roam in, plenty of shade, and a shallow pond where they could fish to their avian heart's content.

Today the birds were sharing their enclosure with fourteen humans. Three vets had already set up at a series of tables, their syringes gleaming against white cloth. Next to the vets, technicians from the Animal Care Building, their faces a mixture of excitement and dread, counted out vials of serum as they eyed the flamingos.

The flamingos eyed the technicians even more warily.

This was all to the good, because it kept the flamingos' eyes off the southwest corner of the enclosure, where a group of keepers stood holding the four plastic panels used to corral the birds. At Manny's signal, the keepers would march forward with their panels in a pincher movement, eventually trapping the birds against the high masonry wall. Once at the wall, waiting keepers would pick up the birds one by one, carry them to a vet for inoculation, then turn them loose. Easy does it, no muss, no fuss. Everybody healthy and happy.

That was the plan, anyway.

As a nonbirder with no flamingo experience, my job was to stand on the visitors' walkway outside the enclosure and act as an outfielder in case one of the birds made it over the fence and headed for the lake. No flamingo had ever escaped since the Great Flamingo Round-Up was initiated several years back, so no one was especially worried. I had plenty of backup, too. Several yards to my right stood Robin Chase, the big cat keeper who for some reason had decided to hate me, and Myra Sebrowski, who disliked any woman she saw as a rival. Equidistant away on my left stood Gunn Zoo hunk Lex Yarnell, who kept casting flirty glances Myra's way.

Once we were all assembled in our proper places, Manny Salinas raised his hand and the line of panel-bearing keepers moved forward. They walked so slowly it took the flamingos a minute to figure out what was happening. By then it was too late.

You seldom see a lone flamingo, because flamingos flock. That's their inbred defense mechanism. This "don't grab me, grab the other guy" strategy works well on the coastal lagoons of Chile, where it helps individual birds defend themselves from predators. It doesn't work so well at a zoo, because it makes them easy to catch. As the keepers and their plastic panels advanced, a tightly packed pink sea flowed ahead of them, honking in irritation.

Chilean flamingos are tall birds. They can grow to five feet, but they weigh only five to seven pounds; their height is comprised mainly of legs and neck. This lightness of being makes them easy to haul around, which the keepers started doing as soon as all the flamingos were trapped in the makeshift plastic corral. But the birds' spindly legs made them extraordinarily fragile, so I admired the care with which the keepers handled them. They grabbed the flamingos while their wings were still folded around their body, the best way to avoid breaking fragile wing bones. Most birds were carried away, long yellow legs dangling, with little struggle, but not all went peacefully. Several long pink necks snaked around keepers' backs as vicious hooked beaks attempted to find purchase on human flesh.

The noise was deafening, because flamingoes don't chirp—they honk.

Imagine, if you will, a forty-car traffic jam with each driver leaning on his horn in frustration. That's what forty trapped flamingos sound like. Add to that the yelps from keepers when flamingos did manage to bite them, and you had one heck of an atonal symphony.

"Some racket, huh?" I called to Lex over the din.

He flashed white, perfect teeth at me. "Anything that pretty has to have a downside." Then he winked at pretty Myra.

Robin, hunched over like a female wrestler ready to rumble, ignored us all.

The Great Flamingo Round-Up was going so smoothly that I relaxed. *Let's see, as soon as we were finished here, I'd go over to Tropics Trail and take care of Lucy and Baby Boy Anteater, then I'd...* "Watch out!" someone shouted.

When I snapped to attention, I saw a flurry of pink cascading over the fence.

"Get her before she reaches the lake!" Manny yelled, as someone nearby called into a radio, "Code Blue! Runaway flamingo!" I opened my arms to grab the bird but she saw me and swerved to the right. With what seemed like a sneer on her beaky face, she rushed by, wings flapping, honking like a Hummer.

Did I tell you that for short bursts, flamingos can run twenty miles an hour?

There was no way I could outrun her, but I could redirect her course. Except for the meandering dirt path she'd found, access to this side of Gunn Lake was obscured by brush. If I could manage to steer the flamingo off the path, she might get caught up in the weeds. But reaching the lake wouldn't necessarily be a bad thing. Flamingos are shallows waders, preferring not to get deeper than their knees in the wet stuff. Once they're in the water, though, they're just that much more difficult to catch.

When I yelled my intentions to Lex and Robin, they and three other keepers charged through the brush from opposite directions. They reached the lake ahead of the flamingo, and shooed her back up the path toward me. Letting her reach the wide visitors' walkway wasn't an option. If she did, it would turn into Girl's Day Out. She might even be able to wander the entire zoo until a feral raccoon—the bane of zoos everywhere—chewed off her spindly neck.

More worried about her safety than my own, I waved my arms and drove her away from the dirt path and into the deepest part of the brush.

It worked. Not only did the weeds slow her down, but they stopped her dead.

The moment I went into the brush after her, I discovered why. The ground here was morass of mud, standing water, and cattails. Bullfrogs and minnows fled before me as I sloshed along, up to my shins in muck. With her thin legs, the flamingo might have been able to elude me, but she'd somehow managed to get entangled in the cattails.

Now was the time for caution. If I spooked her further, she could struggle and break a leg.

Cooing softly, I moved toward her.

"Pretty Bird wants to go back to her friends, doesn't she? Oh, yes, she does. Pretty Bird is soooo lonely out here."

Through eyes almost the same color as her pink plumage, the flamingo shot me a mean look.

No skinny bird was going to scare me. "Just let me untangle those lovely legs of yours, honey, and we'll be out of here in no time."

I could swear she sneered.

By the time I reached the flamingo, she seemed ready to accept her fate and stood calmly, wings folded around her body. All I had to do was strip the cattails away and pick her up. Piece of cake.

As soon as I bent down, I was rewarded by a nip to my fanny. Because of my thick cargo pants, it didn't hurt too much, so I just kept working on the weeds until I got her untangled. One cattail, two, three, four... Finished!

"Goin' home, Pretty Bird." I wrapped my arms around her torso.

Not to those needles, Pretty Bird honked, hooking her neck around.

"Hey, what are you...?"

Pretty Bird's beak grabbed my earlobe. "Ow!" I screeched.

"Don't scare her!" Robin yelled, as she and Lex sloshed toward me, and I didn't think she was talking to the flamingo.

"She's got my ear!" I howled, leaning toward the bird's

head to take some of the pressure off. The wily thing just pulled back and tightened her hold.

"Ow, ow, ow, ow!" *Don't hurt the bird.*

What do you do when a five-foot-tall flamingo has you by the ear? When you're a zookeeper—nothing, that's what. Defending yourself could hurt the bird, so you just endure and wait for rescue. At least I wasn't wearing ear studs; Pretty Bird might have choked.

"Oh, ow!" *Don't hurt the bird, don't hurt the bird.*

Half out of my mind with pain, I leaned forward again, but this time I leaned too far, because my feet slipped in the mud and I started to fall. Yet I didn't let go of the flamingo. Somehow I managed to twist my body around so that I landed on my back with the flamingo on my chest, still attached to my ear.

"Ow! Ow!" *Don't hurt the bird, don't hurt the damn bird.* "Honk, honk!" The flamingo increased her hold. If she'd been human, I'd have slapped her. "Somebody get this bird off me!"

I lay half-buried in mud, slime, and run-off lake water while tadpoles swam around my head and bullfrogs croaked. When you're in misery, the strangest things pop into your head. Such as… When I was ten, my parents had taken me on a trip to London. Dad wanted me to learn about history, Mother wanted me to meet the Queen. On the final day, we had wound up at the British Museum. I'd been fascinated by the body of the Bog Man, who'd been found in amazingly intact condition after more than two thousand years. He'd been buried in a peat bog, with a rope garrote around his neck. Was that how I would eventually be found, with a preserved flamingo?

I heard splashing from my right. Please, Lord, don't let it be Robin. She'd just finish me off.

"Love your flamingo earring," Lex said.

Rescued! *"Get her off!"*

"Hold tight. I'm workin' on it."

As I lay there muttering imprecations in the slime, Lex oh so slowly and oh so carefully pried Pretty Bird's jaws apart. After that, he gently lifted Pretty Bird out of my arms and hurried off with her to a waiting vet.

I struggled to my feet just before Robin arrived. Was it my imagination or was she smirking?

"You better not have hurt that flamingo," she said.

THIRTY MINUTES LATER, after showering and putting on the clean uniform I always kept in my locker for situations such as this, I plodded over to First Aid and had my ear seen to. That took another ten minutes, so by the time I arrived at the giant anteater enclosure, I was almost forty-five minutes late and Lucy was furious. From behind her holding pen gate, she threatened me with four-inch claws.

"Hssssss!" she added for emphasis.

"Now don't you start," I said, stuffing a starter helping of termites into a faux log. "Just hold on…"

"Zoo One to Keeper Fifty-Two. Report to the office immediately."

Zorah's voice squawked so loudly over my radio that it sent Lucy scurrying for cover with Baby Boy Anteater clinging to her back. The two would have to wait for their second helping of termites.

After arriving at the Administration Building, I parked my cart and wove my way through the maze of desks to Zorah's office. "Keeper Fifty-Two reporting for duty, ma'am," I announced, saluting.

She stopped shuffling papers. "Don't get cute with me, Teddy. We have a lot to discuss."

"And I have hungry mouths to feed."

She looked at her watch. "You'll be out of here in fifteen minutes. Lucy can hold on that long. Sit."

I sat.

Wrinkling her nose, she said, "You smell like cheap soap. And what's that bandage doing on your ear?"

When I told her about my morning's adventures, she smiled. "Man, I would have given anything to see that, but…" She waved a hand at the mounds of paper on her desk. "Those Chilean flamingos are wonderful animals, aren't they?"

"Divine. What did you want to see me about?"

"Aster Edwina called this morning…"

Remembering the conversation at Caro's party, my mood soured even further.

Oblivious, Zorah continued, "…and she wants you to take over Kate's job permanently."

I knew where this was going. "Temporarily, like I agreed yesterday. Permanent, no way. I like working with animals, not paper."

She ignored me. "So in addition to some of the Down Under animals and the TV segment, in the future you'll be the editor of *ZooNews*, keep our website up to date, and generate at least one press release a week. Don't look at me like that, Teddy. Aster Edwina has approved a hefty pay increase, and besides that, you'll make a fortune in overtime. You used to be a teacher, so I'm sure your writing is at least grammatical. You already have some computer skills, but I know there'll be a learning curve, especially with the web site. Helen will help with that."

"Helen Gifford? Your executive assistant? But isn't she…?" I was about to say that Helen was pushing seventy, and couldn't be any more Web-literate than I already was, but Zorah must have read my mind.

"Don't be ageist. For the past ten years, Helen's been

teaching Web site design in the evenings at San Sebastian Community College. Several of her students have even won awards. And in case you didn't know, she's the very person who designed the zoo's web site. Kate just kept it current."

"Then Helen should take over Kate's job."

"A good executive assistant is too valuable to lose. Besides, part of Kate's job was to take care of the koalas, and Helen can't do that. She's allergic."

Not for the first time, I opened my mouth before I engaged my brain. "But Bill…"

"Bill's in jail, and the way things are going, he may be there a while. Now, here's how it's going to work." Zorah outlined a schedule that had other keepers taking over various Down Under animals, as well as some of my own. "So you'll just be left with the koalas, the wombats, the numbats, and the wallabies."

"But Lucy…"

"If you insist, you can keep the giant anteater and her baby. As I was saying, Aster Edwina has already approved overtime for up to fifteen hours a week. Isn't that generous of her? You'll have that old boat of yours in ship shape—ha!—in no time." Zorah stood up, signaling that our meeting was finished. "On your way out, stop by Helen's desk and have her show you where Kate kept her *ZooNews* file. Take it home, and this evening, log onto the zoo's web site and blog to familiarize yourself with the material. Tomorrow, as soon as you finish feeding everyone, come back here and get started. Don't look so glum, Teddy. It'll be fun!"

With that, she came around the desk and ushered me out the door.

THAT EVENING, AFTER studying the zoo's website on my laptop and deciding that yes, with a little help I could keep it updated, I went through the *ZooNews* material that Kate kept in a manila folder. Helen had explained that Kate did most of her writing at home, but fortunately the file included a rough draft for the next issue. From what I could see, the newsletter needed a serious rewrite—the syntax was all over the place, and the accuracy was slipshod. The snow leopard we were getting was a male, not a female. The Egyptian geese were in the African Veldt enclosure with the giraffes and ostriches, not on the Serengeti Plains with the Grevey's zebras. Our zebras, zoo-born, hand-raised, and spoiled rotten, weren't big on sharing.

Kate was also a believer in the power of Post-it notes. Every other page in the file was plastered with them, in various colors that had seemingly nothing to do with their subjects. Some looked old, some new, some were zoo-related, some not. Sorting through the mess, I shuddered at the clumsy phone text spelling.

Koal, mayb Tues. Koala, maybe Tuesday. Possibly a reference to the TV segment she had never lived to appear on.

Frilld liz & snk? Frilled lizard and snake. Back-up animals in case the koala didn't work out, or possibles for a later show.

Frshn sho wi dangr anmals. Kate wanted to freshen up her segment with dangerous animals, instead of a parade of cute and cuddly. As if Zorah would allow such a thing.

Tel Z re prob wi Bill? Uh oh. It looked like Kate was considering telling Zorah about some problem with Bill. What could that have been? A personal problem, or a problem with the koalas?

Emu egs, mt b gd. Emu eggs might be good. On toast, or on *Good Morning, San Sebastian*?

Mnks? Minks, or more probably, monkeys.

Bengl cb pos. Bengal cub a possibility on the TV segment? Over Robin's dead body, I bet. But Kate was the one who had turned up dead.

C Robn Tues. A meeting with Robin planned for the day after Kate died?

T Doris t at party? Talk to Doris Grimaldi at the boat party? Tell Doris "t", whatever that meant. The truth, maybe? But about what?

C Lex. It sounded like she was going to console herself with the park ranger. Or something.

Cst 4 teak? Cost for teak? I had almost forgotten that Kate owned a boat and that it was berthed right here in Gunn Landing Harbor. It had escaped my mind because she didn't have a liveaboard permit and was seldom at the harbor, but the boat was the *Nomad*, a twenty-seven-foot Newport sloop with a hull painted in an incongruous, orange-and-blue psychedelic pattern. Come to think of it, how had Kate, on little more than a zookeeper's salary, been able to afford it?

None of us made much at the zoo; we worked with animals mainly out of love. Altogether, the combination of slip fees on a purely-for-pleasure craft, plus the rent on Kate's Castroville apartment would run a pretty penny. And upkeep, my God! These days the upkeep on a boat was enough to send a millionaire to the poorhouse. My father had given me the *Merilee*, otherwise I'd be sharing a tiny inland apartment with another keeper or living with my mother. Perhaps Kate had inherited *Nomad*, too. Maybe her parents were deceased, which was why no one had been able to find them.

I frowned. Once the medical examiner had declared Kate's death a homicide, surely Joe and his deputies would have already searched her apartment, as well as the *Nomad*, for clues. He would also have looked for family records in order to contact next-of-kin. But at the party last night, Aster

Edwina—who was always the first to know anything—had stated that Kate's next-of-kin remained a mystery.

Shrugging, I turned to another page.

Orgs, banas & prs, vdka. Shopping list.

Pikup unfrm clnrs. Due to our messy jobs, we keepers almost lived at the laundromat but due to Kate's lighter schedule with animals, she was able to afford to send hers out.

When I arrived at the last page, the Post-it note there made me gasp.

Tdy's mom noz.

My mother knows what?

EIGHT

FIRST THING THE next morning I called Caro and asked, "Did you know Kate Nido?"

"Who?" She sounded groggy. No surprise there, since it was only six.

"Koala Kate. The zookeeper who was murdered."

A whine. At first I thought it was my mother, distressed at being awakened so early. Then I realized it was Mr. Trifle, grumpy for the same reason.

"Of course I didn't know her, dear. Why in the world are you calling me at this hour with such a foolish question?"

"Because you popped up on one of her Post-it notes. Here, let me read it. 'Teddy's Mom knows.' What information do you have that Kate might've been interested in?"

"I'm half-asleep and you expect me to answer something like that? It could be anything. A recipe for pâté, the whereabouts of a spa, the name of a good cosmetic surgeon, a…"

"Kate was a zookeeper, Mother, not a beauty queen."

"How many times do I have to tell you, it's *Caro*. And as for that unfortunate Kate person, don't be so certain she wasn't interested in cosmetic surgery. From the picture they ran of her yesterday in the *San Sebastian Gazette* I could see that her nose needed work. Her chin, too. She appeared on that TV segment on *Good Morning, San Sebastian*, so perhaps they were pushing her to get some work done. TV people are shallow that way."

I forced myself not to laugh.

"Keep thinking, Moth… Caro. Maybe you'll come up with something else."

"I'm going back to sleep now. Bye, Theodora." She hung up.

Frustrated, I paced back and forth in the *Merilee*. Three-legged Bonz hobbled close behind while Miss Priss watched us haughtily from her one good eye. Was Caro keeping a secret, one that might wind up hurting her? If so, I had to nip it in the bud.

A plan occurred to me. I wasn't due at the zoo until eight—the drive took only fifteen minutes—and I'd already showered and dressed for work. The weekends were always busy at the harbor, but the fog would keep most folks away until it lifted. The Sunday sailors wouldn't show until then, and most of the liveaboarders still remained snug in their cabins. But would putting my plan into execution be the right thing to do?

Of course it wasn't.

Not only was it ethically wrong, it was illegal. If caught, I'd find myself sitting in the San Sebastian County Jail, explaining my actions to an enraged sheriff. But if Bill hadn't killed Kate, who had? He, or possibly she, was still on the loose, and no matter what the consequences to me, my mother's safety had to come first. Caro might be a pain in the neck, but she was *my* pain in the neck, and anyone who wanted to hurt her would have to get through me!

There are times when having a crook for a father comes in handy, and this was one of those times. After scooping up a flashlight and a handful of hairpins, I pulled a slate-gray sweatshirt over my zoo uniform, slipped out of the *Merilee,* and quietly made my way down the dock to the garish *Nomad.* Best to conduct my search now, under cover of the fog, before Joe had the boat removed to the county evidence yard.

Kate's boat was only seven slips down from mine. Sails sheathed, it bobbed gently on the morning tide. I peered through the fog. Nothing stirred, except for the shadowy figure of a harbor seal swimming alongside the dock and a lone pelican perched on *Nomad*'s bow. When I stepped on board, it flapped away.

The *Nomad* was ringed with yellow police tape, but I ducked under it. My only difficulty was in picking the lock on the hatch cover, not as easy as it looks in the movies. Thankfully, Kate had settled for a flimsy lock, unlike the *Merilee*'s heavy Schlage. Once I'd managed to release its grip, I slid the hatch aside and peeked inside.

Due to the morning fog, the cabin was dark, so after clambering down the ladder, I clicked on my flashlight. Keeping the beam low, I began my search. As I'd expected from what I'd seen of Kate's neat habits at the zoo, *Nomad*'s cabin was immaculate. Although stuffy from being closed up, the salon and galley were spotless. Teak walls and cupboards gleamed, and I could smell the faint scent of lemon wax above the damp. I wasn't too surprised to see that *Nomad*'s interior matched its exterior. It looked like an aging hippie's retreat. Faded tie-dye patterns were everywhere; on the curtains, the seating, over the narrow bunk in the stern. Multicolored love beads dangled from draw-pulls. Peace symbols decorated several cracked coffee mugs.

It was like stepping inside a time capsule.

As I continued taking inventory, I spied a boom box sitting on top of a cabinet between the galley and the head. Stacked on top were reissue CDs of music from Jefferson Airplane, Blind Faith, and Uriah Heep. Taped to the cabinet door was an elderly poster of Quicksilver Messenger Service that announced in psychedelic script, LIVE AT THE FILLMORE!

Since I hadn't broken in for a trip down Memory Lane,

I forced myself out of the Sixties and into the present by opening the cabinet door. Eureka! Crammed inside were a scuffed laptop and two thick manila file folders: one labeled ZOO NEWS, the other BLOGS. After a brief tussle with my conscience, Caro's welfare won out. I grabbed everything and headed for the exit.

I had just started up the ladder to the deck when *Nomad* gave a sharp lurch to port. The wake of a speedboat? Through *this* fog? But try as the harbormaster might, she couldn't keep boaters from cranking up the speed before they were out of the channel and into the Pacific. Shaking my head at reckless human folly, I continued up the ladder.

Just as I stuck my head out of the hatch, a shadow loomed out of the mist.

A tall man.

Brandishing a crowbar.

NINE

"TEDDY BENTLEY! WHAT the hell you doing snooping around Kate's boat? I was about to bash your head in."

"Just looking around," I squeaked in alarm.

Heck Liddell's craggy old face remained stared down at me. "No, you're not. You're stealing something."

"These?" I hung onto the ladder with one hand and with the other held up the file folders in a gesture of complete openness. "No, no, no, I'm not stealing anything. These are just some files I need to write *ZooNews*. I'm taking over Kate's job, so I have to…"

"What'd you mean, you're taking over Kate's job? She was a good writer, and you're nothing more than a monkey's ass-wiper."

"Thank you so much for that enlightened job description, Heck, but would you please put the crowbar down? It's making me nervous."

With a grunt he put it down with one hand, and stretched the other toward me. "Gimme those files."

Now that my head was no longer in danger of imminent bashing, my courage returned. "These files are property of the Gunn Zoo." Not a total lie.

For a moment it looked like Heck was about to brandish the crowbar again, but then I heard a hatch slide back on the other side of the dock and a voice call, "Shut up out there! We're trying to sleep!"

"Shut up yourself!" Heck yelled back. At the caller's renewed demands for silence and a threat to call the police,

Heck gave an exasperated sigh and turned away. Before stepping off the *Nomad,* he motioned me to follow him.

I was tempted to scurry back to the *Merilee,* but my curiosity got the better of me. Why was the old man so protective of *Nomad*? Consumed by curiosity, I scrambled up the ladder, locked the hatch behind me, and followed Heck down the dock toward his houseboat.

To put it baldly, *My Fancy* wasn't.

More than just plain, Heck's home was a floating slum. Little more than a shack on pontoons, the eyesore had enraged the yacht owners at the northern end of the harbor. We liveaboarders at the southern end weren't crazy about it, either. Once, over a bowl of chowder at Fred's Fish Market, the harbormaster had admitted to me that four-fifths of the complaints she received involved *My Fancy.* They ranged all the way from the houseboat's outdoor appearance to the stench emanating from its cabin. Heck's own behavior didn't help. When approached about the possibility of cleaning up *My Fancy*'s act, he never just said "No," it was always "Hell, no, and you know where you can shove your complaint!"

So it was with some trepidation that I accepted his offer of a cup of tea. While I was no longer afraid of the man, I was afraid of catching something.

When I stepped inside, I saw that he had cats. *Lots* of cats. The smell of ripening kitty litter just about knocked me down.

Now, normally I like cats. I even have one myself. But Heck's cats—I counted seven—were very "catty" cats, by which I mean that they looked semiferal, and appeared never to have been groomed. So they shed. Oh, did they shed. When I nudged aside a fat calico so that I could rest my butt on a tattered cushion, my hand came away covered with hair. The chipped coffee mug Heck handed me—it

said STOLEN FROM THE SAUSALITO DEPARTMENT OF CORREC-
TIONS—had a hair stuck to its side. Another hair floated in
the weak tea he poured.

But Caro had raised me to be polite. "Thank you," I
said, taking a faux sip. Then I sneezed. A little white cat
that looked part Siamese sneezed, too.

"Asthma got you, Teddy?"

"Something tickled my nose." My eyes began to water,
making me wonder if I was developing an allergy to cats. I
hoped not. I loved Miss Priss and I'd rather sneeze my life
away than give her up. I loved hairy little DJ Bonz, too.
And don't even get me started on the anteater, the monkeys, the koalas… They were all my babies, my beloved
babies. *No, Teddy, come back to the present. Here you are,
sitting inside the houseboat of the harbor's most disrepu-
table resident. He's armed with a crowbar, and you've lost
your mind.*

Come to think of it, Heck's quick arrival on the scene
should have tipped me off to something. Now that he'd
stashed the crowbar under the galley sink, I asked, "Heck,
were you actually guarding the *Nomad*?"

"Damn right. Kate was my friend and I don't want anyone messing with her boat, even now she's dead."

"Friend?"

"For years and years."

Puzzling, considering that Kate's *Nomad* had only been
berthed in the harbor for two months. Before I could ask
him to explain, he added, "Look, Teddy. I gotta talk about
what's happened and how the cops have it all wrong. That
buddy of yours never touched her, and you can take that
to the bank."

Why did everyone keep calling me Bill's buddy? I barely
knew the man. In this case, though, the mistake might come
in handy. "I don't think he killed her, either," I said, "but

if you wouldn't mind telling me, why are you so sure? Do you know Bill?"

"We've shared a few beers."

That came as a surprise. "You have?"

"Sure, while he was dating Kate. They used to drop by here every now and then."

"Here?" I looked around. Besides the bow-to-stern cat hair, the houseboat was furnished with amateurish built-ins that were coming apart at the joints. The sickly green galley table tilted to starboard, and the long settee that ran almost the length of the boat was covered in disintegrating purple Naugahyde. The only halfway attractive item in sight was taped over an unmade bed in the bow: a Quicksilver Messenger poster identical to the one on the *Nomad*. "Did Kate give you that poster?"

He nodded. "Said her father had two of them so I could have the extra. Ty really liked ol' Quicksilver. I did, too. Even saw them in concert, once. 'Course, that was a long time ago, when everybody and his brother was wearing hair down to their asses."

"You knew Kate's father?"

"We lived in the same harbor. Canaan, up by Sausalito. Three years back slip fees at Canaan got too high, so I hauled ass down here."

"Heck, excuse me if I sound rude, but how old are you?"

"Seventy-five next month." He gave me a big smile. His teeth were brown, but they were his own. "I been living on boats since I was in diapers."

"Was Kate's father, ah, *mature*, too?"

"Hell, no. He's about twenty-five years younger than me. I was close with Grover, his dad, is what it was. Grover was my fishing buddy. But that Ty was a real good kid. Smart, too. 'Course, most of the kids around the harbor was smart in those days, but none smart as him. Terrible, what happened."

"What was that?"

"He got that Alzheimer's thing, and him so young. Wasn't much more than fifty. Poor shit."

I winced. An elderly aunt of mine on my father's side had developed Alzheimer's; it was a long, slow sadness before she finally forgot how to breathe. "What about Kate's mother?"

"She died early on. Drowned in Canaan Harbor. Got stoned and fell off the boat, just like they first believed Kate did. But that turned out to be wrong, didn't it?"

Mother and child, both said to have drowned in safe harbor, not at sea. The coincidence unsettled me.

Oblivious to the way my mind was running, Heck continued. "Kate was less than a year old when it happened. Let's see, her mother woulda been…" He counted on his fingers. "Don't know for sure, but she was young and she drowned right around the time Ronnie Reagan became president. Me being a Socialist, I didn't vote for the jerk. Power to the people, I say. Hey, what's wrong with your ear?"

"A flamingo bit me."

"Birds peck, they don't bite."

"Tell that to the flamingo. So you're saying Kate's an orphan?" If so, who would take care of her funeral arrangements? Aster Edwina, maybe. If not… Well, I couldn't let Kate molder away in Potter's Field. I'd just put off purchasing a new engine for the *Merilee*, and use my overtime money to give Kate the sendoff she deserved.

Heck's outraged voice startled me. "She wasn't no orphan!"

"But you said her father…"

"Just because you get Alzheimer's doesn't mean you

drop dead on the spot. Ty's alive, if you can call it that. Kate'd suspected something was wrong, but since he seemed to be taking care of himself all right she let it slide for a while. Ty always was the eccentric type, so I guess she just thought he was just getting more that way. It wasn't 'til she got back from Australia that she saw how bad he'd got. Losing weight 'cause he was forgetting to eat. She had to work and all that, and she couldn't take care of him herself, so she put him in this nursing home in Oakland. That's why she left her San Diego job and signed on with the Gunn Zoo, so she could drive up there to see him every week. I went with her, once. Don't plan to go again 'cause this Ty ain't the boy I used to know. Tell you this much, if that Alzheimer's thing ever starts with me, I'll take *My Fancy* out for a cruise past the breakwater and we'll let the ocean do what the ocean's gonna do." A sea dog's preferred death. Who was I to judge?

"If Kate's mother drowned when she was just a baby, who raised her?"

"Ty did, him and what other woman he could coax into staying on the *Nomad*. He wasn't all that good-looking and like I said, kinda weird, but there's women can get past that. The one that stayed the longest was Peony Moonbeam. At least that's what she called herself. Fixed the *Nomad* up like it was the *Love Boat* or something, she even talked Ty into letting her paint the hull like that. Christ Almighty!" He vented a rare chuckle.

"'Course, Ty was a one of those retro-hippies himself," he continued. "Never cared for money or anything 'cept Kate and tinkering around in that workshop he rented. Anyways, after about ten years or so, Peony Moonbeam ran off with some other guy and that was the end of that. No more women for Ty. Kate was pretty much old enough to take care of herself by then. Not having a mama, maybe that's the reason she turned into such a little runaround!" He chuckled again, as if her behavior didn't bother him.

The single cat hair floating in my coffee mug had somehow multiplied into three. I fished them out with my finger and wiped it on the purple Naugahyde settee. "Does Kate have any other living relatives?"

"Aunts and uncles're all dead. Ty's own father died early on, same with his mother. That family tended to burn out fast, but they sure blazed bright while they was alive. Smart as whips, the whole pack of them. In the genes, I expect. Anyway, it was just Ty and Kate." All traces of humor gone, he shook his head woefully. "Now it's just Ty. You never know how life's gonna turn out, do you?"

No, you don't. "Do you remember the name of that nursing home? They'll need to be contacted about Kate's death and new arrangements will have to be made for her father's care."

He scratched his head and dandruff flew. "Let's see. Was it Sunshine Acres? Sun Peak Acres? Sun Acres? It was Sun something Acres, I know that much."

"In Oakland itself? Or just somewhere around there?"

"Outside of town a little ways. Oh! You know what? I just remembered that she had to move Ty a couple months ago 'cause the Sun something Acres was being tore down to build another damned shopping center. Pretty soon, that's all this country's gonna be, one big shopping center Atlantic to Pacific, nothing but glass and steel connected by thousands of miles of asphalt. Damn Republicans. Not that them Democrats is any better."

That explained some of the confusion over Kate's next-of-kin contact information. She'd died before she had a chance to update it. One thing puzzled me.

"Did Kate know you lived in Gunn Landing Harbor? Is that why she moved *Nomad* here?"

He bared brown teeth at me. "Nah. I 'bout fell over when I saw her steering *Nomad* into that slip. And I gotta tell ya, I wouldn't have recognized her if it hadn't been for that thing. How many psychedelic orange and blue sailboats you ever seen?"

None, as a matter of fact. Sailboat owners usually had more restrained tastes.

"So, Teddy, you gonna find out who killed Kate?"

"Me? I'm a zookeeper, not a cop. Sheriff Rejas is working the case."

"Yeah, and went and arrested the wrong man. I heard about that thing you did last year, finding out who murdered that rich guy down at the zoo. My girl was worth ten of him, so why don't you get her some justice like you did that other creep."

I was growing increasingly uncomfortable, whether because of the catty air or Heck's suggestion that I become Kate Nido's avenger, so I put my hairy coffee mug down on the ugly green table and gathered up the file folders. "It's been nice visiting with you, Heck," I said, standing up. "But if I don't get going, I'll be late to the zoo."

"You pay attention to what I said, hear?"

Before I could stop myself, I said, "I'll see what I can do."

ONCE AT THE ZOO, I visited the Administration Building to tell Zorah what I'd discovered about Kate's father. By the time I left her office, she was already on the phone with the Oakland Police Department.

The day was a beautiful one and fairly uneventful. Nothing escaped and no one fell into the bear pit. As a result, I was able to put Kate's murder out of my mind while I visited with the animals in Down Under. In fact, I was having such a pleasant time cuddling Wanchu that I almost forgot to attend the monthly lunch meeting of CAZK, the California Association of Zookeepers. After putting Wanchu back in her tree, I headed for the auditorium, stopping only to grab a couple of tacos.

Due to my late arrival, most of the keepers had already finished eating and had moved on to finalizing plans for the upcoming Bowling for Rhinos, CAZK's yearly fundraiser. Rhino keeper Buster Daltry was telling them that the Grimaldis were giving us a 50 percent discount on alley rental at Lucky Lanes plus another 25-percent discount on food.

"That'll boost our donation even more," he said. "We're hoping to double last year's contribution."

"We'll get 'er done!" yelled Jack Spence, to a flurry of applause. In the past ten years, this national bowl-a-thon hosted by zookeepers across the U.S. had raised almost three million dollars for various rhino sanctuaries, including Lewa Wildlife Conservancy, Ujung Kulon National Park, Bukit Barisan Selatan, Way Kambas and others across Africa, Java and Indonesia. With rhinos on the endangered list, we keepers knew how much our help was needed. As Buster kept reminding us, "Endangered means there's still time. Extinction is forever."

But Bowling for Rhinos was fun, too. It was a great excuse for us to make fools of ourselves in front of our friends, bowling gutter balls, and eating our way through mounds of nachos and chili dogs. Participation wasn't limited to zoo employees. Anyone who liked animals, or bowling or both was invited to pay the registration fee and lace up a pair of bowling shoes. KTSS-TV and KRSS-AM gave the event free airtime, and the week before the bowl-a-thon, the San Sebastian CinePlex always ran a rhino documentary showing the animals' plight and donating the take to the sanctuaries.

Taking a seat as far away from Myra and Robin as possible, I gobbled my tacos and joined in the discussion only when necessary. Not being particularly organized, I left the heavy lifting to others. I just helped raise money, which in my case, was fairly easy because all I did was hit up Caro's friends. And Caro herself, of course. Although my mother wouldn't be caught dead in a bowling alley, she liked animals as long as I wasn't being trampled, pecked, or bitten by one.

As if reading my mind, Buster called over, "Teddy, can we count on you for, well, you know?"

"I'm sure Mother will donate her standard five thousand. Roarke Gunn, Aster Edwina's nephew, is kicking in ten, Sheridan Parker's giving six, and Lorena Haskell Anders popped for fifteen. She wants to bowl with us, too."

Everyone chuckled, because Lorena, one of the Gunn Zoo's major donors, was pushing eighty. She was, however, in great condition, probably a result of lugging around all those heavy diamonds. "You think we can lure Aster Edwina down to Lucky Lanes this year?" Jack Spence asked. "We'd let her give a speech."

"Don't hold your breath on that one. But I have an appointment to see her Tuesday, and I'll wring whatever I can out of her. I'm hoping for upwards of fifteen thou this year. She's pretty happy with the amount of publicity our rhinos have received." The room fell silent. Too late I remembered that Kate had engendered all those press releases and made the follow-up calls. Embarrassed, I lowered my head and pretended to be busy with a taco. After a brief moment of discomfort, the keepers continued discussing their plans for Bowling for Rhinos. Once that topic had been exhausted, they began talking about the upcoming television marathon to raise funds for the San Sebastian No-Kill Animal

Shelter, which would take place three days after the rhino fundraiser. Bad timing, perhaps, but what you gonna do?

I volunteered my services for the marathon, then resumed worrying about Kate's death.

EARLY THAT EVENING, after taking care of Miss Priss and DJ Bonz, I climbed back into my truck and drove inland along Bentley Road toward San Sebastian.

A winding, fifteen-mile stretch of narrow, two-lane blacktop, the north side of Bentley Road paralleled the remains of the old Bentley cattle ranch. Formerly twenty thousand acres, three generations worth of bad investments had reduced it to a narrow strip of pasturage that did little more than serve as a barrier to the encroachment of Bentley Heights, a ticky-tacky housing development situated high atop a ridge a mile back from the road. This ugly development was the bane of the Gunn family, whose estate bordered the south side of the road. Things could have been worse. No connecting road ran down from the Heights, and the Gunn's eucalyptus forest kept the offending houses out of sight.

Ordinarily I liked driving along Bentley Road because it held a bucolic charm, but never in the evening or late at night. Other than a thin rush hour in the morning and late afternoon when zoo workers and visitors traveled this relatively unknown hookup to Gunn Road, few drivers chose this isolated byway. The road boasted no gas stations, no call boxes, and no other motorists to hitch a ride with in case of a breakdown.

But my Nissan pickup was mechanically sound, if a bit raggedy, and twenty minutes later, I arrived at the San Sebastian County Jail.

It being Sunday, the jail's lobby was crowded with visitors anxious to see their loved ones. Women wept, men cursed, babies shrieked. Some, like myself, stood in sad silence while awaiting our turn to pass through the metal detector. The crowd didn't bother me because it meant that there was a chance Joe wouldn't catch sight of me among the herd.

Alas, he did.

As I signed in, a big hand gripped my forearm. "What are you doing here, Teddy? And what happened to your ear?"

I gave Joe a weak smile. He looked so exhausted that it was all I could do not to reach up and caress his tired face. "Flamingo bit me."

His face softened with concern for a moment, then hardened again. "And the answer to my other question?"

"Visiting a friend."

Without giving my bandaged ear another thought, he said, "Oh, golly, gee. Could that 'friend' possibly be Bill McQueen, the man who's just been indicted in the murder of one Katherine Nido?"

"How'd you guess?" If there's one thing I hate, it's an argument with the man I love, but that doesn't mean I back away from one. Meeting sarcasm with sarcasm, I said, "Get that big paw off my arm and let me get patted down. It's always such a thrill."

"Didn't I tell you to keep your nose out of this?"

"Tellin' and gettin' aren't the same." As the line shuffled forward, me with them, Joe's hand remained on my arm. I nodded toward his gun belt. "You go through that metal detector with me and you'll set off the alarm."

"Mr. McQueen's guilty, Teddy."

"Like the last Gunn zookeeper you arrested for murder?" The erroneous arrest of a zookeeper several months earlier had cast a shadow over Joe's career.

"This is different."

"Not to me. Look, I visited a friend then and I'm visiting a friend now. Hey, it looks like I'm up next for the metal detector. Please don't make a scene."

He dropped his hand. "We'll talk about this tomorrow."

"I'm sure we will," I said, miserably.

"You remember our date, do you?"

"Of course. And you'll have all day to lay down the law." I tried to make it sound witty, but from the look on his face, I failed.

Without another word, he stalked off.

Unlike some others in the visitors' line, I made it through the metal detector without setting off any alarms. Instead of being shown into the large visitors' area with the rest, I was escorted by one of Joe's deputies to a more secure room, which contained a small table and two chairs. I sat down. The deputy left, closing the door behind him. Before long, he and another deputy led in a shackled prisoner.

Jail isn't good for people. Within days, the color fades from their faces and the whites of their eyes turn yellow. But jail is great for losing weight. Bill looked like he'd already lost ten pounds. "Hi, Teddy. Nice to see a mate. What 'appended to yer ear?"

"Flamingo."

"Coo-er. Them's vicious birds!"

"No kidding. But I'm here to see about you. Are they treating you right?" I tried to smile but don't think I had too much success at it.

A sneer. "Everything's just corker."

"Is there anything you need?"

"Money for chewies would be bonzer. And a case of Foster's if you can smuggle it through."

Behind me, one of the deputies guffawed. This made me even more depressed because their continued presence proved that they believed Bill was too dangerous to be left alone with me. Bill, a man who'd never hurt a hair on a koala's head.

I ignored the lump in my throat and asked, "What did they set your bail at?" Maybe I could do something about that.

"No bail, cuz I'm, like, one a them 'resident aliens.' Bastards took me passport, too."

"I'm sorry, Bill."

"Not 'alf as sorry as me, little sheila."

In an attempt to make him feel better, I caught him up on Wanchu, Abim, and the rest of the animals he loved. From the dampness in his eyes, which he manfully tried to hide from me, I'd just made him miss them all the more. To change the subject, I asked, "Bill, do you know what nursing home Kate's father lives in?"

He shook his head. "She never talked about him. Bloke coulda lived on the moon, for all's I know."

For a moment, I wanted to curse the woman for not having any foresight, but who among us realizes they're about to die? I bit back my disappointment and continued on. "Have they given you a public defender yet?"

"Yeh. She seems fair dimkum. Bit young, though."

"You didn't kill Kate, did you?" Not that he'd admit it with those deputies two standing there.

"That's what I been shoutin' about, not that anybody's listening. Not even me brief believes me."

Attorneys always want to believe their clients are innocent so that they can mount a righteous defense. If an attorney—especially a young, possibly idealistic one—had doubts about her client's innocence, there could be a problem. Still, I tried to paint a rosy picture.

"It seems to me there's a pretty good case for your innocence. You don't have a key card to the electronic harbor gate, and you live in Castroville, twelve miles from the harbor. You don't even own a car, just that old bike."

He shuffled in his seat, another bad sign. "Weeeel, that's a bit of a balls-up, in't it? Seems some bloke saw me ped-dlin' down Highway One toward the harbor a couple hours before they say Kate carked it. He ID'd me in, whatyou-callit, a line-up."

Ominous, but not necessarily critical. "It was dark, so I don't see how that's possible, Bill. Who is this guy, any-way, somebody driving home from a bar?"

His already long face grew longer. "Some preacher tailin' it back home after visiting a dyin' parishioner. Wasn't all that inky where he saw me, either. I'd stopped to tighten me bike's chain underneath that streetlight by the harbor turnoff." He sighed. "I've come a crapper, haven't I, Teddy?"

"It could be worse." But I didn't know how. "Does the sheriff say how you could get into the harbor without a key card?"

"No prob there. Them Grimaldis had it propped open with a rock the size of a wombat's arse."

With the two deputies listening right behind me, I knew I shouldn't ask him my next question, but I had to know. Bill would either answer me or not. "What the hell were you doing at Gunn Landing Harbor?"

"Kinda needed to talk to Kate," he mumbled.

"Why not call her?"

"Called five or six times, but daft sheila wasn't answerin' her phone, was she, so what else was I 'sposed to do, send up smoke signals? See, I knew she spent Sunday nights down at the harbor, but when I got there the damned hatch to her boat was locked from the outside. I hung around until I heard Kate's voice coming from the *Gutterball*, but there was all kinds of other people talkin' round her, so... Well, what I needed to see her 'bout was private, so I hung back, waitin' for her to come over to the *Nomad*. When she never showed, I gave up and legged it. I told that wanker sheriff she was alive and shootin' her mouth off when I left, but he didn't believe me."

Talk about an absolute wreck of an alibi. "What did Joe say your motive was?"

"That I killed her 'cause she dumped me for that dumb park ranger."

"Lex isn't dumb."

"Wallabies is smarter. Besides, Kate didn't dump me. It worked the other way round. Women don't leave Outback Bill—he leaves them."

I ignored his heartless arrogance. "What was so important that you couldn't wait until Monday to talk to Kate? Especially since you live only a couple of blocks from her apartment. You could have talked to her then, before she left for the zoo."

Foolishly open until now, Bill sat back and folded his arms across his chest. In formal, non-Aussie he said, "On advice of counsel, I will not answer that question."

And that was the end of that. With Bill refusing to say another word, I saw no reason to prolong our visit, so after bidding him a polite goodbye, I let a deputy escort me back out. As I forked over the last of my cash into Bill's canteen account, I heard a woman tell the desk sergeant that she was here to see Mr. McQueen. Like so many other women in the jail that night, she was crying. I forced myself not to turn around because I recognized her voice.

It was Robin Chase, the big cat keeper.

Why hadn't I realized she was in love with him?

TEN

On my day off, Joe arrived at the harbor early enough for us to spend some quality time together on the boat, then wander over to Fred's Fish Market for an après-love-making breakfast. It being a Monday, the restaurant wasn't overly crowded, but I did see a few harbor regulars. Among them was Ford Bronson, dressed in yachting clothes, and preening slightly as he talked to a similarly-clad blonde who looked enough like Madonna to actually be her. Was she? After taking note of a booth filled to overflowing with bodyguard types, I realized she was. Not wanting to be a bore, I resisted the urge to walk over and request an *a capella* version of "Like A Virgin."

At a table across the room sat Melanie Gideon, owner of the Captain's Inn, the nautical-themed bed and breakfast that had won so many awards. Melanie was deep in discussion with Fred himself, probably trying to cadge his recipe for bouillabaisse.

When my eyes drifted back to Bronson, I waved.

As he always did when he was seen with someone famous, Bronson smiled and waved back.

Joe scowled. "That guy sure lives up there where the air is rare, doesn't he?"

"No kidding. Last week he was in here with the Secretary of Defense; the week before that, Oprah. A month ago, it was Clint Eastwood and Brad Pitt. At the same time! He takes them cruising on his yacht, the *Lady B Good*."

Joe's scowl grew deeper. "Don't those people have their own boats?"

Did I detect a hint of jealousy? Excellent! "Just birds of a feather, flocking together," I murmured, nuzzling his neck. "Anyway, you're cuter than Brad and more masculine than Clint." With that, we returned to murmuring sweet nothings over our eggs ranchero, but as soon as the waitress took our plates away, our idyllic morning almost fell apart.

Joe waited until she'd disappeared behind the swinging door to the kitchen, then leaned over the table and said, "I'll ask again. What were you doing at the jail last night?"

We hadn't let the waitress take our coffee cups away, so I was able to stall for time by taking another sip of hazelnut decaf. "I told you, just visiting a friend."

"Just 'visiting'?" As he mimicked my voice, he made a face. "Teddy, I don't want you mixed up in the Kate Nido case."

Not liking being told what to do—I'd had enough of that from Caro over the years—I said, "I'm not 'mixed up' in anything, Joe. And I wasn't the only zookeeper visiting poor old Bill, by the way. Robin Chase was there, too."

"You understand that visitors' conversations are videotaped?"

"Of course."

"Then you know what your questions sounded like."

Another sip of hazelnut decaf. I sloshed the liquid around in my mouth for a few seconds, then swallowed and took a deep breath. With as much time killed as possible, I answered, "I was curious, that's all."

"Since I never insult your intelligence, please don't insult mine. Remember what happened last time you involved yourself in a murder investigation?"

"I found the *right* murderer is what happened."

Joe sighed and ran his hand through his thick black hair.

The disarray made him look sexier than ever. "I love the way you summarily dismiss three attempts on your life."

"There were only two real attempts. The other one was faked."

Hands through the hair again. "Have you ever heard of 'magical thinking'? Just because you think someone's innocent doesn't mean he is. Mr. McQueen's phone records indicate… Well, I can't discuss those, Teddy, but believe me, he had M.O.M."

The seeming non sequitur set me back. It had never occurred to me that after Joe's father died so many years earlier, his mother would finally embark on a new love life, and with a much younger man. An Australian, at that. "You mean to tell me that Bill and your mother…?"

This scowl out-scowled all the previous ones. "Get your head out of the gutter, Teddy. M.O.M. is an acronym for means, opportunity, and method. Bill had them all."

"A woman having a love life is 'gutter' material? If that's so, what about you and me?" Now I was really mad.

"I didn't mean…"

"Yes, you did."

The waitress, a pretty blonde, interrupted our glaring contest by asking if we wanted a refill. I said no. Joe held out his cup. "To the brim."

She smiled at him. Much too warmly, I thought. "For you, Sheriff, anything."

My frosty stare didn't scare her away, so holding out my own cup, I snapped, "I changed my mind. More for me, too."

Unsmiling, she dribbled a few more drops in my cup, which didn't even bring it to the halfway mark, then with a flick of her hips, sashayed away.

Joe's voice roused me from my jealous funk. "No arguments, Teddy. Back away from the Nido investigation before you get hurt." Furious, I put my cup down and crossed my arms across my chest. "Let's see. The zoo trusts me to take care of the wolves, the tigers, and even help out with the rhinos from time to time, but you don't think I'm up to conversing with a human being."

"Not the *murderus humanus* subspecies, I don't, no."

"Bill's not a murderer," I snapped. "A cad, but not a murderer."

"You're kidding."

"Then why aren't I smiling?"

"Teddy, if you don't stop messing around in this case, I'll…"

"You'll what?"

"I'll… I'll…" He stopped, baffled.

There's nothing sweeter than a baffled cop, so I blew him a kiss. "I thought so. You'll do nothing, because as long as I don't break the law, there's nothing you can do. And I don't break the law, do I?" I decided to keep quiet about my evidence tampering on Kate's boat.

Joe stared at me for a moment, an unreadable expression on his face. Then he leaned across the table, took my hand, and kissed it. "I'm doomed."

I blinked. "What does that mean?"

"It means you're impossible and I love you anyway."

The next time the waitress came by, he demanded she fill my cup to the brim.

Earlier, after a much friendlier squabble, we'd decided to take his children to the zoo for the afternoon. At first he'd hung back, saying that for me, it would be too much like work, so why not take them to the Monterey Bay Aquarium instead. I'd stuck to my guns and by one o'clock, we were all munching cotton candy from the zoo's Gumdrop Gorilla's Candy Emporium. Eight-year-old Antonio, who looked just like his blue-eyed, black-haired father, handled his cloud of blue fluff well, but three-year-old Bridget, who bore a heart-rending resemblance to her deceased mother, got more cotton candy on her face than in her mouth.

I fared little better. To the children's glee, my frizzy red hair kept springing forward and draping itself across my own blue goo, so much so that I gave up and tossed the remainder into a trash receptacle.

After the children had glutted themselves on empty calories and we'd wiped them down, we braved the crowd at Friendly Farm, where Antonio rode a docile pony around in a circle and Bridget fed a chicken. We had our pictures taken by a zoo photographer while we sat astride various mounts on the Endangered Species Carousel. Joe chose a dragon (very endangered); me, a snow leopard; Bridget, a roly-poly panda; and Antonio, the South China tiger, which he advised us, was already extinct in the wild.

"How did you know that?" I asked, shocked. Most adults couldn't tell a South China tiger from a Sumatran, let alone an eight-year-old.

As we rode round and round to the music of the calliope, he answered, "Dad bought us a book about endan... endan..."

"Endangered," Joe said softly.

"Endangered animals," Antonio finished up.

I gave the boy a kiss on the cheek, then leaned over from my snow leopard and gave Joe a one-armed hug. "A gold star for you." Joe grinned. "If I'd known you're react that way, I'd have fessed up earlier. Can I have another hug if I admit that last week I contributed twenty dollars to Bowling for Rhinos?"

"But did you?"

"Call me George Washington, because I cannot tell a lie." He got his extra hug.

"You'll get better than that if you pledge a matching twenty during the marathon for the No-Kill Animal Shelter."

A wink. "Oh, I might be able to arrange that."

Now aware that our little group included a budding zoologist, I led them to the giant anteater's enclosure. By the time we arrived, three-year-old Bridget had already fallen asleep in the wagon Joe had rented, but Antonio was delighted when Baby Boy Anteater climbed off Lucy's back and scampered across the compound. When Lucy caught up with him, they both flopped down on their sides and scrabbled at each other with their feet in Lucy's favorite game, "Let's Box And I'll Let You Win."

"Cool," Antonio said.

When the boy moved further along the fence to get a better look, I glanced down at sleeping Bridget. So peaceful, so innocent. So like her mother.

"Have any leads turned up yet on Sonia's killer?" I asked Joe. Only three months after Bridget's birth, Joe's wife—an assistant prosecuting attorney—had been found shot to death in her car near the I-5 off ramp. Her killer had never been identified.

Joe shook his head. "Not a thing."

"How are you...?"

"I'm handling it, Teddy. I..." His face changed. "Antonio's coming back. Say something happy."

I'd led enough school tours through the zoo to know what would sound happy to an eight-year-old boy, so I said, "Hey, Antonio, did you know that a giant anteater is the only animal in the Amazon rainforest who can bring down a jaguar? The anteater rises up on its hind legs, and when the jag attacks, the anteater rips its belly open with its four-inch talons and scatters jag guts all over the place."

While Joe stared at me aghast, Antonio clapped his hands and said, "Waaaay cooooool!"

I had just started to tell him more fascinating facts about anteaters when Joe's cell phone rang. After glancing at the caller ID, Joe stepped off the pathway and into the brush, but I could hear him using his official voice. "Yes, Deputy." Silence for a moment, then, "Give me the details." A longer silence, ending when he said, "Oh, hell. Yeah. Yeah. Right. I'll meet you there in twenty minutes. For now, keep them in separate rooms."

When he came back he apologized, then hustled us toward the zoo's exit. "So much for my day off. Ordinarily I'd take you back to the *Merilee*, but there's an emergency, and I need to meet two deputies at a crime scene. It's a domestic turned ugly."

"They're calling you out on a *domestic*?"

"It's…complicated."

Knowing he wouldn't say anything else, I let the matter drop. As we walked along, he said, "I have to get the kids back home, but what about you? I can either deposit you at the jail—I know how much you like to hang around there—or you can visit Mom until I'm done, which might take up to an hour. Maybe two."

Colleen and I had always gotten along well, so I almost agreed, but I knew what a cop's life was like. What at first looked like a one-hour call might turn into eight, which would leave me stranded in San Sebastian, fifteen miles from the harbor and my own babies. Checking my watch, I saw it was two-fifteen.

"Slow down a sec," I said, digging my cell out of my handbag. "Give me enough time to make a call."

After my brief phone conversation, a bemused Joe left me sitting on a bench at the zoo's entrance while he shepherded the kids across the parking lot. Feeling a bit bemused myself, I sat back and waited for Caro.

Fifteen minutes later, when I climbed into the silver

Mercedes next to Mr. Trifle, the first thing Caro said was, "What's wrong with your ear?"

I was getting tired of hearing about my ear. "It's just a scratch."

"But…"

"Drop it, Mother."

"*Caro.*"

"Drop it, *Caro.*" But I smiled to take out the sting, because the only thing worse than an over-protective mother was a mother who wasn't protective enough.

Borders established, we drove along comfortably enough for a while with Mr. Trifle sitting in my lap. When she'd called and told me about today's appointment in San Sebastian, I'd had a good laugh. But now, with the Chihuahua dressed like my mother in a silk Chloe jacket and matching beret, I didn't find it so funny. Something needed to be done about the poor dog, and quickly. But was taking him to see a dog psychic the solution?

As we entered the San Sebastian city limits, I broke the silence. "Caro, are you *sure* you didn't know Kate Nido? Not even casually?"

She took her eyes off the road long enough to stare at me like I'd lost my mind.

"How many times do I have to tell you, I didn't know the woman."

"You're sure?"

"Theodora, you've become such a nag."

The idea that I might be turning into my mother silenced me, but I remained uneasy. I might not have known Kate all that well, but she had appeared to have a rigorously logical mind. She must have written *Tdy's mom noz*, for a reason, but for now, the meaning of that Post-it note remained a mystery.

The small city of San Sebastian is crowned by San

Sebastian Mission, which perches on a hill overlooking the business district. Founded in 1798 by Padre Bautista de Sosa, the Mission has withstood earthquakes, fires, locusts, and other natural disasters. Now it endured yet another invasion: tourists. As Caro maneuvered her silver Mercedes SL along Main Street, she had to contend with rentals from Enterprise and Avis dueling for parking spaces at the bottom of the hill. The narrow road leading up to the Mission had been closed to traffic two decades earlier. "I hate tourists," she grumped, as a teal-colored Chevy Cobalt cut her off.

"Our ancestors built the ships that made tourism possible. And our family rich."

"Wealthy, Teddy. *Rich* is so vulgar."

"No kidding."

She shot me a look. "Are you insinuating that I'm…?"

"Wouldn't dream of it, Mother."

"*Caro!*" she barked.

"Whatever."

As we drove along the street, I spotted a lavender storefront decorated with a mural that featured dogs and cats romping happily together. The sign on the door read, SPEAKS-TO-SOULS, ANIMAL PSYCHIC. The same words were emblazoned on a lavender cargo van parked just down the street.

"There's a parking spot right in front of the store, Caro."

"Place of business," she muttered. "*Store* is so…"

"I know—vulgar. Better grab that spot before the black Accord does."

After shooting another dirty look toward her insolent daughter, she successfully beat the Accord to the parking spot and angled the big Mercedes in. Before we exited the car, she straightened the beret on Mr. Trifle's head, expertly avoiding his snapping teeth. At that moment, I decided that if Speaks-to-Souls couldn't help him, I would kidnap the poor animal and find him a sane home before Caro lost a finger.

My concern about Speaks-to-Souls intensified when we entered the store. I bear no animosity toward New Thought philosophy, and God knows I'm a fan of the animal kingdom, but the store's blending of the two jarred what little remained of my artistic sensibilities. Bamboo and copper wind chimes clacked and tinkled over a sound system playing Peruvian flute music, while paintings of dogs wearing angel wings hung on dark purple walls. Kapok-stuffed white tigers crouched next to a bookshelf filled with books on animal chakras, tofu recipes, and vegan candle making. A closer inspection showed the books had all been penned and self-published by Speaks-to-Souls.

More down-to-earth was the swarm of cats and dogs that rushed to greet us. A retriever mix with a battered snout and sweet expression licked my left ankle as an aged tabby with one ear rubbed against my right one. Close behind them were three mongrels of various shapes and sizes, and five alley-type cats. Judging from their scars and grateful natures, all were rescues. Well, good for Speaks-to-Souls. She might be a phony but at least she was a compassionate phony.

When the woman herself swept toward us, her orange-and red-patterned sari fluttering in the kitty-litter-and-patchouli-scented air, my doubts about her increased. If she was American Indian, I was a Sumo wrestler. She wasn't India Indian, either, because she looked Norwegian. At least six feet tall with pale gray eyes and what appeared to be natural blond hair, she was as sturdily built as a lumberjack. There was something familiar about her face, too, but I couldn't quite pinpoint it. No matter. In deference to her obvious animal-rescue activities, I would sit politely through her spiel, urge Caro to write a fat check, then hustle my mother out the door as soon as possible.

And lay my plans for a dog-napping.

"Caro, how wonderful to meet you and Mr. Trifle in the flesh," Speaks-to-Souls said, with a voice as deep as a man's. "It's so nice that you've brought your sister along."

Accepting this transparent flattery as truth, Caro simpered. "Sweet of you to say so, but Theodora is my daughter."

I didn't simper. "Call me Teddy. And in the spirit of full disclosure, I'm an animal keeper at the Gunn Zoo, and therefore I'm a bit leery about all this dog psychic stuff."

Penetrating gray eyes met mine. "The Gunn Zoo? How interesting. Oh, well. Let's take Mr. Trifle into the treatment room and get started. Alyse will watch the shop while we work."

A younger woman who looked enough like Speaks-to-Souls to be her daughter, although dressed in tee shirt and jeans, stepped from behind a unicorn-filled étagère. Her own gray eyes danced with amusement. "Will do, Mom."

Then she winked at me.

The treatment room, as Speaks-to-Souls had dubbed it, was carpeted and painted a deep, restful blue. The furniture looked like rejects from a La-Z-Boy factory but for a shiny CD player nestled between two white, patchouli-scented candles. On the floor lay several doggie beds in varying sizes, ranging from teacup Chihuahua to great Dane. Scattered around them were a selection of doggie toys, including balls, ropes, and several stuffed animals. Mr. Trifle, still snarling after Caro lifted him from her tote, ignored them all.

"My, what a fierce fellow you are," said Speaks-to-Souls, bending down to look him in the eye.

Mr. Trifle gave her a worried glance, then went back to snarling at Caro.

With a fluid move, Speaks-to-Souls flicked on the CD player and Peruvian flute music filled the room. She then lit the candles and switched off the overhead light. Settling herself into one of the big loungers, she said, "I believe I already know what the problem is, but I'll need to go into a trance to check with the spirits. If you could both sit quietly, please?"

Caro and I sat, leaving Mr. Trifle standing at Caro's feet.

Ignoring my warning, Speaks-to-Souls picked up the Chihuahua and placed him in her lap. For a moment Mr. Trifle seemed to consider biting her, then to my amazement, gazed into her eyes with an adoring expression. That surprised me more than anything I'd seen earlier.

Then, in the candle-lit room, Speaks-to-Souls slumped against the headrest of her La-Z-Boy, rolled her eyes back, and chanted, "*Um mah, um mah, um mah!* Oh, Great Animal Spirit, visit me now!"

I kept a straight face, but it wasn't easy.

As the minutes ticked by, we were treated to more chants, more eye rolling. And more self-control from me. Caro, however, looked enchanted. So did Mr. Trifle.

"*Um mah, um mah, um mah!*"

Despite my best intentions, I yawned. The deep blue room, the patchouli air, the Peruvian flute music—I was desperate to go beddie-bye.

Suddenly someone—or some thing—answered in a deep, growly voice. "*Um mah zezezzer acupopo zeezix!*" Looking more carefully, I saw Speaks-to-Souls' lips move.

She embarked upon a long conversation with whatever was hiding out in the ether. A sperm whale? Border collie? A vole? Whoever he/she/it was, he/she/it certainly liked to talk.

Stifling yet another yawn, I wondered how much longer this could continue. Would I be trapped in this dark room for eternity with an unseen spirit, a phony dog psychic, my nutty mother, and her just-as-nutty Chihuahua?

Speaks-to-Souls' eyes suddenly flew open. "That's it!" she proclaimed. "The Great Animal Spirit has revealed the problem!"

"Wha... What?" Caro asked, her voice unusually hesitant. Without answering, Speaks-to-Souls began stripping Mr. Trifle of his Caro-clone clothing. Off flew the white jacket and matching beret. I had never seen Mr. Trifle look so relieved.

"His name is not Mr. Trifle," Speaks-to-Souls declared. "The Great Animal Spirit has informed me that this noble animal is the reincarnation of a great Aztec warrior named Feroz Guerrero. Caro, you must begin calling him by his rightful name. And, my dear, stop dressing him up as if he were nothing more than a fashion accessory. Feroz Guerrero was known for charging into battle naked."

Caro's mouth, already open, dropped further.

So did mine, because I had realized that while Speaks-to-Souls was undoubtedly a charlatan, her animal skills—as well as her tact—were the real deal. "Ever think about becoming a zookeeper?" I blurted out.

Turning her head so that Caro couldn't see, Speaks-to-Souls mirrored her daughter's earlier wink. "Actually, I did give it some thought at one time. Then I decided I could do more good by channeling the Great Animal Spirit."

After the performance I'd just seen, I wasn't about to argue. Before we left with a naked Chihuahua renamed Feroz Guerrero—who looked much happier now, by the way—I made certain that Caro wrote Speaks-to-Souls a large check. Surprisingly, the woman had her make it out to the building fund for the San Sebastian No-Kill Animal

Shelter, explaining that she preferred not to profit from her work with the Great Animal Spirit. She did, however, talk Caro into purchasing several scented candles, and for those, had another check made out to her store. As I slid into the Mercedes with a naked Aztec warrior tucked under my arm, I said to Caro, "Did Speaks-to-Souls look familiar to you?"

A bit stunned from her introduction to the spirit world, she shook her head and started the car. She remained silent as we drove back to Gunn Landing. Half an hour later, when Caro dropped me off at the harbor gate, I still couldn't remember where I'd seen Speaks-to-Souls before. But then Caro couldn't remember knowing Kate, either, so I guess we were even.

As I walked down the dock to the *Merilee*, I noticed that the *Nomad* had been taken away to the county's evidence storage yard. The slip where Kate had berthed her boat now lay empty, except for a harbor seal swimming back and forth between the pilings. As much as I enjoyed wildlife, I found the scene depressing.

"Sad, isn't it?" a voice said.

I turned to see Ford Bronson. He'd halted his evening run along the southern promenade and was jogging in place next to me.

"Very sad," I replied.

"Life can be dangerous, Teddy. I'm surprised your mother lets you live down here all by yourself."

"*Let*?" I shook my head. "Oh, please. I stopped asking for permission two decades ago."

"Still…" He looked off toward the channel, where a whale-watching excursion was just returning. "Promise me you'll be careful."

While it was flattering to know a handsome billionaire

worried about me, it was also annoying. But to keep the peace, I nodded. "Will do."

Satisfied, he jogged off.

Once back aboard the *Merilee*, I changed into my sweats and settled down with the first of Kate's files to work on *ZooNews*. I'd done the bulk of the rewriting the evening before, so I had just finished when Joe called to make certain I'd arrived safely home. I assured him I had.

"It's just as well you caught a ride with your mother, because I didn't get away until a few minutes ago," he said. "The deputy was right. That domestic was one of the hairiest I've ever experienced."

"A fatal?" So many domestic disturbances turned tragic these days.

"Not at all. Just…complicated."

"That's what you said at the zoo."

"That's all I'm going to say, too. How'd things go with the dog?" We both had a good laugh as I described the "séance."

"Sounds like Speaks-to-Souls or whatever her real name is performed a public service," he said, when I'd finished. "But she'd better watch her step. Our White Collar Crimes Division has started cracking down on fraudulent psychics."

I smiled. "How can you tell if a psychic is fraudulent?"

"The amount of money they charge for a reading is a good tip-off."

Remembering the large check Caro had written to the San Sebastian No-Kill Animal Shelter, I didn't say anything. As far as I was concerned, any money donated to an animal shelter was clean money, even if procured in a liquor store holdup.

"So what's your evening look like?" he asked.

I told him I'd almost finished rewriting the zoo's newsletter, and after that, I would work on Kate's blog. In a meeting between Zorah and Aster Edwina, the two had decided to change the online diary's name from *Koala Kate's Outback Telegraph* to *Tiger Teddy's Telegraph*. Since I rarely worked with tigers, the name wasn't all that appropriate but it would have to do.

"I'm not looking forward to it, because you know how I feel about more paperwork," I said. "But at least I've found all of Kate's files…" Oops. I'd found most of them during my break-in at the *Nomad*, but he didn't need to know that. "…uh, at the zoo, so I'll go over them and try to match her style. By the way, I noticed that the *Nomad*'s gone."

"Yeah, they winched it out around noon. Not that I think we're going to find anything helpful. Judging from where you found her and which way the tide was running, it's probable that once she left the party she never made it back to her boat." Then he abruptly changed the subject, and we talked about more personal things for a while.

When we rang off, I went back to work.

Once I opened the second of Kate's manila files—the thickest one—I received a surprise. The printouts inside weren't from *Koala Kate's Outback Telegraph* after all; they were printouts of a blog I'd not seen before: *The Tasmanian Devil*. Curious, I began to read. Halfway through the first page, I began to understand the skeptical looks that had passed among the other zookeepers when I had talked so blithely about how much "fun" Kate's blog was. The Tasmanian Devil was just the opposite.

> *Koalas enjoyable as usual, B annoying as usual. What's up with men, anyway? Considering their own non-monogamous natures, isn't it rather hypocritical of them to demand fidelity from their girlfriends? Like male lions, men want mating rights with every female around, but woe betide a lioness who casts*

come-hither glances at the new stud on the block.
You know what I have to say about that, Dear Read-
ers? ROAARRR!!!

Stunned, I took out my laptop and signed on to the Internet. Typing in the URL for *Koala Kate's Outback Tele-*
graph, I found it no different than I remembered: a field
of warm beige headed by a picture of Wanchu at the top.
Colorful Aboriginal designs trailed down the right side of
the copy, which contained nothing but cute stories about
some of the zoo's most popular animals. I saw nothing
even faintly derogatory, either of animals or humans. In
short, the blog read nothing like the printouts I'd found in
the folder.

Checking the folder more carefully, I found something
I had missed earlier. Written under the URL for the blog I
was looking at now was another URL. When I typed that
one in, *The Tasmanian Devil* popped up.

This blog was not only darker in tone, but darker in
design, too. At their best, Tasmanian devils, an Australian mammal about the size of a small dog, are rather unattractive, but the one gracing the site's menacing gray
background looked positively repulsive. Its fangs had been
lengthened in PhotoShop, and blood dribbled down the
side of its mouth.

The Tasmanian Devil's posts were bloody, too.

After describing koalas' mating ritual in blunt words—
sometimes the females darn near rape the males—Kate segued onto the mating rituals of the human species.

Yes, Dear Readers, it's mating time at the zoo and not
just for koalas. Cat Girl has fallen hard for B, while
Rhino Man has the hots for Our Glorious Leader.

*Nothing like a little unrequited mating to liven things
up, is there?*

After my experience at the jail the other night, I realized
"Cat Girl" was Robin Chase, observed by Kate in Robin's
first swoonings over Bill. But if "Rhino Man" was Buster
Daltry, surely Kate hadn't been under the assumption that
he'd fallen for Zorah! From what I'd been able to see, our
zoo director's love life was about as titillating as a nun's.

In a post dated a week later, Kate indulged in more mischief making. After few paragraphs about sweet Tulang,
the roly poly wombat, she started sniping at people again.

*If there's one thing you learn about working in zoos,
Dear Readers, it's that the world is growing smaller
by the minute. No, I'm not talking about the shrink-
ing Rainforest, sad as that may be, or other areas of
our endangered eco-system. I'm talking about how
we run into Familiar Faces in Unusual Places. Sometimes those FF's aren't happy to see you, and for
good reason. There's more to come about this, because I have a very special post planned to reveal the
dastardly deeds of THIS particular FF. As they say on
television, "Stay tuned for an important announcement." I'm unsheathing my claws and am about to
pounce. ROAARRR!!!*

Biting back my distaste, I continued scrolling through
more posts, noting a mixture of tender essays about Down
Under animals—especially Wanchu—intermixed with increasingly harsh snipes at unnamed animal keepers, concession owners, volunteers, and even the denizens of an
unnamed harbor.

Love can be blind, can't it, Dear Readers? Especially when older women are married to younger men. A certain boat-owning woman I know is having trouble keeping Younger Hubby in check, which in her case, will be about as easy as picking up a 7-10 split. YH was recently seen boozing at a local watering hole and kanoodling with a girl who looked half his age. But as we all know, men are actually admired for that kind of behavior, aren't they?

Given the 7-10 bowling reference, Kate had to be talking about the Grimaldis. Was Sam being unfaithful to Doris? Intrigued despite myself, I remembered the Post-it notes I'd found in one of Kate's files. *T Doris t at party.* Could that have meant, *Tell Doris the truth at party*? This possible translation of Kate's note brought about another question: had Kate died *before* she could tell Doris about Sam's wanderings?

Shuddering, I read another post, this one dated only two weeks back. Kate spent several sweet-funny paragraphs on our new lion cub, then unleashed her claws on humans again.

If you ask me, Dear Readers, firefighters don't belong on boats. They're fine on calendars or when your stove catches fire, but that's pretty much the end of their usefulness. Forget about sailing. Most of them couldn't hoist a sail to save their lives, so they prefer gas-guzzling power boats. And a certain firefighter, who owns a boat named something like Berserker, is one of the worst of the species. Why, he's so high on himself that he thinks "Hello" is an invitation to join you in the sack.

I ground my teeth. Walt MacAdams, the San Sebastian firefighter whose *Running Wild* was berthed near the *Merilee*, had once saved my life. And as far as being "high" on himself, as the old saying goes, "Point your finger at someone and you'll find three fingers pointing back at YOU." Maybe Kate had hit on him and he'd declined. Walt *was* pretty fussy about the company he kept.

With her snipe at Walt, I thought Kate had reached the epitome of her nastiness, but the last lines of the next post took my breath away.

Rich people are so boring, aren't they, Dear Readers? The town where I've ended up is full of them. They try to act sooooo respectable, but when you dig into their backgrounds, you discover that almost all of them are the beneficiaries of past crimes. Typical of this pack of jackals is a certain multilast-named ex-beauty queen who, not content to live off an embezzling ex-husband's ill-gotten gains, is currently looking for a fifth husband to fleece. Parasites like her make you suspect old Karl Marx had it right.

Oh, the bitch!

I was so enraged that for a moment I forgot about the Post-it note that mentioned Caro, but it came back to me in a flash.

Tdy's mom noz.

Could Kate have been considering writing a follow-up post, one that might suggest Caro knew where my on-the-lam father was hiding, and thus set her up for a round of questioning by the Feds?

I swallowed. *Tdy's mom noz.* The answer to that question was a definite "Yes." Caro knew which country Dad had fled to after his last sneaked visit to Gunn Landing because she had orchestrated his escape.

But "parasites"? We were talking about love here, and where love was concerned, morality went out the window, which Kate would have known if she had ever truly loved someone. As I sat there fuming over her treatment of my mother, more uneasiness crept into my mind. How far would Caro go to keep my father's whereabouts a secret?

After studying the situation, I decided to pay a visit to Heck to see if Kate had ever discussed my mother, or the Tasmanian Devil's other victims, with him. Stepping topside, I walked down the dock to *My Fancy*, where I found its owner daubing some sort of compound on the seal of an aft window.

"Damned rain blew in last night while I was sleeping," he said. I'd slept so deeply that I hadn't noticed the rain. Also, the *Merilee* was a much tighter boat than *My Fancy*.

Swallowing my anger at Kate, I asked Heck if he needed any help. "I'm pretty good with a putty knife."

He straightened up with a groan. "All done. How 'bout some tea?"

Remembering all the cat hair I'd found in the last cuppa he'd served me, I started to decline, then changed my mind. However unpalatable, the tea would give me plenty of time to talk about Kate's blog. "Sounds delicious, Heck."

When his gnarly face creased into a relieved smile, I realized how lonely he was. Kate had been his only friend. Making a mental note to visit with him more often, I followed him into the cat-hair museum he called a houseboat. Within minutes I found myself sipping another questionable cup of tea while a catarrhal cat made phlegmy sounds in my lap. After a bit of chatter about the difficulties of harbor life, I steered the conversation around to the blog. Now that my anger had faded, I decided to leave her comments about my mother to the last.

"What the hell's a blog?" he asked.

When I explained it was just an online diary, he grunted. "Don't have a computer. Things are a big waste of time, if you ask me."

I tried a different tack. "Yesterday when we talked, you mentioned that Kate and Bill both used to drop by and visit. How'd they get along?"

He shrugged. "Fine, I guess. For as long as it lasted, anyways, Kate being like she was."

"What do you mean?"

He shrugged again. "You know, goin' from man to man, just like her daddy always done with the ladies."

Having known Kate for only two months, all I had seen was the end of her relationship with Bill; nothing ominous about that. Then again, endings could get rough, and given the Aussie's size, well… I didn't want to ask my next question, but did anyway. "What caused the breakup? I found something that makes me think she might have been, well, *flirting* with another man. Did Bill get rough with her over it?"

"Girl's got a right to go after who she wants to, doesn't she?" Sure. If she was, as they say, unencumbered. And the other party was, too.

"If she was dating Bill at the time, he wouldn't think so."

"Nah, she broke up with him before she started seeing that other guy."

This was something new. "The way I heard it, Bill broke up with her."

"Then you heard it wrong. One thing she complained about was he kept callin' her all the time. Drove her nuts, that did."

Joe had said something about Bill's phone records. Is

that what he'd meant, that Bill was harassing Kate? Or was it all just a 'he said, she said'?

"Who was the other guy she'd started seeing?"

"Some good-lookin' stud at the zoo. Forget his name." Other than Bill, the only other truly handsome man that popped into my mind was the park ranger. "Would his name have been Lex?"

"That sounds about right. Yeah. Lex something or other."

I frowned. Lex Yarnell hadn't seemed the slightest bit disturbed about Kate's death. Either Kate had been lying to Heck, or… "Her blog also mentioned that Kate, let's see, how did she put it? Oh, yeah, she ran into 'familiar faces in unusual places.' You know anything about that?"

He gave me a proud, snaggle-toothed smile. "What with the TV show my girl was on, she'd got kinda famous, ya know. She said folks was always coming up to her sayin' did she remember them from grade school or high school or shit like that."

I soldiered on. "How about Sam Grimaldi? Did she ever talk about him?"

"Young guy has the *Gutterball*? Married to that old bitch?"

One day I would give Heck a lecture on political correctness, but this wasn't the time. "Right, the *Gutterball* guy with the older wife. Kate wrote a note saying that she was going to tell Doris the truth about something at their party the night she died."

"Truth about what?"

"That's what I'm asking you."

Heck shook his head. "Mostly she just yammered about them animals down at the zoo. But sometimes we talked about the old days back in Canaan Harbor. She missed them. Can't say I did." I plucked another name from Kate's blog. "How about Walt MacAdams? She have any trouble with him?"

"Firefighter guy lives on *Running Wild*?" At my nod, he continued. "She might a been sweet on him, him such a manly man and all. That's the kind of guy she always went for. Big strong studs, like the Aussie and that other guy at the zoo. Come to think of it, couple weeks ago I did see her talking to that firefighter over at Chowder & Cappuccino. She looked all dithery."

"How'd he look?"

"Not so dithery."

Being rejected could have explained the wrath in the *Tasmanian Devil*. Rejection was something few people took well, except maybe poets, who used it as fodder for their work. The next time I saw Walt, I'd ask him about Kate, but it would probably turn up to be a dead end. Inwardly sighing, I realized it was time to bring up the subject of Kate's last Post-it note, however much it pained me: *Tdy's mom nos*.

"Do you know if Kate ever had a run-in with my mother?"

Heck's old face morphed into an expression of pure lechery. "Wouldn't be surprised if any woman had a run-in with your mother, but it'd be all about jealousy. Kate wasn't bad-looking, but she wasn't nowhere in your mother's league. You don't mind me saying so, that's one hot broad, regardless of how old she hasta be. Too bad you don't look anything like her."

He must have seen me wince, because he immediately covered his slip. "Not that you're not cute, Teddy, what with all that curly red hair and them freckles, but your mom was Miss San Sebastian County once and she doesn't look much different now. Why, every time the paper runs an article about your dad and what he done, they run her old pageant photo, and Christ on a crutch, what I wouldn't do for a piece of…" At my expression, he trailed off. "Well, any man who's at least half alive would want a go at her."

Diplomacy, thy name is Heck. "I'll convey your compliments."

His rheumy eyes lit up. "You'd do that for me?"

"Don't get your hopes up. She's dating somebody else." Prospective Husband Number Five owned a national chain of upscale women's shoe stores. "Anyway, back to Kate. Did she ever say anything about my mother—or my father—to you?"

"Never talked about your father, and the only thing I remember her ever sayin' anything about your mom was when she saw that big car of hers, that big silver Mercedes. Kate thought the gas-guzzling thing was eating up the rain forest and driving out the monkeys, or something like that. Hell, even when she was a kid, she was like a lot of us at Canaan Harbor, didn't care for the hoity-toity types, thought the power should be with the people, and damned right, too! But comes the revolution, I'm willin' to let your mother keep that Mercedes. She looks awful foxy drivin' it."

Beauty, the great class leveler.

"Heck, are you sure there's nothing more you can tell me about Kate that might help me finger her killer? Given that the killer isn't Bill, of course."

"Bill ain't who done it, you can make book on that. He was crazy about that girl, maybe too crazy. But nah, I can't think of anything else, exceptin' lots people around here didn't like her because she tended to say what she thought. Kate was honest, she was. The thing she hated most was people who acted like they was one kind of person when they was really something else. Couldn't stand hypocrites, Kate couldn't."

Too bad she hadn't named them in *The Tasmanian Devil*.

Out of a fear of legal action, perhaps? Setting the murder case aside for a moment, I decided to take a stab at something that had been bothering me for the past couple of hours. "Say, this might not have anything to do with Kate's death, but do you by chance…" I gestured at the cats occupying every seat, shelf, and otherwise flat surface in the houseboat. "…know anything about that animal psychic who's set up shop in San Sebastian?"

"Animal psychic? What the hell's that?"

Deciding not to get into an explanation about the Great Animal Spirit, I just said, "A kind of animal psychologist. Helps them out with their problems."

"This damn world's getting crazier and crazier, innit? But nah, I never heard of anybody like that. My cats have problems, I fix them myself."

From the aft bedroom I heard a feline sneeze. Then another. It probably had asthma from all that loose hair floating around.

"I'm sure you take great care of your cats, Heck." Then I sneezed, myself.

"Got a cold, Teddy?"

"Might be coming down with one. You know, I've got an idea. Why don't you let me come over tomorrow night after work and help you clean up this place? I've got a special vacuum that's terrific with pet hair." If I was having trouble breathing, I knew he was. "What do you say?"

He flashed those brown teeth of his. "Why, that's damned neighborly of you, Teddy!"

"Tomorrow, then." Good deed planned, I returned to the issue at hand. "Heck, search your memory. Are you certain Kate didn't say or do anything strange, even if it didn't seem so at the time?"

"Hell, Teddy, whenever my girl came over she mainly talked about the zoo and the animals. That koala, Wanchu, was her favorite. Couldn't say enough about the ragged-ass thing. Just about the only time she mentioned humans was when she was gripin' about Bill. Oh, yeah, and your mom's car. Come to think of it, she did talk about her dad a lot, was worried half to death about him. Have you found him yet? Poor guy needs to be told she's dead, not that he'll understand or anything, what with his Alzheimer's, but still…"

"The zoo director's working on it. We'll track him down, don't you worry. Well, it's been nice visiting with you, Heck, but I need to get back to the *Merilee* and take care of my own menagerie." I stood up, dislodging the cat that had taken up residence on my lap.

Heck, who retained some tiny semblance of manners, rose too. "Maybe you could bring your mother by some time?"

What a lech. "Caro's pretty busy these days, but I'll extend the invitation."

With that, I sneezed and left.

ELEVEN

WHEN I PICKED up the animals next morning to take over to the television station, I discovered that not only would Bernice be accompanying me but Robin Chase, too. The big cat keeper looked thunderous as she toted Rusty, a young Capuchin monkey, to the van. Loyal Bernice followed with Dolores, a white-frosted marmoset, while I carried Marcus Aurelius, a ring-tailed lemur.

On the drive to the station, I asked Bernice if she'd read Kate's blog.

"Which one do you mean, *Outback Telegraph* or *Tasmanian Devil*?"

I blinked in surprise. "You knew there were two?"

Bernice laughed. "Everybody did except you, Teddy. And maybe Zorah and Aster Edwina. The *Devil* was one of the main topics of discussion in the volunteer's break room." She turned and said to Robin, "You guys read it, didn't you?"

The string of cursing that issued forth from Robin's mouth was enough to convince me that she was well acquainted with Kate's second blog.

"How did you two find out about it?" I asked.

Bernice shrugged. "One of the other volunteers told me, I think. It sure wouldn't have been a keeper, because none of them are happy about it, and for good reason. Right, Robin?"

More cursing.

"Well, no one ever told me," I complained.

Robin stopped cursing long enough to snap, "They would have if you'd spent more time in the employees' lounge!"

For the rest of the drive, I wondered what else everyone knew that I didn't.

COMPARED TO LAST week's disaster, today's program went smoothly. Before we stepped on set, I warned anchorwoman AnnaLee not to touch the animals so we wouldn't have a repeat of the Abim incident. After telling me crossly that she knew how to handle a live TV program and I didn't, she obeyed for a while. The monkeys behaved well, which allowed me to deliver educational information without a hitch. The only problem arose when Marcus Aurelius climbed on top of my head and wouldn't get off. He only weighed around five pounds, but that's a pretty heavy hat, and I struggled to keep my head up.

Pushing his two-foot-long, black-and-white-ringed tail aside—he'd draped it down over my face—I continued my spiel, "As you can see, lemurs are agile animals, both on the ground and in the trees, although they do prefer the arboreal habitat. This, plus their high intelligence, leads many people to think that they're monkeys, but they're actually a monkey's cousin. Or a monkey's uncle, as the saying goes."

A glance at the monitor showed that Marcus Aurelius had settled in nicely, his snout turned toward the camera, his black-banded eyes lively. He was enjoying this.

His happiness gave me an idea. I said to one of the stage hands, "If you could get one of those mikes? Ah, thank you, sir." I held the proffered mike up to Marcus Aurelius' throat. "Lemurs have something in common with yet another species. House cats! Hear our boy purr?"

"Why, that's the most adorable thing I've ever heard!" AnnaLee said, after the stagehand took the mike away.

"Those purrs mean he's happy, as well he should be. He's been fed a full-fruit breakfast, given clean water, and now he's sitting on my head under these warm studio lights, everything a lemur could wish for. Except a girlfriend, of course. By the way, did you know that during mating…"

"Better not go there!" the alarmed anchorwoman interjected.

"Don't worry, I'm not going to get clinical. But when male lemurs fight for mating rights, my, my, you'd pay top dollar to watch that! They have these powerful, almost skunk-like scent glands, and during mating season the males rub their scent all over their tails and wave them in the air to out-stink each other. But back to more mundane topics. As I was saying earlier, lemurs live in trees on the island of Madagascar—perhaps you've seen the Disney movie of the same name, which I highly recommend—but as in so many other places around the Earth, the forests of Madagascar are being decimated by agricultural development. Lemurs are giving way to cows and crops, and as a result, all lemur species, especially the red-ruffed lemur, are endangered. That's why breeding programs…"

As if afraid I'd start yammering about mating rituals again, AnnaLee interrupted. "Say, Teddy, what kind of name is 'Marcus Aurelius'?"

Didn't they teach history in school any more? To maintain Gunn Zoo/KTSS-TV harmony, I merely said, "Marcus Aurelius was a Roman emperor/philosopher considered so intelligent that he was nicknamed 'The Wise.' Since this particular lemur is so smart, and because his keeper is a fiend for the classics—try reading Aurelius' *Meditations* some time, you'll simply adore it—he named the lemur after him."

"Oh."

A line running underneath the monitor revealed there

were three minutes left for the segment, so to kill time, AnnaLee leaned forward and took a sniff of Marcus Aurelius. The lemur, that is. "Wow. I see what you mean about those scent glands, Teddy. He is rather, ah, highly-scented."

"No kidding. I'll have to shower when I get back to the zoo or I'll be unpopular all day. Big difference from the eucalyptus-scented koala, right? Uh, AnnaLee? Remember what we discussed earlier. Don't touch him!"

She shot me an irritated look. It was *her* show, her body language said, and I and my animals were just guests. Remembering her high-handed treatment of the elderly author last week, I gave in and let her do her thing.

"I just want to feel his fur," she said, smiling at the camera. "It looks so soft." Ignoring the lemur's stench, AnnaLee raised her hand toward him, which was a mistake.

Interpreting the raised hand as an invitation, Marcus Aurelius grabbed onto her arm and swung himself up on her head, where he assumed the same position he'd taken on mine: nose toward the camera, black-and-white-ringed tail drooping down across AnnaLee's face. He looked cute and he knew it.

To AnnaLee's credit, she didn't shriek. But from the expression on her face, I knew if she'd had a gun she would have shot him. I realized then that the anchorwoman didn't like people or animals. To her, we were all just props.

"He won't bite me, will he?" she asked, her face tense.

"Any animal can bite," I told her. "Even birds, as you can see by the bandage on my ear. That came courtesy of a flamingo. But in Marcus Aurelius' case, he seldom bites humans. Not enough that they bleed, anyway. Like so many of the animals I'll be bringing on this show, his mother rejected him at birth, so he was hand-raised by his classics-loving keeper. As a result he likes people. I mean *really* likes them. He'd hang with them all day if allowed to. But you bring up a good point, AnnaLee. It's never a good idea to attempt to make friends with wild animals. When a wild animal loses its fear of man, it can turn dangerous, which is why the rangers in Yellowstone National Park don't want you feeding the bears. The bear that looks so adorable while he's begging for a slice of peanut-buttered bread might be the same bear that bites a toddler's hand off ten minutes later. As for Marcus Aurelius here, he confines his acting-out to climbing on people's heads and swishing his tail in front of their faces, as you can plainly see. Is he still purring?"

Her fears allayed, she smiled at the camera again. "Oh, yes."

"He's got a crush on you, AnnaLee. Good thing there aren't any other male lemurs around or we'd have us a big ol' stinkfest, wouldn't we?"

"Not at KTSS-TV, we wouldn't!" She seemed to take a lemur's natural behavior as a personal affront. I wondered if she had any pets. None, I guessed. Probably the only animals in her house were fashioned into fur coats.

Another twenty-two seconds left.

"Back to the subject of names, AnnaLee. I'll bet you don't know what the word 'lemur' means."

AnnaLee's eyes crossed as she stared at Marcus Aurelius' long tail dangling less than an inch from her nose. When the tail started to swing back and forth, so did her eyes. She looked like she was watching a too-long tennis match and itched to retire to the bar. "No, but I'm sure you'll enlighten me." She didn't smile.

In a Zen-like moment I decided that whatever was going to happen would happen, and as long as the lemur wasn't hurt, the universe would remain in its proper place. "Well, AnnaLee, 'lemur' means 'spirit' or 'ghost.' That's because when a lemur calls out in the forest, it makes this awful ghost-like shriek. Like this."

I imitated a lemur's cry.

My faux lemur language must have sounded authentic, because Marcus Aurelius immediately flicked his tail up and shrieked back.

AnnaLee winced. Six seconds left.

The timing was perfect, so I called out again. So did Marcus Aurelius.

Three seconds left. The camera's red light was about to go out.

C'mon, Marcus, baby. Do your thing.

At the end of his third warning cry, Marcus Aurelius hunched over and took a massive, odiferous dump on AnnaLee's head.

Mission accomplished, I smiled and waved goodbye to the red light.

A FEW MINUTES LATER, when Bernice, Robin, and I were leaving the studio with our charges tucked safely into their carrying cages, we ran into Ford Bronson. He was accompanied by my mother, who for once, didn't have a dog stuffed into her handbag. Bronson smiled. Caro frowned.

"Hello, Mr. Bronson," I said, hoping he'd had the monitor on in his office. "How's tricks?"

Caro's frown deepened, but Bronson's smile widened, making him look more handsome than ever. Lucky Izzy VanStoeller! "I'll always be Ford to you, Teddy. Thanks to your segments, viewership for *Good Morning, San Sebastian* has risen sharply." Increased viewership not being part of my game plan, I said nothing.

Caro grabbed my arm. "Theodora, Ford and I happened to be watching the monitor when you pulled that trick on poor AnnaLee Harris. How *dare* you!"

"Then you heard me warn her. Besides, that was nothing a little shampoo can't take care of." After four or five washings, anyway.

Bronson's blue eyes danced; he was enjoying this. "We have a hairdresser on the premises, so no harm done. She'll be camera-ready again in a half-hour. Until then, George Hendershot, the weatherman, will work the program alone. He did it before, when Ronnie Simms, the seven-year-old chess Grand Master, threw up on her."

Remembering that program, I had to laugh. Since joining the early morning lineup three years earlier, AnnaLee had turned into a regular poop-and-vomit magnet. Karma, perhaps? All of a sudden I was struck by the oddity of running into my mother at the television station. "Mother, what are you doing here?"

Sensing a possibly long conversation in the offing, Bernice and Robin left me standing there and hustled the animals out to the semi-fresh air.

Mother sniffed. "It's *Caro*, Theodora. How many times do I have to tell you?"

"Well, then, *Caro*, what, I ask, are you doing here? Surely you're not looking for your own fifteen minutes of fame. Haven't you had enough?"

My mother had suffered through considerably more than fifteen minutes of fame in years past. Her television exposure began in her beauty pageant days, then re-emerged in earnest when Dad embezzled his firm's fortune and every reporter west of the Mississippi camped out on her doorstep. Yearly, on the anniversary of his escape to Costa Rica, a gaggle of reporters reassembled in her yard for fresh quotes. They'd have done the same to me if it hadn't been for the electronic gate leading to the harbor. Many times I'd offered the *Merilee* to Caro as refuge, but she always turned me down, claiming that she wouldn't let the jackals drive her out of her own home.

Bronson saved her from answering my question. "Your mother dropped by to give me a programming idea."

At her smug expression, I tensed. "It better not have anything to do with me." I was trying to get out of one program, not onto another.

"Don't be so self-centered, Theodora," she snapped. "You can't be the star of *everything*. I simply recounted my experience with Speaks-to-Souls and suggested to Ford here that a program on animal psychics might do well in this area."

"I promised to give it some thought," Bronson said.

Seeing my possible liberation in the offing, I said, with as much enthusiasm as possible, "It would be a hit! Emmy material! And Mother should be one of her first guests! Put it in my time slot! Well, gotta go!"

As I headed out the exit, I heard Bronson laugh.

Bernice and Robin were waiting for me by the van, into which they'd already loaded the animals. During the ride back to the zoo, the atmosphere felt more relaxed than earlier. All three of us were smiling, pleased that the *Good Morning, San Sebastian* segment had gone well.

"You're a bad, bad girl, Teddy," Bernice said, trying hard to wipe the smile off her face. "Granted, AnnaLee refused to follow your instructions, but did the punishment fit the crime? When you mimicked the lemur call, you knew what would happen."

"I can't predict when an animal's going to take a dump."

From the back seat, Robin snickered. "I've never seen a keeper who couldn't." Then, as if remembering she hated me, she forced a growl. "But I agree with Bernice in that you behaved unprofessionally."

Pleased, because Robin would no doubt lodge a complaint about my behavior with the zoo director, I said, "You're absolutely right. I shouldn't be allowed anywhere near a television camera. God knows what might happen next time. I might even be crazy enough to make AnnaLee perform a dental inspection on a full-grown Bengal tiger."

"Not Maharaja, you won't! The silly bitch might hurt his jaw."

"Girls, girls," Bernice cautioned. "Play nice."

In deference to her greater age and wisdom, we withdrew our claws. But once we'd delivered the animals back to Animal Care, I saw Robin head up the path to the Administration Building to tattle on me. I hoped her complaints would be successful.

Although Zorah didn't require me to work a full shift after my television appearances, I did anyway. The day, cloudless and crisp, was too beautiful to spend anywhere else, so for the next few hours I communed with my furry friends.

Lucy and Baby Boy Anteater were happy to see me. Lucy especially loved the mashed banana I fed her through the fence. Over in Monkey Mania, Marlon showed his appreciation for his fruit snacks by picking leaves out of my hair with his tiny fingers. In Down Under, Abim sat rapt while I serenaded him with "Waltzing Matilda," after which I had a brief visit with Malka Malka and Tulang.

I'd saved the friendliest for last.

"Cooeee, Wanchu!" I called, as I entered the koala enclosure. For once, she was already awake. Upon hearing my voice, she scampered down her tree and bounced over to me, then rocked back on her haunches and opened her arms.

"How's my good girl?" I said, as I picked her up. Burying my nose in her fur, I smelled eucalyptus, a considerable improvement on lemur. "Does Wanchu miss Kate?"

"Eeep."

I took that as a yes. "Kate loved Wanchu, didn't she?"

"Eeep." She nuzzled her leathery snout against my neck.

"And Wanchu loved her back."

"Eeep."

"Did Kate ever tell Wanchu what happened between her and Bill?"

No answer this time.

I tried again. "Was Kate having trouble with anyone else?"

"Eeep."

This might have been helpful information, but unfortunately, I don't speak koala. "Poor Wanchu. Losing two friends in a week." First Kate, then Bill. "But you've got me now, Wanchu, and as soon as I find out who murdered Kate, you'll have Bill back again." I scratched her behind the ears.

"Eeep, eeep!"

Our conversation continued like this until she dozed off. Taking the hint, I carried her over to her tree and nudged her nose against it. "Climb on up, Wanchu."

It took three nudges to rouse the koala out of her stupor, but she finally shook herself and scrambled up to her favorite limb. She wrapped her arms around it, the same way she'd wrapped them around me, and dozed back off.

It was only when I left Down Under did I realize that she'd peed down the front of my shirt.

AT THE END of the day, when I was clocking out, Zorah approached me.

"I hear you engineered a lemur 'accident' for poor AnnaLee Harris," she said, disapproval on her broad face.

"I'm not responsible for everything Marcus Aurelius does. Especially after someone ignores me when I tell her time and time again not to touch the animals."

"A little bird told me you fed him fruit and gave him plenty of water just before you went on. All he needed to let loose was to hear another lemur's call, which the same little bird told me you so graciously provided."

"Who is this little bird who's been telling tales on me?" As if I didn't know.

"That's confidential information, Teddy. Seriously, don't pull a stunt like that again. The Gunn Zoo is getting great publicity because of the TV segment."

"Which is just another reason you should find someone who wants to do it, and that's not me. How about Myra?"

At the mention of the great apes keeper, Zorah's eyes shifted. "Why her?" she asked.

I ticked off the reasons on my fingers. "One, she's better looking than I am. Two, her vocabulary is excellent, and she certainly has the required zoological experience. Three, she wants the job badly enough to stab me in the back with a pitchfork."

"Oh, I wouldn't go that far, Teddy."

"She would."

Frowning, Zorah said, "The problem is, it's not my call. Aster Edwina is determined that you do the program. Could that be because your mother suggested it?"

"Caro thinks having a Bentley on TV is déclassé."

She laughed. "Yeah, that sounds more like her. But bottom line, you're stuck doing the program unless you can convince Aster Edwina that someone else would be better. In the meantime, quit torturing AnnaLee Harris. It's not her fault you have to do something you'd rather not. You're both in the same boat, metaphorically speaking."

The idea had never occurred to me. "What makes you say that?"

"Last week, after she'd done that remote from outside the rhino enclosure to publicize Bowling for Rhinos, we got to talking. She told me that she has a Master's in film from USC and what she wants to do is to go into film. Write and direct her own material, independent-type things that explore the inner torment of the individual in the face of an uncaring world. Shit like that."

"You're kidding me, right?"

"I was very impressed."

"But if that's what AnnaLee wants to do, why is she wasting her time at a local TV station?"

Zorah shrugged. "The usual reason, I guess. People get themselves in traps, then don't know how to get themselves out." Her face fell into sadness, reminding me that she regretted letting the higher salary of a zoo director lure her away from her real love: the direct care of animals. She was right. We all have our traps. "To change the subject, Teddy, thanks for finishing *ZooNews*. You have any trouble sending it out?"

I shook my head. Sending out a newsletter via email was simple.

"How about the blog, then? I need you to finish *Tiger Teddy's Telegraph* by tomorrow afternoon so I can check it before it's posted to the blog site. Which animal are you going to focus on?"

"Wanchu, and koalas in general." Knowing it meant a long night's work ahead, I added, "It'll be in your office first thing in the morning." I started toward the exit, but a sudden thought made me turn around. "Have the Oakland police found Kate's father yet?"

She shook her head. "There's no 'Ty Nido' on record anywhere."

"'Ty' sounds like a nickname. Did they try 'Tyler' Nido?"

"The sergeant I talked to said they'd tried Tyler, Tyrone, Terrell, and a slew of other 'T' names, but there're no

'Nidos', period, at least not in Oakland. They gave up and turned the whole thing over to the state police, or CHPs, or whatever they're called these days, to see if those guys can track him down. If they can't, the FBI's next. For now, the mortuary's hanging onto Kate's body until notification of next of kin, but there's a limit as to how long they can do that. Aster Edwina says we need to find her father by the end of the week, or we'll have to hold the services without him. Since she's paying for the whole deal, her wishes rule."

"Wasn't Kate's father's full name on her Emergency Contact form?"

Her face twitched in exasperation. "Just that bad phone number and address. You want to know the truth, she didn't finish filling out the Emergency Contact form, just the first couple of lines, and then she stopped. I couldn't figure out why it'd been left that way until I looked at the date. She'd started to fill it out the same day you found that dead guy in the giant anteater's enclosure, and as I'm sure you remember, everything went south mucho quicko, especially for me. Human Resources meant to have her come back and finish the form after things calmed down, but it looks like they forgot and so did she. So here we are, S.O.L."

Paperwork. We hate it, but we need it. "Tell you what. I'll drive over to the jail and ask Bill…"

She raised her hand. "Not necessary. I asked yesterday when I visited, but it seems Kate never discussed her father with him. He didn't even know the guy was in a nursing home."

What irony. With all the gossip about others Kate had written in *The Tasmanian Devil*, she'd been closed-mouthed about her own life. Maybe she had her reasons.

Then I remembered something. "Say, I'm going to be seeing Heck Liddell tonight. He and her father used to be friends. Want me to call you at home if I find out anything?"

"Absolutely. The sooner we can get that funeral squared away the better. One other thing. Now that you're making a little more money, have you bought a new engine for the *Merilee*, yet?"

With everything that had been going on, I'd actually forgotten. "As soon as I get the time, I'll start checking prices. But as you know, I've been busy." I'd meant that last bit as a jab, but she just smiled.

"Speaking of busy, Helen says you haven't gotten together with her yet to learn how to update the zoo's website, so I've made you an appointment for noon tomorrow. Here. On the dot. No excuses."

"Zorah, I…"

"Didn't I say no excuses? If you're worried about lunch, don't be. I'm ordering out for pizza."

After my mumbled assent, Zorah let me escape. Thinking about boat engines, blogs, and complicated relationships, I collected my trusty Nissan pickup from the parking lot and made a beeline toward Gunn Landing Harbor. I'd quiz Heck again while I vacuumed cat hair out of *My Fancy*.

But as it turned out, I was too late.

TWELVE

"AHOY, HECK! PERMISSION to come aboard."

By the time I'd taken care of my own animals, the sun hung just above the western horizon and the sky had turned crimson. Heck should have been waiting for me, but except for a chorus of cats, his houseboat was silent.

"Heck? I brought the vacuum!"

Rapping at *My Fancy*'s door again, I heard nothing but plaintive mews. I looked over at the parking lot and the bike rack where Heck kept his aged Schwinn chained. It was still there.

I knocked one more time. No answer.

I was just getting ready to knock again when Linda Cushing stuck her head out of the *Tea 4 Two* and shouted, "Teddy Bentley, why don't you shut up already? Can't you see the old fart's not home?"

Old fart? Heck was a mere five years older than Linda. But I let it slide. "Heck's expecting me. I promised to help him tidy up his boat."

She nodded toward my vacuum cleaner. "With that little thing?"

"It may be small, but it's great with cat hair."

"This I have to see." She stepped onto the dock and joined me at *My Fancy*'s door. Knocking, she yelled in a voice that sounded like a sea lion's bellow, "Wake up, you old bastard! Teddy's here to clean up your act!"

When Heck still didn't answer, her face grew concerned. "All I hear is the cats."

A true houseboat isn't like a regular boat-turned house-boat. It has a door instead of a hatch, and a small rear window instead of a porthole. I'd been sensitive to Heck's need for privacy, but the less delicate Linda leaned against the window, cupped her hands around her face to cut out the sun's rosy glare, and peered inside. "Dark as a dungeon in there," she said. "Maybe he turned in early. Wait. There's some light over by... Oh!"

She jumped back, her eyes wide. "He's fallen! We should..." Shoving Linda aside, I opened the unlocked door and rushed inside the cabin, where I found Heck lying face down on the galley floor, surrounded by his mewling cats. When I pushed them away to render aid, I saw a deep red line around his throat. Heck was beyond help. Judging from the coolness of his skin, he'd been dead for some time.

"Heck! No!" A scream from Linda, who had followed me inside.

"Linda, don't touch..."

Blind to the evidence of her eyes, she bent down and clutched his shoulder. "Wake up, honey! Oh, honey, honey, I'm so sorry, honey, wake up now, wake up!"

As the woman who had acted so calm during the recovery of Kate's body continued wailing, I grabbed her hand and forced her to let go. "We have to call the sheriff."

"No! The EMTs! Or get Walt MacAdams, that's who we need! He's a firefighter, he knows how..."

"Linda, Heck's dead."

"He's not! He's just, he's just..." As suddenly as they'd begun, her wails then ceased. She took a deep breath. "He's really gone?" I had misjudged the relationship between Linda and Heck. Love doesn't always present itself with pretty words.

"Yes, Linda, he's gone, and I'm so sorry." I put my arm

around her and turned her toward the door. "We have to get out of here."

"But I don't want to leave him!"

"We must."

"I want to stay with him until…until…"

"No. And don't touch anything else, because…" Because *My Fancy* was a crime scene, but I didn't want her to know that yet. "Well, because you shouldn't. I need to call the authorities now, so let's go. Reception will be clearer outside." Linda was a big woman, much larger than I, but she was so weak with grief that her feeble protest didn't amount to much. I guided her through the door and onto the dock where several boat owners had gathered, alerted by Linda's screams.

"What's going on?" asked Sam Grimaldi, as his wife Doris stared at me through frightened eyes. As I'd carried my vacuum over to *My Fancy*, I'd seen them enjoying their evening cocktails on the deck of the *Gutterball*.

"Is anyone hurt?" This, from Larry DuFries, owner of the *Texas Hold 'Em*.

Waving aside their questions, I pulled my cell phone from my pocket and punched in 9-1-1. After giving the necessary information to the dispatcher, I then called Joe, who told me to do exactly what I was already doing: stay off *My Fancy* and keep the others away, too.

"You're sure it's a crime scene, Teddy?" he asked.

My back was turned to the crowd on the dock so they couldn't see my lips move. "It looks like he was strangled. By something thin, like a wire."

A grunt. "Keep the boat clear until I get there, all right? Get those folks off the dock and back to their own boats." Without waiting for my answer, he hung up.

My next call was to MaryBeth O'Reilly. The harbormaster had a right to know I'd found a second murder victim.

When I briefed her, she said she would notify the Harbor Patrol, then she hung up as abruptly as Joe. I knew that within minutes I'd see her marching toward *My Fancy*.

I turned my attention back to Linda, who had pulled herself together and was slapping away the many arms reaching out to comfort her.

"Leave me alone, you bastards," she barked. "I'm fine."

She didn't look fine. Her eyes were red and her broad shoulders slumped with grief. My heart ached for her almost as much as it did for Heck. Pushing my own emotions aside, I followed Joe's orders and began herding the onlookers back to their boats. Since boat owners, especially liveaboarders, don't like being told what to do, they grumbled as they shuffled away.

"Don't know who you think you are, Teddy, ordering me around like this," Larry DuFries muttered, as I nudged him toward his *Texas Hold 'Em*. "You're not the boss of me."

Sam and Doris Grimaldi were less argumentative as I escorted them to the *Gutterball*, but Doris was curious. "What's happened?"

"The sheriff will tell you everything you need to know."

"Is Heck sick? Shouldn't someone stay with him? Or did…?"

"Doris, I can't…"

Thankfully, the arrival of the harbormaster, flanked by a khaki-clad foursome from the Harbor Patrol, interrupted us. MaryBeth looked as pale as the hull on *Ghost Rider*, her all-white Catalina sloop. Leaning close, she whispered, "Teddy, what makes you think it's murder?"

"Someone looped a wire around his neck," I whispered back. "Or maybe a thin cord of some kind."

Always level-headed, she didn't let her face reveal her shock. "Have you notified the sheriff?"

"He's on his way with crime techs and the coroner. And,

I guess, an ambulance. For Heck's body." It wasn't easy keeping my eyes dry, but I managed.

MaryBeth turned and issued orders to the men from the Harbor Patrol, three of whom stationed themselves at varying points along the dock, the other at the electronic gate. The harbormaster herself stood sentinel in front of *My Fancy*, her face grim. Linda and I joined her. Until Joe arrived with his yellow crime tape, our harbor posse would keep anyone from contaminating the crime scene any more than Linda and I already had.

Joe's arrival seemed to take forever, but a glance at my watch proved it had only been fifteen minutes before a cascade of sirens swept toward us down Bentley Hill, the setting sun casting a pink glow across the black-and-whites. If you hadn't known why they'd been summoned, you might have thought their lights pretty.

The first thing Joe did when he arrived on the dock was to separate Linda and me. "Go on back to the *Merilee*, Teddy. I'll be over to interview you later." He glanced toward Linda. "Is that Miss Cushing? The woman who was with you when you found him?"

I nodded.

"Isn't she the one who helped you with…?"

The other body, he meant to say, but didn't. I nodded again. He raised his voice so Linda could hear. "Ma'am, don't go anywhere. I need to talk to you."

MaryBeth put a comforting hand on Linda's shoulder and answered for her. "Can't you see how upset she is, Sheriff? Her own boat's just a couple of slips away. I'll keep an eye on her." After a brief pause, Joe nodded and disappeared into *My Fancy*.

For the next few minutes, while I cuddled a nervous Miss Priss and DJ Bonz in the *Merilee*'s salon, more sirens screamed toward the harbor. Myriad feet clomped past.

Voices issued orders. Miss Priss, normally the most aloof of cats, tucked her head under my armpit as if to deafen the noise.

"There, cat, there, everything's fine," I said, stroking her trembling sides.

Bonz looked worried, too, so along with a few comforting pats, I directed some reassuring words his way. "Nothing to worry about, Bonz. Just some unpleasant human business that doesn't concern you."

It was full dark by the time Joe got around to me. When he and two deputies stepped onto the *Merilee*, both my pets fled into the aft bedroom. At Joe's first question, I regretted that they'd abandoned me so quickly because I needed comforting myself. Especially since the larger of the deputies was taping our interview on a hand-held digital recorder.

"Ms. Bentley, approximately what time did you leave Gunn Zoo?" Joe said, in a chillingly neutral voice. He was taking notes, too.

With a wary eye on the tape recorder, I answered, "At the usual time. Just after six."

"And you went straight to Mr. Liddell's boat?"

"First I fed Miss Priss and walked Bonz. *Then* I went to see Heck, um, Mr. Liddell."

He didn't look up from his note pad. "That would be at about what time?"

"Maybe five minutes before 9-1-1 received my call. Maybe three. I wasn't checking my Timex, and you know darn well that conversation was time-tagged."

"Describe your movements yesterday, say, from two-fifteen until this morning."

"You mean after our trip to the zoo with the kids?"

He didn't look up, but I saw the tips of his ears turn red. "Just answer the question, Ms. Bentley."

"But I don't understand."

"You don't need to."

"Joe, don't tell me you think I killed that poor old man!"

His next few words proved why he refused to look at me. "In a murder investigation, no one is above suspicion, Ms. Bentley." Swallowing my anger, I gave him a rundown on yesterday's activities. Visiting Heck and promising to help him clean the filthy *My Fancy*. Surfing the Internet and finding *The Tasmanian Devil*. Going with Caro to visit Speaks-to-Souls in San Sebastian. I did skip, however, the more ridiculous details of the doggie séance.

"That's your vacuum cleaner on Mr. Liddell's boat?"

"Yes." I knew better than to ask for it back. The vacuum cleaner, along with *My Fancy* and everything on it, would soon be joining Kate's *Nomad* at the county impound lot. Then I remembered something much more important than any old vacuum cleaner. "Joe, Heck's cats. They can't be left on the boat."

"Animal Control's on their way."

Here was the problem. Building on the San Sebastian County No-Kill Animal Shelter was months away from completion, and in the meantime, strays were being housed at the county pound. And due to overcrowding... Well, it didn't bear thinking about.

"Tell Animal Control to turn around. I'll take the cats."

He turned his attention away from his note pad and looked me full in the face so I could see the disapproval on his own. "You can't be serious, Teddy. There must be a dozen cats on that boat, and the *Merilee*'s too small for the animals you already have."

"Seven."

"What?"

"Seven cats. And there's more room on the *Merilee* than you think."

Theoretically *Merilee* offered around four hundred

square feet of living area, most of which was taken up by decks, bulkheads, the galley, and various fittings. I'd once estimated that there was less than twenty feet of actual walking-around space. But crowded cats were better off than pound cats. I'd find them good homes, beginning with zookeeper friends who had proven to be soft touches for needy animals. Come to think of it, Zorah was down to three cats. She had room for at least two more.

Joe's voice interrupted my kitty placement plans. "If you want to bring in more animals, I can't stop you, but you're cra…" After a glance at the tape recorder-wielding deputy, he looked back down at his note pad and changed the subject. "Right. Let's talk about Ms. Cushing. Didn't you once tell me she and Mr. Liddell hated each other?"

"You must've heard me wrong."

"How about Ms. Cushing's relations with Kate Nido? Any problems there?"

That question made me wonder if Joe was beginning to doubt his case against Outback Bill, but any joy I might have felt was replaced by a new concern for Linda. The last thing she needed was to take up residence in the San Sebastian County Jail.

Joe's official voice pulled me back from my worries. "Ms. Bentley? You didn't answer my question. How did Ms. Cushing get along with Ms. Nido?"

Oh, *Ms, Ms, Ms*. He sounded like a beehive. "They were the best of friends."

Apparently he didn't see my fingers crossed behind my back, because he then proceeded to ask me about Heck's and Kate's relations with everyone at Gunn Landing Harbor, including the harbormaster.

"We all get along great."

"Yeah, you're just a 'Kumbayah'-singing bunch. Anything else you can tell me that might be pertinent to the investigation?"

Now that the roughest part of the questioning was over, I opened up and told the tape recorder everything Heck and I had talked about the night before, leaving out Heck's comments about my mother and her car, of course. I also didn't tell Joe the probable reason for Kate's animosity toward Walt MacAdams. But now, after Heck's murder, I felt duty-bound to confess that I had been hiding something. Well, not actually *hiding*, just not being completely open, and those were two different things, weren't they?

"Ah, Joe, have you read Kate's blog?"

"Sure. It being within my jurisdiction, I read that zoo stuff all the time. Besides, it makes a relaxing departure from all the heavy material on *LawOfficer.com*. By the way, I've got an article in there this month about the new reactive skin decontamination products. You should read it." Belatedly remembering the tape recorder, he cleared his throat. "What does *Koala Kate's Outback Telegraph* have to do with anything?"

"I mean Kate's other blog, *The Tasmanian Devil*."

He looked up, his eyes narrowed so much that I wondered how he could see through them. "Are you telling me that Kate Nido had two different blogs?"

"I just found out myself." My voice was so tiny that even I could hardly hear it.

His eyes narrowed even further. "Tell me everything." With a sigh, I started in.

BY THE TIME Joe left—after escorting me over to *My Fancy* to pick up the cats—I couldn't tell if he was angry with me or merely disappointed. I was left alone on the *Merilee* with a boatload of furry angst.

"Dog, cats, can't we all just get along?"

Miss Priss, recovered enough from her fright to bristle with indignity at this multi-cat invasion of her turf, stood on the galley counter and yowled her displeasure. Fluffed out to twice her size, her one remaining eye stared daggers down at the newcomers. They weren't happy, either. Three stood mewling in distress on the steps leading up to the hatch, while the other four found comfort behind cushions in the triangular-shaped sleeping quarters at the bow.

Bonz stared at them all in stupefaction. "More cats?" his expression seemed to ask. "They're gonna steal my food!"

After shutting up my own outraged pets in the aft bedroom and leaving Heck's cats to make peace with their new environment, I headed over to the *Tea 4 Two* with a pot of freshly-brewed tea. I found MaryBeth just stepping off the boat. The look the harbormaster gave me was as dour as Joe's. "Don't stay too long, Teddy, and for God's sake, don't ask her any questions. She's had to answer too many already."

For a fleeting moment, I wondered if Linda's story matched mine. But why wouldn't it?

While MaryBeth headed toward her office at the northern end of the harbor, I called across to *Tea 4 Two's* hatch. "Linda, it's Teddy, with a pot of tea. Permission to come aboard?"

"Yeah." She sounded soggy.

The tidy *Tea 4 Two* was a far cry from the slovenly *My Fancy*. A Catalina 30 that was almost the twin of Mary-Beth's, it was a sloop-rigged boat that had almost worn itself out from thirty years of sailing up and down the California coast. Last year, after unexpectedly coming into a small inheritance, Linda had repaired the keel, installed a new mast, and refurbished the interior with sea-blue carpeting and color coordinated appointments. She'd spiffed up the teak fittings, too, so much so that the interior looked like it had just left the showroom. Now she seemed oblivious to her splendid surroundings. Accompanied by her faithful German shepherd Hans, she sat in the galley, huddled into a blanket.

"It's all my fault," was the first thing she said.

Survivor's guilt. I had a touch of it myself. As I set down the teapot on the galley's Formica table, I responded, "There's no way you could have done anything."

She shook her head. "I heard it, Teddy. Only at the time I didn't realize what I was hearing."

When I sat down next to her, Hans licked my hand and whined. He was worried about her, too. "That's impossible," I said, pouring us both some tea.

"Around one in the morning I heard someone walking along the dock, but I didn't pay any attention. I figured it was just Sam Grimaldi sneaking someone over to the *Gutterball* for a midnight screw."

Linda had just confirmed my own suspicions about the Grimaldis' marriage. Doris was the one with the money and big house, while Sam had youth and a boat. Since it was impossible that Doris didn't know what was going on, the two had probably come to some sort of "modern" understanding. "Maybe you did hear Sam."

Linda shook her head again, this time so hard that I feared she would hurt her neck. "No. A few seconds later, I heard someone rap against a door. Then I heard it open and somebody whispering. It didn't sound like Sam. Then everything went quiet and I fell back asleep."

"Did you tell the sheriff?"

"Of course. But I could have stopped it, Teddy." A tear trickled down her furrowed cheek.

I'd brought tissues, so I handed her one, then poured us both some tea. Like me, she took hers black. After making certain she'd taken a sip, I said, "Look, Linda, if you'd gone over there, you'd have been killed, too. Do you really think that you'd have been allowed to live if you'd gone barging in?"

At the shocked look in her eyes, I softened my tone. "You would have done that if you'd believed Heck was in danger, wouldn't you?"

"Of course!"

"Which means you had no inkling of what was going down. So don't you ever feel guilty. There was nothing you could have done."

"But…"

"Drink some more tea, Linda."

Some of the old spirit flooded back into her ravaged face. "I've already had so much tea I'm about to float away. MaryBeth got two pots down me before she took off."

"Decaffeinated, I hope."

"Do I look like a decaffeinated kind of gal?"

I was about to apologize for casting aspersions on her honor when she said, "The sheriff says you're keeping Heck's cats on the *Merilee* until you find them good homes. Thank you for that, and I'm sure the old fart—wherever he is now—thanks you. In case you're wondering, as ratty as they look, they're all in good health. Since Heck didn't have a car, I was the one who took them to Dr. Wypath, that vet over in Castroville. They've all been neutered and are up to date on their shots. To make it a little easier for you, I'll start you off by taking two."

"Two cats?" I looked at the massive Hans, who appeared oblivious to her offer. "But what about Hans?"

Hearing his name, the German shepherd raised his shaggy head. From where I was sitting, it looked as big as a Mexican gray wolf's. His teeth were almost as big as a wolf's, too.

Linda must have noted my concern, because she said,

"Oh, don't worry about Hans. He's always liked Spike and Estelle, but he has no time for any of the others." At my blank expression, she added, "Spike's the short-haired gray, Estelle's the calico. They're a couple."

Just like Linda and Heck. "I can take one, myself. No more, though, because as you know, I already have…"

"Bonz and Miss Priss. Might I suggest little Toby? He's the white part-Siamese. Has a bit of a mother complex from being weaned too early. Priss can give him all the mothering he missed." Priss had never come across to me as the motherly type, but I was willing to try it. The more boat babies, the merrier. "Toby it is, then."

Casting off the blanket, Linda stood up. "Great. Let's go get Spike and Estelle."

We trooped over to the *Merilee*, where Heck's cat herd had pretty much taken over the entire boat, with the single exception of the aft bedroom, where from behind the door, the outraged Miss Priss continued to yowl.

Unfazed, Linda said, "Toby will calm her down."

If she didn't kill him first. But I had sense enough not to voice my thoughts. "We'll see."

It wasn't too hard separating Spike and Estelle from the herd. After a few nervous hisses, they allowed Linda to scoop them up and carry them over to the *Tea 4 Two*, me following with two cans of cat food and an empty coffee can I'd filled with kitty litter. As soon as she released the cats, Hans walked over and nuzzled Estelle. She purred. He did the same to Spike, but Spike just stood there in stoic silence. Then the three, led by Hans, trooped into the aft sleeping quarters where they all curled up together on Linda's blue blanket.

"That's surprising," I said.

For the first time since we'd found Heck's body, Linda attempted a smile. "Things aren't always what they seem."

I set the cat food down on the galley sink and poured the kitty litter into the cardboard box she'd found under the sink. "You're going to need a litter tray."

Her smile disappeared. "I'll pick one up in the morning on the way to the funeral home. Heck doesn't have any family, so it's up to me to make arr…arr…arrangements." After clearing her throat, she continued more steadily. "Speaking of arrangements, what's the holdup with Kate's funeral? She wasn't here long, but she was one of us. All the live-aboarders want to attend."

I explained the problems the police were having finding Kate's father. "They've called every nursing home in the Oakland area looking for an Alzheimer's patient named Nido, and there don't seem to be any."

"Have you considered that 'Nido' might not be his last name? Heck once told me that when Kate was seventeen, she had a big falling out with her father and ran off and married some kid from San Francisco. Apparently it didn't work out, because she was back on the *Nomad* less than a year later. Maybe she never took her maiden name back. Some women don't. After they go to all that rigmarole of changing their maiden names to their married names on their drivers' licenses, Social Security cards and other stuff, they don't want the trouble of doing it all over again."

"That would be pretty rare, don't you think? Especially these days."

A bitter laugh. "You think so? Well, I wasn't born with the name 'Cushing', Teddy. That came courtesy of a marriage when I was old enough to know better. And don't bother asking about it. That's a part of my life I simply won't discuss."

We never know as much about our friends as we think we do, do we? Moving beyond my surprise at Linda's secret past, I admitted that her theory about Kate might be correct. "Did Heck ever mention Kate's husband's name?"

"He…" She gulped, then recovered herself. "He just said once bitten, twice shy, and that was why she had trouble sticking to one man. Myself, I think it might have had more to do with the way he said she was raised, with her dad bringing all those girlfriends onto their boat and none of them ever staying more than a few months. When you're raised around revolving door relationships, that's what passes as normal for you." She sighed. "Oh, well. Thanks for the tea."

I know when I'm being dismissed, so I left her with a new menagerie to comfort her through the long, lonely night.

When I returned to the *Merilee*, I discovered that the yowl-fest I'd left behind had diminished in energy. From behind the aft bedroom door, Miss Priss muttered imprecations at the invaders, but the other cats were silent. To help them feel at home, I set out several saucers of cat food. One by one, they crept forward and began to eat. Toby was easy to spot. He was the smallest, a pale enough cream color to pass for white, and with a less wedge-shaped head than a full Siamese. Within seconds he let himself be bullied away from his saucer by a larger cat.

Later, after I'd hand-fed Toby at the table so that the feline bullies couldn't take his food away, I retired to the aft bedroom, where I found Miss Priss so angry that she refused to let me pet her. Instead, she stalked to the corner of the bed and lay there in a huff.

Believing it would help me keep my mind off Heck's murder, I stayed up half the night to write the Tiger Teddy column for the zoo's blog. It dulled my unhappiness, but never quite made it disappear. At three I finished the blog and sent it to Zorah via email. Then I turned in, with Toby curled against my left side, Miss Priss at my right, and DJ Bonz at my feet. Snug and warm, my three babies and I drifted off to sleep.

My dreams were not good.

In the worst, it was late at night. I was walking along the dock toward the *Merilee* when I saw a man and two women floating face down in Gunn Landing Harbor, wires wrapped around their necks.

As the incoming tide nudged at them, the three bodies slowly rolled over to stare sightlessly at the moon-lit sky.

Kate. Heck. And me.

THIRTEEN

ZORAH WAS ALREADY in her office when I clocked in at six the next morning. A blank note pad was positioned in front of her, pen at its side. Unlike myself, she looked like she'd had a good night's sleep. Then again, she'd only heard the news about Heck on KTSS just this morning, while getting ready for work.

Concerned, she said, "You need to get off the *Merilee*, Teddy. It's too dangerous. Stay with your mother until they find out who's been doing this."

When I shook my head, she added, "Oh, yeah. I forgot that you and your mother don't always get along. Too bad. She's a nice woman. Generous to the zoo, too. Tell you what. You can come stay with me. I don't have much room, but the couch makes into a comfortable bed. You can even bring your dog and cat." I thanked her for her kind offer, but turned her down, explaining that the *Merilee* was my home and I wasn't going to be driven from it. "By the way, what are you doing in the office so early? What happened to the perks of management?"

"Two reasons. One, I checked out the *Tiger Teddy* blog before I had Helen post it to the Net. Good job! Two, I had a brainstorm last night. This thing with Kate's father…"

"Zorah, I think I may have…"

Without letting me finish, she said, "We've been going about this the wrong way because like most people, we've expected the cops to do everything for us, and even they have their limitations. I have to take the blame, because I should know better, but I'm new at this job, which, yes, was a big mistake. I need to get back to taking care of animals."

"Zorah, about Ka…"

"Don't argue with me, Teddy. It's the Peter Principle. 'In a hierarchy, every employee tends to rise to his highest level of incompetence.' Well, I'm bailing as soon as we get Kate buried and I can find a replacement. Two, actually. One for her, one for me."

"But…"

"Will you stop interrupting me? God, you're rude. Why can't you behave with your mother's good manners? Until you learn how, remember that I'm still your boss, so just be quiet and listen. Anyway, while I was lying in bed waiting to drift off to sleep last night, I figured out how we can find Kate's father. All I needed to do was…"

"Zorah?"

"Quiet! As I've been trying to tell you, all I needed to do was call the San Diego Zoo and speak to the head of Human Resources. That's Nancy Perez, who used to be in Human Resources at the Omaha Zoo when I worked there." Zorah checked her watch. "She's like you, a real early bird, and I've left a message on her voice mail, so she should be calling me any minute."

"But…"

"You're obviously deaf, so I'll say it louder. *Shut up, Teddy!*"

Ears ringing, I shut up.

Zorah smiled in satisfaction. "Nancy will…"

This time, the phone interrupted her, not I. She snatched it up midway through the first ring. "Nancy? Zorah here." A long pause while she listened to the other end. In the meantime, she picked up her pen.

"Yes, Nancy, a terrible thing. We're all in shock. Tragic, I agree. So young. Well, the police arrested Bill, but I doubt sincerely if he's the one..." Another pause. "I know. Bill has a foul mouth, but that's all. He's as gentle as a hand-raised kinkajou. But back to business. Do you have that info I asked for?"

Another pause, this one much shorter, as Zorah scribbled a name and number on the notepad. "Got it. Thanks so much. Think you'll make it up for the memorial? Oh, sorry. Well, tell Denziel hi, and give my love to that brand new grandkid. Bye." She hung up and looked at me, satisfaction on her face. "Well, Little Miss Rude. Nancy Perez came through for me, as I knew she would. She pulled Kate's files, and they had a completed Emergency Contact form. Kate's father's actual name is Tyler Everts. Seems Kate was married at one time and was still using her ex-husband's name. I'll pass this info on to the sheriff, and that should take care of it. Now, what was so important that you had to keep on interrupting me?"

My mouth flapped up and down a few times before I could make a sound. Then the first thing that popped out was, "Uh, want a cat?"

An hour later, I was telling Wanchu about my new part-Siamese and Zorah's two new tabbies, Roger and Ebert, when Joe arrived and called to me over the enclosure fence.

"We need to talk, Teddy."

The use of my first name meant the discussion was going to be personal, and Joe's tone meant that I wouldn't like the subject matter. But if it wasn't about Heck—which would have been an official conversation—what could it be? Surely not our relationship, not at this time. Joe wouldn't be that insensitive.

"Her name's Wanchu," I called back. "Isn't she cute?"

"Adorable. Now, come over here. I don't want this conversation conducted in shouts."

"She smells like eucalyptus leaves, doesn't she?" I said, walking with the koala over to the fence. "That's because she…"

"Eats them. You've told me a dozen times."

Trying not to think about something makes you think about it all the more. I kept seeing Heck's dead face, the red line around his neck. He might have been gruff, but I'd been fond of the man, and rather than talking to Joe right now, I wanted to share my sorrows with Wanchu. At least she didn't look so cross.

"Joe, could you ease up on me a bit?" I asked. "Of all people you should know what a rough night I had." Then I remembered something I needed to tell him. "Oh, I've got Kate Nido's father's name."

"Tyler Everts."

"Zorah already called you?"

"And I passed the info along to Oakland PD. Teddy, put that thing down and find us a place where we can have a good, long talk."

"Don't call Wanchu a 'thing.' She's a koala, and a very nice one, too. Did you know she has a backwards-facing…?" There I went again, using an animal as an exercise in avoidance.

"Pouch. Yes, I did. Now put her down and let's go someplace private before I have a total meltdown."

"Sounds to me like you already have," I muttered, as I carried Wanchu back over to her tree. When she'd scampered up, I let myself out of the enclosure and led Joe to a nearby visitors' bench. "All right. What's so important that you have to add more gloom to an already depressing morning?"

"I want you off the *Merilee*."

"You, too?" We had been down this road before. In an

earlier murder investigation, I'd briefly moved in with Caro, but it hadn't worked out. I reminded Joe of that.

"It was your own fault," he argued. "You should have…"

"Shoulda, coulda, woulda. I'm not leaving the *Merilee*, especially not to move in with my crazy mother."

"Then move in with me."

Now I was well and truly shocked. Joe was a bit of an old-fashioned guy himself, but his mother Colleen was more Catholic than the Pope. She had no use for any male/female live-in arrangement that didn't come complete with a church-sanctioned trip down the aisle followed by a drunken reception.

"Oh, c'mon, Joe. Your mother…"

"Suggested it."

My mouth made a little round "O".

He leaned forward, his beautifully chiseled face blurred with misery. "She's as worried about you as I am, Teddy. In case you're wondering, which judging by your expression you are, she says you can bunk down in the spare bedroom. But that any, um, *romantic activity* between us must be conducted somewhere else."

"In the garage, maybe?"

"Don't wisecrack at a time like this. Within two weeks, two people have been murdered less than ten yards away from the *Merilee*. I don't want you added to the body count."

I immediately felt contrite, and considering last night's dream, almost gave in. Then I remembered that most of my friends at the harbor didn't have the luxury of running away and staying with the sheriff. Whatever happened, they'd hunker down for the duration. I would, too.

The misery on his face increased when I told him. "Teddy, you can't…"

"Can and will." To redirect his attention away from me,

I said, "Now that someone else has died in the same way as Kate, what are you going to do about Bill? Since he was locked up at the time, it's obvious that he didn't kill Heck. And don't tell me there's a copycat killer running around, because we both know better."

Further resistance being futile, Joe just sighed and said, "First thing this morning I placed a call to the county attorney. She needs to read a copy of my report on Mr. Liddell's murder before she takes any action but, yes, it looks like Mr. McQueen is off the hook."

Relief swept over me with such power that it was a good thing I was sitting down. As soon as I could breathe again, I asked, "When will he be released?"

"Let's not get ahead of ourselves, Teddy. There are procedures…"

"When?"

He sighed again. "Tomorrow, possibly. Friday at the latest. But I'll have to hang onto his passport. Just in case."

A precaution even Bill would understand. "He'll be able to come back to the zoo?"

"If Zorah will have him."

"Oh, she will." After a brief pang at the prospect of losing the privilege of caring for Wanchu and the rest of the Down Under gang, I managed a smile. "All's well that ends well, then."

Joe didn't look as happy. "Except that the murderer's still on the loose. And you're living in Ground Zero."

ZORAH WASN'T THE only person who could have a brainstorm. During lunch, when I tried without success to get other zookeepers to take the remaining two cats ("I'm all full up, Teddy. Six cats and three dogs."

"Sorry, no can do. My lease doesn't allow more than two dogs and/or two cats, which I already have."

"What, are you nuts? I have six geckos, two snakes, four dogs, and a cat."), I realized who might be able to help me. After wolfing down what was left of my Borneo Burger, I placed a call to Speaks-to-Souls and related my problem.

"How's their health?" she inquired, sounding more businesslike than woo-woo.

"Both cats are neutered and up-to-date on their shots. They sneeze some, but that's because of the environment they were living in. Their owner wasn't a very good housekeeper, and he had too many cats for the space."

"Hmm. You realize that I have a lot of animals myself? Both here at the shop and at home?"

"It would be better than the pound." Guilt works well with animal lovers.

"What do they look like?" Yep, she was softening.

"They're tuxedo cats, mostly black with white chests and paws. They even come when you call their names."

"Which are?"

"Kennedy and Rockefeller."

A giggle. "Oh, all right. I'll take them."

My heart gave a happy little bounce. "Can I drop them off after work this evening?"

"Tomorrow would be better. I have two evening appointments tonight, and I'll be bushed afterwards. Channeling the spirits takes a lot out of me."

I bet it did. But Thursday was the evening I'd promised the Bowling for Rhinos committee that I would hit up Aster Edwina for a donation. I did a quick time calculation in my head. The meeting with Aster Edwina would take thirty minutes at the most, the drive back to the *Merilee* to pick up the cats about fifteen minutes, then the drive from the harbor to San Sebastian another half hour. "I can have them there tomorrow evening between seven-thirty and eight. Would that work for you?"

Another *hmm*. Then, "I close the shop at five unless I have a client, which I don't tomorrow, so you'll have to bring them to my house."

She started to give me directions, but I stopped her half-way through. Having lived in San Sebastian County most of my life, I had a pretty good idea of where she was leading me; a small piece of the old Bentley ranch that had been deeded to Carlo DiGiorno, a much-loved family retainer back in the 1850s. Since then, the property had passed through his descendants' hands. The original house remained on its hilly lot, crumbling slowly, encumbered by Draconian phrases in the old deed. To paraphrase the legalese, not only did the property have to remain occupied by a DiGiorno at all times, but no new building could commence until the house was declared unsafe for habitation by three board-certified county engineers. Even then, the house's footprint could not be enlarged.

"You're living in the old DiGiorno place, aren't you?" I said.

"You know it?" She sounded surprised.

"My last name is Bentley."

"Oh. That's different than your mother's."

No surprise there, since Caro had undergone several name changes since being born Caroline Piper. And I'd been married once, myself, but didn't feel like explaining all that to a woman I hardly knew. "That's right."

I vaguely remembered old Elizabetta DiGiorno dying, as they say, "without issue," several years back, and the house sitting unoccupied until the estate's attorney's dug up a relative who was willing to take on the crumbling property. "You're a DiGiorno, then?"

A momentary silence, then, "Can't keep any secrets around here, can I? Not that I need to."

From the cautious tone of her voice, I wondered about

that. With her Valkyrie features and build, she sure didn't look like a DiGiorno, but I just said, "So seven-thirty is fine with you? For the cats?"

"I'll be waiting with two new bowls and a tray filled with fresh kitty litter. After they work out the territorial situation with my other animals, they'll feel right at home."

Mission accomplished, I left the employees' lounge and drove my cart to the rhino enclosure to discuss Bowling for Rhinos with Buster Daltry, the event's chairman.

I found him working with Notch, the smaller of our two Southern white rhinos—if you can call a two-ton animal "small." Respectful of Notch's bulk, Buster was kneeling behind a safety rail fashioned from an old wooden telephone pole, attending to a small scrape on Notch's foot. The big rhino stood on the other side of the rail, peacefully chewing timothy hay, her three-toed hind foot raised. Watching them from the other side of the enclosure was Half-Ear, her somewhat bigger friend.

"Nice training job," I called across the fence. No way was I going in there. White rhinos may have calmer temperaments than black rhinos, but they're still tanks on legs. Tanks squash people.

Buster, who was used to the great beasts, just nodded. "Notch will do anything for a little timothy, won't you, my little piggy?" He reached over and patted the inside of her hind leg, a rhino's "sweet spot."

"How long did it take?"

He looked up, a frown on his sad lump of a face. "To train her to lift her feet? Six or seven months, I think. It took Half-Ear even more, 'cause she's more stubborn. But it's easier than having to lure them into a safety chute every time I need to attend to their feet or horns."

Ah, yes. Rhinoceros horns, the main reason rhinos were nearing extinction. Used in the Near East for decorative dagger sheaths and in Asia as Chinese "Viagra," a single horn—which is made out of a hair-like substance, not ivory—sold on the Black Market for as much as $55,000. Because of the great demand in 1970 alone, half the world's rhinos disappeared. During the next four decades, most of the surviving 50 percent were slaughtered to accommodate the vanity of men who strutted around with knives on their belts or had trouble getting it up.

"Zorah told me you have the latest figures for Bowling for Rhinos," I said. "How much have we raised so far?"

It may have been my imagination, but Notch glanced over at me with what seemed a hopeful expression on her face. Buster didn't look as optimistic.

"I don't have the exact dollar amount, but we're down in contributions this year. The biggest lump sum donations so far have been five hundred and fifty from the Foot Fetish and three hundred twenty from Cappuccino & Chowder. How are your own fund-raising efforts coming along? Have you put the touch on your mother yet?"

"We can count on her for her usual contribution, but even better, I'll be seeing Aster Edwina tomorrow, and she's always good for a few thou." Something else occurred to me. "Come to think of it, right after that, I'm visiting an animal psychic who might…"

Buster scowled. "That fraud over in San Sebastian? More likely, she'll relieve *you* of your hard-earned green!"

His scowl disappeared when I related Caro's experience with Speaks-to-Souls and the woman's offer to take in two orphaned cats. "Okay, so maybe I'm wrong. But didn't you say she was collecting donations for the No-Kill Shelter? Unless someone's stinking rich, they tend to limit themselves to one charity. Two at the most."

"Like you?" He blushed. Although Buster, like most zookeepers, had very little money, he donated part of each paycheck to rhino and elephant sanctuaries. He also spent his week nights amassing sponsors for the marathons he ran, then donated the proceeds to various children's charities. With his great bulk, Buster always came in at the back of the pack, but with his just-as-great heart, he always finished.

"Zookeepers are different," he said.

I was about to reply when a loud noise made me look over at the other side of the enclosure, but it was just Half-Ear taking a dump, and since each rhino defecates more than fifty pounds of dung a day, the dump was large. I also noticed that the spot she picked was the same spot our dearly-departed Kehtla, the big male, had always used. A game of Follow-the-Leader? Or just a grumpy female's editorial comment on the entire male gender?

Both animals liked Buster. Regardless of his less-than-handsome countenance, most females did, even females of the human species. But to Buster's ongoing sorrow, women liked him only as a friend. God only knows how the poor man managed to get a date. If he ever did.

As soon as I left Buster and drove down the hill toward the giant anteater's enclosure, something began to nag at me. What was it? My conversation with Buster? Zorah? Speaks-to-Souls? The discomfort remained while I was preparing Lucy's evening meal of termites, but as soon as I'd stuffed her dinner into the small hollow log we kept in her night house, I figured it out.

Caro. Her name had come up twice during the day: once with Joe, once with Buster. I hadn't heard from my mother since I'd run into her yesterday at the television studio, which was odd, since it was her habit to call during the day to complain about my job at the zoo.

I checked my watch and saw that it was a little after five. Apparently she hadn't watched the morning or noon news.

When I'd dressed for work this morning, Heck's murder had headlined every local news program and newspaper. KTSS's newscaster had proclaimed, "Second murder at the Harbor of Death!" KTRM had inaccurately brayed, "Yachtsman shot to death in Gunn Landing." The *San Sebastian Gazette* had printed in a sixty-four point red Gothic font, SERIAL KILLER LOOSE IN SS COUNTY? All this should have had Caro showing up at the zoo with two burly cousins and a net to haul me away to the safety of Old Town, but as yet, I hadn't heard a peep from her. This maternal silence was so unlike her that I began to worry, especially in the light of Kate's Post-it note: *Tdy's mom noz.*

Once I'd locked Lucy and Baby Boy Anteater in their night quarters, I hauled my cell out of my cargo pants and punched in Caro's number. It rang four times, then switched over to voice mail. As Caro's voice began to explain that she was away from her phone, I disconnected. Knowing that she'd be furious for what I was about to do, I called her nearest neighbor, Mrs. Gwendolyn Wexford-Smythe.

"Have you seen my mother today?" I asked Mrs. Wexford-Smythe, once her maid Yvette fetched her to the phone.

"Shertainly nosh." It was well known among Old Town denizens that Mrs. Wexford-Smythe often began drinking well before the sun moved past the yardarm.

"Are you sure, ma'am? Not this morning, not this afternoon?"

"Don't keep trash of your musher's wherea…wherea… where she ish."

"Could I speak to Yvette again, please?" The maid had once worked for Caro, and knew her habits well.

"Shertainly."

A crash, probably of the phone being dropped or Mrs. Wexford-Smythe's plump butt hitting the parquet, then

Yvette came to the phone. "'ow can I help you, Meez Bentley?"

In her thick French accent, Yvette related that she'd seen Caro's Mercedes back out of the driveway and turn south toward Monterey around noon. "I was in front watereen ze potted plants. Zat's when I saw 'er."

"Actually saw my mother or just her car?" After all, anyone could be driving it. A car thief, a serial killer… "I zee your *maman*, Meez Bentley."

"How'd she look?" Sick? On her way to the hospital, perhaps?

"Like always, zee so hair so sleek, zee dress so debonair! Was zee Halston, I theenk. But zaire was one differeence. Zee was not carryeeng ze *petit chien* zees time."

Not carrying the dog? Thank God for small favors. Caro must have left the fierce little Chihuahua to guard the house. "Thank you, Yvette. I usually hear from my mother by this time of day, but perhaps I'm just overreacting and she's merely out shopping again. Could you do me a favor and not mention this conversation? If she knew I called to check up on her, she'd have my scalp."

As Yvette promised to keep it on the down low, I heard Mrs. Wexford-Smythe bawling for her to hang up the damned phone and gesh her anuzer gin and tonk, so I said a quick goodbye.

My comments to Yvette notwithstanding, I felt uneasy. Shopping had never proven a barrier to Caro's overprotective instincts, and many was the time she had called me from a fitting room. Once she even snapped a picture of the dress she was trying on and sent it to me via her picture phone for my opinion, which I gave. She bought the dress anyway.

I've never finished my day with such dispatch. When

I clocked out, I jumped in my pickup and headed for Old Town. The minute I pulled into Caro's driveway, I saw that my fears were unfounded. Mother, in the midst of pulling shut the living room drapes, waved a cheery hello. I waved back, and as I approached the door, tried to dream up an excuse for my unannounced visit.

She and her Chihuahua greeted me at the door. Mr. Trifle—excuse me—*Feroz Guerrero*—looked relaxed for a change. The formerly crotchety dog even wagged his tail at me, possibly remembering that I was the one who had accompanied him to his liberator, Speaks-to-Souls.

Caro clapped her hands like an excited child. "I've bought the most wonderful dresses for you, Theodora! Shoes, too. And naughty lingerie." Mother? Buying me naughty lingerie? What was going on?

Out of the corner of my eye, I saw the newspaper lying untouched on the hall table, which meant that she hadn't yet read it. She probably hadn't heard the news, either, since boutiques don't keep television sets in their dressing rooms. I decided not to enlighten her. As someone once said, sufficient to the day is the evil thereof.

"Did you say dresses, plural?" I asked. Actually, I was more interested in the lingerie. Joe loved naughty lingerie.

Her eyes danced. "Come see!"

A row of brightly-colored shopping bags, pastel-colored clothing spilling out of them, perched on the massive Victorian sofa. "Some haul! What brought all this on?"

"I received the best news this morning!" She clapped her hands again. "Lorena Haskell Anders called me and actually got me out of bed, but when I heard what she had to say, I didn't mind in the least. Oh, Theodora! Yesterday Isabel Van Stoeller, the woman Ford Bronson's been dating? She eloped with an Argentine polo player! The man's penniless, too."

"Izzy and a polo player?" I had to grin. The Van Stoellers were notorious snobs, and the elopement would put a crimp in their collective tails. Well, good for Izzy.

As Caro began pulling clothes out of the bags, I caught a whisper of peau de soie here, a rustle of lace there. "She met him at a match in April and has been seeing him on the sly ever since. Isn't it wonderful?"

Amusing, yes, but *wonderful?* "I'm missing something here."

She held a cloud blue sundress up to me, tucking it under my chin and draping it around my bosom. "That's always been the problem with you, Theodora. You're a bit dense. You never see the great shape of things, and therefore never plan ahead. Instead, you just stumble through life willy-nilly, letting this thing happen, then the next. Sometimes I despair of you, I really do." The dress was pretty, but I peeled it away and dropped it back into the bag. God knows what animal stains were on my uniform. Come to think of it, her obliviousness to my condition added to the mystery. Caro liked to carp about how dirty my job was, but today she hadn't even noticed.

"Mother, what's going on?"

Her ebullient mood dimmed slightly. "I've told you a million times not to call me that."

Sigh. "Sorry, Caro. What's going on?"

Pushing the clothes aside, she took my grubby hands into her perfectly-manicured ones, and looked deeply into my eyes. "We must start our campaign immediately, Theodora. Once news of Isabel's elopement spreads—and with Lorena working the phones it'll spread fast—every debutante on the Coast will be making a beeline for him."

"Him?"

"Ford Bronson, of course! With Isabel out of the picture, he's available again!"

I wanted to scream and run, but my marriage-minded mother held my hands too tightly. I was too appalled to make a sound anyway.

"Here's how we're going to play it, Theodora. Unfortunately, your television segment was only yesterday and you're not due at the station until next Tuesday, but I've taken care of the problem. Before I went shopping, I called Ford and said I wanted to meet with him tomorrow about my program idea, you know, the one about animal psychics. Being the lovely man he is, he agreed to see me at SoftSol headquarters. What he doesn't know is that I'm bringing you, but not dressed the way he usually sees you, in that baggy zoo uniform or lugging along some smelly animal."

She took a deep breath, then prattled on. "Definitely that blue linen sundress. So cunning. Since you wouldn't let me take you to Dr. Markgraf for implants, you're a little light in the bosom, but you have good shoulders and can carry it off anyway. Underneath, you'll wear a sweet blue brassiere with lace straps that peek out in a ladylike way, because men like that sort of thing. I've also arranged for Miss Evelyn, you know, the brilliant cosmetician down in Carmel, to get here early and do something about your freckles. Mister Guy himself has promised to drive up to fix your hair, and…"

Envisioning a battalion of makeover artists setting up shop in Caro's house brought my voice back. "Excuse me for interrupting, but how in the world are you going to explain my presence at a meeting which is supposed to be about a proposed television program that I have nothing to do with?"

"When Ford sees you, no explanation will be necessary." Mother's continued belief in my irresistible female charms was both touching and infuriating. Touching because regardless of her incessant money-grubbing, the woman loved me; infuriating because she refused to accept the fact that I loved Joe every bit as much as she loved her disapproving daughter.

"You're forgetting something, Mother."

"*Caro*, Theodora. *Caro*."

"This little piggy ain't going to no market, no, not ever again."

"There's no such word as 'ain't', dear. You also used a double negative. Triple, actually."

Another thing about my mother. She hears only what she wants to hear. "Then let me restate my feelings in a more grammatical fashion: I shall not do it. Or, as the hipsters say, *hell to the no*!"

"You will."

"Nope. *Nada. Non. Nyet.*"

She smiled. "Remember a few months back, when you bailed your friend out of jail?"

"Yeeessss."

"Remember where the money came from?"

"Yeeessss." It came from the secret account my father had set up for me in the same offshore bank as Caro's. I used it only for emergencies—other people's emergencies, not mine, because we're talking dirty money here. As Joe so frequently reminded me, *someone* in the Bentley family should at least attempt to live a law-abiding life.

Now that she had my complete attention, Caro brought out the big guns. "I can block your account access, Theodora."

"Big deal." I wasn't certain she could, but even if she was right, I didn't care.

"You'll think it's a very big deal when something ghastly happens to one of your friends and you're unable to help."

The woman knew me well. I tried for one final reprieve. "If Mrs. Anders' information is correct, Izzy just eloped last night. Don't you think Ford might still be a little, well, *upset*?"

"Men recover from these things quickly."

Talk about a one-track mind. "Oh, all right. What time do you need me here? I do have a job, you know."

She sniffed, whether as an editorial comment or at my gamey odor, I couldn't tell. "There's no hiding what you do for a living, is there, dear? But since you are kind enough to ask, our appointment with Ford is for ten, so be here at six." Squinting her eyes, she looked me up and down. "Miss Evelyn and Mister Guy have a lot of work to do."

FOURTEEN

I'VE HAD BETTER EVENINGS. At first, Zorah was annoyed when I called her from the *Merilee* and told her that I couldn't make it to the zoo until early afternoon, when I'd also deliver the two tabbies she'd so generously agreed to take. She brightened somewhat when I promised to hit up Ford Bronson for a donation to Bowling for Rhinos.

Not realizing that she echoed my mother, she said, "He's a billionaire, girlfriend, so work him hard."

"I will."

"Aren't you seeing Aster Edwina tomorrow evening, too?" I reassured her that I was.

Now Zorah echoed Buster. "Do what you have to do. Our donations are running 20 percent down from last year, and we've only got four days to go. If it doesn't work out with Bronson, Aster Edwina's our last chance."

"Well, there *is* Caro." I told Zorah I planned to talk to my mother about Bowling for Rhinos on the way to the television station. In order to ensure my good behavior, she would possibly cough up plenty herself. If—and it was a mighty big if—she hadn't yet heard about Heck's murder. Then all bets—and donations—would be off. I could only hope that in my mother's frenzy to snag me a rich husband, she'd not notice anything else. "Your mother's always come through for us, and we're very grateful, Teddy, but it's Bronson and Aster Edwina who have the really big bucks."

After Zorah rang off, I was tempted to call Joe, but what would I tell him? That Caro was about to dangle her daughter in front of yet another billionaire, and that for reasons of my own, I was forced to play the game? Better to go to sleep without the comfort of hearing his voice. Steeped in the bitter brine of self-pity, I checked on my menagerie.

Miss Priss was sulking in the aft bedroom, but Roger and Ebert, Zorah's designated tabbies, were playing with a catnip mouse in the salon while Kennedy and Rockefeller watched. Toby, however, was nowhere to be seen.

"Kitty, kitty," I called, as I wandered through the *Merilee*, looking under this, on top of that. "Toby? Toby? Wherefore art thou, Toby?"

I finally found the part-Siamese in the forward area, curled up next to DJ Bonz. The dog was licking him. The little cat was purring.

"Well, aren't you the proud papa!" I told Bonz.

Wagging his tail, he looked up at me for a moment, then resumed licking his cat.

Confident there was peace in the valley, I joined the disgusted Miss Priss in the aft bedroom and read a few chapters of a Jack Hanna book. It had a picture of a koala on the cover. If I hadn't known better, I'd swear it was Wanchu.

THE NEXT MORNING found me at my mother's house in Old Town, being preened and primped. When Miss Evelyn and Mister Guy finished their work, Caro paid them a small fortune and they departed smiling, unaware that a naked Aztec warrior followed them to the door. As Caro slipped the blue sundress over my shoulders and Feroz Guerrero returned to stand sentry next to her left ankle, I went for the kill.

"How much do you plan to donate to Bowling for Rhinos this year?"

"Is it that time again already?"

"We bowl Saturday."

Humming a tune from *My Fair Lady*, she zipped the sundress up the back. "A perfect fit! Theodora, I know you'll think it's just a mother talking here, but you look absolutely gorgeous. Pure, but with a hint of spice. Ford would have to be blind not to snap you up."

She stepped back, searched through her Coach handbag, took out a decorative glass vial, and spritzed me with a cloud of Annick Goutal's *Eau d'Hadrien*. The perfume smelled as expensive as it was.

"I was thinking maybe five thousand."

"Five thousand what?" She stepped forward again and tugged at the hem, straightening it.

"Dollars. For the rhinos. You spend that much a month on clothes. And perfume."

"Do not."

"Do."

A frown. "It's been a bad year for my portfolio, Theodora."

"That's why I'm only asking for five."

"Five hundred, then."

I reached around and started to unzip the dress. "All right! Five thousand!"

I held out my hand. "Check, please."

Grumbling, she took her checkbook out of her handbag and began writing. "You promise to be charming to Ford Bronson?"

"I'll be the epitome of charm." Until her check cleared the bank. Then I'd revert to my usual charmless self.

WE ARRIVED EARLY at the corporate headquarters of SoftSol, the software company Ford Bronson had founded in the late 80s. A fifteen-story glass and steel cube, its entrance plaza sprinkled with several Henry Moore sculptures, it outshone any other building in San Sebastian's new business district.

Bronson's top floor office, once a phalanx of security

guards allowed us to reach it, was glorious, too. Paneled and bookcased in Brazilian rosewood—which the ecology-minded billionaire was quick to explain had been reclaimed from some other billionaire's demolished mansion—the plush carpeting was so deep that Caro and I sank in it up to our ankles. But none of that matched the large array of photographs lining the walls, which showed Bronson with various movie stars, Nobel Prize winners, U.S. senators, and three presidents, including his golf buddy. Crowning them all was a reprint of the famous AP photo that caught him as he was testifying before Congress about the sharp rise in software piracy. He looked more statesmanlike than they did, with his chiseled chin, flinty eyes, and authoritative nose. No Quasimodo, he.

The whole high-toned office/handsome-available-billionaire setup was so impressive I feared that at any moment Caro might fall on her knees and plead for Bronson to *please, please, please* take her recalcitrant daughter off her hands.

However, the woman proved herself a trouper. As soon as we sat down, she launched into a rehearsed spiel about her television show, making a strong case that San Sebastian's very own Speaks-to-Souls should be the subject of the premiere episode. Her passion for the project was so intense that I began to wonder if using me as marriage bait was nothing more than an add-on to her visit. The idea made me relax enough to have some fun. On the drive over, she'd ordered me to flirt, a skill I'd never mastered. But thinking that I might later try some of the more successful moves on Joe, I decided to get in some practice.

When Caro began describing Mr. Trifle/Feroz Guerrero's temperament turnaround, I cocked my head and simpered.

Bronson smiled, whether at me or at Caro's recital, I couldn't tell.

When Caro, who had done her homework, quoted the large audience share of *Meerkat Manor*, the popular Animal Planet series, I batted my mascaraed eyelashes.

Another smile from Bronson.

Caro finished her pitch with "And I'm certain you'll agree that programs about the Other Side do every bit as well as animal programs, so why not combine the two?" I tried to toss my red locks, but unfortunately, Mr. Guy had sprayed them so heavily they couldn't move.

With yet another smile on his lips, Bronson dropped his intense study of my simpers to focus on my mother. "Well, you've certainly presented a very attractive package, Mrs. Petersen, and I'll definitely give it some thought."

Mrs. Petersen? Who was Mrs...? Oh, right. Caro's last husband's name was Petersen.

After expressing her gratitude, Caro stood to leave.

That's when I made my Bowling for Rhinos pitch. After all, I didn't want the visit to be wasted.

Ten minutes later we were climbing back into Caro's cavernous Mercedes. Judging from her tone, she was not happy. "For God's sake, Theodora, that was crass!"

"Crass, perhaps, but I kept my promise to be charming." I tucked the check for ten thousand dollars into the Versace handbag she'd loaned me.

"A person can't be crass and charming at the same time!"

"A person can when an endangered species is involved."

She fumed all the way to Old Town, but as we pulled into her driveway, she relented. "I guess your appalling manners made no difference because he was definitely smitten. Why, he could hardly take his eyes off you! I'm so glad I had the foresight to plan that little do tomorrow night. You'll wear the lavender satin. That color looks particularly ravishing on redheads. And I'll loan you my diamonds, of course. They leave no doubt as to the kind of people we are."

Right. Cattle thieves. Tax evaders. Embezzlers. Serialmarriers. "What little *do* are you talking about, Caro?"

"Um, perhaps I forget to mention it. I've invited Ford and a few close friends over for cocktails. I expect you to be as charming as you were today, but without the crassness. Understood?" Since I had yet to turn hers and Bronson's checks over to the Bowling for Rhinos treasurer, I agreed. But I would rather have spent the evening with Joe.

AFTER RETURNING TO the *Merilee* and changing into my uniform, I scooped Roger and Ebert, Zorah's two tabbies, into an animal carrier and took off for the zoo. Imagine my surprise when I clocked in and found TV host AnnaLee Harris talking to Zorah. "We're announcing the winner of the Name the Baby Anteater Contest today during KTSS-TV's noon broadcast," Zorah explained, as she took the cats into her office. "The station sent over a remote van and the cameras are already set up in front of Lucy's enclosure. Since you're her main keeper, I want you there. I'd planned to do it, but you're much better at this sort of thing."

Exhausted from my flirting practice session, I merely said, "Want me to say anything special?"

"AnnaLee will ask you a few questions. This is a public relations event for the Gunn Zoo, but if you can, get in a pitch for the San Sebastian No-Kill Animal Shelter Marathon, too. About half our staff have volunteered to man the phones."

"I have, too."

To my surprise, she shook her head. "No. You're taking Wanchu. You two will be in that lineup of movie stars and whatnot Ford Bronson has arranged to put in an appearance."

I blanched. "Me? With movie stars?"

"Yeah, you. And make sure you behave yourself. Drew

Barrymore is emceeing, and if you pull anything cute with her, she's liable to hit you upside your head."

"But…"

"Don't 'but' me, Teddy. Just do your job."

With that, Zorah turned Roger and Ebert loose, expecting them to hide underneath her desk. Instead, they immediately ran to the window to watch the monkeys, who in turn, watched them. Cats and monkeys thus entertained, we humans walked up the hill to Lucy's enclosure, where a small crowd had gathered. A cameraman, his camera almost as large as he, leaned precariously over the rail.

"Be careful!" I warned. "The last man who fell into Lucy's enclosure lost his skin."

The cameraman swiveled around until the lens pointed straight at me. "This is the same anteater that killed that guy?"

"Lucy never killed anyone. He was shot. Lucy was just trying to scrape some ants off his face." Too late, I noticed the red light flashing. "Hey! Turn that thing off!"

"Taping for stock. I'll let you know when we go to live feed." Lucy, attracted by all the fuss, had moved to the edge of her moat and was peering up at us. Baby Boy Anteater, riding on her back, looked sound asleep. I hoped he would move around when the live feed began, because his diagonal gray, black, and white shoulder stripes blended so perfectly with his mother's that you could hardly tell where he began and Lucy left off.

"Let's get this party started while she's facing the camera," AnnaLee said. "Better now than a shot of her big hairy ass as she walks away."

For that uncalled-for remark, I wanted to pick up her own big hairy ass and toss her to Lucy, but since it was against the law, I didn't. Unlike my parents, I have scruples.

"Little Ricky, get over here!" AnnaLee snapped to a small tow-headed boy.

Dressed like a miniature gangsta rap artist in a Raiders team shirt, enough bling to sink the *Titanic* all over again, and Levis three times too large for his tiny self, Little Ricky looked thrilled. When he smiled into the camera, it was with all the sincerity of a child actor.

"And four and three and two and we're live," the cameraman said.

"Good afternoon, San Sebastian!" AnnaLee bubbled. "We're here *live* at the giant anteater's enclosure in the famed Gunn Zoo, to announce the winner of the Name the Baby Anteater Contest! With us is Teddy Bentley, the giant anteater's keeper, and seven-year-old Ricky Hartounian, who came up with the winning entry. First, Teddy is going to tell us all about giant anteaters, aren't you, Teddy?"

Fulfilling my promise to behave myself, I went into my standard spiel: giant anteaters have yard-long blue tongues; give birth while standing up on their hind legs; are basically peaceful, solitary animals but using their four-inch talons, they can disembowel a jaguar if attacked, yadda, yadda, yadda.

"My, that's fascinating!" AnnaLee said. "And now, Little Ricky is going to tell us the new name of Lucy's baby, aren't you, son?"

"Damned straight," Little Ricky said.

AnnaLee blinked. "Uh, so go ahead, Little Ricky."

Little Ricky puffed out his little chest. "Little Ricky!" The kid was naming the anteater baby after himself?

"That's right!" AnnaLee enthused, as if self-centeredness was the most delightful trait a child could display. "You see, loyal KTSS-TV watchers, a long, long time ago, there was a television show called *I Love Lucy*, and in it, an actress named Lucille Ball played Lucy, a New York housewife, who was married to a Cuban bandleader named Ricky Ricardo! When they had a baby, they named him Little Ricky, which also just happens to be the name of our winning contestant here! Isn't that adorable, Teddy?"

"If you say so."

AnnaLee smiled madly. "And now a word from our sponsor, Clive Clam's Seafood House. If Clive's clams were any fresher, they'd walk off the plate." Her smile vanished when she looked down at Little Ricky—the human one. "We're done with you, you little shit. Get out of my sight."

Television appearance accomplished, I headed to the rhino enclosure to give Buster Daltry the checks I'd received from Caro and Ford Bronson. The big man took them with a mixture of awe and gratitude. After shoving them into his cargo pants pocket, he gave me a slap on the back that nearly knocked me down.

"You sure hang with the richie-riches, don't you, Teddy?"

"Only when holding a WILL MINGLE FOR DONATIONS sign." The next time I ran into Zorah was in the zoo parking lot when we were entering our respective pickup trucks for our journeys home. Roger and Ebert were vocal about being separated from the monkey show at the window. Zorah told me that the monkeys weren't happy about it, either.

"These sure are loud cats," she said, as she placed the tabbies in the passenger's seat.

"That's what Heck's neighbors always said."

Suddenly serious, she said, "I watched the news coverage this morning while I was getting ready for work. So sad. Think the sheriff will let Bill go now? From what they said on the broadcast, it's obvious the same person killed Kate and that poor old guy."

I nodded. "Joe said he needed to talk to the country attorney first, but that it was pretty much a done deal. Bill could be back here as early as tomorrow."

"Really? If I were Bill, I'd fly straight back to Australia and hide myself somewhere in the Outback."

"Not without your passport, you wouldn't."

Around us, other zookeepers were hurrying to their cars, eager to get home and feed their own menageries. On the other side of Zorah's pickup, Buster Daltry climbed into his battered '93 Dodge Shadow; after several cranks and groans, it finally started, and he waved goodbye to us as it chugged away. Robin Chase, grumpy as usual, slammed the door of her rust-bucket Pinto, studiously ignoring everyone. Across from us, beautiful Myra was putting the top down on the sleek Corvette that a former boyfriend, a hockey star, had given her.

Watching the Corvette—it was silver with white racing stripes—Zorah sighed. "So pretty."

"Myra?"

"The Corvette. Look, just so you'll know, I received news that the Oakland police found Kate's father, but as it turns out, he's too sick to leave the nursing home. I called Aster Edwina and told her so she can get started on the funeral preparations." I thought about Kate's father, a man too ill to see his only child buried. While nothing would change his failing condition, there might be something I could do for him. It would entail a trip to Oakland, but if it helped, even a little, what was a two-hour drive compared to the comfort it might give a grieving father?

"Zorah, do you still have that photo we took of Kate when the koala enclosure had its grand opening?"

"Of course. I had several copies made for publicity purposes, but why…" She got it. "You want to give one to Kate's father."

"Exactly. She looked great, smiling broadly with Wanchu in her arms. He'd be so proud." If he even recognized his daughter, that was. Alzheimer's wasn't only a thief of memory, it was a thief of the heart.

Zorah breathed what sounded like a sigh of relief. "Tell you what. If you drive the photo up there tomorrow, I'll count the trip as work time and you won't have to report in at all."

"I'll come in, all right." Being with my animal friends would give me the strength I needed to survive Caro's next Let's-Find-Teddy-a-Suitable-Husband party, where she would dangle me in front of Ford Bronson like a worm on a hook.

The drive to Gunn Castle took five minutes, since it was more or less right next door to the zoo. Set on the highest hill in the center of the massive Gunn estate, the castle lorded over everything: the Gunn Zoo, the Gunn Eucalyptus Forest, the Gunn Winery, even the thousand-acre Gunn Vineyard, with its undulating rows of Chardonnay, Pinot Noir, Syrah, and Grenache grapes.

It was a spectacular drive, but an uncomfortable one, because what lay at the end of it was the castle, which looked like something out of an old Dracula movie. Hauled over stone-by-stone from Scotland by railroad baron Edwin Gunn, the dynasty's founder, the castle sported six towers, a crenelated roof, and rows of archers' windows. I'd never enjoyed my childhood visits here to play with the Gunn children, but the dour architecture and the moldy smell of ancient walls was only partially the reason. To tell the truth, Aster Edwina scared me half to death.

As a child, I'd been a friend of the younger Gunns— Aster Edwina's great-nieces and nephews, since she had no children of her own—and whenever there'd been a falling out, the formidable old woman had no qualms about swatting me with the same enthusiasm with which she swatted them. Even now I was careful to keep more than an arm's length away from her.

Memories churning, I finally made it to the end of the eucalyptus-lined road and parked my pickup behind an elderly but still-gleaming Rolls. Seconds after I had pulled at the massive door's entry bell the just-as-elderly butler let me in. He led me through the marble-tiled entryway, past the immense drawing room, and into the castle's dark, multi-fireplaced library, where Aster Edwina sat waiting for me on a Jacobean armchair every bit as stiff and formal as herself.

Her silver hair was almost the same shade as her dress, but the library's dim light was merciful to her wrinkle-ravaged face. "And now comes Theodora Bentley, metaphorical tin cup in hand. How's the begging going, dear?"

Having been subjected to her rudeness for years, I didn't bother to blush. "Not well, Aster Edwina. Thanks to the crummy economy, everyone's broke. And that's a tragedy, because rhinos are…"

"Endangered. Have you forgotten that I oversee the zoo, endangered rhinos and all? And therefore I can tell you exactly how many rhinos remain at which sanctuary or zoo, and which of them are pregnant?"

"I didn't forget."

"Of course you didn't. You were just warming up for your sales pitch."

Despite the library's lone stained-glass window, I detected a slight smile on Aster Edwina's face. She had always enjoyed seeing people squirm, but since the result of my humiliation would be a big donation for Bowling for Rhinos, I didn't mind. "How well you know me, ma'am. Now about that contribution…"

A thin shaft of sunlight struggled through the stained glass and illuminated the portrait above the fireplace

mantel. Painted when Aster Edwina was in her early forties, it portrayed her with a handsome elegance that made
mere beauty seem irrelevant. With her gray eyes, hawk
nose, and hair just beginning to gray, she looked like an
aging Valkyrie.

But there was something…something…

Oh, my God.

"What is it, Theodora? You look rather foolish with your
mouth hanging open like that."

"It's just that I…that I… Hey, how come you never married?"

She drew herself back as if she'd just confronted a leper.
"My personal life is of no concern to you."

Remembering the rhinos, I forced myself to calm down.
"Um, um, I'm sorry and all that, Aster Edwina. I, um, I
don't know what came over me. Maybe this past couple of
weeks has been more of a strain that I believed."

Her eyes grew hard. "I would have believed you'd be
well-acquainted with murder by now."

"You never get…" Better not go there. This conversation was tanking fast, and I had to turn it around. "The
rhinos, Aster Edwina. They're in desperate shape and we
need to do something to help them, that's why I'm here,
not to reopen old wounds. Bowling for Rhinos is day after
tomorrow, and we're having trouble selling raffle tickets,
but even worse, we're abysmally behind in our donations,
so I was hoping…"

"Your mother didn't contribute?"

"Of course she did, but…"

"Her portfolio took a big hit, right?" A thin smile. "Excellent. A little humility will be good for her. So how much
do you want from me, Theodora, to make up for your mother's lack of economic foresight?"

I took a deep breath. "Ten thousand."

"Pardon me while I laugh." She forced out a raspy sound that might have been a chuckle. "Try again, you foolish girl."

"But Aster Edwina…"

"I said, *try again.*"

The old harridan was enjoying herself, all right. "Nine thousand."

"Keep going, Theodora, in a downward direction."

"Eight?"

"Five. Not a penny more."

"Oh, come on. Even Caro gave me five."

She raised her eyebrows. "I suppose you believe that I'm obliged to trump her, am I correct?"

"You always did before."

She nodded. "And I will again, because that gold-digging social upstart needs to be taught her place. But I won't do it with more money. I have something even better. A seed that can grow into a rather large plant if your finance committee handles it correctly." Remembering the rhinos again, I swallowed the insult to my mother.

"Late last year I purchased something that for business reasons I am now unable to use. So I've decided to offer it as the grand prize at the Bowling for Rhinos raffle. Thus, I'll see your mother's five thousand, but I'll raise her an all-inclusive, two-week safari to Africa. For two. All land and air expenses paid."

"Africa?" I squeaked.

"It's that big continent on the other side of the Atlantic, dear. The one with rhinos."

"Holy shit!"

"Language, Theodora."

"I meant to say, wow, that's very generous of you, Aster Edwina."

"It most certainly is. Now, in order to get the most financial mileage out of the prize—and the Africa trip is worth quite a bit, you understand, bringing my total con-tributions to Bowling for Rhinos to around twenty-five thousand dollars, which leaves your mother's paltry five thousand in the dust. And it should, as that appalling tele-vision chef says, kick raffle ticket sales up a notch. Now, will you call the media or shall I? Folks up in San Francisco or down in Monterey will need at least a day's warning to participate in the raffle, and we don't want my generosity to go to waste, do we?"

We most certainly didn't.

AFTER A QUICK dash back to the *Merilee* to pick up Kennedy and Rockefeller, I barreled down the dirt road that led to the DiGiorno property. Located at the far eastern edge of the old Bentley cattle ranch, Speaks-to-Souls' stone cottage was tucked into a shallow valley. Although it was partially hidden by a large stand of live oaks, I could see the warm glow of lights peeping through the trees.

From the outside, the cottage looked little different than the one I remembered from my childhood. There could have been new paint on the window sashes, and the front door might have been new, but in the growing dusk, I couldn't be certain. Behind the house stood a series of shaded, roomy corrals that held a collection of animals ranging from bur-ros to llamas to some very big dogs of indeterminate breed-ing. Chickens, ducks, geese, and even peacocks strolled free on the grounds. One small gray rooster—I think it was a speckled Hamburg—strutted up to me as if expect-ing to be fed.

Nudging him away with my foot, I hauled the cat car-riers out of the pickup and approached the door. It opened before I had time to knock.

"Welcome to Casa de Castaway," Speaks-to-Souls said, her face shadowed by the light behind her. She cradled a cat in her arms while several others swirled around her feet. Further on in the house, I saw at least four small dogs and a few more cats. This was a woman who not only talked the talk, but walked the walk.

"Thank you, Speaks-to…"

"Call me Josie, but never in public. It's short for Josephina."

"Okay, Josie, where shall I put Kennedy and Rockefeller?"

"God only knows, but if you come in, we can start working on the problem."

The house's brightly lit interior wasn't too bad. Decorated much like the zoo's employees' lounge with a collection of mismatched furniture and animal posters, it made its own original design statement with the small reptile aquariums that lined the walls, the largest of which was the size of a casket and contained a green iguana easily two feet long.

At my quizzical look, she said, "I found her in a San Sebastian Dumpster, cage and all. Some people have no conscience."

No, they didn't. For all their reptileness, iguanas were friendly animals that grew deeply attached to their keepers. Not being literate, they couldn't write or speak about the heartbreak they experienced when discarded like trash, but there was little doubt they suffered.

I set the cat carriers down by the sofa, then plopped myself into its own pillowy softness. Within seconds, a small Pekingese mix jumped onto the sofa to keep me company. He turned a few times, then rested his head on my thigh.

Patting him, I said to Josie, "Green iguanas can grow to more than four feet in length. What are you going to do then?"

She carefully lowered herself and the black cat onto a recliner. "I have a call out to several zoos, the Gunn included."

"Good luck with that." People were always trying to foist their animals on zoos, unaware that the zoos were already full up.

"If I can't find a zoo to take her—I've named her Eve, by the way—I'll soon have to move her out back. Alyse is building several more pens, and it won't be too much trouble to outfit one for her." She smiled. "For Eve, not Alyse."

I smiled back. "Where is your daughter, by the way?"

"At the library. She's a volunteer and helps them shelve books twice a week. The rest of the time, when she's not working with me, she's running around trying to raise money for the San Sebastian No-Kill Animal Shelter. She's even going to take part in that television marathon next week, answering the phones, I think. So am I, for that matter."

Not knowing how much or how little her daughter knew, it was a relief to be able to speak freely.

By now, every one of the room's felines had approached the cat carriers to inspect Kennedy and Rockefeller. Other than a hiss or two, the introductions were peaceful. After all, every cat in the room was used to being part of a menagerie.

"Looks like it's going to work out," I said.

Another smile. "It always does."

With the light from a corner lamp shining her full on the face, I could see that she was older than she'd appeared at her dimly-lit shop, as much as forty, even forty-five.

Old enough.

"What are your plans?" I asked.

She feigned puzzlement. "Plans for the cats?" I shook my head.

"My, aren't you being the Sphinx."

The Peke-mix in my lap stood up, wagged his tail, and gnawed gently at my hand in an invitation to play. When I told him no, he settled himself back down. I patted him and told him what a good dog he was. He wagged his tail again, but this time kept his teeth to himself.

"You have a way with animals," Josie said, admiration in her voice.

"I like to think so."

"You were asking about plans?" She looked rather Sphinxlike, herself.

"Right. Now, let's see. To take possession of this property, you had to present a birth certificate proving that you were a DiGiorno by birth, which means your father would have been one of the DiGiorno boys. I'm guessing Giannino. From what I hear, he was a handsome devil. Very popular with the ladies."

"Yes, Uncle Giannino was quite the Romeo. He's married now and has a large brood of children, none of whom wanted to be bothered with this run-down place. I'm Delmazio's daughter. And before you ask, he and his wife are getting up there in age, so he didn't want to go through the trouble of moving back here. Especially not to this hovel."

She said "his wife," not *my mother.*

"He didn't want to move back here from where?"

"Mt. Pleasant, New York. He owns a restaurant there. Italian, of course. My two younger brothers manage it, but food's never been my thing. Animals are."

A township forty miles north of Manhattan, Mt. Pleasant was the seat of Pocantico Hills, the family home of the Rockefellers. I'd once spent a weekend on the estate as a guest of one of the Rockefeller girls, a friend of mine from

Miss Pridewell's Academy for Young Ladies. No wonder Josie had laughed when I told her the cats' names.

"How did a DiGiorno wind up that far east?" As if I hadn't already figured it out.

"The Gunn family wanted him as far away from here as possible."

I decided to go for it. "They wanted *you* as far away as possible, am I correct?"

No smile now. With her thinned lips and straight spine, she was the twin of the portrait I'd just viewed in the library at Gunn Castle. "Oh, yes. The Gunns definitely wanted me out of sight."

"So they paid your father off."

"Yes."

"How did your mother feel about that?"

"My mother?"

I softened my voice. "Yes, Josie. Aster Edwina. Your mother."

FIFTEEN

IF YOU DRIVE fast enough you can reach Oakland, a neighboring city of San Francisco, in little over an hour, but with the engine in my Nissan pickup being little better than the *Merilee*'s engine, we crept along the slow lane for the entire distance. It gave me plenty of time to think about last night's conversation with Aster Edwina's long-lost daughter.

All Josie/Speaks-to-Souls knew was what her father had told her. When he and Aster Edwina were both in their forties, they'd had a brief affair that ended when Aster Edwina had left to visit relatives in England.

"But she wasn't in England," Josie had said. "She went somewhere to have the baby. My father, who was married to his first wife at the time, didn't know anything about it. He thought Aster Edwina had grown tired of fooling around with the peons, so when old Edwin showed up on his doorstep one night with a big check and a baby, he was shocked. Dad didn't want the money, but his wife talked him into using it to buy his uncle's restaurant in New York, so we became New Yorkers and we all lived happily ever after. End of story."

But it hadn't been the end of the story. After repeated questioning, she explained that as a rider to the check, Josie's father had to promise Edwin that he would never contact Aster Edwina again. She wanted nothing more to do with him, Edwin said.

Josie gave me a bitter smile. "To set Aster Edwina's mind at ease, and also to placate his wife, Dad promised. Not that it did much good. Not long after we arrived in New York, his wife left him for another man, and he raised me alone."

When I'd asked her about her plans, she refused to answer.

THE GOLDEN RULE Rest Home was on the western edge of town in an industrial area that hadn't yet seen gentrification, but from the FOR SALE sign in front of the shabby building, its time would soon be up. Just like its residents'.

As the stoutly built manager, whose name tag announced her as MRS. MORTHLAND, ushered me down a dark hallway toward Tyler Everts' room, I banished Aster Edwina and her daughter from my mind to concentrate on another parent and child. Judging from the shabbiness of Golden Rule Rest Home, Kate's father must have lived a hand-to-mouth existence. At least he'd loved his daughter and she'd loved him. It was too bad neither of them had been able to afford a nicer place for him to end his days.

Not that the Golden Rule was a bad place; it wasn't. The staff appeared compassionate, but the hallway carpet was threadbare, the ceiling water-stained, and the air musty with the smell of boiled vegetables and decaying flesh. When we reached Tyler's room, I saw two narrow beds. In the far bed, an old man lay staring sightlessly at the ceiling. The other bed was empty.

"Looks like Mr. Everts is in the rec room watching TV," Mrs. Morthland said.

Before we headed to the rec room, I noted that the wall on Kate's father's side of the room was plastered with snapshots of boats. Some I recognized from Gunn Landing Harbor, others I didn't. The largest photograph was of the *Nomad*. Standing in front of it, arms around each other, were Tyler Everts and the child who grew up to be Koala Kate. They looked happy.

The television in the rec room was turned to the Nickelodeon cartoon, *The Penguins of Madagascar*. Several elderly men and women sat facing it, their aged faces almost indistinguishable from each other. One man appeared at least two decades younger than the rest. He was holding something in his arms. A doll?

Mrs. Morthland pointed to him. "That's Tyler. The fellow with the plush koala. It was a gift from his daughter."

In a way, Kate's father was still a handsome man, leaving aside the vacant look in his eyes and the thin vein of drool that escaped from his mouth. He had a straight nose, a well shaped, if slack, mouth, and broad shoulders, and he was wearing a blue Canaan Harbor tee shirt with a picture of a sailboat on it. He cradled the stuffed koala as if it were a child.

I showed Mrs. Morthland the picture I'd brought. "Will he recognize her?"

"It's hard to say. Sometimes he's with us, sometimes he's somewhere else. This morning he was alert enough to remember the names of some of the food he was having for breakfast. Eggs. Toast. But he believed the sausage patty was a cookie and complained that it wasn't sweet enough. That's how it is with these Alzheimer's patients."

She gave me a kindly smile. "If you need me, I'll be in the office filing medical records. But be sure and stop in to see me before you go. I have an envelope I meant to give Kate. She put it down on his night stand the last time she was here, then forgot to take it with her when she left. Since she's passed over, you might as well have it. When the police told me what had happened to her, I looked through it and saw several receipts, including one from a funeral home and another for a double cemetery plot not that far from here. So you see, someone has to..." She trailed off.

"I understand. Let me know when Mr. Everts, ah, passes over. The zoo will take care of the arrangements."

Mrs. Morthland thanked me and started to leave, then paused at the door. "When you talk to Tyler, don't bring up what happened to Kate, okay? When the police first told him, he cried and cried, but now he's forgotten all about it. Reminding him will just break his heart all over again." Then she left me on my own.

Summoning up the skills I had learned when dealing with the elderly aunt who'd suffered from the disease, I approached him slowly. Stopping in front of his chair, I stooped down so as not to loom over him. "Hello, Mr. Everts. My name is Teddy, and I used to work with your daughter."

He gave me a vague smile. "Are you my daughter?"

"No. Her name is Kate."

His brow creased for a moment, then he shook his head. "I don't think I know anyone by that name."

It's never a good idea to argue with an Alzheimer's patient, so I simply said, "That's a very nice koala you have there. What's his name?"

"Wanchu."

"Isn't that the name of the koala your daughter takes care of?"

He beamed. "Yes! My daughter gave it to me, but I keep forgetting her name. Do you know her?" Just like that, his memory had snapped back.

"Oh, yes, we're very good friends." A stretch there, but a well-meaning one.

"Is she coming to see me today?"

Remembering Mrs. Morthland's warning, I said, "She couldn't get away from work, but she gave me this to bring to you." I slid the framed photograph out of its manila envelope and held it in front of him.

"Wanchu," he said. "And Koala Kate."

"Yes, Wanchu. And Kate, your daughter."

He beamed at the photograph for a few seconds, then the blank look slid across his face again. "Who did you say you are?"

"Teddy. I'm a friend of Kate's."

He turned to the television, where one of the penguins was upchucking a partially-digested fish. "I don't know any Kate." A few minutes later, I realized he wasn't coming back, so I left him to watch television with the other residents.

"How'd it go?" Mrs. Morthland said, looking up from her filing as I entered the office.

"As well as expected, I guess." I handed her the photograph of Kate and Wanchu. "Can I put this up on his wall?"

"It's against regulations to let visitors nail anything to the walls, but I'll put it up myself as soon as I'm through here. Which reminds me, here's that envelope I told you about. The one Kate forgot."

She handed me an envelope. It felt thick enough to contain funeral arrangements for a hundred dying men.

I WAS IN such a somber mood when I drove into the parking lot at Gunn Landing Harbor that I almost slammed into the big Mercedes taking up my reserved parking space. But there was no way I could miss the whirlwind of anger and recrimination that headed for me in the form of Caroline Piper Bentley Hufgraff O'Brien Petersen, otherwise known as Mother.

"Did you think I wouldn't see this?" she screeched, shaking a newspaper in front of my face so violently that several seagulls flapped away in alarm.

SERIAL KILLER LOOSE IN SS COUNTY? The *San Sebastian*

Gazette bawled, in big red type. Second victim found in Gunn Landing harbor sobbed the lead.

"That paper's two days old, Caro. And here I thought you kept up on current events."

"I've been busy putting your party together!"

"It's not my party, it's yours," I muttered, trying to sidle past her. "Don't get smart with me, missy." She grabbed my sleeve and gave a yank, almost making me drop Kate's envelope. "You're coming home with me whether you like it or not. Whoever that killer is, he's either going after people connected to the zoo or to that Koala Kate person. It says right here in the article that Mr. Liddell was a friend of Kate's. And you were, too."

Not really, but Caro had no way of knowing that. "Look, Mo... Caro, I can't just move out of the *Merilee* and leave my animals behind. I have a new cat..."

"Bring them. Wait, did you say a new cat, it's now *cats*, plural? Don't you have just the one, that Miss Priss or whatever the fluffball's name is?"

"My new cat's name is Toby, and he belonged to Heck."

"The second victim?" Her eyes widened. "Don't worry, I can handle an extra cat. The only question will be, can Feroz? Since I took him to see Speaks-to-Souls, he's a different dog."

Change the environment, change the behavior. "If worst comes to worst, I'll confine the animals to my room. I also need to bring some things, like my uniforms and my computer. I'm supposed to be working on the zoo newsletter." The minute the words escaped my mouth, I realized that she was right. Despite my earlier defiance of Joe's edict, I did need to leave the *Merilee*—if only to keep my mother from having a heart attack.

With my acquiescence, the tension left my mother's face. "I'll help you pack, Theodora."

An hour later DJ Bonz, Miss Priss, Toby and I were ensconced in my old room at Caro's house. For a woman addicted to serial marriage, she remained remarkably faithful to her memory of me as a teenager. The turquoise and lime green color scheme remained, as did the posters of Jon Bon Jovi, Gloria Estefan, and the Thompson Twins. Bonz and Miss Priss had holed up here before, but little Toby, having just started getting used to the *Merilee,* looked scared out of his wits. The Aztec warrior sniffing hungrily outside the door didn't help, either.

I picked Toby up and cuddled him. "Don't worry, I won't let mean old Feroz get you." Eventually, he relaxed enough to purr. I continued holding him and talking to him until Caro rapped at the door.

"Lunch time, Theodora! Grizelda's made tuna salad." Grizelda was her new maid. Due to temperament issues coupled with an odd perfectionism about household matters, my mother blew through an average of six maids a year. She never fired them; they just disappeared, sometimes turning up employed by one of Caro's friends.

I set Toby down, and without thinking, opened the door. A snarling Feroz headed straight for the little cat.

He never made it.

DJ Bonz, usually the most peaceful of dogs, placed himself between Feroz and Toby, teeth bared.

The Chihuahua slid to a stop. Hackles high, he froze in place on the lime green carpet, mulling over the situation. Bonz was twice his size, with teeth two times as long. Moreover, the three-legged mongrel appeared willing to fight to the death for the safety of his cat.

Even naked Aztec warriors know when a situation is hopeless, so with a face-saving growl, Feroz turned and walked out of the room with all the dignity he could muster.

"If that mutt of yours hurts Feroz, I'll kill him," Caro huffed as we walked downstairs to the dining room.

"Not if I kill you first," I answered genially.

Formal lunches aren't my thing but they are Caro's, so I sat at the long dining table as Grizelda fussed about with a lace tablecloth made by French nuns, monogrammed linen napkins, old Bentley silver, and an irreplaceable pattern of Royal Doulton china.

For tuna frickin' salad.

"What's the big hurry?" Caro asked, as I speared the last pea.

"I'm late for work."

She sniffed. "Surely you're not going in today, not after everything that's happened."

"I'm as safe there as I am here, Mother."

"*Caro*, dear. If I remember correctly, you were almost killed at the zoo once. That awful anteater tried it, too."

After patting my lips with a napkin, I stood up. "Lucy is a perfectly reasonable animal, unlike a certain Chihuahua I could mention."

"I thought you liked Feroz."

"Not when he's about to kill my cat." Good deeds never go unpunished, do they?

As I headed up to my room, Caro's voice followed me. "Don't forget the party tonight. All the right people will be here."

She was more correct than she realized. To make the evening bearable, I'd compiled a guest list of my own, and had been delighted when no one turned down my offer of free food and free booze. To make certain there would be enough, I'd also called the caterers and told them to double everything. When Caro received the bill she would not be pleased, but I figured her dream of marrying me off to a billionaire would help ease the pain. My only disappointment had come during my phone call to Joe, when he warned me that with two murder investigations going on, he'd arrive at the party late, possibly not at all.

Humming "Baby Elephant Walk," I changed into my zoo khakis, grabbed Kate's envelope, and sped out of the house. Fifteen minutes later I was hurrying through the zoo's Administration Building to Zorah's office, where I found her just hanging up the phone.

"How'd it go at the nursing home?" she asked.

"It was sad. Sometimes he remembered Kate, sometimes he didn't. But at least he now has that picture of her and Wanchu to look at during the times he does. The director of the place gave me some papers that Kate left there by mistake. Apparently she'd already made plans for her father's burial, so I need to contact Aster Edwina right away and let her know. Mind if I use your phone? I didn't want to call from Caro's."

She shoved the phone across the desk. "On a happier subject, what time's your mother's party?"

"People will start arriving around seven."

"What with all I have to do here, I doubt if I can make it that early, but I should be able to get there by eight. Speaking of which, I wondered how long it would take your mother to lure you back up to Old Town."

"It wasn't so much a luring as it was a kidnapping."

When I reached Aster Edwina, she thanked me for the update on Kate's funeral arrangements. For a moment I was tempted to ask if her own daughter had gotten in touch with her yet, but common sense advised against it.

After hanging up, I rose to leave, but Zorah waved me back down.

"We need to talk about your work schedule, Teddy."

"Can't it wait? I need to see to the anteater, then the koalas…"

"Robin Chase is taking care of Lucy as we speak, although she's not happy about it, and Bill is with the koalas."

"Joe released him!" I punched my fist into the air.

Zorah followed with a similar gesture. "With only one caveat. Sheriff Rejas made me promise to keep an eye on him. There's irony for you."

Considering Zorah's past encounter with Joe, irony was the word. "I'll call Joe and thank him."

"You do that. Now sit down again. We have things to discuss." Her smile vanished. "The job you did on *ZooNews* was terrific, and we posted it online without any changes. But, damn it, Teddy, you sent the thing into me at midnight, after putting in a full day's work. You can't maintain that kind of schedule."

I wholeheartedly agreed with her, and once again put forth my argument that someone else should be hired to take over Kate's duties. "Get a PR professional, not a zookeeper. We have other things to worry about." A new idea occurred to me. "Hey, how about your executive assistant? I know Helen can write because she's constantly fixing up your letters. And as for the *Good Morning, San Sebastian* segment, well, mature women are the new Big Thing on television now. They're called cougars."

"Forget it. You've gained quite the following from your appearances on KTSS-TV, and regardless of how much you hate it, you're stuck. But we need to fix your schedule. Speaking of *Good Morning, San Sebastian*, AnnaLee Harris called and told me she got a new job as morning anchorwoman at the CBS affiliate in San Francisco. Thanks to you, she's moving up in the world."

A pang of guilt coursed through me, followed by a pang of relief. "What do you mean, thanks to me?"

"During her interview, the station manager at KTSF said she displays great calm under extreme circumstances. You know, such as continuing to broadcast with a pile of lemur poop on her head."

"Then all's well that ends well."

"For now. But if you try any of those tricks on her replacement, she'll rip your head off and spit down the stump. Ariel Gonzales, who starts next Wednesday, happens to be an old friend of mine. She just got back from Iraq."

I was impressed. "A war correspondent?"

"A Marine. Ex-Marine, as of last month. During her two tours in Iraq, she received a Purple Heart and a Bronze Star. Like I said, watch your ass."

"But how does a Marine…?"

"Girlfriend received her degree in broadcast journalism from USC and did remotes for KTSS-TV for two years before she enlisted. Now, about that schedule of yours."

What my new schedule boiled down to was this: From now on, I'd work Monday through noon Saturday, skipping Sundays. When I said that I preferred Monday as my day of rest, Zorah turned me down flat.

"Sunday is our busiest day, and I want you home resting. Your Mondays will be devoted to all the PR stuff. Tuesdays, you'll continue the segments on *Good Morning, San Sebastian*, and once you're back from the station, you'll revert to your old schedule for the rest of the week. Except for the koalas. Now that Bill's out of the pokey, your services down there are no longer required." As happy as I felt for Bill, I was sad, too, because cuddling Wanchu had turned out to be one of the bright spots of my day. But you can't have everything, can you? With a sigh, I left Zorah's office and headed down the hill to congratulate Outback Bill on his release. For a just-freed man, he was in a grumpy mood.

"Wanchu looks ragged," he grunted, holding her to his broad chest. "What you been doing to my girl, ya silly sheila? Dragging 'er around to the telly, I hear."

The moan of a didgeridoo floated through the surrounding eucalyptus trees. In the next enclosure, I could hear the wallabies sounding off. Were they mimicking their keeper?

"Nice to see you, too, Bill."

He grunted again—yes, he sounded just like the wallabies—but when Wanchu nuzzled him, it chased away his frown. "And what's this about another murder down at the 'arbor?"

My explanation brought his frown back. "Crikey. Gunn Landing's gettin' too rough for this old Aussie. Soon's everything's cleared up and I get me passport back, I'm scarpering off to Sydney. You Yanks got no sense, killin' folks all the time when you could be settlin' yer differences with a good bar fight." If Bill left, Robin would be heartbroken. Did he know how deeply she felt about him? Resisting the urge to play Cupid—Caro had shown me how irritating that game could be—I simply invited him to Caro's party as a way of celebrating his release from jail.

At first, he didn't sound interested. "I'm not one for them fancy American cocktails."

"There'll be all the free beer and hard liquor you can drink. You can bring a date, too." Being with Bill again might soothe Robin's temper.

He reconsidered. "Then mebbe I'll stop by. Like you said, to celebrate."

Just the thought of Outback Bill hefting a few brews under Caro's prim roof made me smile, so I gave him directions to Caro's house, then I started on my afternoon rounds. Although Zorah had told me Robin was already taking care of Lucy, I headed for the giant anteater enclosure anyway. No day was complete without a visit to my sweet girl and Baby Boy Anteater, now known as Little Ricky.

As luck would have it, Robin was sweeping up the

enclosure while Lucy and Little Ricky watched through the holding pen gate. Perhaps it was wishful thinking, but I would have sworn that Lucy looked happy to see me. Robin wasn't.

"Look what the cat dragged in," she sniped. "Miss Goody Two Shoes finished with her road trip?"

"Bill's back," I said, hoping that the mere mention of his name would get her mind off me.

It didn't. "No thanks to you."

"Have you talked to him lately?" He might not have had a chance to call her about the party.

"None of your business." But her red eyes gave her away. Bill had talked to her, all right, and she hadn't liked what she'd heard. So much for my attempt at calming troubled waters. I couldn't blame her rudeness. As a woman who sometimes has love troubles of her own, I experienced a surge of sympathy.

"Sorry, I didn't mean to pry. Anyway, Zorah rearranged my schedule, so starting tomorrow, I'll resume full care of Lucy. In the meantime, I hope to see you at my party tonight. Lots of people from the zoo will show. Buster, Lex…"

"Hmph."

"Bill will be there, too."

"Tell me why I should care." With that, she resumed sweeping up giant anteater feces.

SIXTEEN

YOU KNOW WHAT they say: time flies when you're having fun, so the rest of the day sped by. By seven-thirty, I was back at Caro's, primped to the nines and acting as greeter at her "little" do. More than twenty Old Town aristocrats had already arrived. If there's anything the rich love more than tax loopholes, it's free booze. Among them were George Baffin, the former action star-turned-Old Town mayor, in attendance with his second, thirty-years-younger wife; Magda L'Entrado, the former soap star and Baffin's wife no. 1, shooting eye-daggers at her replacement; and U.S. Senator Harrison Hedley Grainger, who—as rumor had it—was on the verge of resignation following an unseemly public bathroom incident at an airport in Atlanta. Rumor also had it that the "complicated" domestic, which had interrupted my zoo date with Joe and his kids, resulted from the senator's confession to his wife.

All in all, it was a typical Old Town party.

Stomach growling because I hadn't eaten yet, I stood next to the rent-a-butler, murmuring welcomes as servers rushed about refilling champagne glasses and topping off the harder stuff for those so inclined. Me, I was drinking organic orange juice from a champagne glass, hoping the pulp would help fill the pit in my stomach until I could make a dash for the food table.

One of the first to arrive was a relatively sober Mrs. Gwendolyn Wexford-Smythe. "Theodora, you look like a tart," she said, eyeing the scarlet Valentino dress Caro had insisted I wear.

"Why thank you, ma'am. That's what Mother was aiming for, so it's nice to know she hit the bull's eye."

The corner of her mouth lifted in a sneer. "With that low cut Valentino *she's* wearing, she doesn't look very ladylike herself. Then again, she never does, does she?" Before I could reply, she bypassed the food table and headed straight for the open bar.

The air was redolent with the scents of Glenlivet, smoked salmon, and outrageously expensive perfume. To add to the evening's smarmy ambience, the string quartet from San Sebastian Community College was playing Andrew Lloyd Webber show tunes intermixed with Strauss and Debussy. Given the political beliefs of the crowd, I thought a few John Phillips Souza marches might be more appropriate, but Caro had demanded a romantic play list.

Just before eight, Aster Edwina Gunn herself arrived, looking eager. She'd never found a week satisfying until she and Caro had traded barbs. "Caroline is up to her old tricks again, I see," she sniffed at me. "That dress of yours is decidedly whorish."

"I'll tell her you said so."

"Don't bother, Theodora. I'll tell her myself." Off she went. By eight-fifteen, the party took on some life, at least as far as I was concerned. Arriving en masse was the first wave of my own invites: Zorah Vega, looking managerial; Buster Daltry, smelling faintly of rhino; Jack Spence, wearing a Pooh Bear tie; Robin Chase, looking surly; and Lex Yarnell, who immediately began scanning the crowd for unchaperoned women. All were dressed in their slickest civvies. Give or take a scattering of scratches and bite marks, they looked as respectable as the Old Town residents.

Right behind them, but arriving separately, was Outback

Bill, in his zoo uniform. No problem there, since it was relatively clean, but I was appalled to see him hand-in-hand with beautiful Myra Sebrowski. Did the man have no sense at all? As the couple approached the bar, Robin, hovering over the hors d'oeures table, pretended not to see them.

Hard on the zoo staff's heels came my favorite harbor residents: Linda Cushing, doing her best to hide her grief over Heck; firefighter Walt MacAdams, serving as her escort; Larry DuFries, less blustery than usual; and Harbormaster MaryBeth O'Reilly. Bringing up the rear were Doris and Sam Grimaldi, the hosts for tomorrow's Bowling for Rhinos.

As I waved the mob toward the bar, Caro hurried over, bristling with outrage. "Who are all those people and what are they doing at my party?" she hissed.

I hissed back, "It's *our* party, so I used the occasion to invite a few guests of my own. Joe might show up, too. If you want me to play nice with Ford, whom I notice isn't even here yet, you'll play nice with my friends."

"This will cost me a small fortune! Don't you realize that the recession has…" The outrage on her face suddenly transformed into bliss, and I didn't need to turn around to know who had just entered the room.

The guest of honor, Ford Bronson. Caro's prospective son-in-law.

Since I liked the man despite her fixation on him, I bid him a warm welcome. "Look how popular you are," I said, gesturing at the crowded living room.

"Hmmm. If they're here to see me, why are they swarming the bar?"

I glanced at my nonexistent watch. "Because it's eight-thirty. Here, let's get you a drink, then I'll introduce you to my friends. Every one of them would make great fodder for a television interview."

"Are you talking about the zookeepers or the townies?"

Caro broke in, "She means our wonderful Old Town residents, of course. Don't you, Theodora?"

"No, I don't. At some time in the future, we're going to run out of exotic animals to feature on *Good Morning, San Sebastian,* so what better way to fill the gap than with their keepers? For starters, Buster Daltry, the guy with the Heineken, he starts the day by sanding the rhinos' horns. And those horns, by the way, are made from…"

"A hairlike substance," he finished. "I do watch your segment, Teddy."

As he smiled at me, white teeth gleaming, graying hair as sleek as a seal's coat, Caro looked so delighted I was afraid she'd pee herself. "Well, I'll leave you two alone now and see to my other guests," she said, then tottered off on her five-inch Gallianos.

"Your mother is a force of nature," Bronson said, hooking his arm around mine as we walked toward the bar.

"That's one way of putting it."

He smiled down at me—did I mention he was six-foot-two? "You don't approve of her."

"Let's just say we tend to disagree when discussing what I should do with my life. She wants me to marry and settle down, but I'm content to work at the zoo."

"And live on a houseboat."

Oh, dear. He had been checking up on me. "The *Merilee*'s not a true houseboat. She's a converted CHB trawler."

"I have a boat, too."

At that, I had to laugh. "You call that enormous Okell yacht down at the harbor a *boat*? What is it, a hundred feet long? It's bigger than some people's homes! How in the world do you steer that thing?"

"It's less than eighty feet, actually, and I seldom 'steer' it, because the crew takes care of that. Didn't your mother tell you? My, my, she must be slipping." He grinned to take the sting out of his comment.

I was beginning to smell a rat. "How much do you know about my mother?"

He began to count off on his fingers. "Born a Piper, crowned Miss San Sebastian, married several times—the first to your rascal of a father, whom I suspect she continues to love—and despite the Feds that are always breathing down her neck, she appears to have unlimited cash reserves. Off-shore accounts, perhaps? What I find most fascinating about your mother is how determined she is to snag a rich man for her daughter, who just happens to be dating the county sheriff." He leaned closer and leered comically, wagging his eyebrows up and down like a melodrama villain. "I love your red dress, by the way. Your mother has good taste."

Despite my shock, I had to laugh. "Did you hire a private detective to check us out?"

"Unnecessary. Besides owning several television stations, I own newspapers, too, and it's truly amazing some of the things they print. Beauty contest results. Marriage announcements. Crime reports. All digitized, on line, and accessible to anyone's prying eyes."

Had he subjected Isabel Van Stoeller to the same sort of scrutiny? Not that it mattered anymore, since Izzy had run off with her polo player. "I can't keep any secrets from you, then, can I?"

"You don't need to. I already find you delightful."

The crowd at the bar parted as we approached, and after we'd been handed flutes of champagne, I led him toward the hors d'oeuvres. During all that time, he kept commenting on my various charms. My hair, my eyes, my freckles, my well-developed biceps.

"From hauling around hay at the zoo," I explained.

"They're still nice," he said, helping himself to some caper-sprinkled smoked salmon.

As much as I loved Joe, it was a pleasure having such a handsome man take an interest in me. Bronson was a self-made man who had worked hard for his money, not a lay-about lout like Jason Jackman McIlhenny Forbes IV. Then, as if the mere thought of Joe had made him materialize, I saw him heading straight for me, dressed in a dark suit I'd never seen before. The room fell silent. Everyone there knew the reason for the party, and the fact that the sheriff had taken such trouble with his wardrobe meant that they might—just might—be treated to a jealous outburst. Or even better, that Outback Bill might take a poke at the man who'd jailed him.

"Hi, Joe," I said.

"Good evening, Teddy. You're looking, ah, interesting tonight. Good evening to you, too, Mr. Bronson."

"Call me Ford. All my friends do." A smile.

"So, Mr. Bronson, how are you finding the party?"

No smile. "Everything's delicious."

Somehow I didn't think Bronson was talking about the smoked salmon. Deciding that I didn't want to be in the middle of a brawl, I grabbed Joe by the arm and led him into a quiet corner far away from either Bronson or Bill. "Do you have to act so bullish?"

I'd swear I could see steam coming out of his ears. "He was putting the moves on my girl. And what the hell are you wearing a dress like that for? Do you know what it makes you look like?"

"A tart. Mrs. Wexford-Smythe already told me. You look good, too, in that new suit."

That stopped him. "I do?"

"Good enough to get you somewhere alone so I can…"

"Theodora Esmeralda Iona Bentley!" Caro bore down upon us.

I gave her a big smile. "Joe was just telling me what a lovely party this is, weren't you, Joe?"

"If you say so."

Caro drew herself up in a belated attempt at dignity. "While I'm happy that you are enjoying my party, Sheriff, we can't have Theodora neglecting the guest of honor, now, can we?"

"The hell we can't," he muttered, just loud enough for me to hear.

"I'm happy you agree, so I'm going to march her right back over there. In the meantime, if you must stay, why not mingle? There must be someone here who enjoys tales of cops and robbers. Theodora's friends from the zoo, for instance. Or those—what are those people called?—*live-aboarders* down at the harbor."

With a studiedly blank face, Joe said, "I was just about to get myself a ginger ale. Talk to you later, Teddy." When he made a beeline for the bar, only Caro's grip on my arm prevented me from following.

Bronson's eyes danced with mischief when Caro hauled me back to him. "Ah, the lovely lady of the manor returns with her dutiful daughter."

"I know you'll take good care of her, Ford," she cooed. Her voice took on a grittier tone when she said to me, "Don't you dare leave his side, you naughty girl. Trying to make our guest of honor jealous like that!"

This time Bronson laughed outright. "Girls will be girls, won't they, Mrs. Petersen?" Then he winked at me.

He obviously understood my situation, so I winked back. Caro noticed, but ever hopeful, misinterpreted the exchange.

"Well, how nice! I'll leave you two love birds alone now."

Throwing a triumphant smirk at Joe, she sailed off into the crowd.

"She's rather obvious, isn't she?" Bronson chuckled.

"Unfortunately, yes."

Under Joe's watchful eye we chatted until Mrs. Wexford-Smythe, herself the mother of a divorced daughter, spotted the guest of honor and headed his way.

"Buckle up your chastity belt," I warned. "She's worse than Caro."

Upon reaching us, Mrs. Wexford-Smythe immediately began to extol the charms of her daughter, whom I knew to be a spoiled college dropout who, ten years later, remained unemployed because she was trying to "find herself." Zoning her out, I began to pay more attention to the conversations around me.

To my right, Aster Edwina loudly congratulated herself on quadrupling the Bowling for Rhinos raffle ticket sales in a single day. "By the time of the drawing I wouldn't be surprised if sales jumped to the high five figures."

"That all-inclusive African safari for two is quite a draw," the Mayor said. "Did you by any chance bring any tickets along, Aster Edwina? I'd like to try my luck."

When Aster Edwina said that she, by chance, just happened to have an entire roll of tickets, several hands delved into pockets and handbags, Senator Harrison Hedley Grainger's among them. After all, he was going to have a lot of free time in the future.

Behind me and just in front of the hors d'oeuvre table, Zorah was telling the zoo staff about an upcoming memorial for Kate. "We'll have it at the zoo, but the actual intern-ment will take place in Oakland, not far from her father's nursing home. Teddy drove up there this morning and vis-ited with him. Apparently he didn't make much sense—

Alzheimer's, you know—but at least she was able to come away with some papers Kate left there."

A collective murmur of sympathy spread through the group. On the opposite side of the table, several denizens of Gunn Landing Harbor were huddled together. They were also talking about death, but the subject this time was Heck, not Kate. "Why did I let him stay by himself that night?" Linda moaned to the Grimaldis. "I knew something wasn't right."

"I don't understand," said Doris Grimaldi.

"Don't you remember what Heck said about Kate's father? That Tyler…"

Suddenly a woman's strident voice pierced the air. "Why, you *bitch*!"

The string quartet stopped in the middle of "Memory."

I turned to see Robin Chase, her face swollen with anger, push Myra Sebrowski. Myra pushed back. Robin lost her footing and fell onto the hors d'oeuvres table. Caviar splattered, and capers rolled. As Robin tried to struggle to her feet, she clutched at the front of Myra's dress, pulling her down on top of her. With that, the fight was on.

Zookeepers don't fight like most women. Instead of such relatively harmless endeavors as scratching, biting, and pulling hair, they slug. Myra landed a hard right to Robin's cheek. Robin retaliated with an uppercut to Myra's jaw. Both then punched each other in the nose. Myra's aim proved superior to Robin's, because blood spurted at the moment of contact.

The blood flow didn't slow Robin down. As the two rolled around on blood-spattered paté de foie gras, she gouged at Myra's eyes, yelling, "I told you to stay away from him!"

The table, never designed to hold both a full spread of hors d'oeuvres and two full-grown, fighting females at the same time, gave a sharp crack and collapsed onto the floor. Prosciutto-wrapped figs and crab bruschetta flew everywhere.

The entire room, silenced at the first curse, erupted into shrieks and shouts.

"Stop them!"

"They're killing each other!"

"Somebody call 9-1-1!"

"My beautiful table!"

"Is this great or what?"

Joe, Bill, Bronson and I reached the struggling women at the same time. Pushing me aside, Bill leaned over and hauled Myra up by the hair, tearing her away from a death grip on Robin's neck. "What ya think yer playin' at, ya silly sheila?"

Hearing the contempt in Bill's voice, all the fight went out of Myra and she began to cry.

Joe helped Robin up a bit more gently and passed her over to me. "Hang onto her and don't let her anywhere near that other one. I have to call this in."

Robin, as stunned as Myra, began to weep, too. "Dy node. I dink id droden."

As Joe reached for his cell, Caro rushed toward him. "No, you don't! I absolutely forbid it!"

"You can forbid all you want, Mrs. Petersen, but I'm getting a squad car and an ambulance down here right away. Ms. Chase needs medical attention."

"You can't…"

"Shut up."

Caro's jaw dropped in shock. "How dare you speak to me like that, Sheriff!"

"That's my title, all right, and you'd be wise to remember it." With that, he turned to Myra and informed her that she was under arrest.

"But she hit me first!" Myra blubbered. Her pretty pink dress was smeared with food.

"That was a shove, not a hit. But if it makes you feel any better, I'll be arresting Ms. Chase, too. Just as soon as she's released from the hospital."

At the sound of Myra's voice, Robin began to struggle in my arms. Since she was covered in caviar, capers, and curried eggs, some of it rubbed off on my red Valentino. Oh, well. I hadn't liked the thing anyway.

"Hold still, Robin," I said, looping one arm around her waist and the other around her neck, the standard hold for a recalcitrant howler monkey. "If you bump your nose, you'll just make it worse."

"Da ditch dook Dill daday dud de," she said, which I translated as *The bitch took Bill away from me.*

Deciding that even the sight of Myra would serve to keep Robin infuriated, I frog-marched her down the hall into the powder room and leaned her against the sink. "Breathe through your mouth. I'm going to clean you up."

Robin gave me a wild-eyed look. "Dutch dy node ad I dit doo!"

"Hit me and I'll hit you back. On your nose."

The threat, which I would never have carried out, settled her down enough for me to wash the blood and food off her face. It would not only make things easier for the Emergency Room physician, but would also return some of the dignity she'd lost in the brawl. Despite the tension between us, I recognized real heartache in Robin's eyes, and I knew from my own experience how deeply it hurt to be passed over for another woman.

"He's not worth it," I told her, the standard comfort on such occasions, but which in this case, had the added benefit of being true.

"Id too."

"Id not."

She stared at me for a moment, then managed a weak grin. "Doan do dock de."

"I'm not mocking you, Robin, I'm sympathizing." After giving her face a final pat with the washrag, I blotted her dry with a guest towel. "Bill doesn't have it in him to be faithful to anyone. Before you, there was Kate. After Myra, there'll be someone else. And another, and another, etcetera."

She sniffed. "Den Id ad ass."

"When it comes to love, we're all asses. Now, can I trust you to go back out there without trying to kill anyone?"

"Des."

"Promise?"

"Dodise."

My arm around her more for moral support than anything, we exited the powder room just as the ambulance arrived, trailed by a squad car. I handed Robin over to the EMTs. She gave me a grateful wave as they trundled her off on a stretcher.

The next group to leave was a handcuffed but struggling Myra Sebrowski, two deputies, and my boyfriend, looking official.

He didn't wave goodbye.

SEVENTEEN

I WAS LOADING up Caro's dishwasher when an early morning phone call from Zorah informed me that while both Robin and Myra had been released on their own recognizance, Robin's broken nose meant that she wouldn't make it to the zoo until noon, and even then, wouldn't be feeding the big cats.

"No point in letting the cats smell human blood and get ideas," she said. "She'll be working with the hoof stock for a couple of days. In the meantime, you're taking over the ocelots."

"Who's getting the other cats?" I asked.

"Myra gets the lions, and if one of them eats her, that's fine with me. Bill's taking the rest of the cats, which means you're back on Down Under duty."

I almost cheered, then remembering Caro's black mood—she was sitting across from me at the breakfast table reading the account of last night's party on the Mean Streets page of the *San Sebastian Gazette*—kept my glee to myself. "I'll get to them as soon as I finish with the giant anteaters."

"Teddy?" Zorah sounded hesitant.

"What?"

"Uh, considering the circumstances, should I send your mother a thank-you note? You know, for the party?"

I glanced at Caro, who after putting the newspaper down, looked as if she was planning a murder: mine. "It wouldn't hurt."

"First your father, now you," Caro said, as soon as I hung up. "I'm getting tired of this family being mentioned in the crime reports. By the way, I'm billing you for the damage."

"Of course you are."

She shook the paper at me. "Your friends are hooligans!"

"Unlike Senator Grainger, for example?"

"At least he didn't create a scene in public."

"He might, once the Ethics Committee gets through with him."

"Theodora, the very least you could do is help me finish cleaning up. Since Grizelda worked so hard setting up for the party, I gave her the day off. But…" She motioned toward the wreckage in the other room. "Even though I just called and humiliated myself by begging her to help out, she turned me down flat, saying something about taking her grandchildren to the zoo. As if that could be more important than this."

Good for Grizelda. "Unfortunately, I'm expected at work within the hour. You can forget this evening, too, because I'm pulling registration duty at Bowling for Rhinos. Tell you what. Considering the fact that two of my coworkers started the fight, I do feel a bit responsible, so I'll foot the bill for Maids R Us." At Caro's continued glare, I added, "Oh, all right, I'll pay for the table's repairs, too. By the way, before Ford Bronson left last night, he told me he couldn't remember a more fun party. He meant it, too."

With her mood considerably brightened, I left.

It being a warm, sunny Saturday afternoon, the zoo was crowded. Families wandered by the various enclosures, fascinated by some animals, bored by others. Observers were three deep at Lucy and Little Ricky's enclosure. Baby Boy Anteater showed promise at matching Lucy's stardom when he lifted his snout and snaked out his long tongue toward the crowd, making them ooh and aah. The ocelots were strutting their stuff, too. Smaller than leopards, yet every bit as wild, the mated pair prowled the perimeter of their enclosure, snarling and snapping at one another like an old married couple.

By ten o'clock I'd worked my way to Down Under, where Wanchu and Nyee were both sleeping the sleep of the innocent.

Neither looked up when I tied fresh eucalyptus browse to their trees. Like the koalas, the wallabies were napping, too, although Abim did rouse himself enough to hop over, possibly in hopes I would sing a few stanzas of "Waltzing Matilda." Being a pushover for big brown eyes, I indulged him.

I had just finished the first chorus when he gave a start at some noise and fled. Looking back over my shoulder, I saw Robin's zoo cart headed toward us. She was such a fearsome sight with her two black eyes and nose splint that I was tempted to flee, too, but once she braked, she lifted both hands in the universal sign of harmlessness.

"Thank you for taking care of me last night," she said, her voice trembling. "I can't apologize enough for my behavior."

Anxious to smoke the peace pipe myself, I exited the enclosure and walked up to her cart. "These things happen at parties." But rarely at Old Town's parties.

Sniffling, she handed me an envelope. "What's this?" I asked.

"Some money toward the furniture repair bill. I'll give you more as soon as I get paid."

Knowing how little zookeepers make and how much the banquet table would cost to fix, I gave the envelope back. "In case you didn't notice, Robin, my mother's loaded, and fixing the table won't put so much as a blip in her budget."

I'd already promised to pay for the table myself, but didn't tell Robin.

"Are you sure, Teddy?"

"Absolutely."

"I sent your mother a note of apology this morning. Do you think I should call her, too?"

"The letter will be enough. After all, you weren't the only person involved in that brawl."

"I'm used to paying for my mistakes, Teddy."

Taking note of the tears in her eyes, I gave her a squeeze on the shoulder. "You already have."

We chatted for a few more minutes, and I confirmed that she planned to attend Bowling for Rhinos that evening. Before driving away, she said, "What you told me last night? You're right. He's not worth it."

Not long afterward, I saw Myra as I was driving by the mountain gorilla enclosure. She only had one black eye. I slowed and waved, but she didn't wave back. Nor did she attempt an apology for last night's behavior.

At the end of the day, after I had fed the squirrel monkeys and returned them to the Monkey Mania night house, I went in search of Bill. I found him cuddling Wanchu, who was the only female he's ever remained faithful to.

When he saw me, his face curved into a sneer. "Well, if it isn't Little Miss Heiress. Here to hobnob with us commoners?"

I refused to take the bait. "Are you going to be at Bowling for Rhinos tonight?"

"Yeh. I'm going to show you Yanks what's what, rub your uppity noses in the dirt."

That set me back. "You bowl?"

Now it was his nose that poked up in the air. "Been a dab hand at tenpins since I was a kid. Yer looking at the winner of the 2006 Gold at Joondalup and the 2008 Melbourne Silver. Gonna win me that trip to Africa."

"Bill, that prize is for the winner of the raffle, not the bowler with the highest score."

His face clouded. "You sure about that?"

"Aster Edwina was very clear that the trip would be the Grand Prize for the raffle. But all zoo employees and volunteers who registered for Bowling for Rhinos will receive one raffle ticket when they sign in. You can buy extras if you want. Two for a buck, twelve for five dollars."

He exploded into curses, which disturbed Wanchu enough to give him a leery look.

"There, there, little sheila," he cooed to her with lowered voice, but his words to me remained harsh. "You bloody cheatin' Yanks! Yer all like that, stealin' a man's chance ever time he turns around. Lockin' him up for nothin'…"

Considering how hard we'd all worked to get him out of jail, his ingratitude annoyed me enough to indulge in a minitantrum of my own. "If you'd cooperated with the police in the first place, you probably wouldn't have been arrested! But no, you had to pull the I'm-Not-Talking-to-the-Cops routine, which—considering that you were seen near the harbor at the same time Kate was killed—made you look guilty as hell. So don't give me that 'locking you up for nothing' crap!"

I expected more vitriol in response to my outburst, but it had an unexpected effect on him. "Ah, Teddy, now look what I've gone and done. I've made ya sound just like that hellion Kate." The roughness of his words contrasted with his suddenly sad expression.

My anger fled. "I'm sorry, I didn't mean to…"

He waved my apology away. "Not yer fault. Was me out of line. Want to know why I wasn't sayin' naught to the sheriff? That court-appointed attorney *told* me to keep me trap shut. But I wasn't all that bumblin' anxious to fess up, anyways. Hell, I'd been callin' Kate for hours that night, tryin' to get her to pick up the phone, wantin' to crack onto her."

"Crack?" That was a new one to me. Did he mean *hit*?

He rolled his eyes. "Put the moves on, ya dumb sheila! Anyways, instead of waitin' around anymore, I biked down to the harbor intendin' to beg her to take me back—yes, *beg* the bitch—but when I got there, it's like I said, she was prancin' around on that damned *Gutterball*, and I never saw her again. Yer satisfied now?"

The idea that Bill would beg anyone for anything—especially for a woman to take him back—rattled me. "You told me you were the one who'd dumped Kate."

His shoulders slumped enough that Wanchu had to scramble to keep her hold. "Was the other way around, Teddy. Kate musta tired of me Aussie charms 'cause she was movin' on, most likely to that pretty-boy park ranger, Lex what's-his-face."

"Lex Yarnell?"

"Yeh. Him."

This surprised me, because Lex had always appeared more interested in Myra Sebrowski than in Kate. "When did she tell you this?"

"Couple weeks before she died. Without a by-your-leave she turned up at the Amiable Avocado when I was slaggin' 'round behind the bar and told me it was over, that she had other fish to fry."

"Those were the words she used, 'other fish to fry'?"

"Yeh."

"Did she actually use Lex's name?"

"Nah."

"What else did she say?"

"Nothin'. That was it. And I was at work, right? I

couldn't hang around grassin' with her, so I went off to deliver some idiot's mojito."

There had to have been more to the conversation, because a woman doesn't normally walk into a bar and deliver a Dear John without any explanation. "Didn't you ask Kate to explain what she meant by that 'other fish to fry' remark? Maybe she wasn't talking about leaving you for another man. Maybe it was something else."

He gave me an incredulous look. "Are yez daft, Teddy? Damn bar was swarmin' with blokes orderin' fancy drinks with fruit and such like. Think I'm gonna start mewlin' and whinin', tryin' to get me woman back front of 'em? Hell, after she hit me with the bad news, I kept meself down at the other end of the bar 'til she took off, like any self-respecting Aussie would do."

In other words, he'd hidden his hurt feelings under a steaming heap of, well, false pride. What idiots men could be. But considering everything Bill had undergone the past two weeks, I kept the observation to myself. After making a few sympathetic comments, I left him to Wanchu's less judgmental company.

As I PULLED into the parking lot at Lucky Lanes, I was startled to find it already three-quarters full even though the doors wouldn't open for another thirty minutes. Anticipating the rush, Zorah had sent her executive assistant over to take care of last-minute sales, which was a good thing because the line of eager ticket-buyers snaked halfway around the building. Helen, Zorah's assistant, sat at a canopied table in front of the entrance, dressed for the occasion in a leopard-print blouse, matching leopard-print hat, and a zebra-striped pair of leggings that added twenty-pounds to her already robust figure. She was having the time of her life.

Seeing me approach with my arms full of Bowling for

Rhinos registration materials, Sam Grimaldi unlocked the double doors and let me in. The only other time I had visited Lucky Lanes, which was to finalize the Bowling for Rhinos arrangements, I'd heard balls striking pins, cheers of triumph, and a sound system playing a combination of rap hits and golden oldies. The place seemed eerily quiet now, but from the scent of hot cooking oil that wafted to me over the smell of rosin and polished hardwood, the chefs were already busy deep-frying the vitamins out of potatoes and zucchini.

Locking the doors behind me, Sam led me past a shoulder-high inflated rhino—it had a lei hanging around its neck—to the sign-in table. He then disappeared into the office. Before he closed the door, I saw a flashy young blonde sitting on the office sofa with her skirt hiked up to the equator.

What gall, flouting his playmate more or less under Doris's nose! I fumed for a bit, then something Sam had said—or almost said—flashed through my mind. Right after Kate had been murdered, I'd talked to him and his wife on board the *Gutterball*. He had said something about Kate being "sweet," then added, "Every time I…" At that point, Doris had cut him off. Had Sam been involved with Kate? If so, how much had Doris minded? She was a big, strong-looking woman, and… Buster's voice interrupted my dark musings.

"Welcome to Bowling for Rhinos, ma'am," he cracked, taking the cartons and putting them down on a table next to a WIN AN AFRICAN SAFARI! poster. His lumpy face was alight with smiles. Of all the zoo's many fundraisers, this one was closest to the rhino keeper's heart.

"My, my, aren't you the early bird," I said.

Crooked teeth flashed. "The girls were more than happy to go into their night house. 'Course, that might have had something to do with the new shipment of alfalfa hay the suppliers brought in this afternoon. Usually I have to coax them to leave their enclosure, but Notch and Half-Ear both love alfalfa, and when I put several flakes in their mangers, they almost knocked each other over in their hurry to go in. I was out of the zoo by six and drove straight here. Don't worry, I showered first!"

We spent the next half-hour arranging various door prizes and raffle gifts on the long tables: a necklace with tiny rhinos a-dangle; a bright watercolor executed by Indu, our painting elephant; a glass snow globe with two rhinos inside; a pink plush rhino; a ceramic tiger; an autographed copy of Jack Hanna's *Monkeys on the Interstate*; a plethora of gift certificates from local businesses; and a year's pass for four to the Gunn Zoo. After these prizes were awarded, the winning tickets would be put back in the raffle hopper so that everyone would have the chance at the African safari.

"Ticket sales will continue until half an hour before the drawing, won't they?" Buster asked.

"They'd better, or there'll be a riot. You should see the crowd outside."

Buster looked around at the jammed prize tables, then rearranged them so that the evening's trophies were more visible. The design for Best Male Bowler, Best Female Bowler, and Best Bowling Team had been Buster's creation: bronze-covered rhino turds the size and shape of a softball, elegantly mounted on teakwood stands.

"Beautiful," I sighed, knowing that with my poor bowling skills, this was as close as I'd ever come to one.

A clamor at the front of the alley made me look up. Sam Grimaldi had just opened the doors and people were thronging in, led by eager members of the zoo staff.

"Let the games begin," Buster said.

The first to arrive was Bill, his arm around a smug Myra Sebrowski. Next came Monkey Mania volunteer and part-time television aide Bernice Unser. Following close behind were our married zookeepers: Haylie Hewitt, desert tortoises; and her husband Mark, black-footed ferrets. Behind them came Robin Chase, nose splint, black eyes and all.

"You bowl?" I asked Robin, as she signed in.

"More or less. And more less than more, if you understand what I mean." She bought ten extra raffle tickets, explaining, "Considering how little I make, winning the raffle is the only way I'll ever make it to Africa to see cheetahs in the wild."

I wished her luck.

For the better part of an hour, as Lucky Lanes came alive with the sound of crashing bowling pins, curses, and cheers, I manned the registration table. After paying the $35 registration fee, each Bowling for Rhinos participant received a canvas tote bag filled with coupons, pens, one free raffle ticket, and a gold tee shirt showing a rhino knocking down bowling pins, with the legend, BOWL LIKE A MUTHA FOR DA RHINO!

Midway through registration Aster Edwina arrived with Caleb, her chauffeur, a stoop-backed man who didn't look much younger than she. Having donated the evening's big prize, she would choose the winning ticket. She grandly paid her registration fee and demanded three extra totes for Caleb's grandchildren. Knowing which side the zoo's bread was buttered on, I handed them over without argument.

"How is Caro doing after last night's fiasco, Theodora?" she asked, passing the totes to the chauffeur.

"She'll survive."

"It was a shame about that table, especially since I hear

it belonged to one of the Romanovs." The malicious smile on her face revealed that she didn't think it was a shame.

"I'm having it fixed. At my own expense."

The smile disappeared. "That will cost you a pretty penny. Can you afford it without dipping into that hush-hush offshore account your father set up?"

"You know I don't use that money, Aster Edwina." To keep her from needling me some more, I added, "We all appreciate everything you've done for Bowling for Rhinos, but please move along. You're holding up the line."

Gratified at having annoyed me, she patted my cheek and moved off. Out of the corner of my eye, I saw Caleb settle her into a reserved booth near the drinks window so that she could sip cheap wine from a plastic glass while missing none of the action.

The registration continued with no more unpleasantness. Most of my harbor friends showed up: Linda Cushing, looking a little less grief-stricken than she had at Caro's party; firefighter Walt MacAdams, with his latest girlfriend; harbormaster MaryBeth O'Reilly, who bought several extra raffle tickets; and *Texas Hold 'Em*'s owner, Larry DuFries, who slipped his tee over his shirt even before he stepped away from the registration table.

Also present were Mayor George Baffin, followed by Senator Harrison Hedley Grainger, attempting to curry popular support before the Ethics Committee began its public castration process. Mrs. Wexford-Smythe even showed, and purchased one hundred extra raffle tickets.

"I've always wanted to see Africa, and winning would certainly be a cheap way to do it," she explained.

Just before the registration closed, Josie/Speaks-to-Souls and her daughter Alyse walked in. Alarmed, I gave a quick glance at the drinks booths, and was somewhat comforted to see Aster Edwina deep in conversation with

Sam Grimaldi. To give Josie fair warning, and to keep her from wasting her registration fee, I whispered, "Aster Edwina is here!"

"Here's a twenty for extra raffle tickets," Josie said. She looked serene, as if the thought of publicly confronting the mother who'd given her away at birth didn't disturb her. Being raised in New York inured one to shock, I guess.

On the off-chance that she hadn't heard me, I delivered my warning again, this time in a normal voice. "Aster Edwina is sitting right over there by the drinks window."

This time there was no doubt that she heard me. "Isn't it nice to run into family? Thank you for letting me know where the drinks are." She turned to her daughter. "I'm dying for a Budweiser. How about you?"

"Parched." Alyse's eyes danced with mischief.

At my disapproving frown, Josie added, "Like myself, Alyse is older than she looks. Twenty-two, as a matter of fact. Come, dear." Hooking her arm around her daughter's, Josie headed straight for the drinks window.

When they neared Aster Edwina's table, I held my breath. At first it looked as if the two might pass by without her noticing, because Sam Grimaldi was still talking to her. Unfortunately, he moved off just as Josie and Alyse arrived alongside the table.

Aster Edwina gave the two an idle glance and began to say something to her chauffeur. Then she stopped, her mouth open.

The color drained from her face.

Josie smiled and leaned over the table. I'm no lip-reader, but I'd swear she said, "Hello, Mother."

The plastic wine glass Aster Edwina had been holding dropped from her hand and rolled across the carpet. When Caleb leaned over to pick it up, she grabbed him by the shoulder and whispered into his ear. Nodding, he helped her out of the booth, and with a spindly yet protective arm around her waist, ushered her out the door.

She never looked back.

Registration closed at eight, just after Zorah came in from the parking lot, staggering under the weight of the hopper that held the bulk of the raffle tickets. I added my collection, then helped her carry the hopper over to the proper table. Official duties done for the evening, I walked over to the lanes to find out whom I would be bowling with. To my chagrin, I'd been paired at lane thirty-nine with Myra Zebrowski, who had never apologized for her behavior at Caro's party.

"Hope you can bowl better than the loser I was paired with last year," she said.

"Which loser was that?" I asked, choosing a bright orange bowling ball that matched the color of my hair.

"Robin."

I resisted the temptation to drop my bowling ball on her head. "Then you're out of luck. I've only bowled once in my life, and that was one game when I was fourteen. If I remember correctly, my score was somewhere in the low fifties."

"Then that's two years in a row I have a snowball's chance in hell to get the Best Team trophy. Why couldn't you have done everyone a favor and stayed home?"

Women like Myra irk me to no end. In front of men they act all sweetness and light, but with women—who exist for them as nothing more than competitors—they set free their Inner Bitch.

I refused to rise to the bait. "You go first. Maybe I'll learn something."

"As if." With a sneer, she hefted her personal bowling ball and approached the lane. With a fluid motion, she sent the ball rolling straight down the alley. As it neared the pins, it hooked slightly to the left. Pins went flying until only one remained.

"Rats," she grumped.

I rose to take my turn but she ordered me to sit back down. "Oh, for Pete's sake. Don't you know *anything*? I get another chance."

"Sorry."

She picked off the last pin with ease. "*Now* it's your turn."

I did my best, but my pretty orange ball went straight into the gutter. The same thing happened on my second attempt.

"Jesus," Myra moaned.

"Sorry again."

The rest of the evening's four games—or were they called *sets*, as in tennis?—pretty much went the same. Myra knocked pins down, I left them standing. During the second game I saw Josie and her daughter take up position in the lane next to ours. I waved, but Josie appeared too distracted to notice. Her daughter waved back. From the number of pins they proceeded to knock down, I figured they were no strangers to bowling alleys.

Two lanes away, Bill bowled expertly with Buster. Further along, Jack Spence bowled with Robin Chase. They both looked like relative beginners, although neither approached my level of ineptness.

The event grew even more interesting during the third game, when Aster Edwina's chauffeur walked back into the bowling alley, handed a note to Josie, then left again. After a brief glance, Josie put it in her pocket, and resumed bowling. Her expression was so blank I couldn't guess at the note's content. A plea for forgiveness? A bribe? A demand to leave town? Deciding to mind my own business for a change, I resumed bowling.

"Last chance," Myra finally said, signaling that the night's humiliation was at end. "Try not to screw up again."

By then, my aim had shown improvement, and the orange ball knocked over two pins.

"My, my. Only eight to go," Myra sniped.

When the orange ball knocked down four more, I gave a loud cheer. Josie and Alyse applauded for me, as did Buster.

"Beer frame!" Buster shouted, and told the waitress to bring me a brew.

Myra was less enthusiastic. "Oh, wow. That brings your game score to forty-three."

Once I stopped jumping up and down in triumph, I asked, "What's yours?"

"Two sixty-five."

"That's good, isn't it?"

She stared at me in disbelief.

A few minutes later, the last ball had been bowled and Zorah, through a microphone, announced it was time to award the prizes.

You know how these things go. The smaller prizes were handed out first, starting with the Snuggie, which went to a delighted zoo volunteer. Park ranger Lex Yarnell won a year's free bowling at Lucky Lanes. After that came more gift certificates, the elephant's painting, various pieces of animal jewelry and statuary, and other animalesque odds and ends. As each prize was collected, the winner's ticket was put back into the raffle hopper. Then came time for the bowling awards.

"Best Male Bowler, with the high game score of two eighty-seven, goes to Outback Bill!" Zorah announced to cheers. "Step forward, Bill, and collect your very own rhino dung trophy!"

With a swagger, he did, but he made certain Zorah returned his ticket to the hopper.

"The next trophy, for Best Female Bowler, goes to Myra Sebrowski, with a high game score of two sixty-five!"

The cheers for Myra were nowhere as loud as those for Bill as she simpered up to claim her prize.

"The trophy for Best Bowling Team, with a combined high game score of five hundred and thirty, goes to the mother/daughter duo of, um, do I have this right? Ms. Josie Speaks-to-Souls and Ms. Alysa Speaks-to-Souls?"

"That's us!" Alysa whooped. "Gimme the dung!"

To a chorus of laughter, Alysa ran forward and clutched the rhino dung to her chest as if it were solid gold. When she returned to her mother, she received another award: a maternal kiss on the cheek.

While I was thinking about mothers and grandmothers, the microphone squawked. Zorah silenced it with a shake, then said, "That's not the end of the awards, folks! Tonight we're going to initiate two new trophies. The award for Most Successful Money-Grubber goes to Teddy Bentley, who—boasting several millionaires among her many acquaintances—raised in excess of $34,000 for Bowling for Rhinos! Teddy is the person who talked Aster Edwina into donating that wonderful African safari for two that we're all so excited about, a trip that accounted for raffle ticket sales throughout our great state of California. Because of Teddy's shameless money-grubbing, the Gunn Zoo will now be contributing more than $67,000 to the Lewa Wildlife Conservancy in Kenya. Let's hear it for Teddy!"

To a loud chorus of cheers, I rushed forth and scooped up my beautiful trophy. Rhino dung looks so nice when it's bronzed.

When the crowd settled down again, Zorah said, "The award for Most Successful *Non*millionaire Money-Grubber goes to rhino keeper Buster Daltry, who raised the sum of $12,257.56 by going from door to door throughout

San Sebastian County spreading the word to households, offices and schools about the rhinos' plight. And, I would like to add, he personally bought $100 worth of raffle tickets for himself."

"Way to go, Buster!" someone yelled, as the rhino keeper blushed. "Bet you're going to be living on peanut butter and jelly sandwiches for the next month!"

"Get up there and get your bronzed shit, mate," Bill ordered, giving his bowling partner a good-natured shove.

The cheers increased as Buster clomped his big feet forward to receive his trophy.

When the hysteria died down Zorah picked up two pencils and drummed them on the table in an inexpert but rousing take on "Ruffles and Flourishes."

Knowing what was coming next, the room fell quiet.

After stashing the pencils in her pocket, Zorah picked up the mike again. "Time to award the big prize we've all been waiting for, an all-expenses-paid, two-week African safari for two—*two* people, mind you—*two!* to Mother Africa, where two lucky people will gaze upon elephants, rhinos, giraffes, big cats and all the other wonderful animals that roam the veldt. Are you ready, folks?"

The loudest cheers of the evening erupted from the crowd. "All right. As you know, we'd planned for Aster Edwina to pick the winner, but an emergency came up and she needed to leave." The crowd *awwwed*.

"So I brought in a substitute. For this final best-of-all prize, and to assure you that there's no fishy business afoot, the long arm of the law will now reach into the hopper and pull the winning number."

To my delight, Joe emerged in full uniform from the back of the crowd and jostled his way to Zorah. At his appearance some people cheered again; a few others booed. I guess it all depended on how traumatic their experience with the long arm of the law had been. Since Joe looked so dangerous and sexy in his uniform, I delivered a wolf whistle. He winked back.

As Joe turned the crank on the hopper, Zorah used the pencils as drumsticks again.

"Turn! Turn! Turn!" shouted the crowd.

Joe kept turning and the crowd grew louder.

I had no horse in this race, myself. If I won, it would be disastrous public relations situation for the zoo, so I'd given my tickets to others. Joe, who had earlier purchased twenty tickets from me as I'd stopped by the police station on my way to Lucky Lanes, had done the same.

Some people were more deserving of good fortune than others. But Luck was a fickle lady, as was proven every time a divorce attorney won the Powerball.

"Pick it! Pick it! Pick it!" everyone screamed.

Experienced at crowd control and the riots that sometimes broke out when excited people lost their common sense, Joe stopped the roll mid-crank. The tickets slid to a heap at the bottom of the hopper. Turning his back, he reached behind him, fumbled the wire gate open, and after rustling through the tickets for a few more excruciating seconds, pulled one out.

Joe looked at the ticket for a second, then said, "Want to know the number?"

"Read it! Read it! Read it!"

He grinned, enjoying the chance to make people happy for a change.

"One five oh…"

People scanned their tickets. Several tossed them with disappointed expressions.

"two…"

More tickets were tossed. "seven…"

Even more tickets hit the floor.

Perhaps I imagined it, but I thought I heard an indrawn breath.

"…three."

"Say again?" A voice from the back, too choked up to be readily identified as male or female. Heads turned toward the voice as Joe reread the number.

"One-five-oh-two-seven-three."

A long silence, then—*"Oh, my God, I won!"*

It was Buster Daltry.

EIGHTEEN

IT TOOK SIX of us more than two hours to clean up Lucky Lanes and its parking lot. In the celebration that had followed Buster's win, people ripped up score sheets and rained them down on him like confetti. After being doused with beer, the big man was hefted on the shoulders of other big men and paraded around the bowling alley like a king, then out the double doors and into the parking lot, where the other ticket buyers roused themselves out of their collective funk long enough to congratulate him.

The cleaning crew, comprised of me, Robin, Helen, Bernice, and Haylie and Mark Hewitt, was now one short. Buster had planned to help out before Fate intervened. After his royal progress through the parking lot, he'd been carried down the street to the Amiable Avocado, where he was working his way toward a world-class hangover.

"I'm glad Buster won, aren't you?" Robin said, sweeping up the last scrap of paper into a black garbage bag.

"Couldn't have happened to a nicer guy, and I say that without irony," I answered. "Let's hope he gets to see both black and white rhinos, not that I could ever tell the difference. And elephants. Buster loves elephants."

"Maybe he'll see cheetahs on the run. And a lion pride. With cubs." She sounded wistful.

Poor Robin. After Bill and Myra had treated her so shabbily, I had been secretly rooting for her. To get her mind off her losses, I said, "Well, this is it. All that's left is to take this stuff out to the Dumpster."

For the next few minutes we hauled bag after bag, until Sam Grimaldi declared the job finished. "A professional crew couldn't have done better," he said.

He ushered us out the door, and while we climbed into our vehicles, stayed behind to lock up.

With the exception of the block where the Amiable Avocado is located, the small city of San Sebastian is pretty much deserted after midnight. My journey through town would have gone faster, but I hit every red light between the main drag and the turnoff to Gunn Landing. The lights were long ones, too. I didn't mind, because the city's strict zoning regulations kept the heart of San Sebastian authentic, so with my window down to admit the fresh night air, I enjoyed the picturesque view.

Renovated adobe buildings erected in the mid-1800s reflected the area's Spanish influence, with adobe storefronts connected to each other by tiled archways. The city had its share of statuary, too, and I drove by life-sized bronzes of Horace Bentley, my paternal great-great-great-grandfather; Abraham Piper, my maternal great-great-great grandfather; and the infamous Edwin Gunn, from whose loins sprang the indomitable Aster Edwina. The real star of the city came at the intersection of El Camino Real and Via del Sosa, where stood a floodlit, life-sized bronze of Padre Bautista de Sosa, the Spanish priest who had founded San Sebastian Mission. As always, I gave the padre and the trio of adoring Indian children at his feet a salute as I drove by.

The end of the city's older section signaled the new business center, flag-shipped by the corporate headquarters of SoftSol. Although it clashed with the Spanish-themed buildings that came before, at least it was attractive enough not to be an eyesore.

But the view degenerated once I passed the YOU ARE NOW LEAVING HISTORIC SAN SEBASTIAN sign. This signaled the less aesthetic side of the Modern Age, which was represented by fast-food restaurants and strip malls. Idling at the last endless red light before the turnoff, I found myself staring through the window of a laundromat, watching what appeared to be the entire San Sebastian Community College's women's soccer team doing their laundry. A black woman with hair as red as mine stood at the sorting table near the window, folding an SSCC red-and-black regulation jersey. As the light changed, she looked up and waved. I waved back.

I was just about to release the pickup's clutch when a dark sedan pulled along beside me and I heard a loud *crack*. Before I could react, the driver's side window of my truck disintegrated, covering me with powdered safety glass.

"Wha...?"

The sedan pulled forward, then angled in, effectively cutting me off.

Before I could breathe again, I heard another *crack*, and my windshield splintered into a web-like pattern. Shocked, I released the clutch too fast, and my Nissan stalled. Still not understanding what was happening, I turned the key in the ignition and tried again, intending to shift into reverse to give myself room to pull around the dark car. The pickup truck took two hops forward, then stalled once more.

Another loud *crack*, this one followed by the clang of something hard striking metal. Then, without the interference of safety glass, I felt something whiz by, and a nanosecond later, the rear window exploded.

I sat there, too stunned to move.

My mind cleared when someone yelled, *"Get out of the truck! There's a sniper out there!"*

I saw the redhead from the laundromat holding its door open, gesturing frantically for me to come in.

"Get in here, girl! Someone's shooting at you!"

Sometimes I might be a little slow on the uptake, but I'm not stupid, so I followed her instructions. As more *cracks* and *clangs* destroyed the peaceful San Sebastian night I lowered my head, slid along the bench seat to the passenger's side, and bailed out the door. Shielding my head with my Best Money-Grubber trophy, I scurried toward the laundromat in a bullet-ducking crouch while more shots rang out. The redhead's strong arms yanked me inside. As soon as I'd cleared the door, several other women upended a metal sorting table in front of it.

"We've already called 9-1-1," my savior said, kneeling beside me and brushing powdered glass off my shoulders. "Did you get a good look at him?"

"I never saw…" My voice came out as little more than a squeak.

"You're bleeding." She turned to a wiry blonde and snapped, "Jennifer, hand me that pillowcase. No! The clean one." The blonde handed her a snowy pillowcase.

I protested that I was fine and couldn't possibly be bleeding, but the redhead pressed the pillowcase to my cheek, then held it up. "See?"

The pillowcase was now blotted with red. "But I can't be shot," I squeaked again. "I would have felt it."

She shook her red curls. "Just a scratch. Where's the damn cops when you need them?"

"Joe's right down…he's right down…" *The street*, I meant to finish, but I ran out of voice.

"Dina, give her a drink. She's going to faint."

Sorry, Red, I'm not the fainting kind. But I complied with her orders and took a big gulp out of the insulated water bottle Dina—a female bruiser almost the size of Joe—held to my mouth. After I'd swallowed, I gagged. "What the hell's in here?"

"Grapefruit juice and bourbon," Dina answered. "About half and half."

Steeled for the burn this time, I took another slug while Red, whom I guessed was the team captain, snapped out more orders. "Ariel and Brittany, make sure the back door's locked. Lacy and Denise, lift that other sorting table onto the top of the one at the window. We need to block it before that asshole starts firing in here. But make sure you're covered while you lift it. We don't want anyone shot, and God knows how long it'll take the cops and EMTs to arrive."

Accustomed to obeying Red, the women snapped to attention, and within seconds, turned the laundromat into a fortress. They weren't through yet. After breaking open the supply closet, they armed themselves with mops, brooms, and open jugs of bleach. "He comes in here, I'll knock his head off," Dina muttered darkly.

"It would be more fun to bleach his eyes out," Red said, her face fierce. "Wonder if they'd sizzle?"

"What's that thing you're hanging onto?" Dina asked. "A bronzed softball?"

I looked down at my Best Money-Grubber trophy. The teakwood base now sported a round hole just below the rhino dung.

"Rhino shit. I won it."

Dina and Red shared a long look, the kind you give people who claim they've been abducted by aliens.

I started to explain that the heavy trophy would make a good weapon if worse came to worse, but then the sounds of approaching sirens cut me off.

The law had arrived.

NINETEEN

IT WAS HARD to tell if Joe was furious or worried, which is a common problem with cops; you can't always read their faces. "Did you get a good look at your assailant?" he asked again, while redheaded Liz Carroway, the captain of the SSCC's women's soccer team, looked on.

The laundromat had never been meant to hold so many people; an entire soccer team, several sheriff's deputies, two inquisitive crime scene techs, and a fussbudget EMT who kept insisting that I go to the hospital. It was all very irritating.

"Too dark," I said. "Not even sure he was a he."

"How about the car. Make? Model?"

"Big and black? Small and blue? You think I'm a bat or something? Not that they actually 'see,' it's more of a radar kind of thing." I took another deep drink of Dina's grapefruit juice/bourbon mixture. By now, it not only tasted a whole lot better, but I felt a whole lot better, too. So much fuss over a sniper. Hey, I was still in one piece, wasn't I? So no harm, no foul. Except for my poor Nissan pickup truck. All those windows! What was my deductible? Two hundred? Three?

"It's five hundred dollars!" I wailed.

Joe turned to Liz. "Do you know what she's talking about?" She shrugged. "Girl never did make any sense. She even told us that bronze baseball was rhino shit."

I clutched my beautiful award to my chest. "Is too!"

Joe frowned. "Teddy, are you drunk?"

"Am not!"

"Are too," chortled the EMT. "C'mon, Miss Bentley. Let's just get you on this nice little stretcher here and we'll take a nice little ride to the nice little hospital. Just scoot onto…"

"Gonna slap you!"

Liz reached forward and jerked Dina's water bottle from my hands.

"Cruel!" I sobbed, trying to grab it back.

Joe stood up. "Oh, for… All right, folks. Party's over. Ms. Carroway, if you'd give your statement to the deputy over there, I'd appreciate it. Same with the rest of you, ah, ladies." Then, to the EMT, he said, "She's refusing treatment."

"Let it be on your head," the EMT warned. Then he and his partner took the stretcher and left.

After giving his men a slew of instructions, Joe hauled me to my feet. "I'm taking you to your mother's."

I looked at my watch. "Awwww, it's after curfew. She'll *kill* me!"

His face assumed another expression I couldn't read. "Not in front of a witness, she won't."

SEVERAL HOURS LATER, I woke up to see a red-eyed Caro sitting next to the bed, Feroz perched on her lap like a miniature guard dog. She looked like she'd been there all night. Pushing the covers and Miss Priss aside, I staggered past DJ Bonz and his cat into the bathroom. As my mother held my head, I emptied my stomach into the toilet. "Good thing I put the seat up last night, otherwise there'd be a mess on the floor," Caro commented as I re-heaved. "Think you're through now? Heavens, you were drunk!"

"I don't know how that happened."

"Joe said something about grapefruit juice and bourbon."

"I've always hated bourbon. Now I hate grapefruit juice, too."

After I stood up, she dampened a washrag, blotted my face, then handed me a glass of Listerine. "Just gargle, don't swallow." As per instructions, I gargled, brushed my teeth, and gargled again.

Since Caro continued to hover, I said, "I would like to take a shower now, so if I could have a little privacy?"

She pressed her lips into a hard line. "I've seen your naked butt before, Theodora. Remember, I used to change your diapers." At the mention of diapers, my stomach heaved and I looked longingly at the toilet again.

"You see? You're not safe to be left alone."

"You never changed my diapers," I said, waiting for the nausea to pass.

"Between nannies, I did. You can't replace those people right away, you know, what with all the references that need checking." Ceding defeat to a stronger opponent, I stripped and showered. When I stepped out of the tub, she handed me a thick towel. Once I dried myself off, she wrapped me in a terrycloth robe so closely and slowly it felt like an extended hug. But since my mother wasn't into displays of physical affection, I figured I must have imagined it.

"How does buttered toast sound, dear?"

I waited to see what my stomach would do, but when it made no comment, I nodded.

Down in the breakfast room, the toast, albeit somewhat charred, hit the spot. As I started on my third slice, I realized that Caro must have made the toast herself. "Where's the maid? Surely you haven't started giving her Sundays off, too."

"Grizelda quit."

"What was she, your third this year?"

"Fourth. People are so disloyal these days. Myself, I blame the media."

Myself, I blamed Caro. She was enough to drive old Padre Bautista de Sosa to drink.

"Speaking of touchy subjects, how long did Joe stay last night?" I asked.

"Until three."

"That long?"

"We talked."

The very idea that my mother and Joe could remain alone together for that amount of time without killing each other boggled me beyond boggle. "What about?"

"New York Fashion Week, Halston's fall line..." Seeing my expression, she said, "We talked about *you*."

"Come to any conclusions?" I started on my fourth piece of toast, which tasted better now that I'd heaped it with the expensive marmalade Caro had shipped over regularly from London.

"We agreed that you need protection from yourself."

"Oh, ha."

"Oh, ha *back*, Theodora! You could have been killed last night."

"Random violence is just part of modern life."

"Joe thinks you were targeted."

"Cops tend to be paranoid." After a moment's reflection, I added, "Except when it comes to this family, of course. They're right on, there. The Bentleys and the Pipers have been thieving around San Sebastian County since the early 1800s."

"Don't change the subject, Theodora. Someone tried to shoot you last night."

"All he bagged was my poor Nissan." I blinked. "Hey, where is it? I know I didn't drive it home."

"Joe had it towed to the county impound lot. As soon

as the automobile showrooms open today, I'll buy you a new vehicle."

"Save your money. I like that truck."

Caro's face assumed the dreamy expression it always did when contemplating major purchases. "I'm thinking an armored Mercedes with a computer system that will alert the authorities if you run into trouble. Maybe a gun rack for the rear window and a gun, one of those long things you prop against your shoulder to shoot."

"Have you lost your mind?"

"Of course not. I'm not losing my daughter, either."

We argued until she backed down on the idea of an armored Mercedes with a gun rack, but we stalemated over the idea of another pickup truck. Only lawn crews and rednecks drove them, she said, while I insisted that zookeepers drove them, too. Anyway, the entire subject was moot, since I didn't have enough money for a replacement.

Burnt toast breakfast completed, I returned to my room and dressed in a pair of old jeans and a green tee shirt that advertised bird-watching tours of Gunn Landing Marsh. With Sunday my new day off, I wasn't expected anywhere, so I could just relax. After writing a thank you note to the San Sebastian Community College women's soccer team, and a separate, more personal note to Red, I went up to my room and watched *Meerkat Manor* reruns with my dog and cats for company.

The good thing about reruns is that they give you space to think. Despite what I'd said to Caro earlier, I didn't think the attack on me was random. But why in San Sebastian, and why now? While the meerkats went about their meerkatty business, I sat cross-legged on my bed and mulled over the possible answers. Kate had been murdered twelve days earlier, but no one had tried to kill me then. Nine days later Heck had also been killed, yet still there had been no attack on me. Then last night… What had changed?

Determined to keep my promise to Heck to find out who had killed Kate, I ticked off the week's timeline on my fingers.

Tuesday, Heck had been killed.

Wednesday, little of significance happened, other than my visit to Aster Edwina.

Thursday, nothing happened. Friday, ditto.

Satur…. Wait a minute. Friday, Caro had held her Let's-Find-Teddy-a-Husband party. Many of Old Town's residents and other moneyed people around the county were in attendance, along with friends from the zoo and the harbor. Conversations had encompassed everything from Bowling for Rhinos, to rising slip fees to the murders, with Caro acting her usual hostessy self. Zorah had been almost as chatty; she even discussed my visit to Tyler's nursing home, and my finding out about the prepaid cemetery plots.

The party had ended in that slugfest between Robin and Myra.

Yesterday… Wait. I had forgotten all about Thursday, when I'd dropped off the tuxedo cats to Speaks-to-Souls and she'd come clean about her relationship to Aster Edwina. After *that* came the trip to the nursing home in Oakland, *then* the party, and… The trip to Oakland? Could that have been the reason the killer had targeted me last night?

Possibly. But… The trip, other than being sad, was uneventful, and surely the killer wasn't worried about an Alzheimer's patient's scrambled memories. Most of the time Tyler couldn't remember his own daughter's name, let alone feed me information that identified Kate's killer. Then I had a sudden thought: could one of his former neighbors at Canaan Harbor know something?

While I was trying to figure out how I could get to Canaan Harbor without transportation, my restless mind developed another itch. I was forgetting something. I thought and thought, but could find nothing that had any connection to Kate and Tyler other than their old harbor. Yet if I'd never been up there, how could I forget something I'd never learned in the first place?

This conundrum made me frown so deeply that Bonz, ever sensitive to my moods, raised his head and gave me a searching look. "Just thinking, dog," I told him. "Nothing bad is going on."

With a relieved sigh he closed his eyes.

Now I was convinced that, despite appearances, the niggling thing I couldn't quite remember must have had something to do with my visit to the Golden Rule nursing home. Besides my halting conversation with a confused man, what else happened there? Oh, yes. The home's manager gave me an envelope that contained the name of the cemetery where Kate had planned to have her father buried. Try as I might, I couldn't figure out why that kind of information would matter to a killer.

It didn't, I decided. The dead seldom pose any threat to the living, so the killer's motive was probably something else. Could there be another item in the envelope that posed a danger to him? Or *her*, as the case might be. Women, I knew, could be just as murderous as men.

I climbed off the bed and crossed the room to the small suitcase I'd brought with me when my mother had rousted me from the *Merilee*. I rummaged through my clothes until I saw the envelope. Rifling through it, I saw the receipt from the Ocean View Cemetery for two adjoining lots, as well as receipts for complete funeral arrangements, right down to the flowers. Ever the dutiful daughter, Kate had planned every detail.

Searching through the rest of the papers, I came across

the South Oakland You-Store-It receipt I had briefly glanced at. Examining it more closely, I saw at the bottom, typed in capital letters, 6 MONTHS RENTAL FOR C-127.

C-127. The number stamped on the loose key I'd found in Kate's file of newsletter ideas. Maybe something in that storage locker revealed the killer's motive. Unfortunately, that file was still on the *Merilee.* I could walk to the harbor, which was less than a fifteen-minute hike downhill from Old Town, but what good would that do? Without a car, I wouldn't be able to drive to Oakland to see if my hunch was right. Calling Joe to tell him what I suspected would simply elicit more dire warnings about involving myself in police business. Worse, now that Joe was on semi-speaking terms with Caro, he might tattle on me and she'd make my life a living hell. Neither would care about the promise I'd made to a dead man.

Frustration at my helplessness made my head hurt again, so I went into the bathroom and swallowed two Excedrin Extra-Strength caplets. While waiting for them to kick in, I walked over to the window seat and watched the parade of Old Town dog-walkers going by. In the space of ten minutes, I counted two French bulldogs, a matched set of Affenpinschers, one Dandy Dinmont, three Papillons, four pugs, and six Shih Tzus. Not a pound puppy in sight. Glancing over at DJ Bonz, my three-legged Heinz 57, I saw him curled around his cat, bathing the tiny creature with a long pink tongue. What Bonz lacked in pedigree, he made up for in love.

"Good dog," I told him. To Miss Priss I said, "Why can't you be more like that?"

Because I'm a cat, she thought at me.

When I resumed my perusal of Old Town's blue-blood canine population, I saw Mrs. Wexford-Smythe's silver Lexus creep down the driveway next door and turn into the street. For a brief moment, I considered running over to her house and hotwiring her second car, an aged Jaguar, but decided against it. We Bentleys had never gone in for petty theft; if the haul wasn't worth millions, we didn't bother.

Trying to rent one would prove difficult. The closest car rental place was in Monterey, but I had no way of getting there. Roman, owner of Roamin' Roman's Rent-A-Wreck, was an old school friend of Caro's and might be talked into driving a rental over to Old Town, but Caro would probably tackle me before I could reach it.

Happily, a more workable plan to rectify my transportation-challenged state then popped full-blown into my mind. Choking back a giggle, I grabbed my cell phone and dialed Caro's number, hoping that she wouldn't check her caller ID. When she answered, I lowered my voice and did my best to mimic the thick accent of Mrs. Wexford-Smythe's maid.

"Allo, Mees Peterzen? Thees ees Yvette, and I eeese tired of working for Meez Weexford-Smyeeeth, she eeese terrible womans! I theenk zat you bee needing 'elp now, oui?" My fractured French wouldn't have fooled a child.

But it did fool my mother. "Why, yes, Yvette, I would love you to come work for me again, and I can assure you that despite what you may have heard from Grizelda, I've become very easy to work for. When you get your break, walk over here and we'll…"

"Non, non, Mees Peterzen. Zis terrible womans nevaire geeve poor Yvette breaks. You comes ovair 'ere now while sheeze at zee store and we talk, oui?"

"Be right there!" Seconds later, the front door slammed. Hoping it would take several minutes for Caro to realize she'd been had, I raced down the stairs to the end table where she kept her purse, and fished out her car keys. Within seconds I was sitting in her Mercedes with the re-

mote in hand, zapping open the garage door. As I sped
down the street, I could see Caro in the rear view mirror.

She was shaking her fist.

After stopping by the *Merilee* to grab Kate's files,
I headed along Highway One to the 101 cutoff. Once I
made it onto the freeway and hit the accelerator, the tank-
like Mercedes cruised along like an eiderdown pillow on
wheels. In what seemed like no time I was pulling onto the
road that led to the South Oakland You-Store-It, but a check
of my watch showed that I'd committed Grand Theft Auto
almost two hours ago. As I hooked a right into the entrance,
a possible problem disappeared when I saw a pickup truck
loaded with household belongings approaching the closed
gate. When the driver punched a code into the gate's key-
pad and it swung back, I tailgated him through.

Having stored my own belongings in a place similar to
this after moving onto the *Merilee*, I found C-127 with little
trouble. It was smaller than I'd anticipated, but I reminded
myself that before contracting Alzheimer's, Tyler had lived
on a boat no larger than my own. There was no furniture
among his meager belongings, just cardboard storage cartons filled with out-of-date clothing and papers, an old ste-
reo system sitting alongside hundreds of vinyls, and shelves
of computers so ancient they could have been used by Fred
Flintstone. They seemed well cared for, though, wrapped in
plastic and dust-free. Someone had treasured them.

One of the cartons was filled to the brim with tax records, business communications, and receipts of various
kinds. Rifling through them, I saw a few documents that
looked promising, but decided it would take hours to study
them properly. Before closing the box, I was brought up
short by a photograph of two men smiling into the camera.
One was a particularly scruffy teenager with bad acne and
oily hair stood next to an older man: Tyler Everts.

Another carton held a clear plastic box filled with old floppy discs and a series of dot-matrix printouts of numerical coding similar to those I had produced in my college programming class. Not that I remembered much of it. The hand-written notes on the printouts were almost indecipherable. Deferring further study until I was back at Caro's, I loaded both boxes and several of the newer computers into the Mercedes. Rethinking the situation, I went back and grabbed the two oldest computers—a Tandy and a Commodore. Then I relocked the storage unit and headed for Canaan Harbor.

Canaan is a small marina near Sausalito. Surrounded on three sides by the lush green hills of Marin County with the San Francisco Bay on the other, the harbor was similar to Gunn Landing's, populated with fishing boats, houseboats, pleasure craft, and several fancy yachts. Most of the liveaboard vessels were located at the far north end, so after following a couple of Sunday sailors through the card-controlled gate, I headed in that direction.

Now came the hard part: finding anyone who knew Tyler Everts and his daughter.

That, too, turned out to be easier than anticipated. After talking to several people, one of them directed me to a middle-aged woman who was scrubbing the deck of a re-fitted twenty-seven foot Newport. From her hippie mama appearance—waist-length hair, tie-dyed caftan—it was easy to see why she might have been close to the owners of the *Nomad*. Her name was Louise Signorelli, and she had known both Tyler and Kate well enough to shed tears when I told her about Kate's murder.

As she wept, seagulls whirled and danced around her, appearing to mock her grief. Also oblivious was the pelican that flapped to a landing on a piling at the end of the dock. More in tune with the moment came the moan of a faraway foghorn.

"Thank God Ty's too far gone to realize what happened to her," Louise said, once she had recovered enough to talk. "That kind of stuff, he just doesn't take well. Never did. When Silver Dove got drunk and drowned—that's Kate's mother—we all thought he'd lose his mind with grief, so some of us women started 'comforting' him, if you get what I mean. I spent lots of nights on the *Nomad,* not that it was any chore. Ty was just the sweetest man. A bit weird, maybe, but hey, I always liked them weird. The weirdness, I guess, was why it took folks around here so long to notice that something had gone *really* wrong, that he was wearing the same clothing for days, was even forgetting to eat." Louise had been the person who alerted Kate about Tyler's deteriorating condition. Dabbing at her eyes, she said, "We'd been friendly enough that I had Kate's cell phone number, so one day, when Ty started raving about enemies stealing his things and other paranoid stuff like that, I called her. Hell, that man never had anything worth stealing. Kate had just come back from Australia, but when I told her what was going on, she flew right up here. Next thing you knew, she moved Ty into that nursing home. I went over there once to see him, but it was so depressing I never went back. I'd rather remember him the way he used to be."

Estrangement was a common reaction among the friends and relatives of Alzheimer's patients, so I didn't judge her. A visit with someone who no longer recognized you provided little incentive to return. "You said that even before Ty got sick he was 'weird,'" I said. "What did you mean by that?"

"He was always talking about things nobody understood, always tinkering with things over there at that workshop he rented."

"What kind of workshop? Carpentry? Or…"

She shrugged. "Some kind of electronic rigmarole. He tried to explain it to me once, but I just spazzed out. Never did have a head for that kind of thing and never will. Hell, I don't even have a TV, let alone a computer. Owning a cell phone is my only bow to technology, and even there, I've got one of those super-easy Crickets. But Ty? He could have made those NASA people look like they were driving buckboards."

"Do you think the workshop might still be there?"

"Maybe, maybe not. It was years ago, and could be a mall's gone up in its place. Anything's possible these days. Ty used to take Kate over there when she was just a little kid, but I never went with them, so I don't even know exactly where it was. Some place in Novato, he told me. Wait. Come to think of it, he said that the workshop was in a garage."

"Like an auto mechanic's garage?"

"Nah, the kind attached to a house. I remember that part, because he told me that one of the teenagers who lived in the house was always hanging around, watching him work. Ty said he used to let the boy handle some of the easier jobs."

The hairs on my neck began to prickle. "Did he say what kind of jobs?"

She turned her hands out in a helpless gesture. "Beats me. But that's what he called them, 'jobs.'"

"Do you remember the boy's name?"

"Honey, these days I do well to remember my own. Ty did bring him around every now and then to take him out for a sail in the *Nomad*, but that's all I remember. Certainly not the kid's name."

Fortunately, I'd had the foresight to bring the photograph

I'd discovered at the storage locker with me, and I showed it to her. "Would this be the kid you're talking about?"

"Sure looks like him," she said. "And that's Ty he's with. Cute, wasn't he? Ty, I mean. Not the teenager. Jesus, look at the poor kid's skin."

I acknowledged that Ty had been cute and that the teen certainly had a bad case of acne. "Anything else you can tell me?"

She shook her head. "Sorry. I'm surprised I remembered as much as I did."

The conversation having reached its natural conclusion, I thanked Louise for her help. Before I left, we exchanged phone numbers, and she promised to call me if she remembered anything else. Then I headed back to Gunn Landing Harbor to face the music. Instead of making the turnoff to the harbor, I continued south on Highway One to Monterey and Roamin' Roman's Rent-A-Wreck. Roman agreed to follow me back to Caro's in my rental—a chartreuse Kia with a crumpled fender—as long as I drove him back to Rent-A-Wreck afterwards.

When the Mercedes and the Kia pulled into Caro's driveway, she ran out the door, primed for a fight. "The very idea that my own daughter would steal from me!" she screamed, not caring if the neighbors heard her.

Since Roman had gone to school with Mother, her histrionics didn't faze him. He just leaned against the Kia and watched the dog walkers pass by.

While transferring Tyler's belongings from the Mercedes to the Kia, I explained, "I did not steal your car, I just borrowed it. I even filled up the fuel tank for you. Furthermore, I don't know what you believed you'd accomplish by keeping me prisoner."

"Prisoner!" Her eyes bugged.

Roman cleared his throat. "Um, Teddy, can I get that lift back to my lot any time this century?"

Caro turned her ire on him. "And you, Roman, how dare you be a party to this!"

He grinned. "Don't involve me in your family disputes, Caroline. I knew you when you'd never been kissed. Or anything else."

"Why, you son-of-a…"

"Bye, Mom!" I said, hustling Roman into the Kia.

THERE WAS ANOTHER reason I needed a car.

An hour later, Linda Cushing was waiting on the deck of the *Tea 4 Two* as I hurried up the dock. She held an urn in her hand. "I thought you'd forgotten," she said.

"Forget Heck's funeral? Never."

We cast off. Followed closely by a small flotilla of live-aboarders, we motored through the channel, then set sail into the Pacific. Once we were beyond the three-mile limit, Linda dropped anchor. After motoring alongside the *Tea 4 Two*, the others followed suit.

The distant fogbank rolling toward us kept the service necessarily short. After a brief eulogy, Linda tipped Heck's ashes into the waves, while from the deck of the *Texas Hold 'Em*, Larry DuFries, a former Merchant Marine, played a simple seaman's version of "Amazing Grace" on a hornpipe.

When Heck's ashes floated away with the outgoing tide, floral wreaths—including one of my own—accompanied him.

Home was the sailor, home in the sea.

TWENTY

Two DAYS, TWO memorial services.

At noon Monday, Zorah officiated at "A Remembrance for Kate" in the zoo's auditorium. An enlarged version of Kate's portrait with Wanchu—the same pose I'd given her father—took center stage, surrounded by a large wreath of multi-colored blooms. Most of the zoo staff and volunteers attended. So did Wanchu. Confused by such a large gathering, she kept her arms clasped around Bill's neck and didn't make a fuss. Neither did Aster Edwina, who sat next to them in the front row with a face as impassive as Bill's. Matriarchs and Aussies don't cry.

Standing near the door, their eyes on the audience, were Joe and two deputies. Did they expect the killer to jump up in the middle of the service and shout "I did it!" like on the old *Perry Mason* reruns?

One by one, zookeepers walked to the podium to share stories about Kate and her love for the koalas. Deciding to reveal a part of Kate's life that most of the others were unfamiliar with, I talked about the *Nomad*, how Kate had been raised on her, and how after her father became ill, she'd sailed the boat single-handed all the way down from Canaan Harbor.

"Much of Kate's life was on land with her beloved koalas, but she was also a sailor. I'd like to think that wherever she is now, she's at the helm of a craft tall and true."

After the service was over and no one had confessed to the murders, the deputies left. A grim-looking Joe lagged behind to warn me once more about getting mixed up in the investigation.

"Promise me you'll stay at your mother's house until this thing is over."

"I promise."

"Promise again, Teddy, this time with your hands in front of you so I can make sure your fingers aren't crossed."

I did, and I meant it. There was no way I would spend the night on the *Merilee* until the killer was arrested—not that the streets of San Sebastian had proved any safer than Gunn Landing Harbor. I didn't tell Joe about my trip in a stolen Mercedes to Oakland and Canaan Harbor. Or that this morning, after spending the night going through the two boxes I had retrieved from Kate's storage unit, I had turned over the most troubling material to Helen, Zorah's assistant. I wanted an expert opinion before I took my suspicions to Joe.

And I kept the photograph I'd found in the unit.

Just in case.

THE NEXT DAY started off badly and stayed that way.

Although I had promised to appear with Wanchu on the San Sebastian No-Kill Animal Shelter Marathon that evening, Zorah insisted I still show up for my segment on *Good Morning, San Sebastian*.

"Birds this time, Teddy," she said, over my protests. "I've already picked them out for you."

Ear still sore, I felt hesitant about bringing birds of any kind onto the set. But Manny Salinas, head of the zoo's avian collections, assured me everything would be fine.

"That's why Zorah sent me with you, Teddy," he said, as he helped me lift the birds' carriers into the van. "To make sure no 'accidents' happen. She said this was AnnaLee's last day at the station and she doesn't want her to go out with a splatter."

Zorah's plan worked. For a while.

When the segment began, Mei-Ying, the Eurasian scops-owl, behaved herself, as did Godwin, the peregrine falcon. Seemingly on cue, both birds peered wide-eyed at the cameras, stretched their wings, and sounded their genus-appropriate calls. Neither tried to peck anyone. But Jason, the macaw, refused to sing "Mary Had a Little Lamb," as promised. Instead, he launched into an imitation of Miss Piggy serenading Kermit the Frog with "I Want To Be Loved By You."

The only embarrassing moment came when Evita, the Humboldt penguin, ate the sardine Manny allowed AnnaLee to feed her, then regurgitated the fish on the anchor's shoes.

"That's actually a compliment, AnnaLee," Manny said, pained. "She was just feeding you like she feeds her chick."

AnnaLee smiled as if much worse had happened to her, which it had. "And now for a word from Big Daddy's Bait Shop. Big Daddy's got the bait the big fish love."

"You WERE RIGHT, Teddy, that woman's a vomit magnet," Manny said, while we were toting the birds to the zoo's Animal Care Center for their après-TV checkup.

I was about to reply when I saw a familiar figure heading toward the auditorium: Aster Edwina. I hadn't seen her since Bowling for Rhinos, so why…? Then I remembered. Today was the day Buster was to be officially presented with his African safari tickets. Also, the volunteer roster for keepers working tonight's marathon would be announced. I checked my watch. If the vet declared the birds ready to be returned to their enclosure quickly enough, we might be able to make the presentation.

It worked out. After giving the birds a cursory glance, the vet declared them healthy. An hour later, Manny and I hurried to the auditorium, where we took our seats next to Robin. Zorah had just begun reading the list of zookeepers detailed to answer phones during the No-Kill Animal Shelter Marathon, and the keepers unfortunate enough to present an animal.

"Teddy Bentley will present Wanchu, Manny Salinas a mynah…"

Most keepers appeared terrified at the thought of appearing on live television, but Zorah was merciless. In the end, I counted four other keepers doomed to share the spotlight with their charges. The mood lightened when Zorah finally stepped away from the mike, and Aster Edwina came forward to hand over the safari tickets. Buster, big puppy that he was, fairly wiggled with joy as he accepted the thick envelope.

"I have an announcement myself," he said, a sly look on his face. "There are two tickets in here, right, Miss Gunn?"

Aster Edwina nodded. "Certainly, Mister, ah, Buster."

"And I can take whoever I want with me, right?"

She nodded again. "Of course."

"You wanna take your mommy with you, is that it?" called someone from the audience.

"Miami's more her style," Buster shot back. Then his face became as tender as it was when he cared for his darling rhinos. "But I do know someone who's been dying to see Africa, a lady I've admired for a long time but never got up enough nerve to admit it to, a beautiful young lady who deserves all the wonderful things life can give her— especially Africa."

Oh, hell. Buster was going to give that other ticket to Myra. I looked around and saw her sitting right behind me.

The insufferable keeper's expression was so smug I wanted to smack her. But, of course, I didn't.

Zorah must have thought the same thing, because a little of the joy went out of her face. She looked over at Myra, and if glares could kill, Myra was a dead woman.

Aster Edwina didn't look all that happy, either, but she just said, "Don't keep us in suspense, young man. Who have you chosen to be your guest?"

The smile on Buster's face extended all the way to his ears when he said, "I would like Robin Chase to do me the very great honor of accompanying me to Africa."

Robin gasped.

Myra muttered, "Shit."

The crowd erupted in whistles, cheers, and palm-blistering applause.

Once the noise died down, Buster said, "Robin? Will you?"

"Hell, yeah!" she answered, and with that, charged up on the stage, threw her arms around him, and planted a big sloppy kiss on his lumpy face. "I've always been crazy about you, you idiot!"

Later, while we were filing out of the auditorium with the rest of the zookeepers, I said to Manny, "I love happy endings, don't you?"

"Don't make me cry," he sniffled.

I was just climbing into my zoo cart to drive up to Tropics Trail when a voice halted me.

"Teddy! I need a private moment with you." Aster Edwina.

A request for a "private moment" with Aster Edwina usually signaled some form of warning, or worse, punishment. What had I done now? Did she blame me for the penguin barf incident? For a moment, my heart lifted. Perhaps, given all that had transpired, she'd begun to question the wisdom of the zoo's *Good Morning, San Sebastian* segment and decided to pull me off it.

Feeling optimistic, I gave her a big smile. "I always have time for you, Aster Edwina."

She frowned and my smile disappeared. Her next words, delivered in a tone low enough that the departing crowd of zookeepers wouldn't hear them, shocked me. "I thought she was dead, Teddy."

No point in asking who "she" was. The old woman meant Josie/Speaks-to-Souls. Her daughter. "Why…" I swallowed. "Why would you think that?"

"Because that's what my father told me."

The story that emerged was a sad one, although not uncommon in the days when a single woman giving birth was considered a life-ruining scandal. The baby's delivery had been a secret, attended only by Edwin Gunn himself and a private doctor with more debts than ethics. After Aster Edwina had emerged from the heavy sedation, Edwin—seizing his chance to make the scandal disappear—informed her that the baby had been stillborn, its tiny body already "disposed of."

"Why would I doubt him?" Aster Edwina said. "My father had never lied to me before."

Appalled, I wondered why was she telling me this.

My face must have revealed my confusion because she said, "You, of all people, should know that in this day and age, dirty laundry always winds up getting aired. Josie looks just like me. Tongues are probably already wagging, so I've decided to take control by issuing a press release to give the story a positive spin. You'll draft it tomorrow, but let me look it over before you release it to the press."

I nodded. This would be one press release I'd enjoy writing. She surprised me again.

"One more thing. Teddy, I would like to invite you to a

reception in Josie's and Alyse's honor. It'll take place next week at Gunn Castle. You, your mother, and several other of the most prominent local families will receive formal invitations."

My mouth dropped. "Have you run this by Josie?"

Her voice frosted with ice, she replied, "Of course! She *is* my daughter, isn't she? And a typical Gunn she's turned out to be, too." Then the ice melted, betrayed by maternal pride. "She's already made me pledge a ridiculously high sum of money toward the No-Kill Animal Shelter. And my granddaughter—the little imp—actually weaseled another few thousand for the San Sebastian Public Library."

Chuckling, the old woman walked away.

HOURS LATER, CARO having assured me she would feed Bonz, Miss Priss, and Toby, I drove straight from the zoo to the television studio with Wanchu in the back of the last available van, a fifteen-year-old relic. I wasn't looking forward to taking part in the marathon, but at least—unlike the other keepers who'd already quaked their way through their appearances, then fled back to the zoo—I didn't suffer from stage fright. I also enjoyed watching the evening's hosts, Dick Van Patten and Drew Barrymore, both of whom were well known as animal lovers. The odd couple pairing worked well, with Van Patten acting as straight man for Barrymore's more ribald jokes.

Behind the duo, zoo staff—including Buster, Robin, Lex, and a dozen others—answered the phones and took pledges while the two stars introduced a series of Hollywood types. Dropping by with their own pound puppies and kittens were Natalie Portman, Charlize Theron, Katherine Heigl, Mickey Rourke, Meg Ryan, and Christina Applegate.

Myra Sebrowski had been delegated to mop the studio floor. Wanchu and I were enjoying the show so much that we almost missed the introduction delivered by an enthusiastic Barrymore. "And now, the real star of the San Sebastian No-Kill Shelter Marathon, Wanchu the koala, accompanied by her friend, Gunn Zoo animal keeper Teddy Bentley!"

"Showtime, girl," I whispered to Wanchu as we stepped onto the set.

It being early evening, Wanchu was more alert than she had been during her first television appearance on *Good Morning, San Sebastian*. As I carried her toward the mike, she leaned forward and took a swipe at Barrymore's dangling earring.

Barrymore laughed delightedly, although she did step out of koala-reach. "I didn't know koalas were attracted by diamonds. Jackdaws, maybe, but not koalas."

"Animals surprise us all the time, don't they, Drew?"

A blinding Hollywood smile. "Tell me about it! I remember when Flossie, my adopted yellow Lab-Chow, brought home a bird in her mouth. I almost had a heart attack before I realized it hadn't been hurt, just wet."

I returned her smile. "Flossie was giving her favorite human a gift. Tell me, did you let the bird go? Or did you decide to keep it?" When she said that she'd walked the bird into the woods and released it, I turned to the camera and delivered a short sermon on how to deal with "found" wild animals. During this, Wanchu grew bored and reached for Barrymore's earring again. The star retaliated by scratching Wanchu's head, something the koala had always enjoyed.

"Her fur isn't as soft as it looks," she said, once my spiel wound down. "It's bristly."

Donation phones ringing behind me, I took this as a cue to trot out another short spiel, this time about koalas and their rapidly vanishing habitats. Once I had finished, Van Patten handed me a coffee mug with a picture of a dog and cat on it, bearing the legend, ADOPT A FRIEND TODAY. As I left the set, another well-known actress stepped to the mike, accompanied by two small white dogs.

"And now let's talk to Glenn Close," Barrymore bubbled, "and her friends Jake and Bill! Glenn, tell us about your website, *FetchDog.com.*"

With a great feeling of relief, I settled Wanchu in her eucalyptus leaf-filled carrier and headed down the hall toward the exit. Before I reached the door, my cell phone rang. It was Helen, calling from the zoo.

Helen said, "Sorry I couldn't get to you earlier, but I've been so busy helping Zorah coordinate our volunteer roster at the marathon... Oh, well, you don't need to hear about my problems. Now that everyone's down there and taking care of business, I want you to know that I spent the night looking at those discs and printouts you gave me."

"And?" I started to open the door.

"You were right, Teddy. About everything."

I set the koala down to give me time to collect myself. "So it *was* piracy then!"

"Technically, no, but not being an attorney, I'm not sure how criminal courts would have handled the actual crime at the time it occurred, if it even was a crime. Civil court, that's a different story entirely. Remember O.J. Simpson. Found innocent in his state trial, guilty in the civil one. Millions of dollars in damages levied against him. In this particular case, we might be talking billions."

Although she couldn't see me, I shook my head. "Killing Kate and Heck probably wasn't so much about the money, Helen, as it was about loss of face. Now that I've got the proof to take to the sheriff, I think..." Over the sounds of Wanchu's leaf-munching, I thought I heard something behind me. A door closing? When I turned around and looked down the long hallway, I saw nothing. But better safe than sorry. "Look, Helen, I'm still at the television station. I need to get Wanchu back to the zoo before…"

"Call the sheriff first, Teddy."

"As soon as I'm in the van." With that I hauled Wanchu up again and hurried out the exit to the parking lot.

It was almost dark, but the parking lot still bustled with volunteers leaving and arriving for the marathon. I'd left the zoo's van parked under a light stanchion, so it was easy to secure the koala carrier in the back. Once that had been accomplished, I climbed into the driver's seat and speed-dialed Joe's cell, but found myself turned over to voice mail. Instead of leaving a message, I disconnected and dialed his office, where the harried-sounding receptionist transferred me to an old middle school friend, now-Deputy Ralph Lazlo, who told me Joe would be back as soon as the mess was cleared up.

"What mess?" I saw a limo pull into the parking lot next to me, and a woman who looked like Alicia Silverstone emerge with two dogs of indeterminate breed and a carrier containing—from the yowls that emerged—an unhappy cat.

"Apparently you haven't been listening to the news, Teddy," Ralph grumped, bringing my attention back. "There was a big chemical spill at that industrial plant on the east side. Half the department's there with a hazmat team. He accompanied them because it's the company's second spill of the year, and now the Feds are getting involved. Want to leave a message?"

Deciding that Joe would check his phone before returning to the office, I said no and dialed Joe's cell again, this time telling him who had killed Kate Nido, why, and how I'd found out. Before I could add that I was on my way back to the zoo with Wanchu, voice mail cut me off. There's technology for you.

"Okay, Wanchu, we're headed home," I called as I cinched my seat belt. Hearing an answering "Eeep," I pulled out of the parking lot.

Rush hour being well over I made it through town to the Gunn Landing turnoff with little trouble, and we were soon cruising along Bentley Road toward the zoo. The road was deserted by now and, since the gentle dusk of evening had segued into full dark, I flipped on the van's brights. My surroundings were invisible beyond the headlights' arc, but to my right lay the remnants of the old Bentley cattle ranch, now reduced to a strip of pastureland. A mile further back from the pasture was Bentley Heights, the ticky-tacky housing development that so offended the Gunns. On the other side of the road stood the tall blue gum eucalyptus forest that bordered the Gunn family vineyards. Not only did the trees provide meal after meal for Wanchu and her mate, but it created a refuge for wildlife, too.

My headlights suddenly illuminated a doe and her fawn standing in the middle of the road. I stood on the brakes, and the van's tires screeched for several teeth-clenching yards before stopping mere inches from the doe's shining eyes. Oblivious to their near-death experience, the two deer bounded across the blacktop and into the trees.

"You okay back there?" I called to Wanchu.

No answer. Just more gnawing of koala teeth on eucalyptus leaves.

As I pressed the accelerator, I said, "Glad to hear you're fine, Wanchu. Just stay settled down, and we'll reach the zoo in about fifteen minutes. After you're tucked into your night house, I'll…" Headlights behind me, approaching fast. Someone was in a hurry.

Slowing my speed, I edged over to the right to give the driver room to pass. Not wanting to blind him, I dimmed my lights. He, not so courteous, flipped on his brights. He didn't even slow down. When the car closed the distance between us much too quickly, I began to worry. Drunk driver?

I edged even further to the side, so much so that the tires on the passenger's side crunched on gravel. This maneuver should have given the other driver room to pass.

It didn't.

Before I could grasp what was happening, the car slammed into the van's bumper.

My hands clenched around the steering wheel while I fought to keep the van on the road. Out of the rearview mirror, I saw the car back off several yards, then speed up again as if aiming purposely for the van.

Attempts at evasion having failed, I floored the accelerator to get as much speed out of the van as possible, but it wasn't enough. The car's bumper made contact again, this time even harder. The van lurched forward, and I was thrown against the seat.

"Eeeeeeep!" Wanchu shrieked.

"Hang on, girl!" I shouted.

As I prepared for another rear-end assault, the driver changed tactics. Instead of aiming for my bumper, he dropped back several feet, then sped up and pulled alongside me. It was a Mercedes almost twice the size of my mother's, and although I couldn't see its driver, I knew who it was.

Ford Bronson.

The man who had killed Kate and Heck.

The man who only a few nights ago had tried to kill me. For a few seconds we sped neck-and-neck along the narrow blacktop, then he dropped back again, but this time, not all the way. Before I could even gasp, the Mercedes swerved sharply to the right and hit the van's rear left fender so hard that the van began to spin. The steering wheel wrenched itself out of my grasp, and I lost all control. Seemingly in slo-mo, the van toppled over and slid on its roof straight along the pavement, lighting up the night in a shower of sparks.

During the roll, the van's rear doors popped open. Still suspended upside down by my seatbelt, I could only watch, horrified, as Wanchu's carrier tumbled end over end, out the door, and onto the blacktop.

"Oh, Wanchu!" I grieved, briefly distracted from my own perilous situation.

My grief was short-lived. The van continued to slide, but by the time it came to rest facing back in the direction of San Sebastian, its still-working headlights illuminated a terrified koala scampering across the road toward the eucalyptus forest.

At least one of us would make it, then. But I'd try for two. With shaking fingers, I unlocked the seat belt, dropped to the roof of the van, and staggered across the road in Wanchu's wake. No point in waiting for help. None of the keepers working the marathon lived in this direction, nor did any of the guest stars. The keepers who'd needed to return animals to the zoo had already done so, then taken the zoo's rear exit toward their apartments in Castroville. At this time of night, chances were good that no other cars would come this way.

No help would come from Gunn Castle, either. It was still at least three miles away, atop the crest of a steep hill.

I was on my own.

To a certain extent, luck was with me. Other than a few scrapes and sore spots, I hadn't sustained major injuries in the crash. Also, as Bronson's car had hurtled forward, its speed had sent it a hundred yards further down the road. By the time he got turned around, I'd almost reached the trees.

Almost.

Brakes squealed and a bullet buzzed past me as I fled

in a zigzag pattern across the grass verge. Another shot. The gunshots sounded deafening, giving me hope that a Bentley Heights homeowner wouldn't mistake them for a car's backfire and decide to call the police. Then again, those houses were more than a mile away... For the first time in my life, I wished that Bentley Heights was closer to Bentley Road and that—pasturage be damned—the houses marched right down to the blacktop.

That heretic thought disappeared the moment I entered the protective gloom of the forest. It had been dark on the road, but the darkness intensified a hundredfold under the blue gums' broad canopies. Plunging deeper into the forest, I soon realized that the darkness alone wasn't enough to protect me. Blue gums are big shedders; their bark peels off in long, narrow strips, littering the ground. A thick carpet of the things snapped under my feet, providing an easy sound track for Bronson to follow. At least my cell phone was set to vibrate—not that my "Born Free" ringtone would be noisier than this crackling forest floor.

As I ran deeper into the woods, all the time angling up a rise in the vague direction of Gunn Castle, concern for my own safety blurred with concern for Wanchu. The koala had never lived in the wild, and thus never learned how to survive on her own. Yes, given the thick eucalyptus forest she wouldn't go hungry. Water presented no problem, either. But Central California nights were cold and damp, which is why we had placed a heating lamp in her night house.

And then there was the traffic problem.

For a while Wanchu would be content to stay in one tree, but at some point she would decide to move, perhaps even to check out strange scents on the other side of the blacktop. Bentley Road might be deserted most of the night, but come morning it would be a different story. If the koala decided to cross the road at the same time as a car sped along… No, I couldn't think about that, just what was happening now, that a murderer was intent upon making me his third victim.

Because of my labor-intensive job I was in good shape, but Bronson had run the Boston Marathon in little more than three hours, his endurance matched by considerable speed. My chances of making it to the safety of Gunn Castle weren't good, but I saw no other option. I certainly couldn't hide. Since so little sunlight had managed to reach the forest floor, there was not much undergrowth to be found. I saw no friendly thickets, no stands of low-branched pines, nothing but eucalyptus. So I ran on, each gasping breath rivaling my footsteps for noise.

"Hey, Teddy, I just want to talk!" Bronson called, his voice full of cheer. "Those were just warning shots. We can work this out."

Said the cat to the mouse.

I didn't bother answering, just picked up the pace.

A new difficulty presented itself. Despite my resolve to head toward Gunn Castle, I realized there was no such thing as running in a straight line. Men had planted the blue gums in even rows a century ago, but over the years the trees had seeded themselves in random patterns; my surroundings resembled a maze more than an orderly orchard. While dodging around this tree trunk and that, I caught myself in the act of making too many right turns. If the incline toward the castle had been steady, all that dodging around wouldn't matter; I could keep my bearings by continuously heading uphill. But nature stymied me there, too. I was on rolling terrain, with rising and lowering elevations sometimes subtle enough to be near-undetectable. After my last right turn, I belatedly realized I was headed down, not up. Was I running back to the highway, where I would present an easy target for a killer?

My labored breaths began to sound like sobs.

Bronson didn't sound at all winded. Only a few yards behind me, he called, "Give it up, Teddy! You know you can't outrun me!" I turned to the left and felt some satisfaction when the ground began to slope upwards, ushering me into a thick stand of newer blue gums. The trees loomed like massive charcoal pillars against the night's black velvet, as close together as lovers, so close that I...

Ran straight into one.

As I fell, a shriek escaped my lips.

It was answered by a laugh. "Hurt yourself? Here, let me kiss it and make it well."

Another laugh.

He was enjoying this.

I tasted blood. The sandpaper bark had ripped along my face, but worse damage occurred when I'd fallen face down on a rock. The pain told me my nose was probably broken, that I'd look like Robin Chase in the morning.

If I ever saw the morning.

I scrambled to my feet, not only winded, but dizzy, too. There was no way I would make it to Gunn Castle, no way to summon help, no way to... *"Ready or not, here I come!"*

This was just a game to Bronson, a game he'd play to win. But I refused to lose without a fight.

Kneeling back down, I searched through the bark strips and found the rock that had damaged my face. I raised it... And heard something crashing through the forest toward me.

From the other direction.

While I stood there with the rock in my hand, a doe and her fawn—the deer I had braked for earlier?—dashed past me, making an ungodly racket as they fled up the slope. Fooled, Bronson chased after them. Using the resulting noise as cover, I stumbled along in the opposite direction, finally clearing the stand of new growth and entering a grove in the older section of the forest where the blue gums' trunks were thick enough to hide behind.

That was all I could do, now. Hide until found.

Bronson would eventually realize his mistake and double back. When he did, well… I was too sore and tired to run any further.

Kneeling behind the largest eucalyptus in the grove—a monster whose trunk was as wide as a car door—I pulled my cell phone from my pocket. Flipped it open. Got a signal. Hunching over so the light from the display wouldn't give my presence away, I speed-dialed Joe.

Got voice mail.

Punched in another number. Heard the ring. Then… "San Sebastian Sheriff's Department. Deputy Ralph Lazlo speaking."

"It's Teddy," I whispered. "Don't say anything, just let me talk." I told him where I was and how I'd come to be there, told him to dispatch cruisers down Bentley Road, told him Helen had proof, told him… The nearby snapping of dried blue gum bark signaled that my time was up.

"My, my, Teddy. If I'd had a rifle, I'd be dining on venison tonight," Bronson chortled, less than a few yards from my hiding place. "Oh, well. Another time."

"Teddy, is that…?" Ralph began.

"Shhh," I shushed Ralph. The fact that he'd heard Bronson's shout gave me an idea.

"Come out, come out, wherever you are!" my pursuer called.

I placed the cell down as close to the tree trunk as possible and covered its glowing screen with leaves and bark. Then I cleared the remaining bark strips away from the tree so that I'd be able to move around silently. I picked up my rock. If he liked to play, we'd play.

"Don't come near me, Ford Bronson!" I yelled, making myself sound more terrified than resigned. Not that it was difficult.

"Gave yourself away, didn't you?" More laughter. The suave golf partner to presidents had long since disappeared, leaving behind the heartless predator he truly was. As Bronson stepped from behind a tree almost as large as my own, I saw a faint gleam of white shirt. He'd always been a snappy dresser.

"Tell me why I shouldn't just shoot you now, Teddy," he said.

"I've got a rock!"

"Teddy's got a rock! Ooooh, I'm so scared!"

"It's a b-*big* rock!"

White teeth flashed as he erupted into laughter. "Oh, I'll bet it's big. But guess what, sweetheart, my gun is even bigger! And if you think the shots will make those folks in the Castle come running, think again. You're so stupid you doubled back on yourself! We're almost at our starting point, so they won't hear a thing."

Considering the gravity of my situation, it wasn't too hard to fake sobs. "Why, B-B-Bronson? Why are you doing this? I thought we were f-f-friends."

"You know why." At least he stopped laughing.

"No, I d-don't!" I wailed. *The helpless female act might make him drop his guard.*

"Oh, c'mon, Teddy. I heard you on your cell phone down at the station. I was leaving my office, but when I opened the door, there you were in the hall, yammering away to someone about piracy."

"Piracy?" I thought fast. "I was t-talking about that oil t-tanker off the coast of S-Somalia!"

A sigh. "Give me a break. You were talking about software piracy, so stop trying to pretend you weren't. What I want to know is, who were you talking to?"

This was good, very good. He wanted to know so he could kill them, too. "All r-right. I won't lie. I was t-talking to the s-sheriff!"

He started laughing again. "You think I can't tell when a woman is talking to her lover? You were talking to a friend, and it wasn't about some oil tanker. I don't know how you did it, but you figured out why I killed Kate, didn't you? Fess up, Teddy, or I'll shoot you in the knee-cap first. Then the other one. Then... Believe me when I tell you that you will die slow." He jiggled the gun up and down for emphasis.

Time to play the game in earnest. If nothing else, the delay would buy me time—not that it would be enough. I gave a couple of loud sniffles. "Figuring it out w-wasn't all that hard."

"Hmmm. I've changed my mind. If you tell me who you were talking to, I won't shoot you. Hell, I won't hurt you, *or* your friend, whoever she was. And yes, I'm betting it was a 'she,' because I didn't hear any sexual tension." His tone was sly.

"P-promise?"

"Promise. I'll just... Let me see, if I remember correctly, your father escaped to Costa Rica. Maybe that's where I should go. I hear the weather's nice."

Pretending to believe him, I took a deep breath and began. "I found the key to Kate's storage unit on her boat, so I drove to Oakland..."

"Yeah, yeah, I heard about your little excursion at the party. What I want to know is, what exactly did you find, and who did you tell?"

"I found old computers. Discs and printouts. A big stack of Kate's father's software programs, including the one you stole and founded SoftSol with—the PCIFS, the Personal Computer InterFile Search."

Bronson grunted. "Nice try, but no cigar. Tyler didn't bother to copyright it, so there was no piracy. Didn't know that, did you? That little money-maker was just sitting around in his crappy workshop, gathering dust. The hippie fool had no head for business, so I just snuck into his workshop and copied the discs. No problem there, since his workshop was actually my parents' garage. Is that a riot, or what? A few years later, I copyrighted the program myself, making it legally mine. Tyler could whine all he wanted, but it didn't make a damn bit of difference. Over the years, he eventually forgot about it."

Bronson moved closer. "Old history. My company's sold and leased hundreds of software programs since then. Even if Kate had taken me to court and won—which is doubtful, because my attorneys would have tied the case until the end of time—I'd still have billions left over."

"S-so why kill her?" As if I didn't know.

This time the sound that emerged from his mouth resembled a growl more than a laugh. "Don't play coy with me, Teddy. You said it yourself. *Loss of face.* An antiquated term, but hey, I run with some pretty important people, and reputation means everything in those circles. Why should I let that greedy little bitch threaten that?"

Because Kate wanted the money for her sick father's care, you heartless monster. "Okay, I understand. But why kill Heck?"

"Are you dense? Because he and Kate were thick as thieves. I couldn't take any chances."

Keep him talking. As long as he's talking, he's not shooting. "Was that you who shot at me the other night?"

"Aren't *you* the smart one!" With that, he ambled casually toward my tree, secure in his triumph.

My cue.

As I slipped the cell phone from its hiding place under the forest debris, I whined, "You promised not to hurt me as long as I told you who I was talking to!"

"Oops, I forgot. Say, I've got an even better idea. Let's compromise and have a little fun. Who knows? You might even like it. *Then* you can tell me. After that…"

I sidled to the left. With the tree trunk still sheltering my body, I stretched out my left arm, revealing the cell phone and its lighted display. "See this? It's an open line to the sheriff's office. They've heard everything."

At that, Deputy Ralph Lazlo shouted loudly enough that every deer in the forest could probably hear him. "Bronson! Touch that woman and you're a dead man!"

The glee vanished from Bronson's face. "Teddy, you *bitch!*" *Time's up.*

I threw the rock with all my might. My aim was good, but not perfect. I'd wanted to hit him in the face. Instead, the rock bounced off the side of his head. While the blow didn't knock him out, it did make him stumble backwards, where he stepped on… A koala.

"Eeeeeeep!!!" Wanchu screeched. *"Eeeeeeep!!!"*

As furious as she was terrified, she wrapped herself around Bronson's shin, dug in her claws, and began biting. His screams blended with hers. Tossing the cell phone aside, I dashed forward and snatched up Bronson's fallen handgun. I don't know anything about guns, only that this one was big and ugly.

"For God's sake, Teddy, shoot!" Bronson yelled.

"You or the koala?" Wanchu was dug in deep and going in deeper with her sharp teeth. Bronson's frantic efforts to pull her away just made her bite harder.

Figuring that the zoo's emergency mantra "humans first, animals second" didn't apply in attempted murder situations, I answered, "Sorry, Bronson. I might—just might—shoot if I thought she could kill you, but so far, you're looking good, give or take some blood spatter here and there. Too bad about the suit, but you'll soon get fitted with a new one. Prison stripes. *Très chic.*"

While Bronson rolled around on the forest floor with Wanchu firmly adhered to his shin, I picked up the cell phone again. "Ralph, did you get all that?"

"On the speaker phone, no less, with four other deputies listening in. Keep that gun on him, girl. Help's on its way."

Watching as the koala munched on Bronson's leg, I smiled. "Tell them to take their time."

TWENTY-ONE

NOW THAT I was no longer running for my life, and Bronson lay handcuffed to a stretcher while having his leg attended to, I'd begun to feel chilly, so it was nice to have a warm koala wrapped around my neck while giving my statement at the San Sebastian Sheriff's office.

"We need to turn that koala over to Animal Control," Joe said, frowning. "She attacked someone."

I shook my head. "Wanchu's had all her shots. If you don't believe me, they're on file at the zoo. As for that so-called 'attack,' that only happened after Bronson stepped on her, so it was self-defense. Plus, I want our vet to look at her foot and make sure nothing's broken."

Before Joe could protest, I hauled out my phone again and called Zorah's cell, catching her not long after she'd arrived home from the marathon. After I'd explained where I was and why, she volunteered to pick Wanchu up and return her to the zoo. That accomplished, I called Helen.

Fifteen minutes later, Helen—who lived nearby—was sitting across from Joe, explaining the import of Tyler Everts' old printouts in language that even the computer-challenged could understand. She'd brought along two of Tyler's computers and all of his discs and printouts to give to Sergeant Kevin Turow, the department's computer crimes specialist.

Turow didn't look like anyone's idea of a computer geek. Around six-foot-six, he had massive shoulders and hands, but as he walked, he leaned to the side like a boxer who had taken one too many hits. Maybe he had. Joe once told me that before Turow went back to school to obtain a degree in computer science, he'd been a beat cop in San Francisco's rough Tenderloin District.

The big man rubbed his meaty hands in anticipation. He sat down at the ancient IBM-compatible, inserted a floppy disc, and scrolled through the files. Seconds later, he gave a happy little yip. "MS-DOS 3.1! Speak to me, you sexy little bitch."

"Keep it clean, Kev," Joe warned. "And in English."

"Sorry, Sheriff. Well, Helen's right. The shi…uh, the you-know-what's gonna hit the fan over at SoftSol if they wind up losing the rights to PCIFS."

Joe cut in. "Like I said, Kev. Keep it clean *and* in English. What's PCIFS?"

Turow grabbed a printout and flapped it at Joe. "You're looking at it. Personal Computer InterFile Search. Hit a couple of simple commands on any keyboard and within seconds, your computer finds whatever phrase or number series you're looking for, no matter how many files you have cluttering up your hard drive, or whatever mislabeled folder the little bas…oops, the little dears are hiding in."

"Which means?" Joe looked puzzled.

"It means money, Sheriff, lots of it." After emitting a high-pitched cackle that sounded startling coming from a man of such size, he sobered up. "At the time this here Everts guy wrote this program, he obviously didn't think it was worth all that much. And why would he? In 1985, the few PCs out there weren't as crowded with files as they eventually became. But flash forward ten years later, when everybody and his dog were using PCs and files were breeding like maggots on hot sh…, uh, hot stuff, data started getting lost. Congressmen lost the love letters they were typing to their mistresses, their wives lost the

list of assets they'd compiled for their divorce attorneys…
Don't you see? Any program that would help users locate
lost data more quickly would make the designer some serious money."

At the mention of money, Joe's eyes lost their glazed
look. "How much?"

Turow cackled again. "Millions, at the very least. Seriously, have you ever tried to find wordage you used once
but can't remember which file you put it in? And you've
got more than *five hundred* files on your PC? Well, before
Ford Bronson copyrighted what he claimed was *his* PCIFS,
that kind of computer search could take hours. Even if you
had the patience to wait that long, the search might result
in some indecipherable coding—to you, anyway—not the
actual wordage itself."

"I still don't understand."

Turow shook his head in exasperation. "This guy here…"
He placed a meaty forefinger on the computer screen. "This
Tyler Everts, *he* designed the PCIFS. In 1985."

"Which means?"

Turow's mouth fell open so far I could see the gold inlay
on one of his molars. "Sheriff, haven't you ever read the
program copyright notification on your computer?"

Joe looked at Turow like he was crazy. "Of course I
haven't. No one does."

Turow gave another headshake at the willful ignorance
of the average computer user. "According to the time/date
stamp here, Everts designed the PCIFS three years *before* Bronson copyrighted the exact same program in 1988.
Bronson used it to give SoftSol its start, and as anybody
who hasn't been hiding under a rock for the past couple of
decades knows, this here PCIFS was the springboard that
built SoftSol into a billion-dollar business. Just as Windows
did for Bill Gates."

An awed silence descended on the room for a moment, then Joe turned to me and asked, "What makes you think Bronson didn't buy the PCIFS program from Everts?"

That's when I told Joe about the two letters I'd found in the Oakland storage unit, which I'd left at Caro's. "One is a dotmatrix copy of a letter Kate's father wrote to Bronson in 1988, when he discovered his program had been stolen. The other is Bronson's hand-written answer. I guess he wasn't much into formality back then. He asked Tyler if he knew how much it would cost to prove his claim and did he have the money to sustain that kind of legal fight. I didn't find any more correspondence on the subject. From all accounts, Kate's father was a bit of a hippie, so it looks like he walked away from the whole thing."

Turow jumped in. "At the time, there were a lot of guys like that, geniuses who got ripped off because they never realized the financial impact of their software. They were operating under the 'open sourcing' theory, that knowledge wanted to be shared, that it was wrong to charge for it, hippie shi…uh, hippie stuff like that."

"Sounds like you're telling me there was no actual piracy, then," Joe said, frowning. "If Tyler Everts walked away from the whole thing, what was the problem?"

Time for me to speak up again. "Bronson is California's version of royalty. Not only does he golf with the President, but he hobnobs with people like Oprah and Madonna. He revels in that kind of reflected glory. But fame can come back to haunt you if you're keeping a secret, and he was keeping a big one. Just before Kate was killed, he testified on Capitol Hill about the evils of computer piracy and intellectual property theft. He knew there'd be a media feeding frenzy if she unmasked him as the same kind of thief he was testifying against."

Joe still looked baffled. "How did Kate make the connection between Bronson and her father? She didn't seem to be very interested in current events, because when we searched her boat, we found no television set, no newspapers, and no magazines—unless you want to count a couple dozen issues of *Animal Keepers' Forum*."

"There's a TV in the zoo's employee lounge. Maybe she saw part of the congressional hearings on her lunch break, and with the repeated exposure, who knows? And don't forget, Kate was at his television station every Tuesday for two months. Bronson himself told me that he met her there in the hallway and that they'd chatted."

"I don't know, Teddy…" he began.

No one can be denser than a smart man. "Kate would have been around five when her father designed the PCIFS. Louise Signorelli, the woman who had a thing for Tyler, told me Kate used to go with him to the workshop. She also said that Tyler mentioned some teenager who used to do odd jobs for him. Bronson himself, when he thought he'd got me cornered back there in the woods, told me the workshop was in his parents' garage. When you check the property records, I've no doubt you'll find their names."

Joe frowned. "If Kate was only five how could she remember…"

I told him about the photograph I'd found in the storage unit, which I'd left in my room with the letters. "When you run it through an age-progression program, you'll see how it could have jogged her memory."

Satisfied that he had finally seen the light, I continued. "When Kate was clearing out her father's things before moving them into the storage unit, she found everything. Maybe she'd been just a child when he wrote the PCIFS, but being computer-savvy herself, she would have seen the dates and notes on the printouts. She'd have understood that her father should have been able to afford the best residential medical facility money could buy. Instead, he was moldering away in an overcrowded nursing home. Maybe Kate found all this material before the congressional hearings, maybe after. Who knows? But once she did, it must have felt to her like a needle being jammed into an open wound. In her *Tasmanian Devil* blog—the unofficial, non-zoo one—she said something about 'familiar faces in new places.'"

Helen, who up to that point had been silent, said, "Poor Kate. When she contacted Bronson, she signed her own death warrant, didn't she?"

"Heck's, too," I pointed out. *And almost mine.* "Not only was Bronson's yacht berthed at Gunn Landing Harbor, but he jogs there every evening. He must have seen the *Nomad*. How could anyone not notice such a gaudy boat? I'm betting he saw Kate and Heck palling around together and began to worry about how much Kate was telling him. Right after Kate's murder, the harbor was on alert and people were watching out for anything unusual, so Bronson must have been worried about making a move then, but as soon as things began to calm down, he killed Heck. Just in case. He even bragged about it."

"Collateral damage," Joe said.

I nodded. "Later, when Bronson was at Caro's party, he heard Zorah say I'd driven up to Oakland to see Tyler. That probably unnerved him, because he had no way of knowing how much Tyler could remember. When Zorah added that I'd left the nursing home with some papers, he must have panicked, thinking she meant these…" I gestured at the printouts. "But he was wrong. All I'd found by that point were receipts from the funeral home. A couple of days later, Bronson tried to shoot me. I guess he figured he wouldn't be able to get close enough to me to use a garrote, like he'd done on Kate and Heck."

At the mention of Caro's name, Joe's jaw clenched. Through gritted teeth, he said, "One thing still puzzles me. That garrote business. How could a software engineer even know what a garrote was?"

Helen smiled. "There speaks a charter member of Luddites Anonymous. Sheriff, SoftSol has an entire game division. One of my favorites is their *X-Andra, Temptress Assassin.* Her favorite method of dispatch is the garrote. All Bronson had to do was learn from his own game."

Joe's face hardened again. "Influenced by a computer game? Here comes an insanity defense. But I think we're all right there. Too much planning went into both murders to pull that off."

As IT TURNED OUT, Bronson, in his arrogance, hadn't planned well enough.

Although an entire fleet of high-priced attorneys argued that my phone call from the eucalyptus forest to the sheriff's office was inadmissible, the judge let it stand. But even if it had been tossed, enough evidence remained to obtain a conviction.

The bullet from my poor old Nissan's headrest—as well as the bullet found lodged in a blue gum eucalyptus fronting Bentley Road—proved to have been fired from Bronson's gun. Gunshot residue sprinkled his Mercedes' steering wheel and the edge of his driver's side window, as well as his hand. The zoo van's paint was found on the Mercedes' bumper... The evidence was overwhelming.

But I didn't find all that out for another couple of weeks. In the meantime, something extraordinary happened a few days after Bronson's arrest.

TWENTY-TWO

JACQUELINE'S BISTRO WASN'T all that busy when Joe and I arrived for brunch the following Sunday, so we were able to grab a table on the shaded patio. A hundred yards to the south began the steep climb up San Sebastian Hill, where the old Spanish mission overlooked the town.

"I'm thinking the ham and avocado quiche, how about you?" Joe asked.

Uniforms happen to turn me on, but I had to admit that he looked devastatingly handsome in his civvies. Not unaware of his effect on me, he had accented his half-Hispanic, half-Irish genetic mix with Gap khakis, an azure shirt the same color as his eyes, and an off-white linen sports coat that covered his shoulder holster. Just looking at that delicious, dangerous man made me want to drag him back to the *Merilee* for another round of... "Teddy, aren't you going to order?"

Startled out of my X-rated fantasy, I said, "Uh, yeah, ham and avocado, oh my God, yes."

He grinned. "You are so transparent." My face flamed.

"Don't be embarrassed, Teddy. It's one of the reasons I love you. You might fib from time to time, but given your open face, you can never truly lie. By the way, you're looking especially pretty today, face scrapes, bruises, and all."

And he says *I* fib. But I'll admit that the fog-colored Vera Wang pants suit Caro bought me several seasons back did tone down my garish freckles and hair. "You wanted me to dress up, so I did."

"I love an obedient woman." Only his chuckle saved him from being clouted. Wisely, he changed the subject. "How's that feisty koala doing? Settled down yet after her big adventure?"

"Enough so that I caught her in a compromising position yesterday with Nyee, her mate. The zoo might celebrate a blessed event in about a month. Not that we'll see the pup that soon. It'll stay in her pouch for six more months."

Joe asked the waiter for champagne, and soon we were toasting the zoo's good fortune. After drinking the bubbly, he said, "And your mother. How did she feel when you moved back to the *Merilee*?"

"Oh, you know Caro. She had a fit." To dig him a little, I added, "But she's already planning another Let's-Find-Teddy-a-Suitable-Husband party."

A baleful look from Joe. "You'd think that after she tried to fix you up with a killer she'd have learned better."

"Caro never learns. She's still madly in love with my father, wherever he is."

He raised his champagne glass again. "To your fugitive father. May he remain forever free."

I grinned. "That's a lawless thing for a sheriff to say."

By the time the waiter brought our quiche, we'd moved our chairs close enough that our legs touched from ankle to thigh. The fact that Joe and I were able to spend only one full day together per week made the day even more piquant.

"Let's walk up to the Mission," he said, once we'd finished eating and he'd paid the check.

"Firearms aren't permitted on Mission grounds," I tsk-tsked.

"The sheriff's are."

Hand in hand, we strolled up the hill.

The day was balmy, with a soft breeze whispering in from the Pacific. The air was alive with birdsong. Two swallows dove toward the Mission's bell tower, while ahead of us several Indian blue peacocks paraded up the path that led to the chapel, the sun glinting off the lone male's gaudy tail.

"Do peacocks mate for life?" Joe asked.

"Indian blues are polygamous. Not being a birder myself, I don't know much about the other peacocks, but I expect they're the same."

"Hmm."

He seemed disappointed, so I said, "Emperor penguins mate for life."

"I like penguins."

"So do I."

"We need to get married."

I stopped in the middle of the path. "Huh?"

"I'm more penguin than peacock, Teddy. So are you."

"Oh, Jesus."

"There's a statue of him further on up the hill if you want to stop by and say hello, but why don't we head for that bench first, since I think you're about to faint."

"Don't be silly, I'm…" *I'm going to fall kersplat on my face.*

He kept that from happening by slipping a steadying arm around my waist. "Hey, hey! We don't have to get married right away, and considering your reaction, an engagement of several months might be a good idea. Then once you're ready, we'll sneak out of town before your mother catches us. We'll drive to Vegas…"

"I'm not getting married by some guy dressed like Elvis!"

He smiled down at me. "Would that be a conditional yes?"

"No to Elvis," I blubbered, "but *yesyesyes* to you!"

With that, I flung my arms around his neck and kissed

him wildly. He returned in kind. From the gasps around us, I deduced that we had shocked the tourists.

And maybe even the polygamous peacocks.

* * * * *